I0692030

Next!

by

Virginie Snow

Don't underestimate
a woman with a penis chart.

It seemed like too much, too soon, too fast—desperate for a mate, regardless of who she could be. But that rib-crushing hug spoke to me and sent uneasy images to my brain: me in a fifties apron removing cupcakes from our matrimonial oven; my carting the laundry basket with freshly-ironed linens upstairs to our boudoir; my vacuuming the floors devoid of cat hair because my new husband hated all animals; my greeting him with a kiss and a gin and tonic when he arrived home from the office. My imagination went wild with my married state that would certainly jump-start Kenny the widower but would devolve me into *humanus domesticus* overnight. I was scared out of my wits.

But as soon as I revealed the farm girl in me, he lost all oomph for his new bride-to-be. No longer attractive was this pig-prattling, swine-swilling woman who surely had the smell of hog manure clinging to her stilettos. Yep, he must've thought: She can dress herself up, but she can't go out. She ate like Wilbur from Green Acres, chili flying in every direction, melted crackers sticking to her gums, orange chili-foam at the corners of her lips. No doubt, he pictured me, as his new bride, in the nude, too: her leg hairs, no doubt, bristly; her skin dry and flaky as a swine's. She probably belched when she laughed hard. And during sex…well, she would probably grunt and fart like hell.

Chapter One
La Divorcée

Thoroughly convinced something was wrong with me, something that drove my husband into the arms of another woman, I made an appointment with a shrink. Even making the phone call was embarrassing. I had never needed the services of a psychiatrist.

"What is the problem?" the receptionist said after I demanded the first available appointment.

"I'm a schizophrenic. I see flaccid penises protruding from the walls."

There was a leaden pause.

"No, I'm only kidding." I chuckled. "But I should mention the penises are talking about me, too, saying nasty things about my hair and teeth."

"Okay, ma'am." She cleared her throat. "You can come in tomorrow."

Merely walking into the shrink's office and sitting in the waiting room put me in a near panic. Not only was I reeling from worry, self-blame, concern over my finances, my struggle to manage all the farm work myself, or, worse yet, losing the farm, but I hadn't slept in days. I was a walking train wreck.

To make matters worse, I was facing a long drive to Albany, NY, to the Master of the Mindless, Dr. Kraisier, MD, PhD., specialty—psychiatry. I chewed my lower lip. Could I possibly have a personality

1

disorder bordering on psychosis?

What if the shrink diagnoses you with sociopathic tendencies? What if you're an obsessive compulsive and don't know it? Worse. What if you're paranoid schizophrenic? What if you really are *a loon? What if Lance was justified in his abandonment? What would everyone think? They'd think Lance had every reason to have an affair. His wife was clearly bonkers!*

I forced myself to check in and sit down. Then, I mustered my sanest expression.

In his private office, Dr. Kraisier handed me a box of hankies as I sat across from him in an over-stuffed leather chair. Where was the chaise? Wasn't I supposed to be lying prostrate, staring at the ceiling, while he picked away at my subconscious like a torn cuticle? I looked around the shrink's office. Homey, subtly decorated, dimly lit to induce calm and not send his rabid patients bouncing off the walls mid-therapy.

I crossed my legs and smiled weakly, trying in my best theatrical stance to look anything but *bezomny.* Lots of people need help coping with divorce. Just because Lance's crazy cock corked a whore didn't mean there was anything wrong with me.

"So, Mrs. Snow, uh, Doctor Snow," he began.

I nodded and smiled knowingly, like Sir Francis Bacon.

"So, your husband left you, and you'd like anxiety medication so that you can sleep."

Looking up from my lap, I laughed. "Yeah! You could feed horses from the bags under these eyes!"

Wrong thing to say. Wrong thing to say. You sound whacko. Crazy people weren't funny. Nut cases don't joke.

I cleared my throat like a financial analyst. "Possibly I'm suffering from shell shock. Maybe I have Post Traumatic Stress Disorder." I giggled like a nervous school child and ripped out a tissue, twisting the end into a volcano. Then smiling a calm, serene smile, one that convinced him I was coping just fine or revealed a transport of myself into some fantastic kind of psychedelic strawberry field of forever, I leaned forward. "Just give me a few pills to knock me out, and send me on my merry way."

"Tell me how this problem with your husband all went down."

I gulped, blinked wildly, and steeled myself, looking him in the eye. Then the memories of the past few days came flooding back. "My Husband the Fuck *left* me, without two weeks' notice and without an exit interview!"

The shrink was silent.

He's gonna think you have Tourette's syndrome, you ass. Fuck him, too. All men are jerks.

"Sorry about my French."

He smiled. "That's perfectly all right. You're understandably angry. And that's okay."

Okay? He does *think you're nuts.*

I recognized kindness in his eyes. "He said my personality sucks! That I drove him to his whore who is *twenty years* younger than he!" I grimaced and swallowed a lump. "And she's already been married three times!"

Why are you shouting, Ginnie? "If I shout, I cannot very well cry."

His eyes popped. "She's twenty years younger and already married that often? Well, that's not going to

3

work."

I lurched forward, spittle dripping into my lap. "It's *not*?" I said.

He shook his head. "Not from my experience. Once the novelty wears off, he'll likely be miserable with her. They're in the honeymoon phase. She's like a new toy right now."

"She's more like a walking vagina." I chuckled at the image. "Well, regardless, I just need to know I'm not...ya know...like all your other patients." I leaned forward again. "I need a shrink to tell me my personality is all right.

Did you just call the shrink a "shrink" to his face? Real good, Virginie. You just sealed your box.

"Sorry about the 'shrink' term, Doctor Kraisier." My hands were balled into fists. "I feel so lost and ashamed, unsure of myself. I am normally a very strong, assertive woman. She's empty now—gutless. Is there something wrong with me?" I reached into the box and pulled out a bunch of tissues. A flock of them flew from the box like doves from a magician's hat. I scrambled to retrieve them. Staring, I hesitated and swallowed a lump of dry moss. "Uh, we were married twenty-eight years. He's fifty-three, me forty-nine. I'm too old to start over but want to be loved again. Also, I'm facing my own financial demise and may have to go back to teaching after being away from it for ten years. Who will hire me, especially in this economy? And do you know the worst part of all this?" A deep breath escaped me. I wrung my hands.

"Tell me."

I tore out another handful of hankies. "I haven't had sex since 2001!"

4

Dr. Kraisier choked and snatched a handful of tissues. He looked as though he was going to throw up.

Finally, he spoke. "Wow! That's almost sixteen years. Definitely not normal for a marriage."

"You're telling me!" Silence washed over us for one long agonizing second. "My gynecologist scrapes out the rust and finishes with two squirts of Quickie Lube."

Dr. Kraisier stared at me, his eyes bugged. Not even his worst paranoid schizophrenic was this deluded.

I grabbed another fistful of tissues and began to wail. "*One time…one time…*Lance couldn't get it up. It scared the living shit out of him. Ya know, his penis had a mind of its own." I squinted, lips pursed, the memories flooding back. "It was calculating, stealthy, always waiting for the right moment to screw him. After that first moment of impotence and every time thereafter his penis made a dick out of him. Whenever he tried—as hard as he tried—it made an ass of him, hanging there, uncooperative, like a moping child. Finally, I couldn't stand seeing the shame on his face." I sniffed back tears. "So, at the age of thirty-three, I decided to never pressure him for sex. Really, his cock was an *alien*."

The shrink hacked into his fistful of tissues.

"Ya know," I continued, "the little blue pill wasn't well-known then. So, it was either abandon my sex life, get a divorce, or get a penis pump at the nearest gas station. I thought Lance was a good guy, and it wouldn't be right to divorce him because he had a disability. So, I stayed with him but avoided any romance so as not to cause embarrassment. That took the heat off him, but, in so doing, I sacrificed my own sex life. And I stayed faithful to him all those years, too."

I huffed and continued.

"Rotten dirtball. To blame me and my personality when he's whoring around, after what I gave up for him. Now he's probably downing a little blue pill with his breakfast twinkies. It's too late for me to start over with someone else. I'm forty-nine, for Christ's sake, a fucking dinosaur! My skin is hanging, and that's not all. I've lost twenty pounds in two weeks. You should see me naked, a human raisin. Even a mummy looks appealing next to me. On top of it, my personality sucks."

I wailed into a pile of hankies.

Dr. Kraisier cleared his throat and leaned forward.

I looked up, my face stained with tears.

"Ginnie, I don't believe there's anything wrong with your personality. Your insomnia is from your body reacting to a very stressful situation. I'll give you meds to help you sleep. As far as your inability to start over and get affection from a man you deserve…"

I glanced at him, wrung my hands, and waited for the verdict.

He's going to say, "Pack it in, Wrinkle Fest. No one in his right mind—'cause I know what a right mind is—will ever invite you to meet his mama."

"You will have no trouble finding the right person to treat you with love and respect. And that right person will want to make love to the beautiful woman I am looking at right now."

Wha-a-a-a-at?

"Trust me—it's not too late for you to start afresh and find a good man you're compatible with and who

6

can enjoy your body as well as your mind."

I stared at him, mouth agape like a jack o' lantern's. *He thinks I'm beautiful?* Surely my nose was puffed and red, my eyes, too. My hair stuck out like an Irish wolfhound's, and I wore the latest farm fashion statement—jeans and a plaid shirt. *He really thinks I'm beautiful?* Then, suddenly, the room opened to a Montana sky—a ray of sunshine accompanied by the theme song to *Bonanza* shone through an imaginary window and lit Dr. Kraisier up like a heavenly Hoss. A huge smile erupted across my face, and I sat back and stuck out my boobs.

"You really think I'm beautiful and there's life after divorce?"

"Absolutely. You're a very attractive woman. It won't be long. Just have some patience."

"I'm not nuts or anal or fixated or anything shrinkish?"

"No. You're just going through a rough time. I'll write you a script for something for your anxiety. Take two before bedtime."

He really thinks you—we—are attractive? It's not too late? You're not a nut case and don't have a dysfunctional personality? Glory Be to Thee, O Christ!

Dancing out of Dr. Kraisier's office and into the crisp spring air of Albany, New York, I breathed in a good whiff of the nearby Hudson and looked up at a flock of squealing seagulls, obviously lost and searching for the ocean. Glory be! Officially, this woman—me—was not crazy at all, not like that guy in the waiting room hiding behind his magazine. Dr. Kaisier truly believed a life existed after Lance. The purple and cream-colored pansies grinned beneath the aspen flanking the parking lot. Funny how the world worked: all could seem so bleak in one moment. But just the right words, the right gestures, from the right person, could adjust one's perspective so dramatically. Perhaps I shouldn't be looking at this divorce as the end of my forty-nine years of life. Perhaps, in fact, I should consider it as a new beginning, a chance to be free, an opportunity to let the real me sing in a way she's never sung before.

Chapter Two
Best Friends

Days later my parents were still reeling from the news of Lance's desertion. Shaking his head, my eighty-four-year-old father stated his disapproval in a stern, no-nonsense voice. "He's a dirty fuck." My mother, donning oven mitts, raised a fist and said in an uncharacteristically high-pitched, Category 2 tornado voice, "What? What the hell is wrong with the son of a bitch?"

My parents had been stellar in-laws to Lance. All of a sudden my mother yelled a final, stinging caveat from the kitchen. "We want our truck back and the hundred dollars we gave him for his birthday!"

I sat on the couch and cried. "I feel so clueless. All these twenty-eight years married to Lance has made me inept. I don't even know how to keep my farm going, don't know how to pay a bill, never set foot in the bank. Lance handled all the finances. I'm like a monkey with her thumb up her ass!"

My mother turned and stared. "You're not a monkey, dear." There was a long pause. "Would you like a banana?" I looked up, preparing to burst into tears. "We love you, just remember that. He's a jerk. Got his head up his ass."

I had the coolest parents alive.

My father, who resembled Ben Franklin, stood up

9

and cupped his belly. "I got one thing to say. 'He started it, and we're going to finish it!' " My parents on whom I never had to depend for anything financial resolved, then and there, to help me pay my attorney's fees. They weren't wealthy people, my father a retired college professor and my mother, a homemaker, but they had saved their pennies their entire lifetime and invested their money wisely. Now some of that money would help turn a knife toward Lance's balls.

Similarly, a best friend is one a soon-to-be divorcée can count on in tough times. My friends stood faithfully beside me, something I'll never forget. Sharon, having her own share of lousy exes, had mastered the art of surviving on cents a day. The auburn-haired beauty became my advisor on financial matters—what to do as Lance gradually, and without telling me, shut off the cable, the phone, internet, and electric. She advised me who to call to clean away the manure pile, who to phone for a blocked toilet, who to call to fix the horse fencing, and above all, how to pay for everything on the five hundred dollars Lance grudgingly offered as support every month.

Sharon gave me a copy of *Any Woman Can,* a sex book. "Study it," she ordered. "You're gonna need it."

In horror I sifted through the pages, catching sight of some beckoning words—"oral sex" and "furry handcuffs." I shivered. All the years of Lance's impotence had probably re-grown me a new hymen much like a grown-over ear piercing.

"Promise me."

"Okay. I'll read it." I put it in the porcelain reading room.

The kick in the butt was that almost ten years ago,

Lance had encouraged me to stop teaching college English in order to maintain the farm—the landscaping, the truck patch, and all our adopted animals. For the last twelve years I always did the hard labor while he operated on bones and managed our finances. I had no idea what my expenses were or how to write a check. With his leaving, overnight this relatively wealthy orthopedic surgeon's wife morphed into a woman whose life reflected unyielding, suffocating poverty and helplessness. My survival was as uncertain as a newly-hatched turtle trundling to the ocean's edge.

Another friend, Charlotte, struggling to support herself and her recently college-graduated son, called me every morning and evening "Just to check in to see how you're doing."

We met once a week at the local diner for the cheapest meal on the menu: a tuna melt with fries, eight bucks and not a red cent more. I worried, confiding my worst fear, "What man in his right mind was going to date a woman with perennial fish breath?"

Charlotte, also divorced, had resigned herself to the single life and filled her evenings basking before the TV set with her three pot-bellied pigs. "My pigs are a hell of a lot more company *and* nicer than men. They never give me any shit."

Finally, my other friends, Lois and Jack, invited me for dinner a few times a week. Lois was a gourmet cook, though almost every dish overflowed with dainty, differently-carved pastas ending in *illi, elli, ini, etti,* and *oni.* Her man, Jack, was a good-looking, fifty-two-year-old, goateed, atypically over-sexed male, not unlike the Bonobo monkeys of the Congo Basin. He enjoyed Lois' fifty-five-year-old, arthritic body—much to Lois'

11

chagrin—every other night. In private, she complained bitterly about Jack's over-eager penis, which, she said, had a mind of its own. Jack knew his insatiable sexual appetite annoyed Lois, but he secretly liked her chiding him about it during our dinner discussions. Very proud of "Dickie's" stamina, Jack merely sat, listening and smiling like a goat eating a pine cone.

I looked forward to the weekly dinners with Lois and Jack, so filled with honest, open, bawdy talk and laughter. Conversation always gravitated to Jack's wildly ready and ripe cock. Despite Lois' obvious irritation, he beamed throughout her diatribes about his being a stud—not the two by four kind—and his own natural "hard hat." Nevertheless, I loved their company and ability to make me laugh while, at the same time, unknowingly making me feel sexually deprived. Between talk of Jack's twenty-four/seven sexual appetite, I moaned about my own lack of sex the last sixteen years and revealed a nickname for myself—the Queen of Impotence. Throughout the summer with the town of Coxsackie's oaks, maple trees, and pines in verdant splendor, we laughed endlessly, our heads bent, howling, over bowls of orzo.

One evening while Lois concocted her famous broccoli and fusilli casserole, the conversation once again turned to their sexual relations. Their fourth year anniversary of living together was coming. Lois took the Humane Society calendar off the kitchen wall and tossed it at me. "Look at this. It's disgusting." The calendar was loaded with little red stars.

"Do those stars represent your daily bowel movements?"

"No. They represent sex sessions," Lois said. She

glared at Jack. "Proof that Jack's sex drive is extreme, abnormal. Disgusting. I'm taking this to my therapist to show her, too."

I laughed. "This calendar looks like the frickin' Milky Way!"

Jack looked up from his dish and wiped the cream from his lips. "It's the milky way, all right." He giggled. "It's normal for me, been like this since I was a kid, had my first sex at the age of twelve with Lucinda in the back of my dad's convertible."

Lois groaned, rolled her eyes, and directed her attention out the window where, a half mile away, the Hudson rolled grandly toward the Atlantic.

I had to agree with Lois. "Jack, it is a bit much, especially since your sessions average forty-five minutes. Nobody wants to eat steak, either, every day of the week. Can't you just do a quickie once in a while?"

"A quickie would be fine," Lois yelled. She stuffed another forkful of fusilli in her mouth.

I started to howl, and then Lois, despite herself, chuckled.

"So, when did you say the last time you had sex with Lance was?" Jack said.

"Sixteen years ago." They knew the story of my being the sacrificial lamb. "One time it failed him, and…"

"Yeah, yeah, we know all about that." Jack stared at the ceiling. "Don't beat a dead dick."

"And I stayed faithful to him all those years, too."

"We know. We know. Eat some pasta," Jack said. "I can't imagine going without sex for all those years. Dickie would've shriveled up and fallen off by now."

Lois muttered through a mouth full of fusilli. "I

wish he would have."

Jack snorted. A heavy pause followed.

"Did I ever tell you about my high school sweetheart?" I laughed.

"No," Jack said. He jammed a piece of garlic bread in his mouth. "Tell us."

I put down my fork and threw out my chest. I did, after all, have *some* sexual experience, other than my marital one fit for a Stephen King movie. Through no fault of my own it occurred thirty-some years ago.

"The guy was so hot." I picked up the TV's remote, demonstrating like a fisherman showing the size of his caught fish. "His penis was so large…." I paused.

Jack and Lois blurted in unison, "How large?"

I held the remote in both hands. "It dwarfed this thing!"

Jack's eyes bugged, and Lois caught the expression. "Now, Jack, don't be jealous. That was thirty years ago."

I continued. "And the head—he called it Ed—was so big it wouldn't fit through my bedroom door on a good night. In fact, one time when we were kissing and grappling like a couple of drunken football players, I felt his immense penis against my thigh, and…

"Excuse me for digressing, but you know, penises *really* are *strange* bedfellows. I've heard they're very quirky, sensitive, emotional, and come in all different sizes and shapes. Kind of like pears."

Jack winced. "Pears?"

"Yeah." I mustered my most serious face. "I've been told by reliable sources that, basically, they are all the same, but each one is just a little bit different. Each has its own little personality. Ed was the most gregarious."

"He talked?" Lois said. Speaking of fruit, Lois was not the brightest orange in the crate, but I loved her anyway.

"Well, not quite."

"Wow," Lois said. She rinsed her pasta bowl in the sink while the TV blared. Another commercial for the latest erectile dysfunction "snake oil." I stared, thinking.

Have a hard-on for three days. For only thirty dollars a pill. Guaranteed erection or your precious money back. Any erection lasting for more than two years, see your doctor. And may I add, a funeral director with a high-lidded coffin.

Jack was focused on my *Saga of Ed.* He scoffed. "Bunch of shit." He resented any penile competition.

I said, "Jack, haven't you ever heard of 'Talking Heads'? Anyway, that afternoon while we were making out, he took my hand and put it you know where." I snorted a chuckle, my eyes bugged. "I didn't see Ed, only touched him a little. He was bent, almost folded in half, damned near turned inside out, for Christ's sake. It was elbowish."

"Elbowish?" Jack said. He rolled his eyes in disbelief.

"I had said to him, 'Holy Christmas. What's with Ed? We could make a croissant-wich out of him.' " I barked a laugh. "Can you imagine I said such a thing when Ed was at the height of his display, like one of those bower birds. I go and tell my boyfriend we could put his meaty manhood into a croissant roll!"

"Just perfect, *Lorena,*" Jack said. "No wonder

15

Lance left you. You're merciless."

The three of us looked at each other and laughed. I nearly blew my fusilli all over the room.

"Seriously," I said. "Do you think I'll ever meet someone in this small town?"

Lois was always good for an ego boost. "Of course, Ginnie. Lots of good men your age live here around Climax and Coxsackie, but you can't meet someone cooped up at your farm. Let's see…" She sat up straight, her chin in her hand. "Lots of them run barges up and down the Hudson, but you can't park yourself on the side of the riverbank and hope to catch someone. Oh! I have an idea: lots of men roam grocery stores."

Silence.

She continued, "That's it. If I were you, I'd go to Wegmans on a week-day evening around ten o'clock. Scope out the place."

"I hate grocery stores." I picked my cuticle. "Avoid them like the plague. I could hang out in a museum. I like museums."

"That would work."

"You wanna pick up a mummy?" Jack quipped.

"Well, he'd probably have a real nice stiffie. How am I going to introduce myself? 'Hello, I'm Ginnie Snow from Climax, New York, and I haven't had one in sixteen years.' "

"Let's see," Lois thought aloud "Where could you pick up a man, a decent one?"

The TV switched to a commercial. A self-assured, sexy voice challenged the viewer to meet "the person of your dreams." The ad showed a guy and girl meeting for the first time, experiencing love at first sight, and running to embrace. But the stud wrenches his back,

16

knocking both of them into a table of romantically-lit candles. Then the scene switches to three ladies searching the computer for a better dating site than one doling out only clumsy men with lumbar problems. A link for Better Buns flashed across the screen.

"Hey. That's it. I'll go online for a man!" I danced the Macarena in place. "Why not? I bought batteries, make-up, and my father's hemorrhoid pillow online. Why not get a man there, too?"

Jack snorted.

Lois said in a tentative voice, "You *could* try it." She paused. "Why not? I heard eLove really tries to fix people up who are compatible."

"Jeez, that would be terrific. My exact match. I wouldn't have to do all the leg-work. I'll go online first thing tomorrow morning and sign up."

I thought hard. "Let's see. I want someone good-looking, nice, kind, entertaining, no beer belly. Bald doesn't bother me, but I need a nice face, a good face— no rosacea. Straight white teeth. Can't stand crooked teeth. Lance had teeth like Tom Sawyer's picket fence. He should be a few years younger than I, a hard-worker, loyal, trustworthy, a one-woman man since Lance was severely retarded in that area. Having a good amount of money would be nice but is not non-negotiable. He must like cats. He should like gardening, mucking horse stalls, and be fun."

Jack scoffed.

"Oh, and he should be intelligent. I can't live with a dolt." I slammed my fist on the table. "There you go. My man bucket list. All I have to do is scrape up a few bucks to pay eLove, and—*Voila*—they'll do the rest. I should have a new beau in just a few days."

17

Lois and Jack looked at each other and rolled their eyes.

I looked at them. "What?"

"Oh, nothing," Lois said. "But I don't know where you're going to find someone like that."

"*On Mars*," Jack roared.

"Nope," I replied. "Right here on Earth. And I expect to have my Prince Charming yelping at my heels within a week."

Lois said, "Good luck with that bucket list, Ginnie."

"I'll let you guys know how it all goes down tomorrow." I jammed my arms into my coat sleeves and headed toward the door. "This is going to be *so* exciting. Thanks for dinner and entertainment. Hope Dickie behaves himself tonight."

And out the door I went into the moonlight and the good, moist smell misting off the Hudson River.

Chapter Three
Online Dating

The next morning I raced to feed the cats, horses, and goats so that I could get down to the day's work—finding love online. I booted up my computer, put in the link for eLove and got busy. My suitor existed, no doubt, somewhere on the web anxiously awaiting my pictures and information. Similarly, Sir Pantsalot was probably staring at his computer screen praying for the likes of Virginie Snow and her arrival in a virtual Cinderella coach.

I looked at the application form. The questions were endless: What are your hobbies? What level of education do you have? Do you like animals? What is your marital status? I typed in "legally separated." The important questions they didn't ask, like "Do you have rectal polyps?" or "How many pairs of big cotton undies do you own?" And then similar questions came up for what qualities I wanted in a potential partner, but, again, they didn't ask the right questions, like "Does foot size matter to you?" and "Do you prefer a man who shaves his testicles?"

The last step was to post pictures of myself, so I uploaded my most flattering photos—standing with a Cheshire grin amongst my twenty cats, planting a juicy kiss on Joseph, one of my mini goats, and eating a hot dog at the Riverside Festival in downtown Climax,

New York. I posted another wearing a Giants football jersey, a glass of beer raised to my lips—if that didn't get their attention, nothing would—and the pièce de la résistance—me grinning, pitchfork in hand, standing next to a wheelbarrow brimming with horse shit.

Finally I entered the thirty-second photo of my scarfing down a barbequed turkey leg at the Coxsackie Music Festival and hit "Save." Four hours later my profile blossomed—as attractive, alluring, and entertaining as possible—with clever paragraphs about my personality, my motivations, my life-loves, my dreams, and my desires. By the end of the application, I was exhausted, thirsty, ravenous and had to pee like a racehorse. But I was determined to finish the profile before shutting down the computer. Every second counted. Men were out there—in cyberspace—awaiting me.

No two seconds passed after I hit "Save" than a big yellow box popped up. It read, "Sorry, but this site only allows participation by those single, divorced, or widowed. ELove does not accept applications from legally separated persons."

I was furious. ELove was a dating Gestapo. Why wasn't I warned at the start that separated people weren't allowed to participate? I wasted four hours with nothing to show—no date, no flirty winky face, and no pumping red cartoon heart—no nothing. I slammed the lid of my computer and went to pee.

I would not be put off so easily. Surely other sites allowed legally separated people to join and actually *use* the information and photos they uploaded. I just had to find them. Back to the computer I went to google dating sites. Up popped a slew of them, sites for all different kinds of hobbyists: equestrian singles, nudists, professors, financial planners, and canoeists. How else would a nudist find a soul-mate other than through an online site? They couldn't very well hang out at the local latte shop. There were sites for farmers, interracial couples, animal lovers, miners, tin soldier collectors, and other unimaginable groupies.

I finally found one for old farts and clicked it. An image of two older, but very attractive, people appeared. They embraced on a beach. They danced hand-in-hand in the waves. Then a close-up focused on the guy's dreamy eyes, her demure posture. Would I ever be happy like that again? Would I ever find lasting love? Appealing to the ceiling, I offered a short prayer: "Please, hook me up with a charming guy, too—minus the sand."

Time to set to work. I had neglected to save the eLove profile, so I had to start all over. If a good man was out there, I must reveal myself in the most luxurious prose ever written.

I ruminated on my task. What would a potential mate want to hear from another potential mate? I pecked away at the keyboard. "Single, thirty-nine-year-old, good-looking, good woman in search of a good man. Walk with me through the moonlight and into the stars. Drink wine and eat Chee-toes while we gaze at your Big Dipper. This double 'D' lady is looking for a friend, companion, and travel partner to share intimate moments with in front of a crackling fireplace. It would be nice if you like animals and nature and walks in the park or strolls along the beach. This lady loves to cook, clean, dust, and watch war movies, re-runs of *The Dirty Dozen, The Good, Bad, and the Ugly* and The History

Channel. I love beer, Monday night football, motorcycles and make the best chili and homemade pepperoni pizza. I don't care if you can't read or spell "coitus," as long as you can muster a stiffie once a month, though every other day is okay. I come equipped with my own stash of erectile dysfunction medication. Good looks are a turn-off for me. I prefer short, bald men with few teeth and scoliosis. High blood pressure and high cholesterol are requirements. An ample paunch is a major turn-on. Children are my passion. Your kids will be my priority, and I'll procreate with you until my ovaries turn to raisinettes. This woman is independent and self-employed, and she makes a *very* comfortable living. I look forward to sharing myself and all my possessions with you. *Contact me, please. Please.*

I reread my profile. Exquisite. I'd get a ton of clicks on my site, perhaps in minutes. And then the next step would be emailing, giving out my private email to that lucky stud with the ponytail, stars-and-stripes head scarf, and Buddha-belly. In a fortnight I'd meet Sir Sweat-a-Lot at a local beer joint where we'd gaze into each other's eyes and finger-fuck each other under the table. Finally, off we'd ride, together, on his iron horse, into the sunset and to the land of forevermore.

Something in that write-up, however, caused goose bumps to do the "wave" up my arms and down my legs. I shuddered. Who was I kidding? What kind of guy would I be attracting with such a pandering profile? I didn't want a boozing biker boy-toy. Likewise, I didn't want a guy whose formalwear consisted of muscle shirts, thongs, and frayed denims and whose only form of exercise is leaping from the couch after his team scored a touchdown.

Soon enough I would learn that guile in online dating is never productive because it can't exist in cyberspace forever. He'd know after a few dates what I truly looked like, how old I was, what kind of personality I had, and what I really expected in a partner. So, it made no sense to post a picture of Jennifer Aniston if the belly that preceded me into the room resembled Rosie's. If I more resembled Cinderella's step-sister, then I shouldn't expect to land a prince either. If the truth revealed itself, Mr. Right deserved to know his potential lover hated cooking, ignorance, and boozing for its own sake. I also hated any sport featuring a ball. How humans, supposedly the most intelligent species on earth, could entertain themselves for hours, months, and even lifetimes with objects even dogs tire of in minutes is beyond my imagination. At my age and after life with Lance, only one kind of ball was worth playing with.

All was beginning to make sense, logically. If I couldn't project my real self to a man, then I shouldn't really want him because, in the end, the relationship would fail. I really wouldn't want a guy just as content dating Ellie Mae Clampit's ugly cousin as he would me. Besides, actually disliking two-wheeled death-traps, games with a ball, and beer-breath, the last thing I wanted near me were screaming kids, neither his nor his exes'.

Time for a rewrite: "The Truth Be Out."

The computer screen cleared, my fingers beating up the keyboard. "Legally separated, forty-nine-year-old, good-looking woman looking for a good-looking man. I am bodacious, so my mate should be, too. If you don't post a picture of yourself, forget it. You'll get no response because you must be 'fugly.' Until I determine you aren't a cereal killer and haven't killed Tony the Tiger, we will meet for coffee in grocery store cafes for the first year. Incidentally, a mama's boy is a turn-off, so you should not have seen your mother more than once in the last year, or, preferably, she should be dead. I would like someone younger than myself so that he can—*perform sexually and satisfy me three times a day, every day, except holidays and solar eclipses*—keep up with my active lifestyle. I like to hike, ride horses, garden, and walk around in animal shit. My partner should have my same dietary habits, which means, 'No pig or goat meat allowed.' All cultures accepted, except Eskimo and Ethiopian. It helps if you have a 'beyond college' degree and adequate money. If you are looking for someone who loves to cook, tend kids, couch it up to watch TV, and bake, I am not the one for you. No one will be considered who cannot correctly use a semicolon. Email me if you're interested. If not, it's your loss."

I posted three pictures of myself, hit "Send" and retired to the kitchen for a turkey sandwich. After ten minutes and while devouring the sandwich and soda, my computer began burping alerts. I ran to the dating site—jackpot—thirty-seven emails.

With each "hit" popped up a picture with a short explanation of the guy's character and interests. To each of the first ten displays I responded with a nice message, thanking each for his interest. After all, one was obligated to be polite. If they took the time to read my profile and email me, I should really answer, even if their pictures did make me nauseous. We could, at least, be pen-pals.

The first hour of online dating was a hoot. In just a few minutes I was attracting men to my site like flies to a horse turd. To those I wasn't interested in, I dutifully sent a quick reply. "You're very handsome. Actually, too handsome for me, in fact. I will bow out because you deserve better." Soon, however, the hits were coming in so hard and fast this dater found herself frantic responding to each one promptly and politely. Completely panic-stricken, I bit off a nail. "I can't keep this up. The ones I'm not interested in are out-weighing the ones *I am* interested in by twenty to one. I can't begin to answer them all." I decided, then, in the interest of time and expediency, when the profile picture didn't attract, I would just have to delete the inquiry.

I soon discovered men were clueless about posting an attractive picture of themselves. At some I grunted out loud. Why would a guy stand in a public bathroom, his cell phone extended, and take a selfie in the mirror while the urinals stood at attention behind him? And what's with the long-distance shots? Those were taken from so far away the image could well have been one of Big Foot or Justin Bieber instead of "Handsome Is As Handsome Does."

Then there were the ones straddling a "crotch rocket" motorcycle. Y*eah, real appealing. Not!* The guy wearing a huge grin and holding a big fish, chest-height, was a real turn-on, too. And the one sitting on his neoprene sofa with a slew of taxidermied heads behind him really got my clit throbbing, too. The faceless pictures got the "gate"—a guy, his back to the camera and dangling from a rope while rappelling off a cliff, a man encased in a snowsuit while snowboarding through a blizzard, another in scuba gear, his face stretched ghoulish by a mask and regulator.

So many guys had posted blur-o-grams to mask their looks. Not even a human blessed with high-definition vision could discern eyes, nose, and lips from positions so cleverly positioned to hide fat pockets and scars. For those posting pics designed to camouflage body parts, I developed a firm policy—*delete*. If a man posted a picture of himself as small as a stinkbug on a wall viewed from seven hundred yards, he was headed for the "trash."

My initial desire to be polite turned sour quickly. A comb-over, a moustache containing last night's dinner, a mole with a hair—all, with a flick of a finger, flew into the trash bin of cyberspace. Shots of him singing karaoke, pics of him holding a baby with spit-up on its face all faced deletion as well as those posting their high school picture.

Soon I became a reconnaissance dater. Was a big, forced smile an effort to conceal three chins? Was the absence of a full-body shot evidence of a gut the size of a sumo wrestler? As well, photos bearing no calendar dates were suspect as were photos showing discrepancies of body shape, face shape, and age—a questionable cornucopia of a single soul. If the guy wasn't thin in most every picture, or if the face shots clashed, they hit the trash. Finally, I deleted those posing next to any kind of a hunted dead animal.

As well, I deleted men based on red flags in their written profiles. Fifty-year-old men looking for women aged thirty to forty I immediately deleted.

Fuck those Lances. Ginnie, you could run circles

26

around those youngsters. Who needs them? Next! As well I deleted men who began their profile paragraphs with, "Well, here I go again, having to write about myself, which I don't like." Christ, get a grip. You've only been living with yourself for the past fifty years. You can't write a simple paragraph about yourself? Hire a fifth-grader. Anyone sending me a set of cartoon lips got the delete button, as well. Lazy, clueless, illiterate men need not apply.

As well, I trashed the extremists—the triathaloners, the pants-shitting biathletes, the wave-runners, the surfer-dudes, the guys frequenting gyms every night after work. Really? When did he intend to date me if, after work, he was humping a treadmill?

I automatically deleted the "cruisers." *Looking for a cruise partner, are you? Take Pepe, your dog.* Like I really wanted to watch a total stranger eat like a cartoon pig and then fight off a bout of diarrhea on the poop deck. *"Th-th-th-th-th-that's all, folks!"* Similarly, those attributing all their accomplishments to some higher being they haven't even met nor had coffee with just really ground my gears.

Delete...delete...delete.

What I discovered during several minutes of continuous trashing of the clueless, toothless, and hairless, was there were fewer than five men I was actually attracted to. My shoulders slumped after an hour of deleting. Some self-assessment was needed. Perhaps I was being too picky, too superficial. After all, I guess even *I* could turn off some potential mates.

A glance in the mirror found me rather comely. My usual bobbed hair had grown a bit scraggly and in need of a haircut, but, other than that, I considered myself fairly attractive—nice teeth and lips, sparkling hazel eyes. Body was certainly good enough for my age—not too fat, perhaps, even, a bit too thin, thanks to Lance.

Had I been too dismissive? I arrived at a conclusion—better to weed out the detractors right now than waste time dating them later. My *modus operandi* of "vetting out" the five semi-finalists would continue after lunch.

While I devoured a hot dog with Selena, my feline friend, a knock sounded. It was Jack. A whiff of spicey cologne followed him into the room. His goatee was immaculately coiffed, and he was dressed in crispy jeans and a white waffle shirt. He looked inbound to an exotic port of call. In his hands dangled a small brown paper bag.

"Look at you," I quipped. "All dressed up and no place to go."

He smirked. Selena slinked around his leg, and he booted her away.

"Hey! Don't kick Selena, Jack. What's the matter with you?"

"You know I hate cats." His moustache curled into a leprechaun's grin.

"I know. But she's only being friendly. What brings you into the sticks today?"

"Lois is working, and I'm stopping by to see if you needed anything from the store or if you needed any help in the barn or anything." Shuffling his feet, he stared at the floor.

"Oh. Really? That's nice. Thanks, but I think I'm okay today." I shoved the rest of the hot dog into my mouth. "I've already mucked and stuff. Just have to bring the horses inside before it gets dark."

"Well, I was in the area and thought I'd just stop by to see if you needed me."

"Uh, thanks." I wasn't used to seeing Jack without Lois. "What fun we had the other night at your place." I laughed. "Seems we always get onto the subject of sex and your and Lois' sex life, which, incidentally, is always a hoot. That calendar with the red stars is hysterical—material for comedy clubs, for sure."

"Yes, our sex life is sometimes—just between you and me—a sore subject between Lois and me." He scowled. "I like it every other night, and she would be happy with it once a month."

"Well, you gotta give her a break, Jack. She *is* fifty-five years old, ya know. Just do that quickie thing every once in a while instead of your ball-busting marathons."

"You and Lois just don't understand." His eyes closed to slits. "I don't do quickies." His assertion sounded as noble as one swearing off "crack." "If I can't satisfy my partner, I might as well not have sex." He paused and straightened his shoulders. "Sex, for me, is all about satisfying my partner." He stared and handed me the brown bag. "Here. You need to watch a couple of these."

I looked inside—porno flicks—one with the appropriate, salacious title, *Cleopatra Does Tutankhamun.* I gulped and offered a gigantic smile. "Geez, thanks, Jack. Would you like some Chee-toes? I just got a five-pound box at Sam's Club the other day." I leaped to the cabinet.

"No, thanks. Like I said, I just stopped by to see if you needed any help."

"Nope. Nope. I'm good. Good. Real good. Thanks.

29

Really appreciate it."

"All right, then. I guess I'm gonna go." With his hand on the doorknob, he looked down, and I stumbled for the right words. He needed comforting.

"Ya know, Jack, seriously, like I said before, just 'cause you love steak doesn't mean you wanna eat it six days a week."

"Yeah, I know. It's just the way I am. I've had a high sex drive all my life. Can't do anything about it at the age of fifty-two." Suddenly his face lit up. "Back in high school, I remember taking Tina Martin parking on the weekends. I'd park on one road and screw her. Then I took her to another back alley and screwed her again. Then we drove somewhere else, and I'd have sex with her again. Then on Sunday nights, I'd be screwing the minister's daughter at another place. I was *unstoppable*." Jack grinned. He was puffed up like a tom turkey.

"Well, I tend to agree with Lois you are a bit over-sexed. Aren't there any pills you can take to treat that?"

"Oh, I'm not going to take anything. I'm fine the way I am. Lois is the one who has a problem with it."

"Okay, well, just a suggestion, is all."

He opened the door and stepped out. Selena followed him, and I scooped her into my arms. He stepped onto the running board of his truck. He yelled, "If there's anything I can do for you, just let me know. And promise you'll watch those movies."

"I will. I mostly definitely will. Thanks. Bye, Jack."

I stepped inside and scurried to my computer while Jack's truck rumbled down the driveway. The green page of the over-fifty dating site appeared again on my

30

screen. Another twenty "views" to my profile. Another ten emails in my inbox. I hit on the inbox and viewed the first of the ten newest aspiring partners. "Now that one looks interesting. Some hair, nice face, normal-sized body. Says he likes cats and BBQ's. He loves taking walks, nature, relaxing with a special someone in a mountain setting. A bit trite, maybe, but I gotta start somewhere."

With my index finger already poised over the delete button, I switched to "Save."

Chapter Four
To Her with Love

That evening I sent out a message to the fifty-six year-old guy living twenty-six miles north-northeast of Syracuse, New York. His photos spoke well of him—nice chin, eyes, bald except for some fuzzicals clinging like Grim Death to the side of his head. He had straight teeth, a complete set, no less. One shot showed him with his arms around his two sons at someone's wedding. He looked hot—about one thousand degrees hot. His write-up, however, attracted me even more—outdoorsy type, fit, loves hiking, nature, rock-climbing, kayaking, ice-skating, and skiing. When he said he enjoyed the art of scuba diving, he had me hooked. So, I sent him an email.

The next day I received an "Echo" back. He was interested in me, too, and had noted our similar interests. He asked my status, and I told him I was legally separated but had no intention of taking "Lance in the Pants" back should he ever decide to leave his whore.

All he said was "I'm sorry for what you're going through." Then he said, with kind encouragement, "What doesn't kill us only makes us stronger."

I wanted to write such a mantra was all well and good, and it sure is easy to rattle off advice like that in an email, but it was a bit harder to live. A lot harder.

Then, because he wanted to see more pictures, I referred him to my Facebook page in which he could drown himself in a maelstrom of Virginie Snow. He could also google my name and read my life's history, including places I'd taught, books I'd written, accomplishments, mistakes, and gossip concerning my cat being a homosexual—not that there was anything wrong with that.

The following day he sent me an email through the site. His first words were "Hello, Kitten."

I melted.

Kitten! No one ever called you "Kitten" before, Ginnie. Kitten is the perfect moniker for a cat lover. You're lovin' this guy already.

I was really getting to like this internet dating business. No stalking men in grocery stores, the malls, making quick and flirty eye contact with strangers or going through an awkward getting-to-know-you phase. Though the dating site cost twenty dollars a month, this online flirting also saved me big-time gas money traveling to meet men. In the morning while glued to the potty chair and my tablet screen, I perused the messages accumulated from the night before. Like a cancer patient with a new drug, the dating site had become another chance at life.

So, the Mad Bomber, as I later nick-named him, and I corresponded back and forth through emails for a few hours, and then I finally suggested we meet, especially since he wasn't too far from me, a mere three hours, which is really pretty far but not so far when you realize dating sites operate globally. At least he wasn't in Finland or the Czech Republic.

"I would love to meet you, too," he wrote back.

"You're absolutely gorgeous."

My inner voice, my conscience, was ecstatic. *Gorgeous. He thinks you're gorgeous. Holy crap!*

I pounded a reply on the keyboard. "Well, handsome, I'd really like to meet. If you'd like, I have a book signing at the Almond Festival in Schenectady this weekend." My fingers missed half the keys, I was so excited. The email provided him with directions, hours for the festival, and other activities we could do during out first meeting, but I had to guard against over-eagerness. I didn't want to look as desperate as I felt.

Wonder of wonders, a guy whose looks and personality attracted and who found me equally attractive only lived a few hours away. I had visions of his sitting intent and rubbing his hard-on before his computer in the hinterlands of up-state New York. That erection complimented me and me alone. I was flattered and sighed lovingly at the computer screen.

His email burped through. "I'd really love to meet you this week…" My excitement was building, but then I read ahead to the next words. "…but I'm in Iraq."

"He's in Iraq!" Selena leaped from the sofa.

"You're in Iraq." I wrote back without an exclamation point or question mark—my dead-pan voice. "Lovely."

"Yes, but I'll be home for Christmas. I'm managing a privately contracted company over here to collect and de-fuse land mines and IED's. I'm in energetics."

"Energetics?" I scowled. "What is energetics?"

"Explosives."

"Bet you're having a blast." Sometimes I could be

34

so proud of my wit. "So, at any time, you could end up in bits and pieces? I prefer a guy with ears, if you don't mind." A long pause sounded. "So, then, I guess we won't be able to meet this weekend at the festival?"

"Not too likely. All good things take time. I'll see you at Christmas, for sure, gorgeous."

"Okay. I'll put you on my calendar, then. Nice talking to you. And don't get blown up."

"I'll try not to, Kitten."

Smiling, I shut down the computer.

****

I decided fairly early on in this dating game I needed a policy, just as any successful business entrepreneur would, to promote efficiency in dating. In an effort to protect myself and sort out any "Interesteds," I would compile a list of requirements, no matter how superficial or shallow, ones known only to myself. The first requisite was the guy's first name.

My potential mate needed a strong, virile name, one with a sexy ring, capable of being uttered without embarrassment during a romantic moment. On my list of acceptable names were Don, Steve, Mark, Brian, Jack, John, Chris, Antonio, and Paul. All I needed to do—at time of introduction via Internet—was pronounce the name while huffing and puffing as if in an orgasmic fit. If it sounded respectable and sexy, I'd return an email to the lucky-named. If it didn't resonate, I was done. Some would think me callous. Too bad. This was a free country, and I made the deal with myself. The name would have to flow off my tongue during a passionate embrace. "Oh...oh...oh...Mark." I imagined myself whispering in a romantic voice. "Hold me, Mark. Kiss me, Mark. Oh, Mark."

Unfortunately, I could never envision myself moaning or gasping names like Oscar, Elmer, Lowell, Dennis, Bruce, the Hispanic name Jesus, Franklin, Ralph, George, or Feldon. If I couldn't envision myself calling out my man's name during sex without dissolving into hysterics, I wasn't going to go there in reality. Too many good men were available with good, strong names a woman could whisper in the sack without burping a laugh.

Another requirement of my dating policy lay in a prospect's expertise in the field of grammar and punctuation. A profile page littered with spelling errors, run-ons and fragments, and other writing errors became a real turn-off for a writing instructor such as myself. If the guy couldn't build a decent sentence, I didn't want him building a climax with me either. While I needn't date a Shakespeare or a Faulkner, I preferred a guy who could identify "See Spot run!" as an imperative sentence.

Furthermore, my dating rule book included a ban on certain images and comments in a guy's profile. Particularly offensive were references or images to "hogs"—motorcycles. I passed on any guy's profile with only one head shot but twenty pictures of his motorcycle in various erotic positions—a full-on, tilted shot of its headlights, a close-up of its pipes, a shot of its ass-end, or a pic of the cycle on a sunset beach. If a man's motorcycle had become his surrogate wife, I hit delete.

Men surrounded with scads of children got the same boot, too. At the age of forty-nine and after having been sexually ignored by my soon-to-be-ex for sixteen years, I didn't wish to take a backseat to anyone—grandkids or the grandkids' kids. Time is too short and precious for a whole lot of sharing. What I would concede to, however, was sharing space and time with a pet of my beau's choice, for animals are selfless and don't require constant coddling. Nor do they demand cell phones. They also don't scream and holler at the drop of a toy. It doesn't matter what kind of critter it is, as long as it doesn't speak garbled English or walk around with spit-up in its hair.

Finally, I concocted a careful analysis of photos—a profile bearing only head shots signifies dysfunction in the lower parts—perhaps a beer belly, a man with a woman's ass, one or more limbs missing, which is all right if they are up-front about it in their profile. In fact, though I would not question a head shot of a man laughing so hard as to bunch up three folds of chin skin, that same pelican neck in a bland, serious photo would be a turn-off. This was the final countdown. At this stage of my love life I wanted it all, including a man who had kept himself in a respectable, decent-looking state through adequate exercise and wise eating. Chipmunk cheeks serving as storage containers for tomorrow's lunch just wouldn't fly.

****

My bomber guy never did get a chance to come home for Christmas, as he promised, because his company moved him to begin another de-bombing mission in Afghanistan. By that time, which happened sometime after my worst, loneliest Christmas ever, John and I had grown to know and appreciate each other very well through email. He vowed to see me during his February vacation.

I thought it a bit odd Jack and Lois held different

37

perspectives on my "Mad Bomber," as I so lovingly referred to him. While Lois thought he was very handsome and dedicated to his job—"Always a good quality"—Jack disagreed.

"Who would be so dumb as to work in a position where he could be blown to smithereens?" Jack smirked. "He could die and leave his entire family alone and destitute."

Lois frowned and stirred the cannellini. "Jack, you're so negative. Some people love this country. They'd do anything for her. He's probably a very patriotic, conservative kind of guy."

Jack grunted and set the table.

"He is really devoted to his job and family," I said. "And he's coming home to see me in February. He calls me Kitten and Gorgeous every day. I feel a special connection to him."

Jack rolled his eyes. "That won't ever go anywhere."

"Don't say that," Lois shouted. "You don't know where their relationship will go."

"The guy's gonna explode!" Jack yelled. Then, he headed, laughing, into the bathroom and closed the door.

****

John's de-bombing mission in Afghanistan was extended, however, and he missed coming home in February. One day he emailed asking if I knew how to Skype. I am, admittedly, not very computer savvy and didn't know if that was a trendy type of sky-diving or if it was a new, technologically advanced method of wiping one's ass. *Sky-y-y-ype, sky-y-y-ype, sky-y-y-y-ype! Clean as a whistle!* I was wrong on both counts—

it was a computer program for people from remote spots around the world to see *and* talk to each other at the same time.

After I downloaded the Skype program, the computer dialed John's cell number. Like magic the screen lit up, and there sat my handsome guy staring at me from his office chair. I ratcheted my chair up to the screen and squinted, my own computer camera simultaneously picking up my own image and transmitting it to his computer in Afghanistan.

"Oh," I said. I smiled and smoothed my hair. I could see myself in a small box in the bottom right side of the screen and winced. "Can you see me, John?"

"I sure can, kitten." I looked hard at the screen. He leaned toward me and stared—our first meeting. I blushed and crossed my legs in a demure fashion, even though he couldn't see below my chest. I smiled sweetly, straightened my shirt, and he smiled back. His stare was intent, focused, *close,* as though he could reach out and touch me. I blushed again.

This Skyping felt awfully personal, a bit weird. I looked down at my box featuring my talking head and regretted not having the forethought to apply some make-up. After all, I was home alone with no one else to see my divorce-bags under my eyes. How clear and distinct would I show up on his computer screen anyway? Would he be able to make out every wrinkle and naso-labial fold? He was all the way on the other side of the world, for Christ's sake.

As I found out, he could see me pretty damn clearly.

An awkward pause followed, and I tongue-sucked a piece of Frito from between my teeth. "So, how's it hangin', John?"

He smiled, sat back in his chair. It squeaked when he moved. "You are, indeed, gorgeous, Kitten."

Only the socially backward could turn such a vivid shade of red, a dead give-away as to my relative inexperience with men and my lack of flirting expertise. After all, I hadn't dated much at all before Lance, and then I was with him—only—for twenty-eight years. What I knew about men was largely gleaned from information gained through tabloid newspapers, romance novels, and stories relayed from high school and college girlfriends.

"Thanks." I grinned like a jackass eating stickers. I checked my little portrait box on the screen's bottom-right and quickly wiped the piano-toothed, pillow-tucked smile from my face. "I appreciate the compliment. You're handsome, too, just as your photos show."

This Skyping feels very awkward, Ginnie.

I ordered my conscience quiet. After all, how did she expect me to communicate with a guy in Afghanistan—through a walkie-talkie?

Five more minutes of stilted conversation followed. Skyping seemed little more than a glorified peep show—two people watching each other between a few quips—all the while analyzing, thinking, judging for "sparkage" projected through a computer screen. Then, in another awkward moment, John showed me his office/home, a shipping container converted into a living and office quarters. Booming echoed in the background.

"What's that noise?" I said. I checked my little box and tried relaxing my furrowed brow.

Frowning's not good, Ginnie. You're Botox-ready.

"Just some shelling going on out there. We're always taking hits from the enemy."

"Can your little hut—I sometimes *never* have a way with words—withstand a bomb strike?"

"No, not at all."

"Oh, that's not good."

"No, it sure isn't, but the Kandahar Air Force base here is two miles square. So, the chances of anything hitting my container are remote. Nothin' I can do about it anyway."

"Guess not." I felt shamefully safe in my home office in rural Climax, New York.

So the conversation continued for another ten minutes, painfully slow because the computers allowed only one person to speak at a time. Then a lag between one's comment and the other person's occurred. As soon as I began to respond to what John had said seconds ago, he began to say something else. The audio lag was disconcerting, awkward, interruptive, and necessarily repetitive. Conversation dropped in and out with the idiosyncratic poor connection. Skyping was cumbersome. But for someone stuck in a tin can in Afghanistan, I guess it was the only way to socialize and date.

What I really wanted to do was reach out and touch him, smell his cologne, which he probably wasn't wearing anyway since he existed in a steel box, and gaze into real eyes. I wanted to experience his "chemistry." One could scarcely figure "sparkage" with a hard screen and five gazillion miles between her and her potential man.

"Are you there?" John said. He leaned forward in

his chair.

The connection had gone bad—he faded out then popped into focus again. When he did, I found myself looking at an eye the size of a whale, like a deep-sea creature, its tentacles sucked up against the screen. I gasped. He gasped, too, as he evidently caught sight of himself projected on his computer at the bottom right. He ricocheted back in his seat, away from the screen, and smiled. But I had already seen his huge, rheumy eye, its eyelid burdened under a dry, scaly patch of skin. Like the submariner in *20,000 Leagues Under the Sea,* I had looked into the giant squid eye, one whose primalness and depth of experience was as unfathomable to me as the abyss from which it had risen. John was sitting back from the screen—smaller now—his eye normal size, his body relaxed. I breathed relief.

After another few minutes of stilted conversation, I bowed out as gracefully as I could. "I better go now. I had a green apple this morning, and I think it's telling me something. I need to run."

And so I clicked the "away" icon, closed out the program, and shut off my computer. That would be the last Skype date I'd ever have.

You didn't even get a slice of pizza, for cryin' out loud.

As for the Mad Bomber, I had to be realistic. He wouldn't be back from Afghanistan for another year, and I could not continue to date a man through a computer screen.

And that eye. Well, it was just too scary.

Chapter Five
"Honestandfun"

That winter internet dating became my extracurricular activity each evening after a hard day tending the farm and writing for my farm animal advocacy group. After a day mucking horse stalls, scooping goat manure, shoveling snow from the walkways, cleaning litter boxes, and removing cobwebs from the barn rafters, I needed diversion. Grabbing my notebook and "tuning in" to examine the latest "I'm interested in you" dating message had quickly become my relaxing but enticing end to a long day of raking the turds of a myriad of animals.

What tasty male morsel awaited our log-in tonight?

Sitting in my soon-to-be-ex's black, over-sized chair, I switched the notebook to "on." The computer screen lit up in an eerie green glow the color of lime Jell-O, and the living room walls reflected the light like the afterglow of an A-bomb. I ordered Safari to my go-to dating site—five new messages.

I was the queen of the fucking prom!

The usernames men chose were meant to allure, but so many of them had no idea how to pick a moniker. Some names would, no doubt, send their potential dates running as though from Joel Rifkin—Gunslinger45, Rabidforyou. Those with creepy animal names made me choke, as well—Eelskinner,

Scorpionking, Ferdelance, Minimoo. Likewise, I could not flirt with those who couldn't spell a username correctly—Agechallanged, Bukanear58, Shevyman.

Quickly, I scrolled through another list of the love-lorn. Bigjavelin. *You wish.* Fast&furious. *Whoa, big guy.* Sexysilverfox, Badandbald, Onceanddone. *You've got to be kidding, right! Add* not bright *to that moniker, too.* 12just4u. *Three, four, shut the door.* Drillerman. *Yikes.* RammerXXL. *Double Yikes.* And Lickandlap. *What the fuck?*

Then some would never tempt my interest: Chubbs350, Pastamachine, Boneybones, Pckrhd, Loveslasagna, and Applehead. *Yeah, that gets me wet and saucy.*

I yawned and tapped on Honestandfun.

Up popped Honestandfun's profile—a head shot of him standing before an ancient castle on the moors of Scotland. Not bad. Brown hair, not mohawked, in dreadlocks, or streaked purple. Nice smile. Normal-looking expression. I clicked on Honestandfun's write-up.

"I teach high school, love to travel, enjoy nature and taking long walks with that special someone. I love the simpler things in life—pets, wine, and a good, home-cooked meal. Life is short—would love to share romantic evenings with the right person. :)"

This guy was a definite potential date. After all, he did enjoy the company of animals. He couldn't be *that* bad.

I clicked on his email and said "Hello. It's nice to meet you."

Honestandfun wrote back, "Hi, there, Foxylady. Nice to meet you, too. :)"

I had had a very difficult time trying to come up with a suitable username for myself designed to throw axe-murderers, rapists, and other sociopaths off their game. Some names just didn't cut it. For some reason, the name game sent me into a fit of sarcasm. Frenchtwister, Cockbuster, Pussygalore, Hitortits, Tongueandtied. Finally, I forced my brain to think in terms of what a guy would be looking for in a long-term woman. Bornforyou, Justyoursize, Smartandsweet, Cookiebaker, or Cleanandgreen. I couldn't bring myself to use any name that made me seem slutty or "toot sweet."

Though certainly I could use my real name as my username, the website discouraged such openness for fear of encouraging bizarros to be...well...bizarre. After much thought and elimination I came up with something sexy and beguiling while at the same time putting an incongruous twist on it. "Foxylady" satisfied my love for animals, my new vision of myself as alluring, charming, and playful yet fulfilled my perception of myself as a woman of honor—a gentlewoman.

His email appeared in my inbox. "Hey, Foxylady. I see we have like interests in nature, hiking, exploring far-off places and enjoying the simpler things in life. I think we could be a good match. How about if we meet for coffee and donuts?"

Donuts, hot damn! I would at least get a free sugar rush if the date was a drag. Before responding, however, this Foxylady perused his profile again, casing out the "joint," looking for clues of misrepresentation and those advertising his sanity or lack thereof—nothing out of the ordinary. The two photos—one, a torso shot with a castle in the background, and another, a close-up of his laughing face—evidenced a fair to good rating on facial features. No beaver teeth, nostrils of average size, full pouty lips, two eyes—everything in place, symmetrical and appearing functional.

So, I clicked on "Reply" and began my own response. "Hi there, Honestandfun. You sound like a nice guy. Indeed, we do have similar interests, and you don't look like a serial killer. Perhaps we should talk on the phone before meeting just so that I know you're not a nut case." Then I added the rhetorical and protective "lol."

In a minute his reply appeared on my screen, "Dear Foxylady, I assure you I'm not a serial killer. But if you are more comfortable with talking on the phone before meeting, I have no problem with that. Please give me your number."

I tapped out my number and waited.

When my cell phone began to bark, I looked at the display. An unrecognized number. Probably Mr. Honestandfun. I answered in my most sultry voice.

There was a pause.

He said, "Is this Foxylady?"

I replied that, indeed, I was she.

"Hi, my real name is James. How are you this evening?"

"Hi, Jim. I'm just fine. I'm Ginnie."

Though I'd have dreamt Jim would be the most articulate master of phraseology and rhetoric I'd ever witnessed in one of the male species, he wasn't, but that was okay. Though I had hoped for a British accent complementing the complexity of thought the likes of

Henry James, I was surprisingly not too disappointed he didn't sound like Thurston the English butler. This guy actually sounded like an average, sane guy. He wasn't verbose. He used common, everyday vocabulary in order to simply communicate a personality of good spirit and niceness. What I liked was he wasn't out to impress me in any way. He wasn't performing or acting comedic, clever, or witty, like Sylvester the cat. He simply talked...well...normal.

His casualness attracted. He was a high school teacher, taught ninth grade history, and took classes on field trips to Europe—the picture of him in front of the castle had been taken in Scotland—and he loved hiking and bicycling. He said he was fit and active and that he and I—if we hit it off—could take a walk in a park sometime.

Throughout the conversation I had my notebook handy, perusing his two pictures as we spoke. I visualized him speaking, and the vibes I was getting were nice, cozy, comfortable, even a bit sexy. I was as interested as if Mel Gibson, on a good day, had walked into the room.

"Okay," I said. "Let's meet. We only live twenty minutes apart. Wanna do tomorrow?"

The pause sounded as heavy as a concrete block in mud. "Tomorrow? Are you sure you want to meet tomorrow already?"

Uh, would you rather do next year?

"Sure, why not? You've passed the serial killer test as far as I'm concerned. I'm attracted to your two pics, and you sound like a really nice guy. Why? Do you already have something planned?"

"Uh, no. I guess not."

Something in that labored response should've put me wise.

"So, where would you like to meet?" I said.

"Uh, how about meeting for coffee at the Earlman's Wegmans on Route 81, in the café loft?"

"A grocery store?" A laugh erupted from my throat.

Tell him, "Hey, I got it! Let's meet at the butcher counter in front of the liver. Or how about in front of the pickled cow's tongue?"

I told my conscience to stop the comedy act. "Uh, sure. We can we get some donuts. I'd love some donuts—bear claws or anything with cinnamon or raisins. Or nuts. Yes, I just love nuts."

"Yeah. Sure." The silence was as heavy as a donkey's ass.

"Okay, then. We're set. What time?"

"Nine in the morning."

I choked.

Going on a date at nine in the morning—to a grocery store? Is he kidding? Not exactly a pussy-throbbing thought.

I wanted to say, "Hey, do I resemble a rooster?" If I were meant to get up at the crack of dawn, I'd have been born with a flashlight where my beaver is." Instead, I said, "That's pretty early. How about ten?"

"Sure. See you then."

****

That evening Lois invited me over for spaghetti with meat sauce. Flurries began when I stopped at the store for some garlic bread and salad fixings. When I knocked on the door carrying my goody bag, Jack answered, a paring knife in his hand. He looked as serious as Jack the Ripper. "Come on in." He hurried back to the kitchen counter. I placed my bag on the kitchen table, hung up my coat, and began to take out the groceries.

"How're you guys doing? Where's Lois?"

His voice was unusually high-pitched, like Elmer Fudd's. "Lois isn't here right now. She'll be back soon—went to see Wanda. But it's okay you're here. Nothing wrong with that at all. We can cut up the vegetables for the salad."

"Good." I cast him the stink eye. What was eating him? I opened a cabinet and poured the salad fixings into a large bowl. Then I searched the refrigerator, found a stray tomato and cucumber and began to slice them into bite-sized pieces.

Suddenly a dish crashed to the floor. "Damn," Jack yelled. He picked up the pieces and slammed them into the trash. "Lois should be home any minute." He worked furiously at the opposite end of the counter. *Hack, hack, hack* sounded Jack's knife. He was as fidgety as a kid urgent to pee. "Watch any of those movies I gave you yet?"

"Not yet. Maybe tomorrow. You okay?" I turned to face him.

"Fine. Why?" His voice sounded like a mouse caught inside a tin can.

"I don't know. You seem *preoccupado*, and you sound like you've been sucking on a helium balloon."

"No. Nothing's wrong." He rinsed his knife frantically under the faucet.

"Okay. If you say so." I walked over to the sink to wash off some lettuce and accidentally brushed against his leg. He leaped aside and shot me a look as though I had seared him with a hot pan.

"What the fuck's the matter with you?" I yelled. A lettuce leaf fell from my fingers and fluttered to the floor.

"Nothing! You just startled me. I was concentrating on cutting up this head of cauliflower when you bumped me. You could at least be more careful where you're walking."

I frowned. "Make a federal fucking case out of it, why don't you? I'm sorry, I didn't mean to touch your frickin' thigh."

"Lois should be home any minute." He was as strung out as Freddie Mercury.

"Good. That's nice, Jack." *He's really weirded out.* I continued to design a luscious salad of spring mix, tomatoes, Vidalia onions, croutons, and capers. I thought a few walnuts would add some extra zest to the whole thing and had opened a cabinet door looking for a stash of nuts when the front door opened. Lois.

"Hey, Lois," Jack piped. He sounded like Marge Simpson. He announced something Einstein would have puzzled over. "We are cutting up vegetables for the salad."

Lois glanced sideways at him. "Yeah? So? You want a medal?"

"What's up, Lois?" I said. "How's Wanda?" I threw the rest of a bag of walnuts into the salad mix and searched the refrigerator for various bottled salad dressings.

"She's fine, very busy, as usual." Lois threw her coat and purse into a chair. She stepped next to me and poured herself an orange-flavored vodka. "So, what are you guys drinking?"

"Nothing yet," I said. "Jack hasn't offered me anything."

Lois glared at her live-in boyfriend of four years. Before him on a cutting board sat a mountain of cauliflower, enough to feed a platoon of rabbits. "You didn't get Ginnie anything to drink, Jack?"

"Hey, I'm busy here cutting up vegetables." He chopped furiously and then began throwing clumps of cauliflower into a stainless steel pot. Something was eating him. Then, he threw down the knife and headed, with some annoyance, for the liquor cabinet. "Ginnie, what would you like? Your whipped cream flavored vodka?"

"That's fine, Jack." I put the French dressing and my favorite, bleu cheese dressing, on the kitchen table.

Jack hurried back into the kitchen, ripped open a cabinet door, grabbed a snifter, and poured out the vodka. Then he placed it on the table. "Here. Happy?" Scowling, he escaped to his cutting board and began chopping up a head of broccoli.

Lois noticed his weird behavior. "What's the matter with you, Jack? You seem agitated." She mixed a drink for herself, pouring damn-near half the bottle of vodka into the juice.

"Nothing is wrong, I'm telling you! Absolutely nothing. Everything's fine and dandy. Now, will you let me alone?"

We needed to change the subject. I said, "Guess what? I'm meeting a guy tomorrow for a first date."

Lois said, "Is this one of the guys you've met online?"

"Yeah. His name is James—nice looking. Of course, there were only two pictures of him on the site, but what was there was good enough for me. He's a high school history teacher—ninth graders. So, we have teaching in common. He's not a complete dolt, anyway. He speaks standard English. We're meeting at Wegmans in Earlton on 81, up in the café loft. What do you guys think?"

I looked at Jack. He stood stiff as a dead cat.

"He's meeting you at Wegmans?" Jack snorted like Lily Tomlin. "Some date," he roared. "Seems to me he could have tried for a nicer place than a grocery store. What are you going to do? Hold hands while he shops for his toilet paper and deodorant? That's really bizarre."

I was so pissed I could've jammed a piece of cauliflower in his eye, followed by a ladle of hot gravy.

"No, it's not, Jack," Lois scolded. "I actually think it's neat. And decently cautious, too. There's all kinds of time for them to meet in more romantic settings, after all."

I said, "Well, at first I thought it a bit odd myself, but I don't mind. It's neutral territory, after all. All the dating sites recommend daters meet in a public place first—takes the heat off. And, of course, it's safe. A guy can't very well rape a woman in the produce aisle—between the Brussels sprouts and the kohlrabi, right?"

"Hack, hack, hack." Jack's knife sounded like a woodpecker drilling glass.

Lois gulped the last of her Sex on the Beach then mixed herself an even stronger Long Island iced tea. "Well, I think it's just fine. You can meet in a more romantic place later. I hope it works out for you, Ginnie."

"Yeah, would be nice. We're both teachers, and he

52

seems nice. Who knows? Maybe we will become an item. We can use our classroom paddles on each other." I laughed.

Jack snorted. "Yeah, right. These guys on the Internet are only after one thing—sex. You better watch yourself on those sites. Never know what kind of characters you meet. They can tell you anything just to get you into the sack."

"Well, we shall see," I said to neither of them in particular. "I'm new to this game. One thing, though... The whole process is efficacious. It's a giant time-saver. You go through pages and pages of single men living within and right outside your zip code. I keep scrolling them along my computer screen, kinda like herding cattle through a chute. If one appeals, you pop out a message. They write back. You talk a bit online or by phone or Skyping, and then you meet. It really facilitates meeting someone. I don't have to be a bar fly and hang out alongside the drunks. I don't have to get religion, go back to church, and sit through a sermon while perusing men praying alone and jerking off in the pew next to me. And I don't have to hang out in the condom section of the drugstores, either. I actually think this online stuff is an ingenious way to meet people."

"It sucks," Jack barked.

"Quiet, Jack," Lois said. She tipped the last of the Long Island tea into her mouth. "Give Ginnie a chance. I'm sure she can take care of herself out there in the cyber world."

****

The next day—my big grocery store date—I hurried through my morning feeding chores, showered, moisturized, and put on make-up. Grabbing my coat and keys, I headed out the door to Wegmans. Before I left, I took one more peek at James' profile so that I could recognize him in the upstairs café.

I pulled into the parking lot about ten minutes early, so I decided to look for a bear claw in Wegman's renowned bakery section. Their baked goods abounded, displayed in all manners—behind glass cabinetry, stacked high on stainless steel shelves, leaning on slanted boards behind the counters. Every kind of doughy delight enticed the weak of diet—sprinkle-coated sourdough donuts, blueberry muffins, chocolate chip cookies with toffee pieces, cakes of all ethnicities, yeasty concoctions like cinnamon bobka, and gooey sticky buns.

I stopped before the macaroons and salivated like a ravenous St. Bernard. As I stood waiting for a clerk to take my order, I glanced upstairs at the café balcony hoping that my knight-in-shining-armor hadn't already arrived. But I saw no one there looking like James.

Suddenly a short, round, older man burst through the automatic doors and headed, arms swinging, head bobbing, down the main corridor. The guy was really motoring considering he had a gut the size of a steamer trunk. My second impression was incredulity the guy would have the balls to leave his house wearing glorified pajamas. Then my next thought almost put me into catatonia. His face vaguely resembled my date, James.

Oh, heaven, have mercy on me. Don't let that old belly of the penis-shadin'-type be James'.

I stared in horror as the full-buttocked Neanderthal lumbered quickly to the coffee machines. His fleshy paws tore at the Styrofoam cups and jammed one under a coffee urn, anxiously tapping his sneakered toe as the liquid drooled into the container.

Dear Goddess, if it be James, perform miracles! Wave your magic wand and transform him into Tommy Lee Jones. And then clear up the complexion. That's all I ask.

I tried to get a grip. Maybe that wasn't James after all. I never believed in the power of prayer, but in this case I'd make an exception: *Oh, did Lincoln have it wrong. All men in this great nation may have been conceived in liberty, but they were* not *all created equal.* If that was my date, he more resembled Sasquatch than the slim vacationer of his profile picture at the Scottish castle. With those brown sweat pants and triple-X size sweatshirt meant to conceal several baloney-like fat rolls, he certainly wasn't dressed to impress.

Please, let the dough boy not be James. Jackie Gleason's not my type.

A bakery clerk came to take my order. I said, "No, thank you. I better pass on the macaroons. Gotta watch my waistline, ya know."

Hoping against hope, I climbed the steps to the upstairs café and took a seat. Bubble boy was nowhere around. Maybe, after all, that wasn't he. Just some guy hurrying for his morning coffee and a gross of chocolate-filled éclairs. Surely my muse, Aphrodite, the Greek Goddess of Love, wouldn't turn her back on me now.

Trying to look nonchalant, I sat at a table and crossed my legs. Others congregated at their tables overlooking the lower floor of the store—the produce section. If James did rival the love-lost green ogre, at least all would not be lost. Afterward, I could shop for the week's groceries. I watched hordes of people pushing their carts from counter to counter, some ordering crab cakes at the seafood section, others piling their carts high with all kinds of freshly baked bread. Then I saw Cro-Magnon monkey-knuckle toward the steps.

My heart sank like a rock thrown into quicksand.

Reaching the top of the stairs, the caveman I had seen scrambling to the coffee machines looked, smiled, and stuck out a meaty hand. "Hi, I'm James."

"Fuck you, Goddess, you cunt!"

It's just coffee and donuts. You don't have to hug him or kiss him. And he can't expect you to have sex in the canned goods aisle. All you have to do is converse and eat a donut. Buck up.

I put on my happy face and proffered a hand. "Hi, James. Nice to meet you."

"I got us a few things to eat." He plopped three paper bags on the table. Then, he slammed into his chair and pulled it tight against the table. He arranged his abdomen below the table edge and pulled a paper bag to his chest. He was on a breakfast mission.

"Oh, that's nice of you." My voice echoed back at me, forced, uncharacteristically sweet. I opened a bag and peeked inside—chocolate chip cookies the size of Frisbees, three coconut macaroons—*There is a God, after all*—and two gigantic sticky buns.

He dove into his bag and extracted a blueberry muffin. Crumbs dribbled onto the table as he washed the cake down with a mouthful of coffee, droplets hanging from his chin.

"Oops!" he said. He wiped the drool with his sleeve.

I burped a pint of gas. Then I turned my attention toward the sushi bar below. "Look at 'em down there preparing sashimi."

James' chewing mouth resembled a human cement mixer, a maelstrom of gross solids and liquids. My gorge began to rise.

You're on a date with Attila. He can't even eat with his mouth closed. Damn you, Goddess, and your claim to be merciful. Not."

I munched a macaroon, savoring the coconut flavor while Giant James plowed into the next bag of sticky buns. He had not bought a second cup of coffee for me, so I had my treat dry. Just as well. I was losing my appetite faster than an anorexic at a Thanksgiving buffet.

As he devoured the second sticky bun, he described the barbeque he was anticipating that afternoon. Myriad thoughts flit through my brain. "Why?" Why had this guy, obviously wanting to meet a partner of the opposite sex, come here dressed as though he were going to a pajama party? Why was he so focused on the sweet treats instead of on Sweet Me? And what was his ultimate goal by having met me here? Did he want someone to gobble breakfast with, or did he want to woo a potential mate? Did he really expect to entice a woman by stuffing his maw full of fatty goods?

Yeah, that's a real turn-on. Oh, Pussy, calm thyself.

But the biggest question was why did he not look anything like his pictures on his profile?

I turned the questions on myself: Why had I wasted

my time getting ready, driving here, squandering precious gasoline to meet Homo Gigantus? Why hadn't I escaped when I first saw Captain Kangaroo's belly preceding him into the store? I could've feigned sickness, a bout of gas, the shits—anything—to get back home where my animals approached me with grace and honesty.

With a mouthful of masticated macaroons, James detailed the more hilarious moments in his classroom, one of which was an incident during one of his junior high history classes. Coconut shards rolled around in a ball at the back of his throat as he laughed. I was close to depositing my own stomach contents on the floor.

I burped, swallowed hard, and turned my attention to the grocery floor below.

I felt stupid. His profile had cleverly avoided any full body shots. That was the first clue I missed which landed me next to this percolating person of gargantuan gluttony. The second clue was the young-looking face before the castle walls, not the face of a forty-seven-year-old. I felt silly and justified in my annoyance. Watching a huge man eating three bags of sweets was doing nothing for me, so I told him I was late for my appointment with Chris Kringle.

As we walked out to our cars, he pointed out he was much more muscular than what he looked in his sweatshirt, and he urged me to feel the muscles in his arm.

"Oh, my," I said. I forced a smile and pinched his biceps. "You really do have firm arms."

"Yes. I go to the gym several times a week. I want to build muscle. Maybe sometime we can go biking on a Rails-to-Trails path."

I shook my head as I imagined him riding astride one of those adult tricycles built for the unbalanced and athletically inept.

"Maybe." I unlocked my car. I opened the door, and he leaned toward me, his eyes eager. *Think. Deflect. Run.* Instead of taking off like a scared rabbit, however, I smiled nicely and stepped in for a friendly hug. However, in an instant, he pulled me close, much closer than I anticipated. His monstrous belly, wherein I imagined his intestines delightfully digesting a huge mixture of coffee, coconut, dough, and icings, pressed against me, his arms drawing me tighter to him. *Oh, Goddess, you betraying bitch!* Separated from those churning guts by only a mere inch or two of skin and fat, I stiffened, caught in the embrace of Kong's brother-in-law. Coffee-vomit breath surged up my nostrils, and I struggled not to gag. He squeezed me tight and then let go.

Quickly I climbed into my car, started the engine, toodle-dooed, and left.

Ginnie, you brainless wonder, you were careless. From now on, always look for a full-body shot.

As I raced for home, I thought no matter how nice a guy was, if his guts preceded him into the room by two feet, the number one rule applied—*Run.* Then I bellowed louder than the radio, "James, you weren't honest, and you weren't fun!"

59

Chapter Six
Imtoosexyformyshirt

"He was a tub, and he ate like a T-Rex," I said with nonchalance. Lois nearly choked on her wine, her eyes wide.

I paused.

"Holy cow! Spill the beans." Lois rubbed her hands together.

"He made me nauseous, ate like Goober—one of the pigs at the rescue center—mouth wide open with a shitload of food slopping around inside like a churning cement mixer. I almost hacked up my breakfast right there in Wegmans."

Goober was one of the pot-bellied pigs at Pig Haven Sanctuary where I volunteered regularly, and food was his lover. If he could climb into his feed dish at dinnertime, he would. Pigs loved to eat, lived to eat. So, apparently, did James. And, actually, the comparison really wasn't fair to Goober. At least Goober had discriminating taste. He loved vegetables more than sweet stuff. James, however, had a penchant for fatty baked goods and barbecues. "And he didn't really seem all that interested in me. He was courting a sugar high, not a woman."

"Told you you were only going to pick up losers with that online dating crap," Jack scoffed.

"Well, I won't know unless I try, Jack." I glared at

him. "What am I supposed to do in my situation? Online dating is similar to TV dinners. Both are easy and convenient. With all this work on the farm, I can still meet men without wasting a lot of time. I always employed farm help to weed gardens, mow, and muck the stalls, but I have it *all* on my shoulders now. There's no time or money to hang out at malls, night clubs, or hardware stores hoping to find the right guy.

"I just feel so lonely these days," I moaned. Self-pity was not usually my M.O. I picked my cuticle. "I haven't had any affection from a man, any attention, for so long I feel like one of those genitalia-less aliens from *Close Encounters*. After all, no sex for the past sixteen years. That automatically makes me a misfit, an abomination of sorts. I'm like a female eunuch."

"You have just started dating, Ginnie," Lois said "Give it a chance. You'll find someone, eventually. Just give it time."

I cleared my throat. "Well, I have developed a system, of sorts, for this online dating stuff. I view prospects via the gallery method—several men at a time. If one appeals, I click on him and view the rest of his photos. Each photo I analyze, something I obviously failed to do well enough in James' case. If those photos perk up my pussy, I pop him an email. After the James thing, I realize chemistry must be the basis for comparison, not kindness, not niceness. This time around I'm going for good-looking *and* nice. Call me superficial. I don't care." I spread my arms. "I want it all. If he resembles Lyndon Johnson, he hits the 'trash.' After all, I've got some decent looks. I can go through fifty profiles in a half hour, kinda like working in an orange factory and tossing the rotten fruit off the conveyor belt."

"Don't be silly, Ginnie," Lois scolded. She poured herself a second Sex on the Beach. "I think what you're doing is fine, but you're too impatient. Give it time. Don't be in a hurry to get a man. After all, you would rather get the right guy than just anybody, right?"

"Definitely. I told you guys before. I don't care if he has money or a prestigious job, but I want someone handsome, fit, and comfortable in his own epidermis. Hard-working would be nice. He's got to like animals and not mind stepping in horse shit. I want a nice, good guy, too. And I want someone younger so he can keep up with my active lifestyle." This would be my last attempt at snagging a man. I would not settle for a gumdrop when I could have the whole giant jelly.

Jack snorted. "Ha! Dreamer. Never. You'll *never* get that kind of guy. I have news for you. You better lower your standards if you ever expect to get someone, or you will spend the rest of your life alone."

"And why can't I get that kind of guy?" My skin felt hot. "I don't resemble ugly fruit."

Jack stuck out his chin and rolled his eyes. "I'm a guy. I know how men think. A man who's good-looking and young is certainly not going to be interested in a woman forty-nine years old. I don't care if you look like the Queen of Fuckin' Sheba. Men desire younger dames."

"And who are you? Dr. Fill? All of a sudden you're a fucking authority on relationships?"

Lois interrupted. "You're wrong, Jack." She downed the last of her drink. I could always count on Lois coming to my defense.

"But I offer so much more than a younger version

of myself. I am thin, physically fit, educated, hard-working, established, fun-loving, and, most of all, funny. I'm Goldie.

"I've written books, and I'm sexy, if I must say so myself. I'm the perfect meal. I make Marilyn Monroe look like a side salad. I can attract a good-looking, nice, intelligent, younger guy." I swallowed hard and tore at my cuticle.

"Never happen," Jack said. He shook his head as if he were scolding a youngster. "Men can get younger women, but it doesn't work the other way around."

"I wish I knew someone for you," Lois said. "But all the good men I know are married."

"Well, this time around I'm holding out. I've got my bucket list. If I can't find the right man for me, I will just do without one altogether. Yes, siree, I'm getting the ol' fishin' pole out and baiting it with a picture of myself and the smell of pussy. I'm out for the catch of the year."

"Never happen," Jack snorted.

****

Days on the farm found me tending the goats, the horses, and the horde of cats accumulated through many rescues. Had I known six months ago Lance was fooling around with Yvonne the housekeeper—the office dick duster—I would have perhaps turned down a few of the rescues. From the Manhattan animal shelter I had rescued two female kittens with three babies each and had saved from the gas chambers two black and white adult cats. I was Noah in desperate need of another ark. What would have been no big deal to support and care for these discarded animals suddenly became another burden to my already stressed-out purse. Still, I would do as I had promised and care for them as best I could.

As usual, the evenings became my time to play and hunt for my prince via the computer. When I was so tired I could hardly sit up straight, I grabbed my notebook, took it and Selena, my long-haired black cat, and headed up the "woody mountain" to bed. While "Family Dad" blared on the TV, I read the ten or so emails streaming in from guys nursing hard-ons over my pics and profile information. I was determined to meet that perfect male specimen on my bucket list.

In minutes I had a message from "Imtoosexyformyshirt."

Ugh! What a dumb username. Spare my beaver.

After a quick perusal of his profile, I had to admit he sounded tantalizing. I responded to his email, said I was interested, and that, perhaps, we should meet.

His response was quick. *Hooked that tuna. Now reel his fishy ass in.* I began to chum with enticing words and phrases plucked from Elizabeth Browning's "Sonnets from the Portuguese." In the course of about fifteen minutes, we had corresponded back and forth probably ten times. My only concern was that he had only displayed one picture of himself—a good-looking profile shot of him walking along a dock. His face was a bit blurry, but long ago I had come to the opinion that, even if I met someone who didn't so much as light a spark in my panties, at least meeting him would be good practice for the one guy who could singe my drawers. Each one provided a practice session for the real flame, once it fired-up a conflagration.

What this guy had going for him, besides his apparent good looks, was he was a widower. Men on the prowl whose wives had met unfortunate, untimely ends were the ultimate prizes. Rather than carrying behind them balls and chains and Titanic-sized trunks of divorce nightmares and bitchy wives, widowers stood out as the golden boys of the dating scene, having become single through no fault of their own or mistreatment of their women. They were proven good men—solids, having stayed by their women's sides through the worst times and "through sickness and in health." A veil of goodness blanketed a widower, a guarantee of faithful, abiding love.

I would bait this hook with my sweetest voice and the ripe aroma of a chimpanzee in heat.

That afternoon I put in a quick call to Sharon, my best bud and worldly sage. I told her about "Imtoosexyformyshirt," and she agreed that a widower would be a special catch.

"Oh," I said. I licked my lips. "I hope this one pans out."

"Well, do you remember my motto, just in case it doesn't work?" Her voice had become low and wise.

"Uh." I thought hard. "Keep the romance out of your pants?"

"No! Come on, Ginnie. What did I tell you when you started this dating stuff? It's been my motto for years."

"Jeez, I can't remember! How about 'Expect nothing; gain everything.' "

"Well, that is what I told you when you started going out, but that's not my motto."

"For Christ's sake, tell me already."

Sharon shouted into the phone, "Next!"

"Oh, yeah." "How in the world could I have

forgotten the one word wherein eternal hope lived: "Next!"

How could you forget that mantra, Ginnie? Wherever there was one guy, there was always another.

Never again would I forget Sharon's motto that would, forever, keep me sane throughout my dating experiences. If a date went horribly wrong, I, in the voice of Ms. Sills, yodeled "Next!" to the mountaintops and vowed to get on with the next male prospect. If a lover broke my heart, others just like him stood waiting in line ready to knock on my door.

The ocean was loaded with fish. Men were a bunch of anchovies in the sea. Where floated one belly-up, millions more swam strongly, swiftly. So, I took an oath. When I released a scrappy specimen into the water, I baited the hook for the "Next!"

****

Kenny, the Imtoosexyformyshirt widower, and I met days later at a local restaurant. He was waiting for me in the parking lot. He was a young version of Clint Eastwood. If Imtoosexyformyshirt's personality was charming and precocious, he would be a definite keeper.

When I stepped from my car, he walked over, smiled, and went in for the hug. In the parking lot the eager widower held me in a vise grip, like an otter holding onto the last clam on the beach.

Okay, you can let go any day. Back off already

His unctuous embrace felt almost suffocating, hardly just a friendly gesture. I pried myself from his arms, smiled politely, and rationalized that some people naturally give stifling bear hugs smelling of rotten-egg desperation. I just wasn't used to them.

Ginnie, you aren't used to any hugs at all—sixteen years, remember?

Standing before him, I managed to say something witty, to which he laughed. Then he took my hand and led me across the parking lot.

So far, so good. Not bad. Well, except for the wart commanding a post next to his right naso-labial fold. You aren't perfect, either, sister. That chicken pock mark above your left ear isn't exactly fetching.

Kenny and I walked into the restaurant looking like a happily-married couple with a lifetime of leisure in their pockets and purse. He pulled out my chair, proffered it, and I sat down with a demure "Thank you." I was nothing if not polite. After the server took our drink order, Kenny looked at me and cocked his head.

I asked, "Something wrong?"

"Oh, I'm sorry. Nothing at all. I was just admiring you, is all. I'm so lucky. You're absolutely gorgeous."

I smiled, coughed, swallowed hard, and opened the menu. "Thank you, though I wouldn't say I'm gorgeous. I am an older woman, ya know. Pretty, perhaps. Hey, they have lots of good stuff to eat here. Tex-Mex food. Nothing like it around these parts. The chimichanga is the best around. What a weird word—isn't it? 'Chimi-changa.' " I bellowed the word four times—liking the sound of it. This guy needed docking back to earth because, for sure, he thought he was on a date with Mary Magdalene herself.

Reluctantly he opened his menu and asked me to recommend something.

"Quesadillas are always great here." I licked my lips and looked up. He was peering over his menu, steely gray eyes staring, penetrating…desirous.

Oh, dear. If it wouldn't be for the un-Lanced in the Pants, I'd recognize that look anywhere. All righty, then.

Goose bumps danced up my arms.

I squirmed in my seat. Finally, I placed the menu on the table—my dinner choice, a small bowl of chili.

"Same for me." He smiled, as satisfied as a dog chewing a smelly sock. I coughed as a sip of iced tea trickled into my windpipe.

"Oh, excuse me. Went down the wrong pipe." I cleared my throat and giggled self-consciously.

The tension in our corner of the room was suffocating, much like his hug. One could have cut it with a chainsaw, it was so thick. This guy was into me like Brer Rabbit into the tar-baby.

No smell of pussikins for this guy. He's already on me like flies on shit.

But he's a widower. He's got to be sane. Surely not a serial killer or a date raper. After all, he had a loving wife for many years. Perhaps too many years. He's good-looking, except for the mole. But that over-bearing hug: tight enough to qualify as a body corset.

Give him a break, Ginnie. Who could be lonelier than a man who has lost the love of his life, never to have her back again? He needs a substitute, as soon as and as quickly as possible. Get her in there—any body will do—as long as it lives, breathes, and moves swiftly behind a vacuum cleaner, in the kitchen, and in the sack.

"Some place, isn't it?" I said. I glanced around the room trying to keep the conversation light. "The Cork and Corkscrew has always been my favorite place, a bit quirky, a bit hooligan. I like the rebellious feel to the place. I find it relaxing. You like it here?"

Silence.

He was leering at me over his menu.

I deflected the wolf's hungry stare and tried again. "During the summer this turns into the biggest, wildest biker bar around. Tons of motorcyclists stop by after cruising along the Hudson. They are so much fun to watch with their leather outfits and handkerchief hats. Their women are way out there, too." Normally self-assured and totally at ease, even in the company of strangers, I became a chatterbox the likes of a nervous first-grader.

I looked up. He had put the menu down and was staring at me, grinning with a come-hither look. "I love you."

A taco chip caught in my throat. I dislodged it with a cough and swallowed as it scraped my upper palate on the way down.

What the fuck do you say to something like that? He doesn't even know you. He loves you? Oh, Goddess, you dirty, traitorous bitch.

"Thanks," I said. My voice cracked like an adolescent boy's.

"No. You don't understand—I really, really adore you. You're breathtaking." He leaned toward me, anxious—his hand open. Under the table his cock was probably as large as a burrito.

Dare I look? No. Unnecessary encouragement.

I gasped. Did this guy know we were in a public place where they sell gorditas and chili rellenos? At the rate he was going, he would soon be over me like Kong on Fay Wray. Where was my escape route? Sure, he was nice-looking, but he seemed more hungry, more deprived, than a prisoner of war. I'd have bet even a taco shell could've served him as pussy.

I reached for my purse for an immediate getaway yet couldn't muster enough courage to flee. So, instead, I sat there and smiled like a jackass eating stickers. I propped my elbows on the table top and slapped my hands together.

"So, what do you do for a living?" I quipped.

The effect was immediately catastrophic, as though I had taken a tiny hose, inserted it into his left nostril and sucked all the air out of him. His shoulders sank. "Plant manager at Stangway's. I make candles."

"Oh, fascinating," I said with no more interest than a monkey with an empty banana peel. "Tell me what you do most days."

"Oh, it's really not that interesting." Then, he took my right hand in his. His grasp was cold and sweaty. My stomach churned at his touch and the thought of his massive, needy burrito under the table. He clasped his fingers around mine. "I find you much more intriguing than my job."

"Thanks." Where were the exit signs?

In case of fire or fired-up men, Exit Here.

Then he took both my hands in his and smiled broadly as though thinking of something I'd probably be better off not knowing. *Well, he has nice teeth. Good teeth are a selling point.* "I so enjoy your company," he whispered through those strip-whitened choppers.

Suddenly the tune to "Desperado" played in my imagination. This guy was as desperate as the legendary character of the song. He also wasn't getting any younger, and he's imprisoned—all alone—in the world.

"So, do you like pigs?" I said.

"Pigs?" His voice could not have been more bland. "I've known a few in my life." He laughed.

Funny guy. Not!

"Oh." I tossed my head backwards in a masculine guffaw. "I meant animal pigs. I volunteer at a pig rescue once a week."

He dropped my hands as though they were fire irons just off the coals. "You like pigs? Farm pigs?" His smile had turned itself upside down.

"Yes." Sighing a breath of relief, I wiped my slimy hands on my pants legs. *Have to get rid of his sex sweat. Hand sanitizer's in your purse.*

I continued. "No, actually. They're pet pigs. Pot-bellies. Just fascinating animals."

His face drooped, the spark snuffed from his eyes. "Oh, really?" He looked as enthusiastic as a bonobo ape without a mate.

"Oh, yes, quite the pet. Much better than a dog. In fact, I want to add a couple to my menagerie soon. I'll tell ya a story about one of my friends who has three pot-bellies in her house. Her name is Charlotte. You see..."

As his eyes glazed over, I told him all about Charlotte's pigs' shenanigans and the nature of pet pigs, in general. All wonderful pets, not a mean one among them. Just love them to death. I told him the animal sanctuary where I volunteered had one hundred and thirty-two resident miniature pigs and how some come into the rescue as neglect cases in really bad shape, sometimes too late.

I said, "It's horrible enough when a pet dies, let alone a pet pig, which is quite human-like, ya know,

71

like losing a family member." I described how they love to eat, diving into their food dish like an Olympian into a pool, chomping with mouths open, smiling and chomping, smiling and chomping. "They live to eat, kinda like me, too. I have an appetite that rivals Billy Bob, the 2013 hot dog eating champion of Lovett, Texas."

By the time our lunches came, Imtoosexyformyshirt Kenny had withdrawn into a shell of his former, avid self—all amid my enthusiastic descriptions of the sub-species of the domesticated pig, *sus scrofa domesticus*.

Much like a pig, I dove into my chili, downing it in record time and flushing it down my throat with a gallon of beer followed by a shitload of soda crackers. Kenny was totally grossed out, and I grinned like a chimp with chili beans and cracker dough sticking to my gums. Likewise, I made no effort to tongue-suck the food particles from my teeth and then smiled my widest smile ever. Then I threw a huge swig of beer down my gorge and burped like a truck driver.

I thought he was going to puke.

"You okay?" I said through a mouthful of melba toast.

"Just dandy." He pushed his crackers away and took a sip of water. Hard as he tried, a smile eluded him.

I laughed, snorting like one of the porcine breed. This date came as close to a reverse mortgage as any date could. So overcome with anticipation, need, and physical attraction was he initially, I felt physically uncomfortable, caught between his leering smile, his sweaty palms, and his throbbing burrito. It seemed like too much, too soon, too fast—desperate for a mate, regardless of who she could be. But that tell-tale, rib-crushing hug spoke to me and sent uneasy images to my brain—me in a fifties apron removing cupcakes from our matrimonial oven, my carting the laundry basket with freshly-ironed linens upstairs to our boudoir, my vacuuming the floors devoid of cat hair because my new husband hated all animals, my greeting him with a kiss and a cocktail when he arrived home from the office. My imagination concocted my new married state, which would certainly jump-start Kenny the widower but would devolve me into *humanus domesticus* overnight. The images scared me out of my wits.

As soon as I revealed the farm girl in me, he lost all oomph for his new bride-to-be. No longer attractive was this pig-prattling, swine-swilling woman who surely had the smell of hog manure clinging to her stilettos. Yep, he must've thought, she can dress herself up, but she can't go out. She ate like the precocious pig from Green Acres, chili flying in every direction, melted crackers sticking to her gums, orange foam at the corners of her lips. I was also sure his mind didn't stop with that dreaded image. No doubt, he pictured me, as his new bride, in the nude, too—her leg hairs, no doubt, bristly, her skin dry and flaky as a swine's. She probably belched when she laughed hard. During sex, well...she would probably grunt and fart like hell.

After lunch, the whole of mine which I finished, and all of his which he didn't, we walked to our cars. For one who was so eager from the get-go, this guy had suddenly lost all luster for me. With not even so much as a pat on the back, Kenny excused himself to his car and headed out the parking lot.

And I snorted, trotted to my car, and squealed as I tore out of the parking lot.

"Next!"

Chapter Seven
Facebook Friends

Two days later I brought a pizza over to Lois and Jack's. Lois had had me over so many times, and I wanted to contribute toward the dinners, too. When I told them about Kenny the Imtoosexyformyshirt "desperado," they laughed. Jack, of course, knew right away Kenny had only been into me as a quick replacement for his dead wife. Of course, Kenny wasn't interested in the real me, Jack reasoned—after all, I was considerably older than he, so that made me user material.

That evening I gripped the steering wheel tightly and squinted through the blinding, driving snow. Once home I slammed my house door tight against the New York cold, grabbed my notebook and Selena, and scurried under the bedcovers. The only light in the room was the bilious glow from the computer screen. And there, like magic, were three other messages from three different guys—all wanting to meet Foxylady. So, I dutifully complimented each one, gave them my cell number, and logged off the dating site. Then, I went to check in to see how my friends were doing on Facebook.

A person my age doesn't live to be forty-nine without having made some kind of impact on the world. Happily, I left many thousands on former high school and college students, leaving them with a bit of my writerly self. I worked hard those teaching years encouraging each student to love writing as I did, and because I was a devout animal lover, I left other marks on fans of my animal advocacy books.

A few years ago, in an effort to promote my writing, my literary agent requested I frequent Facebook for fans and animal lovers. For a solid summer and much to Lance's chagrin, I spent almost every waking moment "friending" people on Facebook. One afternoon Lance, in his usual dismissive, ugly way commented, "The only things you're good at are Facebook and eating." I should have sensed Lance was fooling around then.

I explained calmly being on Facebook was part of the promotional plan for my books, but the last thing—I now know—he wanted was to see my books be successful. That could have up-staged him. Lance always felt if I wasn't promoting him and his orthopedic practice, then my time was being wasted. I ignored his jealousy and in about six months' time had almost five thousand friends—mostly animal lovers, animal rescuers, and former high school and college students.

As anyone knows who frequents Facebook, when someone adds another as a friend, a list of approximately six other people automatically appears along with a message that reads, "Other friends you may know and add." So, I always took advantage of all these lists as each friend would add me. The whole thing resembled a mathematical process similar to the factorial. With each friend came six more, and with each of those six came another six, and so on. And hardly anyone took the trouble to check if I could be a troll or hack. They all accepted my friendship request, even if they didn't know me from Eve.

Over the years my friends list had grown exponentially. And Lance, being the social turd he was, resented every one of them. Still, it was good advertising for my books, and I really appreciated animal lovers as friends. They are, almost exclusively good, honest earthy people—*my kind* of friends.

So, that evening as I was reading through my "newsfeed," a yellow box popped up. It was from a person I had just friended. And my friending process was so efficient and automatic that, other than quickly glancing down at the name, I rarely even saw the person or profile of the person I was friending. One time I happened to look at the picture and realized I had just friended a blue iguana named Gregory. It was amazing how an animal with tiny, sticky fingers like a lizard's could type on a keyboard efficiently. Anyway, the people I asked to be friends, simply friended me back, automatically. They didn't hire a detective to "vet me out." Accepting another's friendship wasn't rocket science—one click later, and they've made another buddy.

This box, however, came from a guy worried I could possibly be the likes of Bonnie Barrow of Bonnie and Clyde fame. "Do I know you?" he replied in a suspicious-sounding written voice. With all the hundreds of people I was friending on a daily basis, I really didn't have the time or patience to deal with one believing I could be an axe murderer. I felt like writing, "Yes, I'm Lizzie Borden. My best friend is my axe." Instead, I rattled back a quick message, without even looking at his picture. "I ask animal lovers and former students of mine from Southington High School to be friends. If you don't want to be my friend, it's perfectly okay."

This ain't high school, honey. We don't have to be friends if you don't want to.

Soon another box popped up from the same guy. "Well, I'm not particularly an animal lover, and I didn't graduate from Coxsackie High School as you did, but I guess it's okay for you to be my friend. I will add you, then."

Well, aren't I privileged?

I typed back a quick thanks and clicked "send." He was just another of the five thousand friends I already had. And then I sent out a broadcast message to my friends, thanking them for helping animals stuck in kill shelters around the country and encouraging everyone to help make animals' lives easier, even if they couldn't adopt—send old blankets to shelters, donate time at a shelter to walk dogs or play with cats or pocket pets, post links to rescue sites on their Facebook sites, and the like. And then I logged off and popped one of Jack's porno flicks on the TV. I watched for an hour in horrific fascination until I fell asleep to the gasping and groaning.

The next morning a reminder came from Amazon.com to update my author page, so that afternoon Charlotte filmed a video of me describing my current books and up-coming manuscripts. We didn't want the standard video wherein the tight-assed author looks as though she's sitting, constipated, on a toilet trying to eek out the same old promotional book shit. We wanted something down-home and honest. So, I climbed on my horse, handed Charlotte my iphone, and began my spiel.

Riding at a walk around the pasture, I joked about my past books, mentioned my three forthcoming books, yelled "Yee-haw" and rode into the sunset. The video turned out pretty good—reflecting me and my farm mentality. And old Red hadn't farted once during that one-minute tape. In seconds Charlotte and I had it uploaded it to my Author Central page on Amazon.

Not bad. You look decent on Red. Good book information plus a creative presentation. Hopefully that'll draw a crowd to your books.

My conscience always gave good advice.

The next day a private message showed up on my Facebook page—another one from *Mr. Wary.*

Who was this masked man? He was so leery of you, and now you hear from him the very next day? Odd.

Just the day before he was afraid to be my bud. Today he's almost cozy. "I must say you have a wonderful author page. It's so nice to sea someone explaining her books in a way that is not simply sitting down at a desk, arms crossed, explaining stuff in boaring language. Congratulations on you're books. I'm very impressed. :)"

Ignoring the spelling errors, I rattled off a quick "Thank you. I wanted to do something entertaining. Glad you liked it," and hit "send." Okay, onto the next project for the day. But something about that guy piqued my interest. After all, no one else had commented on my Annie Oakley video. So, I looked up his Facebook profile.

When his picture popped up, I sat back, mouth agape. My lower lip had dropped to my knees and my beaver twitched. *Holy cow! He's a good-looking guy. Not just good looking, though—really, really hot!* I opened several of his photos. My admirer, whose name was Richard Downing, was downright, droolingly handsome. He looked to be around my age. I checked to see if he was married—he was not.

I wrote back to him, "Hi, Richard. Out of curiosity I went to your photos. You are quite good-looking, as you probably realize. And your family pic with your sister by your side—she's an equally good-looking woman, too. Very nice family portrait. Again, thanks for the compliment on my author video. Have a nice day."

Within minutes Richard replied. "Wow! That is really something—a woman who thinks another woman is beautiful. Now that is super hot."

Puzzled, I replied, "Well, your sister *is* very pretty. It's true, and I give credit where it's due. Have a nice day."

Before I could log off Facebook, he shot back, "Most women are threatened by other good-looking women."

"I don't see other attractive women as threats," I replied. "I can appreciate beauty in other women because I recognize it in myself. Anyhow, I'm just being honest."

"Oh, that is so frickin' hot!" he typed back. Was he sitting there with a boner over this whole discussion? "Did you look at all my pics?"

I admitted I had not but promised to look as soon as possible. I wrote I was in the middle of hacking my way through my next book and was consumed by a divorce, as well. He responded he was sorry to hear about the divorce. But he was more interested in my next book and thought it so totally cool I was an author. He had never known an author before.

Well, I wanted to tell him I engage in other activities besides writing, like eating sloppy BBQ sandwiches and farting at the crack of dawn. Instead I restrained myself. I explained my advocacy for animal welfare, which he was probably well aware of—having viewed my Facebook site—and that I was penning a book on factory farms, the vegan movement, and my philosophy on how people can give more immediate help to farm animals destined for dinner plates than vegans who demand abstinence. I suggested if we eliminated factory farms and legislated humane treatment of farm animals on site, during transportation to the killing fields, and at the slaughter houses, we could benefit these poor souls in a more immediate manner than hoping and praying for the world to turn vegan at the drop of a fedora.

He agreed profusely with my analysis of the problems concerning farm animals and urged me to look at his information and other photos on his profile. We said good-bye, and I knew, by the tone of his voice, I would hear from him again.

That evening in bed, after I read the final chapter on anal sex in *Any Woman Can* and swore off such barbarian activities, I went to Richard's Facebook page and carefully perused his photos. What I discovered was mind-jolting. He was a colonel in the Army and taught military history at an elite military academy. *Very impressive. No ordinary dummy, for sure. Probably very self-disciplined, physically fit, walks tall and carries a big stick! Hoo-brother. And his status read "single." Yummy.*

The next morning I was putting the finishing touches on a very poignant chapter on pigs' hysterical behavior in slaughter yards. By the end of the chapter, I was balling my eyes out, because pigs, in particular, suffer the most of all farm animals: intelligent enough to realize they've been gathered together to die. Quoting numerous veterinarians employed by food-processing plants as well as a famous animal science researcher, I had enough research to prove these animals exhibit stressed and anxious behavior in the crowded killing yards. A pig is so intelligent, the fifth most intelligent animal on Earth, that he or she is fully capable of understanding his or her own demise. That realization tore me apart.

So, while I sniffed and dabbed my eyes, a message came into my Facebook mailbox. It was Richard Downing. "Hi. Just wanted to see how your next book was coming along. Hope you're having a good day. I checked out you're Facebook site again last night. Must say I am very impressed with your writing background. Have a good day. :)"

This guy is a Facebook voyeur.

As I typed a response to Richard, a knock sounded at the back door. Jack stood visible through the peephole. I opened the door, drying the last tear from my eye.

"What's wrong?" My face was as swollen as a puffer fish.

"Oh, I was just finishing this chapter on pigs' behavior at slaughterhouses. Not fun. I usually break down with this kind of subject matter. What brings you here?"

"I'm so sorry you're depressed." He stepped toward me and gave me a hug. I held him, too, and sniffed back tears. After all these years of zilch empathy from Lance, Jack's friendship and support felt good. "Is there anything I can do?"

I stepped back, but he continued to hold me. "No," I managed a smile. "I just have to get over it."

"I'm sure the divorce stuff is getting to you, as well. I came by to see if you needed me to do anything."

"No, Jack. I'm all right. Want an iced tea or something?"

"Sure."

I went to the refrigerator and took out the pitcher, pouring a glass for both of us.

He said, "And I wanted to tell you something, too."

"Yeah, what?" I said. I sipped my tea. The cool glass felt good against my hot, tear-stained face.

"Remember the bit about my not being able to collect my widower's social security if I ever got married to Lois?"

"Yeah, I remember. As long as you stay single, you can still get your wife's social security. But if you and Lois marry, you lose it?"

"That's right. They just changed the law—a friend I know at the social security office just called me about it. Now Lois and I could get married and still collect."

"Terrific. I know Lois would like to be married."

"Well, I'm *not* telling Lois."

I was shocked. "Why wouldn't you? You could get married then. You want to marry her, right? You guys have been together four years."

"No, I don't want to get married. *Ever*. Promise not

83

to tell her, okay? To tell you the truth—we're having problems. Lois is very jealous—she drinks too much, and she hates my sexual appetite."

I laughed, sniffing back the last tear. "Well, it is a bit much, Jack. Not many women at the age of fifty-five want to have sex every other day. Ya gotta admit that."

"Well, I can't help it. That's how I am—have been since I was young. Always had a huge sex drive."

"I know, I know. We've been over this before—don't beat a dead scrotum." I laughed. "Well, try to give Lois a break anyway."

"I just wanted you to know I refuse to marry Lois, especially with these problems between us. Promise not to tell her."

"Okay. I promise. But I think you're making a mistake. Whatever."

"You sure there's nothing I can do for you outside?"

"Yes, I'm sure—for now. But some of my fence rails are rotting. Perhaps we could work on those someday. I have all the stuff to replace and fix them. I just can't handle those heavy rails myself."

"Sure. I can help you with fencing. Did you watch those movies yet?"

"Yeah, I did." Then I changed the subject. "I'll check my supply of fencing and talk to you and Lois sometime this week."

"Don't mention to Lois my helping you with the fence. She's insanely jealous."

What? Getoutahere!

"I've never known Lois to have one jealous bone in her body, Jack." I shook my head in complete disbelief. "Besides, you and I are just friends—she

84

knows that."

"I'd rather you not mention it, okay? So, I'll talk to you later." Jack turned to go.

"Thanks, Jack. I appreciate your help. And I really think Lois would be tickled if you asked her to marry you. Think about it."

"I already did—not gonna happen."

With Jack out the door, I went back to my computer and Richard's message. I responded as any friend would—thanking him for his interest and his friendship. I also complimented him on his accomplishments and acknowledged that I had never known a military man. And I wished him a good day, too.

****

The next few weeks were routine as they always are on a farm. In between carting wheelbarrows of horse and goat shit to the manure pile, I continued writing and participating on Facebook—posting new pics, commenting on people's comments, posting on my wall every once in a while. Every day was packed full with farm work or book activities. Amid it all were the daily correspondences between my new Facebook friend, Richard Downing, and me—all of it friendly, polite and civil. He was a man of impeccable manners, and he knew how to treat a lady, unlike Lance.

In one of his emails, however, Richard complained of having to write a paper, something all the professors at the academy had to do to retain their teaching positions. This year he was due to be published, and he was having a hard time, not only with the subject matter and research, but also with executing it. He was, however, a master of self-discipline—he would surmount his writing barriers, he told me. However, what I soon discovered, through personal emails, was that his efforts to prevail over writing problems amounted to a kind of self-flagellation of sorts—he would sit nights in the library, sometimes the entire night, laboring over each word, phrase, and comma. And he forced himself to stay there until he had eked out one paragraph. He was punishing himself needlessly, so I offered my writing services, which he refused immediately.

"Oh, don't be silly. Let me help you with it. It's what I have done for a living—taught college English and composition. Why torture yourself when I can zip through it, correct your errors, and you can send it on its way?"

"No, this is something I must overcome myself. He was a typically self-disciplined military man.

"Okay, then, you masochist. Go ahead and suffer, but when you've pulled out all your hair and look in the mirror and see a Dick Cheney look alike, give me a call. I don't mind helping at all. It's a contribution I could make to the military—something my writing skills allow me to do. I'd be honored, in fact."

Days later Richard sent me a frantic email. "Oh, Dear God—I can't take it! Do you mind terribly if I send you this paper as an attachment, and you could look it over? I feel really bad about asking you to do this, especially since you are in the middle of another book, but I'm really in a jam, and I have a deadline."

"When's the deadline?"

"Two days from today."

I rolled my eyes and told him to send it. "I told you to give it to me weeks ago. Now *I* must hurry." I was annoyed. "Okay, I'll get on it right away."

He thanked me profusely, and the next email had the paper attached. I saved it to my computer and began editing it. It was a nightmare—like Faulkner on Five-Hour Energy—almost incomprehensible. Though he was a colonel in the military and a professor, he was no writer. The paper was disorganized, lacked transitions, all disjointed—a fucking mess. And the spelling, grammar and punctuation sucked big time, too. Ninth graders could've done a better job. But I had made a promise, and I was going to keep it—for my new Facebook friend, Richard—and as my gift to the military.

Seven hours later I emerged from my office—brain dead. I looked in the mirror—my hair disheveled, my eyes like pee holes in a snow bank, my face drawn and skeletal. I stumbled into the kitchen, took a swig of iced tea, and collapsed into a living room chair. The paper had been excruciatingly difficult to re-organize and edit. And I needed clarity on subject matter, so while I was editing, I had also been communicating with Richard as to information pertaining to the context. I certainly didn't want to edit out necessary details. So, after about twenty emails between us and hours of analyzing, fixing, and re-sending sentences and paragraphs, I was finally finished. Thank goodness.

Working on a business project can bring people closer together. In the space of three weeks, Richard Downing and I had become very good friends, so good that we traded personal emails instead of contacting each other through the Facebook site. And we joked like a couple of siblings. One email from me expressed exasperation with his former English teachers.

"Did they teach you nothing at all, or did you ignore their advice?" I asked.

"Nope. And yes. I wasn't exactly compliant in my learning how to write. It is as much my fault as my teachers'. I'm a dolt when it comes to writing."

"Well, I won't disagree with that, that's for sure." I mitigated it all by saying that while he did know his subject matter well, he just couldn't verbalize it efficiently on paper."

His response to my editorial criticism sent chills down my arms. "I am trained to kill, not write." Then I sent the finished edit to him. An hour later he wrote back. "Excellent. This paper is so good now, it doesn't even sound like me. And that's a good thing. I can't thank you enough. You saved my ass. You have no idea how much I appreciate what you did for me. No frickin' idea."

He was ecstatic, and I was equally happy I had finished it—cleaning up what amounted to a major editorial abortion. In fact, I had saved the baby from the bulrushes—the paper was publishable now. I was proud of myself for having saved, not only his ass, but his job, too.

****

One snowy but beautiful day I was struggling with a section of my farm animal book, when an email came through from Richard. He wrote, "What are you doing?" I replied I was sitting in my office in front of the computer battling writer's block and watching the snowflakes fall.

"What are you doing?" I wrote back.

He said he was back in his apartment after having taught his morning classes and was re-checking his paper before sending it off to various military journals. I assured him that with the hard work we had both put into it, he would have no problem getting it published. Then, he wrote, "So, what are you wearing?"

What am I wearing? What am I wearing? A bikini—what else? I'm going to go outside and get freezer burn. Who cares what I'm wearing? Did he suddenly become a fashionista?

"Black jeans and a red cashmere sweater. Why?"

"Just wondered." Then the next question. "What are you thinking about?"

I banged out a response on the keyboard. "Thinking about how I'm going to begin this next section in my book. Now that you've interrupted me—which, incidentally, I'm secretly grateful for because I've got writer's block—I'm thinking about you. So, what are *you* thinking about?"

Several minutes passed before another email from Richard appeared on my screen. "I am thinking about *having you* all over that farm of yours—in the woods, the hayloft, the fields around your house."

All my friends laugh at my abundance of naïveté. "Ginnie, you couldn't pick a lesbian out of a lesbian parade or recognize an alcoholic at an AA meeting." And I'm equally clueless, oftentimes—in many respects—about the dreams and desires of men. So, when Richard's comments came across my computer screen, I sat immobile and staring for several minutes—rereading, trying to comprehend what he meant. For such a well-educated woman, I certainly was pretty ignorant—sometimes painfully so. And I had never experienced masculine cyber horniness.

Soon I heard a dull thud—my jaw hitting my

desktop.

What did Richard just say? He is "having" you all over the farm? What does that mean—"having you"? "Having you" for dinner? "Having you" as a friend? "Having you"?

For a full fifteen minutes I sat catatonic at the computer, my mouth open like a basking whale shark. Then, suddenly, I hit the stern of a cargo ship—nearly knocking breath and sense out of me all at once.

In a few seconds another email from Richard appeared. I opened it. "And I want you delivered to me wearing nothing but that furry coat of yours."

I shook my head, reread and re-evaluated the situation again. "Curse you, damp pussy!" I scolded myself. Then I sat bolt upright. Without really thinking and in a very weak, vulnerable moment, I calmly typed two words back—"I wish."

My heart thumped furiously in my chest as I hit "send." Had I misinterpreted his email? We were really good friends. We had worked on his paper together and corresponded many times without their being any sexual innuendos at all. Now this? Perhaps I was mistaken, which, in that case, would make me look like a complete fool for blurting "I wish."

Ten minutes passed without any response from Richard. I had torn my right index finger's cuticle to shreds when suddenly an email popped up. I opened it, gritting my teeth and expected an answer like "Umm— you totally misunderstood me. The damned auto-correct changed my message to something I wasn't intending or would ever imagine. Hey, listen—we are *just* buddies."

I gave the new email a sidelong glance. I didn't

want the rejection to hit me squarely in the face. I winced as his words came across the screen. "Ya know, I'm glad I have a notebook computer so that I can use it one-handed."

Again, I sat, spell-bound—completely dumb *and* dumb-struck.

Why would he want to use a notebook with one hand? Did he hurt his other hand? Did he have a sore thumb? A hang nail? Very weird. Who cares if he wants to use his notebook with only one hand anyway?

I was more naïve than a fourth grader.

Finally, after a full fifteen minutes passed, I clasped my hands to my face. "Oh, my Goddess! He just gave himself a *hand job*. It can't *be*." Then I had visions of Richard dancing deliriously in my head—my good-looking, polite, military-disciplined Facebook friend, sitting in full military regalia, including camouflage cap, behind his computer projecting fetching pictures of me and, next to it, his notebook with our current correspondence. There, behind both, he worked himself over—pumping his penis-piston slippery with a fistful of lube.

With a combination of horror, intrigue, and lust, I pictured his face—slack mouth, eyes closed nearly to slits—focused on the computers while furiously whipping his appendage round and round, onward and upward, marching himself deftly toward orgasm. I allowed my imagination to go there with him as he reached his peak, imagining him yelling in fits and starts, the sexual fluid bursting all over my digitally projected face and dripping down his computer screen. Then I pictured his satisfied, peaceful smile. I swallowed hard, and then my own self-flagellation began.

What's the matter with you? You are one sick broad, you are—imagining all this stuff about Richard—you dirty, slutty, horny thing with your damp, disgusting pussy drawers. And one more thing—as your formerly innocent subconscious, I'm totally grossed out. I'm signing out. No more inside advice for you.

Then I rattled off an email I would most certainly regret. "OMG, Richard! Do you realize we just had sex over the computer?"

Moments later his reply appeared. "It was very nice. Thank you. Now, I really have to do some planning for classes tomorrow. Talk to you later, beautiful."

Just as easily as he had contacted me earlier, he had left me—typical for men after sexual satiation. I bet he was smoking a cigarette, too. Women far more experienced than I have reported men either fell right to sleep, or they got on to the day's occurrences as if nothing at all had happened. In the meantime Richard had left me wanting more, feeling guilty about wanting more, and not knowing *why* I wanted more. For Christ's sake, I had never even met him. He was nowhere near me, yet I had experienced a thrill I hadn't had since Lance and I were teenagers. What was wrong with me? How could I possibly get excited corresponding over a computer so uncaring, so unsympathetic to my needs and wants, and so hard and cold as a clam? It was bizarre.

Except for one thing.

The writing.

How wonderful to live a moment through the written word—the imaginative word—whether that word was written by me or by anyone else. My writing caused me to cry about farm animals treated inhumanely on their way to our dinner tables. My writing and the writing of others could create other intense visions in my brain, images strong enough, dream-like, to imitate reality. Words had powerful effects on me, I had to admit, and so, it followed they could have equal effects on others. And Richard's totally male, come-hither language set up my imagination to envision a kind of cyber-reality, if there could be such a thing.

Still, blurting to Richard that we had just had sex over the computer was a remark uttered by someone the likes of Heidi to her goatherd, Peter. It made me look so naïve and clueless, and at the age of forty-nine, those two traits are about as attractive as cat puke in one's lap. And we didn't really have sex over the computer— he had simply jerked off to my picture.

What a stupid thing for you to say, Ginnie: "We just had sex!" You're as pathetic as you were in fifth grade, for Christ's sake, when Gordon Avalon rode his bicycle to your house one Sunday afternoon and held your hand for ten minutes. You thought you were going to get pregnant—*from holding hands! Once a clueless broad, always a clueless broad. What am I going to do with you, Pippi?*

I clasped my hands over my ears to block out my inner voice's nagging. Then I smiled, stood up at my desk, and closed down the computer. Fuck my conscience and the ship she rode in on. That was really *hot. Really hot.* And I was already dreaming up things I would say to Richard the next day.

Chapter Eight
Expecting the Unexpected

While I was slavering like a Saint Bernard over Richard's emails, I had decided to put the rest of my life, except for taking care of my farm chores, pretty much on hold. The three guys on the dating site had been after me to go out, so I wrote to each and arranged to meet them at local restaurants. Two dates came on back-to-back days.

The first would be with Klaus Phartzinger, a German, originating, I imagined with some anxiety, from Hitlerian rank. His profile photos showed a blond, tall, up-right guy with an up-tight Arnold Schwarzenegger expression—no doubt, one of the supposed superior Aryan race. Sporadic phone conversations with him boasted a man extraordinarily, supernaturally, proud of all things German, particularly his German heritage—his relatives, still living in Deutschland, all originated from historical renown.

In the course of one conversation, he described in excruciating detail the most fabulous German recipes for sausage and schnitzels concocted by his Uncle Ogle who, at the age of ninety-five, was still cranking out wieners—he pronounced them "vieners"—every other Saturday wearing his white chef's hat along with a cuckoo-clock print apron. He said no less than the entire community of Vilseck crowded Uncle Ogle's house every Sunday morning to stock up on his homemade sausages. I found it hard to believe every person in the town could fit into Klaus' Uncle's kitchen on a Sunday morning, but who was I to argue? And I questioned whether the talented and wise Uncle Ogle had had the foresight to arrange for porta-potties for the crowd of wienie-eaters.

When I told Klaus I really wasn't into fatty hotdogs or things like Leberkase, which translated to the stomach-churning term, "liver cheese," he barked that no one in Uncle Ogle's town would ever turn down one of his frankfurters, and that Uncle O. would be insulted by my comment. I apologized and assured Klaus that, no doubt, his Uncle must surely have the most luscious bratwurst around

The next day Klaus and I met at All-Fired-Up Backyard Barbecue, a popular restaurant near Coxsackie, NY. I had been sitting in my car in the parking lot for a half hour before he called to say he would be another half hour late. Already disgruntled by his inordinate defense of his schnitzel-slinging Uncle Ogle, I walked inside to get myself a drink since, by the looks of it, this date was already off to a bad start. I sat down at the bar and ordered Lois' favorite, a Long Island iced tea. After a few swigs of the excruciatingly delightful beverage, I could not have cared less if Klaus didn't show.

With another ounce of the libation coursing down my throat, I struck up a conversation with the bartender, a young, jolly, dark-haired woman. I beckoned her with my index finger, and as she sidled over to my corner of the bar, I leaned mysteriously toward her. "Guess what? I'm meeting a dude here I met through a dating site. I need you to give me a thumbs-up or a thumbs-down when he walks through the door. Always nice to have another woman's opinion, ya know."

I laughed, downed another ounce of the Long Island iced tea, and laughed again, nearly choking. I was feeling no pain and continued in a loud whisper. "He's very German—very Berlin German, in fact. I'm English—with a little Italian mixed in—and I find Germans, Berliners, more than a little annoying. They can be downright obnoxious with their knee-high socks and beer "schteins." They can be so over-bearing at times, ya know. And what's with that wall, anyway?" I snorted. My world was rosy.

The friendly bartender laughed with me. "Well, that was taken down long ago—sometime after Reagan threatened them, I guess. So, you got this guy online, huh? This place seems to be a haunt for people meeting from dating sites."

"Really? Others have met here, too? Well, it is sort of mid-point between Albany and the Catskills. That's pretty cool."

"Yeah. It's fun to see these complete strangers come into the restaurant. Some, I can tell, look uncomfortable while others are fine with what must be a very awkward situation. Some look as though they dread meeting. After all, you have this great fantasy going online with only a few pics of each other and only emails and phone calls. It's like it's not really real. But the reality is in the meet-and-greet—ya know—to determine if there's any…"

"Sparkage," I interrupted gleefully. "Yep." I patted a stray hair into place. "I think it all comes down to chemistry on that first date. It's all about the visual—

nice eyes, decent cheekbones, full lips, good teeth, really good teeth. Yep—all about that alligator smile and that mysterious thing called 'chem-is-try.' And, in this case, I hope he has a nice wiener schnitzel." I snickered into my glass. "Well, he should be here pretty soon. Don't forget about the thumbs-up thing. We gals have to stick together."

Moments later the door opened. In walked Klaus in a black leather biker jacket. I waved, smiled, and motioned to him. He was about five feet nine inches with blond curls and an even, symmetrical face. I didn't see any teeth, but, then, he hadn't opened his mouth yet. He sat down, patted my back, smiled, and said in a thick German accent, "Hallo, Chinnie. Vedy nice to mit you."

"Same here." I choked back a laugh. The next few minutes found me, as usual, analyzing the effects of the first few seconds—something I could only measure from somewhere deep down inside me. I could muster no real details of how I felt, no list of positive or negative traits steaming off my date like aromas wafting off a newly baked blueberry pie. All I could do was feel inside the depths of myself for a generalized reaction to the overall maleness sitting beside me.

Okay. What do you feel, Chinnie? Got any sparks going off in pussikins? You got any fireworks at all, or are they all duds? Do you feel a couple of protons bonding with a bunch of electrons or something? Anything going on in that chemistry set of a bod of yours?

I felt nothing.

I glanced at the bartender for help. Trying to look casual, she was holding her thumb—direction up—

discreetly at her hip. I caught the signal and smiled thankfully. Then Klaus ordered a beer. He wasn't ugly—he wasn't good-looking. He was fair, nice enough. Once he had downed half his beer, he recounted the trials of finding the restaurant—how he had taken the wrong exit and had to retrace his steps and how he wished he had not forgotten his GPS. I shook my head, expressing sympathy at his difficulties and poured back another mouthful of my Long Island iced tea.

Despite my best efforts at jump-starting my libido over Klaus, my batteries were solidly dead. Even with an imaginary key to my heart, my starter had punked out. I felt nada—no interest, no sexual attraction—nothing at all. It was probably wrong to judge a man by the potential chemical stew-pot boiling and gurgling in my groins, but I couldn't argue with the overwhelming vacuity of any desire. Still, I felt obligated to give him a chance—time to get to know him and him me. I hoped his charming personality could magically ignite my cunt-buretor.

"Have you been on any vacations lately?" I asked.

He swallowed another pint of beer, wiped his sleeve on his mouth, and burped. "I youshly gaw to Chermany tree times a year—to see my parents, my aunts and uncles, undt friends. I do collect Cherman recipes undt vudt like to put them into a book for puplication—recipes my ancestors passed down through the age-ess."

"Oh, that's really cool," I lied. "I just love wursts. I remember Uncle Ogle's liver cheese, too. Just yummy."

His eyes sparkled. "Yes. I haf a great recipe for bradt-voorst steamed in creamed blood-pudding—

another of my Uncle Ogle's recipes. Undt then there's pig stomach stuffed mit bacon and sausage. And I haf the best recipe for pickledt pigs' feet."

I burped a liter of gas.

"I'm English." Then I corrected myself. "Well, I'm American with a bit of English and Italian."

He stiffened.

Something about Klaus, besides his notion that Germans were an obviously more gifted race, turned me off. Perhaps it was his tar-thick German accent, which should've vanished by now after living thirty years in the United States. Perhaps it was his avoiding eye contact with me that was off-putting. He seemed cold—a robotron—devoid of much emotion, except when it came to things Deutsch.

"My grandfather still vorks, even though he's close to a hundredt years old. He makes Cherman clocks undt flies for fishing. He's starting to go a little downhill dese days. I vant to make another trip to Chermany soon—before he dies. He's vunderbar."

I shook my head. My attention turned inside myself—searching, examining each crack inside me, hoping to discover the heat of a spark for this guy. But my innards were as dead as sofa cushions.

The bartender served someone a drink and then sauntered over to us two stein-clicking love partridges. "Would you like to order anything for lunch?"

Klaus had already perused the menu and placed it down, having firmly made up his mind. "I vill get de sausage mit peppers." As she busily scratched the order onto her note pad, I frantically searched the menu for something appropriate to eat.

Ordering the right food on a first, real online date is

dicey, at best. A woman had to choose her entrée wisely—no salad with lettuce and creamy dressing churning round and round in a cement-mixer-like mouth. Hardly appealing. Likewise, hot wing sauce ringing one's lips required a hosing-off in the parking lot. If the date progressed beyond the restaurant to a walk in the park, then she would be wise to avoid foods that could cause gas, for farting would be the figurative equivalent of blasting his dangly into oblivion. Nevermore would his appendage enjoy an erection after such a display. A blast of rectal effluvium emitted from one's nether cheeks spelled, not the kiss of romance, but the kiss of death.

What foods would be best to order, from a woman's viewpoint? One could get away with most anything dry and sauceless. French fries were a definite good pick as a woman could pick them up, inserting each one daintily into her mouth. Any sandwich for which one has to dislocate one's jaws like a boa constrictor is not a good choice for a first or even second date.

The worst meal a woman could possibly order had to be French onion soup. There's no grace in shoving a shivering tablespoon of limp onions, broth, and stringy mozzarella cheese into one's mouth. And should a woman manage to ingest it with any kind of elegance, an hour later she will find herself struggling, red-faced, to contain her belly full of gas, for cooked onions produce enough methane to rival that from an eructating cow.

The bartender looked at me, and I winced. "A bowl of chili, I guess."

"Chili it is," she said with too much enthusiasm.

She smiled and walked to the kitchen.

Chili has beans in it, you idiot. No fear, though. His sexual allure resembles a mud pot, so you won't be here long.

Our lunches came, and I ate each forkful with gusto. The cost for the bowl of chili was five dollars and ninety-nine cents, a mere pittance for Klaus, whose job in the medical writing field paid him very well. He would have nothing to complain about with regard to my choice of lunches. Still, I worried about the kidney beans fermenting inside me.

As Klaus bit off and chewed up every inch of his sausage, he talked of his two sons and his deceased wife and how they all used to travel to Germany together. He recounted descriptions of the German mountains and streams and quaint villages in such detail they could've rivaled those of the Discovery Channel. Of course, Klaus' wife was purebred German, as well, and the absolute love of his life. He would never find another woman to rival her, he said.

I wanted to tell him I was probably no match for a ghost, but I stuffed a piece of bread in my mouth instead.

After the bartender cleaned away our plates, she put the check on the bar. I put down a ten dollar bill—just to be polite—to cover my bowl of chili and a nice tip for the thumb signal. Fully expecting him to push away my money, saying something like, "Oh, no you don't. I'm getting the bill," I kept my wallet open. But the offer never came. Klaus looked at his portion of the bill, put money down for his meal, and slapped his wallet shut.

"Ready to go?" he asked.

I put my arms in my coat sleeves and contemplated the floor. "Oh, you betcha." We walked out into the parking lot, and I stopped beside my car. He offered a hug, but I deflected successfully. Then I got in my car, smiled, and started it up.

He arrives an hour late and can't even pay for a six dollar bowl of chili? He's as tight as a cow's ass in fly-time.

On the way home I scolded the imaginary Klaus in the passenger seat next to me. "Well, Klaus, you louse. You can go back to Germany and get yourself a frumpy fraulein who fries fritters 'cause you sure as hell aren't gonna see me again!" And then I ripped out a loud fart and yelled above the drone of the radio,

"Next!"

****

The following day was my date with Adam, a fifty-six-year-old widower who was into riding horses—dressage style. We met at The Cork and Corkscrew, the Tex-Mex biker bar where I had met Imtoosexyformyshirt and where I would grudgingly turn down the hot wings in favor of a plate of fries. He had arrived before I had, so when I walked into the restaurant, he was already seated behind a high-top table for two.

My brain went through its quick second analysis—*nice face, thick, luscious, gray-brown hair, sexy lips, blue eyes*. A spark detonated somewhere down around my appendix.

I stuck out my hand and proffered a charming smile. "Hello, Adam. Nice to meet you."

He stood up behind the table and took my hand. "My pleasure." He blushed slightly—lit from within like one of those night lights in a child's bedroom. Then he offered to pull out my chair, but I waved him away. "Don't get up. I can get it." I sat down and pulled my chair forward. He looked around and said, "Boy, this is a quirky place, isn't it? Look at all these dollar bills tacked up everywhere—ceiling, walls." Then, he looked around at the characters sitting at the bar—a bandanna-wearing guy with stringy hair poking beyond the edges of his hat-scarf. With him was a woman with bleached hair and a paunch the size of Norman, another of the rescue pigs I loved. They were picking away at Behemoth Nachos, the tavern's signature dish.

A server handed us menus, but I was getting their famous fries, so I used the time Adam was perusing his menu to make a good and detailed assessment of the man before me. By the looks of things, he wasn't very tall, perhaps five feet eight inches at most. That, however, didn't bother me because Lance wasn't very tall. Though, unlike George, I could "do" bald, it was refreshing to see a man with a good head of hair. His gray strands had been combed and coiffed nicely into place with a little dip that waved over his forehead in a very mysterious manner. His complexion was ruddy but free of blemishes, wrinkles, and blackheads.

People on first dates or meeting for the first few times, usually focus on one facial feature. For most women, that feature is the eyes, for, I suppose, a woman can gaze down into the depths of her man, sizing up the kindness, the honesty, the trustworthiness behind those orbs. Big, brown cow eyes, bespoke honesty, naïveté, innocence. Blue or gray or green eyes were more sexually appealing—come-hither. And the size of the pupils mattered as well. Slightly dilated pupils meant the male was calm, content, and even sexually attracted to his partner. Then again, I knew enough lay-men's medicine to know that dilated pupils, along with a slumped posture, signified death. I guessed, then, that a woman on a date with a black-eyed man would either think he was nursing an unexpected hard-on or was flaunting rigor mortis. Adam's pupils were deep and medium-sized, so I was safe.

I wondered what he thought of me. When I was by myself at home with the animals, I swore off make-up. As long as they got dinner and a pat on the head, they didn't care if I looked like Hillary Clinton on a good day. But before I went on a date, I contained the redness and puffiness around my eyes by applying cucumber slices to my lids. Though my greenish-blue eyes were not set as wide as a fashion model's, my lashes were mighty—as thick and long as a pigs' tail hairs. After I curled them and applied mascara and liner, I looked like a Victorian dolly—innocent yet very sensual at the same time.

Lucky for me, my complexion was almost pristine. I had the best skin around, with few wrinkles for my forty-nine years—no warts or moles screaming for attention, no obvious birthmarks or scars, except for one faint chicken pock mark above my left ear. And my skin had long ago stopped erupting with pimples from over-worked sebaceous glands. Most foundations I refused because they made me look mask-like, like the matte-mud finish on Queen Elizabeth.

Not only did my eyes and complexion make me visually appealing, but so did my lips and nose. My nose was aquiline—like that of Aphrodite, though I never really met her. My lips, however, did not conform to today's beauty trends which dictate full, round, pouty things able to suction stink bugs off walls. My lips were normal-size, perhaps even a bit on the thin side. Anyway, truthfully, my whole facial concoction came together rather nicely, affording me a rather comely appearance the likes of Marie Osmond.

I could tell Adam thought I was pretty.

"I feel like having a crock of onion soup," Adam told the server.

I gasped.

The server began to scribble it down on her pad. He added, "But I won't. I'm going to get a pork barbecue instead."

I choked on my iced tea.

He's going to eat pig? Doesn't he know I refuse pig meat on moral and ethical grounds? Well, Ginnie, you can't have everything your way. Suck it up.

Before our lunch came, he and I enjoyed a relatively neutral conversation—what his kids did for a living, where they lived, the circumstances around his wife's death—the poor soul had fallen from a porch balcony and hit her head on the concrete patio below— out like a light. In turn, he asked me about my books, the subject matter, blah, blah, blah. All was going well, and then our lunches came.

"That's all you're going to eat? Just fries?" he said. He wrapped his fingers around his huge dripping BBQ sandwich.

"Yeah. I love fries more than anything, and I'm just not hungry for any meat today."

"You're not a vegetarian?" He stiffened as though before the devil himself.

"Not really, though I *am* an advocate for farm

105

animals and their well-being on the way to slaughter and at the slaughterhouses."

He jammed one side of the pork barbecue into his mouth as I placed a fry between my lips and munched. Sauce drooled out the back end of his sandwich much like blood out of a surgeon's sponge. I looked away, diverting nasty thoughts to baseball bats and an imaginary Yankees' game. The blood image disappeared.

I put another salted fry into my mouth, looked up to comment on a pair of biker guys pulling into the parking lot and gasped as Adam took another huge bite out of his sandwich. As he placed the barbecue back on his plate, a thick stream of reddish-brown sauce coursed down his goatee much like the Colorado River cutting a swath through the Grand Canyon. Then he plastered a paper napkin to his chin to sop up the mess.

I swallowed hard and turned my attention to the parking lot beyond. Perhaps if I turned the conversation to something mutually appealing, he'd be more interested in me instead of his food. "So, how many women have you gone out with through this dating site?" I chewed the tip off another fry.

"Oh, maybe five or six so far."

"What do you think of the whole dating thing, ya know—at our age?"

His mouth hung full of shredded pork, sauce, and bread. "I have mixed emotions—sometimes I think it's fun. Other times it's a pain in the ass. I'm really looking for someone who has an interest in horses. I ride dressage horses, did I tell you?"

"Yes, well, sort of. I read that in your profile. Very nice. I respect dressage riders and dressage horses—

takes a lot of talent and versatility for an animal to do that." Just then a large bolus of food traveled down Adam's esophagus. The lump slowly disappeared beneath his neck skin, and I silenced a burp behind my hand. Sure—I knew that when one eats, the food slides down the esophagus and into the stomach: I just didn't want to *see* it. All that was needed to trump the vision was hearing the splash-down, like a space capsule into the ocean.

I had to finish my fries quickly if I was going to keep up with Adam, who was devouring his sandwich as hungrily as Big Foot after a hunger strike. So, I began taking fistfuls of fries and loading them, all seven to ten of them at once, into my mouth. If I didn't eat faster, he'd be finished with his sandwich way before me. Timing was critical in this dating game.

Between stuffing food into our mouths, we somehow managed to get enough conversation going to establish a preliminary connection between us. We had several things in common—the love of good food, an active lifestyle, riding horses, appreciating country life, and good looks. I had a few sparks that had ignited before the pork sandwich entered the scene, so that was good. Men gotta eat, after all. I wasn't the most gracious eater either when ravenous. I could be as forgiving as Jesus himself.

Finally, amid jokes about online dating and expectations regarding love and relationships, the server presented Adam with the check and took away our empty dishes. I offered to pay my half, but he would hear nothing of it.

Good sign, Ginnie. Adam is a keeper.

He slapped a couple of bills on the table and stood

up. I got up, too, put my arms through my coat sleeves, and grabbed my purse, fishing around for my car keys as I walked behind him toward the door.

Vaguely did I recall his opening the door for me and stepping into the frigid sunshine. So intent had I been on finding my keys buried in the depths of my bag, I hadn't noticed the one thing that, had I seen it upon meeting my date, would've sent me galloping off into the next county. Brandishing my keychain as proof, I yelled with delight, "I *finally* found them."

And then I was struck silent.

Adam, all of five feet eight inches in his socks, wore male riding attire—skin-tight beige riding jodhpurs and knee-high black leather riding boots. My shock, which I tried to keep hidden but was probably as evident as a draining abscess on the leg of an Ethiopian, was not so much at the riding attire itself, but at the human frame supporting it.

My date had the body of a pre-pubescent girl, from his knobby knees to his slim, feminine waist. Though I don't like big beer bellies on men either, frailty in a man is not attractive. A guy must be able to wrap his arms around me and let me know he means business. A bit of heft on his body—weight that is palpable—is nice. When he hugs me, I want to be enveloped by maleness.

When with a man for a romantic evening, the last thing I want to feel like is a pedophile. I want a man, not a man dressed in a child's suit. One shouldn't misunderstand: I don't require a muscle-bound guy sporting a Miller pack. Still, I didn't want to dwarf my man like Ma Kettle did Pa. Simply put, my man needs to be bigger than I—larger, and with more heft behind him than I have. I want to feel, in my man's arms, I am a small ship protected in his harbor. His body should be there in all its mass and presence. I don't desire hugs from some flea-guy whose strength lies only in his cologne.

Give me a strong, not-overly-bulked-up man who wears shit-kicker boots, not light, girly riding breeches covering a set of bees' knees. Beneath those jeans and shit-kickers the breadth and depth of his character should be reflected by the bulk of his manhood.

In that area I glimpsed not even the bulk of a thimble.

What I wasn't attracted to, which now stood before me on the deck at The Cork and Corkscrew, was a man who could understudy for Little Red Riding Hood—so dainty, so pale-frail, so slight, so delicately-limbed to even disgust the hungriest wolf.

What would sex be like with someone like that? With me on top, it'd be like Godzilla "doing" the Geico gecko. Even though I weighed less than one hundred and forty pounds dripping moist, at the very least, he would surely sustain severe bodily trauma. What would the sexual act, the tension, feel like between us? I expect a man's weight to press sensuously against me, making me feel consumed, used up. With Adam, however, I might as well be having sex with one of my cats.

I gulped, standing before him, as silent and unmoving as a tree stump.

Sex with Adam would be like having sex with another woman and one *a lot* younger, at that. I was not into lesbian activities—not that there was anything wrong with that—but, for me, penises held all the action. In order to use a penis effectively, it must be driven by a powerful engine—a dynamo. Adam had long ago lost the crankshaft of his locomotive. In fact, I'd bet during the act a solar-powered broom would put him to shame.

What sparks had been coursing earlier through my veins like a torched meteor through Earth's atmosphere suddenly became as devoid of substance as a black hole. I looked up at Adam, smiled as weak as his knees looked, pumped his hand while profusely thanking him, and jumped into my car. On the way home I scolded myself for being superficial. I remembered the nice conversation Adam and I had over lunch and how he actually did eat that pork sandwich like a trucker. But, try as I might, I just couldn't get past his feminine profile—the female waist, the slim, thin-boned hips, the slight, high calves, and the wafer-thin thighs. I did have my bucket list for my future mate and having the body of a ten-year-old girl was not one of them.

I drove home, in fact, entirely disgusted with my fussiness and the lightness of his being. And then I yelled.

"Next!"

Chapter Nine
With Beads and Pearls Popping

Over the course of the next few weeks, Richard Downing or "My Colonel" as I referred to him to friends, pelted me with a continuous stream of curious emails. He was as fascinated by my writing ability as he was by my hundred pictures on Facebook. Almost child-like in his requests for stories, he often pleaded for a good tale, so when I needed a break from my farm animal advocacy manuscript, I succumbed to his demands. Of course, he wasn't interested in the commonplace fables like those of the Brothers Grimm—complete with a moral and concluding in a lovely denouement. The tales Richard wanted involved "the big nasty."

Through my writings with My Colonel, I blossomed like Lady Chatterley with her Oliver. This learned, gramma-aged woman, complete with her sterile, non-sexual existence for sixteen years of her twenty-eight years of marriage had graduated to expressing herself by—horror of horrors—sexting.

My conscience took exception to my newfound self, however, and responded, with typical self-mockery. *OMG, Ginnie! What have u become? Ur nothing more than a writer of smut. LMFAO.*

A psychoanalysis of my subconscious was appropriate. "You're just jealous. You're anally fixated

111

on me as Pippi while I've actually matured into the likes of Linda Lovelace.

While my prudish conscience tormented me, I typed furiously—the Pearl S. Buck of cybersex. After all, the sexting with Richard was about the story-telling as much as it was about the love scenes—at least for me. Had Richard known how much planning went into the plot line, the characterization, the editing of my tales, perhaps his boner would have been less boney. My stories were as well-written as Edith Wharton's, perfectly punctuated—with not a dash nor colon out of place. They were subtlely drawn—not so detailed as to make it lascivious but with just enough scintillating description to allow his mind to wander and create its own sensual world. I became, more or less, a Hemingway of the romance story.

I wrote. Richard imagined.

Richard responded. I imagined—and typed.

And corrected.

A few problems happened, however, with the email exchanges. Always the English teacher, I couldn't drum up a good imaginative orgasm if I came upon a semicolon used improperly. The mistake turned me off like the sight of cellulite on a guy's thighs. At times when he was at the height of his sex scene, his poor writing made my eager pussy scowl and dry up like the Mojave. Though I'm sure My Colonel didn't have impotency problems as Lance had, he obviously wasn't a grammarian. In fact, he proved himself an inept stooge when it came to distinguishing between homonyms—"I want you, two"; "I eight you out"; "I rubbed your but."

Had we met in reality, limited purely to speech and

not writing, our relationship would gallop off like a horse stepping on a hornets' nest. But courting through email put the emphasis on the written word, and in that realm Richard was seriously delinquent. Finally, after he had written, "My Deer, I could dye for you," I had had enough. I wasn't Bambi, after all. So, I wrote back, "Okay, Kernel. I think you need to brush up on you're grammar before oui can ever bee a couple."

He had always hated English but vowed to proofread before he hit "Send." However, the promise was short-lived. Whenever the sexual tension in our emails reached "lift off," and I knew he was engaging, as he put it in his proper military-ease, in "self-releasing" on the other end of the computer, his grammar dwindled all to hell. Did impending orgasms melt men's brains? At times the writing was so misspelled and disjointed I could hardly understand it. Soon, however, I regarded the mistakes as a compliment. I imagined him sitting there with his notepad, thinking of me and my beaver and struggling to strike the keys with one hand while jerking his appendage with the other. How cruel of me to judge when I was the reason for his discombobulation.

Yes, all the flirting and love-making between Richard and me occurred—slowly, deliberately—strictly through email correspondence. The story-telling originated not through chat rooms or online messenger systems or Skyping. Our communication was more mysterious, hidden, powerfully sensual because it was so deliberately secret, occurring so privately, personally. While one piece of the story developed on one end, the other was relished on the other.

Even I marveled at my own scene-setting

expertise—creating a romantic setting for the imaginary rendezvous, pumping up suspense for the meet-and-greet, gradually tantalizing Richard into making his moves. I did it all with fictional rules—plot, conflict, climax, more conflict—all with the magic of story-telling. I created for Richard alone—to stimulate him mentally and sexually, to stir admiration for me, my writing, my creativity—each phrase, word, paragraph united toward a common theme, sexual tension. I was fairly assured that, in the end, Richard would applaud in his own unconventional way.

My first story developed instinctively—the two of us, both described as attractive, fit middle-aged adults, meet in a downtown bar somewhere in New York City. We two strangers sit down together in a shadowed "dive" eerily appropriate for an *ID* episode. We are immediately drawn to each other. Eye contact rages intense, but we prevail over our lust momentarily and order a couple of drinks, more as props than as libations. What we want, from the moment our eyes merge, is each other.

So, with the setting and low lighting presented, I emailed Richard that he takes my hand beneath the bar, and then he slips his hand slowly along my thigh. I typed that a shiver goes up my arms and down my back. I lean toward him, gazing into his eyes. I want to devour him with my mouth.

Then, I sent another email to him. "Tell me, Richard. What is your reaction? What are you going to do with me?"

Richard responded immediately. "I take you by your waste and bring you two me. I see that you have the top button of you're blouse undone. I can see just a

114

sliver of a black, lace bra. And I am hard as iron."

"It is spelled 'waist', Richard. Please watch your spelling. Anyway, I breathe in your ear and whisper, 'Let's go outside, Richard.' And, with your arm around me, we get up and walk toward the door—leaving our drinks behind."

"We leave our drinks *behind*?" Abandoning the drinks *really* floored him—an abomination. I laughed aloud behind my computer.

"Yes, Richard. We leave them behind." I typed more. "And we leave the bar for the back alley."

"The back alley?"

The scenario began unfolding in my brain. While I actually had goose bumps marching along my arms and my pussy sat at attention, I also felt another urge—my love of comedy. I was nothing if not a comedienne. My fingers danced across the keyboard. "Yes, Richard. We are walking down the dark alley behind the bar where all the old drunks pee."

I waited for the laugh.

No response.

Uh-oh. Might've turned him off on that one.

Good move, Ginnie. Just gotta be a clown, don't you?

I continued and attempted to save the moment. "And we find a spot that doesn't smell too bad. You pin me lightly against the brick wall. What are you doing to do me, Richard?"

His response was immediate. "Caressing you're breasts. I am undoing all the buttons on your blouse. I slip my hands under you're blouse, take you're breast in my hand, and then I kiss her, suck her, suck you're neck. I'm so hot for you—boiling hot! I kiss you as I've

115

never kissed anyone before!!!!! And I am hard for you, pressing my manhood into your thigh."

My Colonel was boiling over like a mud-pot in Yellowstone.

And so the sexmail continued until Richard had wound himself so tight—like the E string on a violin—I thought for sure I'd hear it *ping* when he "released" himself some hundred miles away.

I, however, did not engage in any self-stimulation, but Richard was anxious to know if I had worked my kitty over. I told him the truth, a partial truth—I had the talent to climax using only my mind. If I ever allowed my hands to touch my furry reality, the effervescence of my imagination would burst flaccid like a chewing gum bubble. Whatever went on inside my brain had a direct line to my nether parts, not to be spoiled by my own fingers. The mere thought of sex with Richard caused my clam to quiver and gulp air.

Richard was always respectful after he climaxed. He didn't just sign off and fall asleep, his head in his computer. He actually typed a few nice, rather mundane things and then politely excused himself—he did have students to instruct, after all.

****

In the mean time I had been racking up telephone calls and dates with guys from the dating site the likes of which resembled the children's rhyme, "Pickin' up paw-paws, put 'em in your pockets." The calls and invites to dinner accumulated, and to each one I gave my undivided attention until I sized them up, categorized them into "nice guy," "jerk-off," "handsome, arrogant bastard," "user," "dud," and "dwarf."

One of my admirers was Geoff, who worked in concrete contracting—drilling holes and filling them with cement. At first I asked myself whether I really wanted to date a guy who made holes only to fill them in again. He specified in his profile he was interested in a cruise partner. Odd. If he just desired a travel companion, he could ask his mother. He wanted a cruise partner? Why didn't he just take his dog? Escorting his dog would be cheaper—a dog wouldn't demand fancy dinners or any souvenirs. Yeah, he was a long-term candidate for a mate—*not*. So much for my farm, animals, and normal life while sailing the world on a fantasy cruise every day of my life. I wanted a life partner, not a cruise partner.

Personally, I think Geoff had been in concrete work for too long a time. He was as thick as a brick—brain-dense, marshmallow-ish. He really had no sense of how to converse with a woman. His lack of communication skills became apparent in our first conversation when he asked if I had big tits. He laughed so hard he went into a paroxysm of coughing—as if he had said the cleverest thing since Reagan said, "Peace through strength." Then, when I didn't answer, he assumed I was a deaf-mute. "Yeah, how big are your hooters? I like *really* big ones."

"They're teeny-tiny—quadruple A size cup. Flat as the Argentinian pampas. You wouldn't like 'em—they're almost non-existent. Likewise, I wouldn't be interested in your thimble-stick."

I hung up.

"Next!"

Another guy clearly dismissed a lasting relationship with a woman. In fact, the last thing on his mind was love or companionship. This guy wanted to debate me, not make love to me. In fact, he bragged about his father being a state representative. He sounded disappointed when I agreed with him on the awful job our Congress was doing, all the IRS and NSA scandals, and the effects of Obamacare on the middle class. In the course of the conversation, he confided he purposefully used big words in his profile write-up so that "dumb broads" would avoid him.

"Oh, that's nice," I said. "I suppose your eminence has been vicariously acquired, then, from your ancestral legacy?"

"Huh?"

"I have a Ph.D. in English."

"Oh, really?" He brightened. But the arguer in him soon reared its ugly head again. "Yeah, not a *real* doctor, though, are you?"

"Yep, that's what some say."

"I collect Victorian antiques. My house is full of them. Just love them—can hardly move in the house, it's so full of antiques. So, whomever I am with has to love the Victorian Age."

I pictured my great aunts' Victorian mansion in Kinderhook, NY, loaded with junk of that kind. Visions of dark, looming, lacey, rococo-styled stuff haunted me again as they had when I was a kid. I felt nauseous.

I paused. A calm washed over me. "Truthfully—I hate Victorian stuff—it's pompous, presumptuous, and supercilious. And Queen Victoria was a fat slob and probably a closet lesbian, though, of course, there's nothing wrong with that. Have a nice life."

I hung up.

"Next."

****

Andre the architect was new to America, his gray locks still damp from the salty sea air of his maiden voyage. His English language skills were similarly fresh, ingénue. Our first and only phone conversation went as follows:

"Hi, Andre. How are you? My name is Ginnie."

"Bueno." Long period of silence. "How…are…you, genius?"

"My name is *Ginnie*." I giggled to myself and repeated in a louder voice. "It's *Ginnie*, not *genius*, although I may very well be." I laughed at my cleverness.

A soft chuckle sounded on the other end. Then a tentative whispery voice said, "Bueno." Long pause. "I trabajo—work—Newyorkinarchitectura."

He said a few more things that I could barely hear or understand, followed by another long pause and some throat clearing.

"Oh, very nice," I said. Long pause. This was not going well.

Andre's English was so broken, and he was so soft-spoken I had to keep asking him to repeat himself. I tried being polite but soon lost my patience. The prognosis wasn't good—death was imminent. Being with Andre for the long term was problematic—I could never live with someone I couldn't communicate with. In a week we'd both be crazy and ready to rip each other to shreds the likes of my homemade sauerkraut. So, I let him down nicely, all apologetic and stuff.

"Andre, I don't think we are a real good match because—" I wanted to say: *I can't fucking understand you!*"

"ForgiffmeEnglishpooryouverynice. Yesyouverynice."

I couldn't even understand his apology.

"Next."

Days later I met Grover.

Entering from the blinding, sunny outside of the mall into the dimly-lit bar of The Bonefish restaurant, I stumbled to a stool. I ordered a drink and checked my phone for emails from other gentleman callers. Surprisingly, there were none. Then, suddenly, my cell phone barked.

"Are you at the bar at Bonefish yet?" Grover said.

"Yes, I am. Where are you?"

"Here at the door. Raise your hand, so I can see you."

The bright light outside morphed everyone coming through the door into black silhouettes. Feeling as though in first grade, I tentatively raised my hand. I saw a return wave, and a man headed toward me. I put my cell in my purse, and the next thing I knew he stood beside me, smiling.

Nice one. Nice face. Nice hair. Not bad at all. A twinge shivered in my pussy.

He put an arm around my shoulders in a friendly gesture, and I smiled. *Very nice. Yum.* "How was your day?" I asked.

"The usual." He smiled and hopped onto a bar stool. "I work—purchase building supplies—for local contractors." He stared hard. A long pause. I smiled back.

"You're absolutely *gorgeous*."

"Thank you." I smiled like a goat eating stickers. "You are handsome, too."

We dined on sushi and bam-bam shrimp, and though I offered to pay for myself, he flatly refused, so I left the tip. He asked me out for the next evening—done deal.

Dinner the following evening with Grover was tantalizing—a few drinks to loosen the libido and dinner at my old stand-by, The Cork and Corkscrew. Grover loved the rebellious biker atmosphere with its thousands of dollar bills written over with phrases spanning the religious to the obscene. We laughed at so many. "Great hot wings are worth a thousand luscious titties." "Gonna rock my world at The Cork and Corkscrew." "Jesus loves you, this I know."

Grover wasn't enjoying his shrimp fajitas nearly as much as he was enjoying watching me devour my buffalo burger. Daintily sucking in a French fry between mouthfuls of barbecue, I noticed through my peripheral vision a moon face. I turned. Grover faced me, staring—again—his eyes drawn to slits. "I can't get over how beautiful you are." His eyes sparkled.

I spit a reply through a mouth full of bison meat. "Fank you." Then, I flushed down the bolus in my throat with a swig of iced tea. I returned the compliment. "I think you're handsome, too."

He looked desirous—hungry for more than just fajitas—and a spark ignited somewhere along my large intestine. I burped behind my napkin and smiled widely hoping shards of burger weren't caught in my gums.

The rest of the meal played out in normal fashion, except for Grover's fawning behavior—I was so this and that, he loved my personality, I was so much fun. Where had I been all his life? Blah, blah, blah. I downed the last fry, profusely thankful for all the compliments, and then we headed for home.

Grover wasn't a giant man, but he had a nice head of cropped, wavy gray hair and matching moustache. His comely looks, topped by sculptured lips and a virile profile dictated that if he wanted to kiss me, I would, not only allow it but would enjoy the loving to the max. When we came home and said good-bye, he gave Selena a perfunctory pat on the head and turned anxiously to me.

He took me in his arms, pulling me tight against him. I giggled, and he buried his face in my neck. A shiver went through my ribcage.

Not bad. Not bad. This guy is pulling some strings, huh, Ginnie? Pussy has her hackles raised.

It was true.

The first kiss came soft, polite, tentative. I sighed, contented, accepted it, and kissed back—lips firm but not too tight. He kissed back, his head turning to the side—engaged, interested. Pussy twinged, and I responded likewise. I whispered in as romantic a voice as his name would allow, "Gro-ver."

Little did I realize that hearing his name would send him into a paroxysm of desire. With a sudden intake of breath, he folded his arms across my back, his hands entangling my hair, and held my face against his. He consumed me with his lips, furious in his passion. I flicked my tongue against the teeth-doors.

"Let me in. Let me in," sayeth the damsel of the castle.

Little did I know a monstrous, dragon-like being lurked, ready to strike, behind those doors. At the moment I knocked on the pearly gates, the dragon burst through my lips and charged, rabid, into my mouth.

Before I knew what was happening, Grover's overly-anxious tongue writhed, snake-like, in my mouth. The serpent was hard, pointed, knife-like—non-human—wriggling like a giant earthworm frantic to escape a mudhole. And it tasted, as I remembered from one nasty experience in my college days, like crocodile meat, with that fishy, brackish flavor enjoyed by inebriated Louisiana dwellers.

I gagged and pushed him away just in time to save my buffalo burger.

"Sorry," Grover muttered. I stood gasping two feet away, eyes big as flapjacks.

"That was a bit much, Grover. Please, don't do that again."

"Okay. I guess I was just excited."

A few minutes later, still trying to clear the bile from my throat, I escorted Grover to the door, likely never to be seen again. After all, I just couldn't take the chance of meeting that dragon again. And puking all over one's date was probably the greatest faux pas ever.

I leaned against the closed door.

"Next."

The following afternoon an email from Richard awaited me. He was free—no student projects to correct, no lectures to plan. Would I talk with him for a while? I responded I always enjoyed our corresponding. Writing for him nurtured my brain and its neurons much like a full, fresh healthy head of cauliflower. I confided I found our conversations emotionally stimulating on a sexual level, what with Lance's sixteen years of impotence plaguing me like a rampant bout of shingles.

In all those years during which Lance had tried but

failed to bed me, I accepted his disability, reading many books about erectile dysfunction in an effort to fix our problem. Despite the recommendations in the books, however, Lance's penis refused to cooperate. The second "Phil" raised his head, he deflated, leaving both of us exhausted and frustrated. No matter how light I made the problem, it haunted Lance like a horrid specter, like some oceanic ghost ship floating aimlessly with slack sails. While I had vowed faithfulness to my disabled husband, I had also unwittingly starved my beaver and my sexual self.

So, when Richard's plea for an afternoon of titillating email sex came in, I galloped to my bedroom, computer in hand. I sped like Rapunzel dashing up the tower steps from a mad, scissors-brandishing stylist. Though real sex with Colonel Richard Downing was nonexistent, the imaginary sex was a good temporary stop-gap as long as the computer and I were in a romantic mood. I was sure that, in time, the colonel and I would consummate our love in the real world—— hopefully on the main lawn of the famous military college as the bell tower tolled midnight.

For now cybersex would have to do. I vowed to put my literary all into it—thus creating an exquisite experience for us both. So began the tale of all tales. I typed away.

"We are attending a military ball, and I am your date for the evening. We make a handsome couple— you dressed in full formal military attire, and I in my slinky, white chiffon gown covered in beads and pearls. You are extremely proud of the lovely woman by your side and notice the stares I command from your fellow officers and college instructors. You recognize the envy on their faces and are proud to possess a siren by your side." I hit "Send" and waited.

"What are you wearing again?" he emailed.

"A long, sleeveless, tight-fitting white dress covered in white beads and pearls."

"Sounds nice."

"It is. I am describing a dress I have."

"Okay. More. Tell me more."

"Soft piano music plays in the background while servers offer hors d'oeuvres from silver trays. We are sipping wine, and you are introducing your friends and other military men to me. I am not only gorgeous, but I can schmooze with them all, even the generals. I giggle and flirt a little, bat my eyelashes in a shy, modest way. You are titillated knowing they all want me—you can see it in their eyes—the lust, the desire, the admiration for your lovely prize. And you eat it up because you know we are a 'solid'—I only have eyes and intentions for you.

"You can see that the other officers are as impressed with you as they are with me. After all, you must be some impressive man to have a woman of this stature and beauty by your side. You are so proud of me and yourself you're ready to burst out of your military tux."

"I'm wearing a tux?"

"Yes. Whatever is the equivalent in the military. Don't make me google it. Just imagine it—something fancy. Let's get back to the story."

I continued to type. "And as the hubbub of partygoers sounds through the main ballroom, I lean toward you, smiling mysteriously, and say, 'Richard. I'm not wearing panties under my gown.'" I hit Send and waited.

A micro-second later Richard wrote, *"You don't have panties on under your dress?"*

"No, I don't have panties on, Richard. What do you think about that?"

The next email came in, jagged and hurried. "That is so *hot*—that you forgot to put on you're panties."

"Oh, I didn't forget. I did it on purpose. Spell it 'your,' Richard. Now, back to the story."

I typed. "Your heart is all aflutter. All you can do is imagine me, exposed, beneath my gown, and you have an erection you're trying to hide beneath your hors d'oeuvre napkin. I am giggling behind my wine glass. You muster control and encircle my waist with your arm. What are you saying to me, Richard?"

The words flashed across my computer screen. "I want you, Ginnie. Right now, on top of the piano while the player belts out 'Amazing Grace.' I can hardly stand it knowing you are standing beside me without you're thong. You are wearing at least a thong, right?"

"I'm not even wearing a thong, Richard. My pussy is wild and free, unfettered—waiting for you."

He wrote, his written English devolving with the sexual tension, "Your two much, my Deer. I'm like a rock hear! You...make me crazy, but I'm lovin' it, thinkin' 'bout all the other officers smelling you like stud dogs on a bitch in heat. I love it—they can't have you. You are mine."

I typed back. "I whisper you will need patience to have me until we get to your home. And you can hardly stand still because your cock hurts—it's so hard. You say, 'Ginnie, I want you now,' and I say you must wait for a few hours until the party is over."

"I can't weight! I want you now!"

"It's spelled 'wait,' Richard."

I continued. "I lead you outside to your vintage, 1968 flame-orange Camaro and open the door and say, 'I can't wait any longer. Let's make love in the back seat, Richard.' And I follow you inside."

Then the author in me switched gears and began writing in third-person so that he could experience our lovemaking as though he were watching us in a movie. "And he tore at her dress because he wanted her so desperately, so deeply, he could hardly think. He could hardly breathe. 'I need you,' Richard gasped. And she brought him to her, clasped him to her so hard that beads from her dress popped off and sprinkled over the back seat.

" 'I love you, Richard,' she said. 'Make love to me.' She lay down, lifted her dress, and made herself open, penetrable. 'Mount me, Richard, like the animal you are. Take me—make love to me.' "

I expected no more responses from Richard. He was imagining with such intensity he would not even be able to respond through a keyboard.

I continued to allow the cinema to unwind. "And he did. He felt her moistness, her heat. He shivered with desire, with need. This was the ultimate woman—accomplished, beautiful, impressive—*his*. She kissed him hard on the mouth, her soft tongue touching his, slipping inside his mouth like a secret thing. She released him, and he directed his manhood slowly, deliberately, into her. She gasped. He groaned as he entered her, and her back arched as she rose to meet him.

And more beads spilled to the floor—tinkled onto

127

the floor.

"Their movement was in perfect harmony. With each thrust she pulled herself into him, driving to the hilt up into him. He watched, intent, as he moved himself in and out, out to the tip and back inside, way inside her, so hard her breath caught. He closed his eyes, felt her, moved with her, felt the waters rising within her as they rose within him.

"She was boiling hot for her soldier, her friend, her ultimate lover. She had long ago given herself to him completely. And every lovemaking session filled her up until she felt like bursting. The length, the breadth, the depth of him took her breath away. Her attraction to him felt instinctive, animalian. He was a superb lover, and she wanted to satisfy him as she had satisfied no others.

"Her dress lay crumpled on the black leather seat. Richard had long ago on this night lost himself in her, the love of his life, the sexiest being he had ever laid eyes on. He pulled her closer, thrusting himself deep within her, and she let out a cry like a hyena. 'Come in me, Richard. I want you to fly with me, feel my release at the moment of yours. Come in me because I'm on the edge—the edge of you.'

"He thrust twice more, and then the two of them climaxed in synchrony. He covered her with kisses as his fluid flowed, pulsed, into her. She could feel his liquid heat coming inside her—the ultimate, most vulnerable act. He stroked her hair and kissed her neck, and she gasped and rose to him. And as he relaxed in her arms, he said, 'I love you, Ginnie. I so love you.' "

I waited for five minutes before Richard's email finally burst onto the screen, "OMG! That was so hot, babe! You are so good with those stories. I *love* them. Thanks."

"Well, you are good subject matter to work with—good-looking military guy with smarts and status. Not too hard to write a sensual story about the two of us together."

Seconds later I added one more comment, my fingers hesitating for just a moment. "Perhaps, in the near future, we can make that fantasy a reality. :) Perhaps we could talk on the phone sometime soon. Love, Ginnie."

I waited five minutes, but there was no response. "Must've gone back to work," I said to myself. Then, with a smile, I shut down the computer.

Chapter Ten
New Hampshire Bill

The fact Richard hadn't responded to my offer to meet in person or speak on the phone didn't really faze me. Our communication was so sporadic his silence went virtually unnoticed, except when my heart was anticipating a sign of affection and felt somehow, mysteriously, deprived. Time was short: in a few months I would be fifty years old—too over the hill to attract even a cockroach to my dried-out bed. If I wanted to find love, I needed to hurry.

So, back to the dating site I went with renewed vigor as well as apprehension. I sent out what amounted to a broadcast flirt to about ten different good-looking and halfway intelligent-sounding prospects, and sat back, awaiting replies. Within minutes four "echoes" appeared on my screen. I clicked on two of them, and my heart skipped enough beats to qualify as a major cardiac infarct.

Now this is more like it. Eat your heart out, Mel.

I squinted at the screen scrolling through five photos of fifty-three-year-old Bill from New Hampshire. I liked him immediately—pictures of him seated with his teenage daughter and son, his mother, and probably his sister. His close-shaven goatee complemented his crew cut—his eyes sparkled as he grinned, surrounded by his family. *A good-looking family man—nice.* Bill was no idiot taking selfies in a public men's bathroom, the urinals in view. This guy actually wanted to attract women and knew how to exact a photo of himself that was flattering and sane. I felt an instant attraction. But New Hampshire? Quite a distance from New York. Well, who could know? If the sparks flew, they might ignite a fire under his ass to move. I emailed him, urging him to call me.

I waited.

Soon my cell barked—Bill.

Tone of voice, enunciation, and skillful use of the rules of standard English are important to me, what with my background in English. If a potential partner lacks the gift of intelligent gab, my pussy deflates. I don't care whether his house has a Jacuzzi or if he's got a 1979 Porsche—if he can't hold his own discussing feminist criticism as it pertains to Hemingway's *For Whom the Bell Tolls*, he won't cut it with me in the sack. The same applies to the tone of voice and whether he slurs or garbles his words. If I must beg him to repeat himself, and if it's from no fault of a lousy cell connection, then I've got to set him free. Just as it was with Andre the Spaniard, I cannot tolerate gibberish.

"Wannatakeitthenextstepupanddothenasty?"

What did you say?

"Want to have sex?"

No!

The voice coming out of the other end of New Hampshire, however, sounded deep and sexy. I held my notebook in my lap, his family pictures handy, in an attempt to make this phone conversation as real as it could be. Our talk was easy, flowing, with no self-consciousness between us. Bill quipped something funny—I laughed. I shot back a witty observation—he responded in like kind. After several minutes of dueling jesters, I probed for more personal details. I would take on his most prized possession—his mother.

"Bill. I just have to tell you what cute little cheeks your mother has. She seems so sweet."

"Oh, she is a very sweet little old lady." He sounded proud. "I just love her to death. Wouldn't hurt a flea."

I had hit the button and rolled five aces of spades. This payout amounted to a *huge* win.

"And your kids look nice, too. Your daughter is gorgeous. Do you think your son would be interested in dating a forty-nine-year-old woman?"

He laughed and said he didn't think so.

The conversation eventually sprouted from a seedling into a magnificent tropical plant with a multitude of leaves, vines, and berries. We talked about the vices and alluring nature of online dating at a mature age. We also discussed people's misrepresenting themselves on dating sites. One woman, he said, claimed in her dating profile to have "normal" body weight. Her face was pretty enough, but when they met at the local coffee shop and she ordered a double chocolate latte, her belly rested on the table like a sleeping cat.

I assured him that, for my age, I was physically fit, slender, and would not be a disappointment if and when we met. He purred that from all my pics on Facebook and the dating site, he knew I was telling the truth. Could he meet the renowned Virginie Snow?

Distance between us soon became a fleeting problem. He paused before remembering a childhood friend living just a few miles south of me in Catskill. One day he could visit me and his friend in the same trip—it would work out perfectly.

"How convenient," I chirped. "Then that will take the heat off us for sex, too. You can spend the days with me and the evenings with him. We can do day trips—like an old, married couple." I laughed. "We can visit the town of Schenectady or Albany and go hiking in the Albany Pine Bush Preserve. It's a nature enthusiast's dream. And then in the evening you can trot off to your friend. No pressure at all. We can just enjoy each other's company—before getting into...ya know...heavy stuff."

"Yes. I can make a weekend get-away out of it. I'll give him a call tonight. Let's do it." I recommended he take a plane and offered to pick him up at the Albany airport, but he was looking forward to the five hour drive—said he loved driving, and the springtime scenery would be beautiful. We set the date for the third weekend in March and said good-bye.

One bitch about the cyber-dating tease—in reality fantasies quickly become impossibilities. The creators of dating sites don't give a rat's ass if they forge romance between people living at opposite ends of the earth. They don't care a woman from New York can't possibly develop a *real* relationship with a weight-lifter from Bulgaria. Distance seems not to be a problem for the online dating administrators. As long as they throw tons of mate bait, from minnows in the Hudson River to sharks off the coast of Australia, to us poor, hapless, hopeless men and women, they feel they've provided a "product" and are justified in scarfing up a monthly membership fee. No one administering the internet dating site cares I am creaming my undies after a guy who can only meet me via the QE II or by hitching a ride aboard a misdirected Air Force drone. No one is bothered that my potential mate is slavering over me in complete sexual angst—his balls the colors of the Aurora Borealis—on the other side of Serbia.

While cyber space has no limits, physicality certainly does. Before tele-transporters transform us, with a click of a button, into micro-atomic bodies flying anywhere in the world through a FIOS cable—we still must contend with getting a real, one hundred and fifty pound-plus body and all its sensual parts to the person of desire. While the messaging and acquainting oneself with a potential romantic partner can all be done over wires and the "cloud," the actual meeting must occur through snail transport. Cyberity must respect reality.

Therein lies the rub—and the tease.

I can't begin to count the number of flirts and messages I have gotten from Texas, California, Florida, Germany, England, and Israel. When a good-looker from Mars sends me an email, my shoulders slump. Politely I tell him that my rocket ship is out of order at the moment, and he needs to seek a Stargazer elsewhere in the galaxy. Of course, it's okay if he wants to be pen pals, but a couple needs to come together with their bodies when the ultimate goal is kissing, cuddling, and violent sex.

So, earlier on I learned online dating demands compromise with regard to traveling a distance. While New Hampshire Bill was willing to drive five hours to see me, some men are unwilling to drive even a half hour for dinner or nooky. Here's how it boils down—if the goal at the other end of the long trip is worth it—

tantalizing, irresistible, honest, then the trip, though it might demand a two hour haul, should feel negligible. If I knew Mel Gibson awaited on a beach in California, I'd buy a bus ticket and sop up the long haul with romantic fantasies. Once two people meet, assess the spark equation and their abilities and willingness to change venues, then the relationship must logically bloom or wilt forever away.

With the improbability of Bill's and my ever-establishing permanence together, and with his visit three weeks away, I resolved to let no moss grow under my flirtatious feet. So, I perused all the replies from that infamous evening of broadcast flirtations and sent a quick "Hi, there," to a middle-aged stud named Steve. The next morning as I lay in bed rubbing the sand from my eyes, I turned over and reached for the notepad that had long ago replaced Lance's head on the pillow next to me. I tapped in my password, and Steve's shock of thick grayish-brown hair and gray-blue eyes appeared in my inbox. My heart skipped three beats, and I clicked on the message whose subject line read, "I'm interested in you."

We had a world of things in common—love of country life—he had a job in the agricultural industry—a penchant for animals and cats, in particular, and living life according to "seeing the glass half full, not half empty." His profile revealed even more— "My mother raised us three brothers to be good men." I liked that. The three pictures showed him with his arms around his two comely daughters and one playing with a granddaughter. He oozed honesty and was possessed of a natural kind of physical and inner beauty.

My conscience woke up with the birds this

morning. *You got a ringer here, Ginnie.*

In the next few days Steve and I corresponded only through emails. We flirted, commenting on each other's attraction to the other, and he told me all about his grown daughters. He admitted other women had been turned off by his vocation—being a "grunt" delivering agricultural products to farmers as well as spreading pesticides and herbicides throughout the countryside. He remarked, ironically, those tree-hugging women wouldn't enjoy starving to death after all the bugs finished devouring our nation's crops. I commiserated, saying, as a country girl, I understood the farmers' plight and how they struggle, especially battling weather, infestations, and failed crops.

Our common connection to the land finally sealed the deal for him—he wanted to talk on the phone. In the weeks preceding Bill's visit Farmer Steve and I developed a slow, strong bond, but a rendezvous during the week was nearly impossible because springtime sent him and the farmers into a frenzy. He worked seventy to eighty hours a week, sometimes not arriving back home in Connecticut until eight at night. And then, exhausted, he grabbed something to eat and went right to sleep. I was as disappointed as a monkey in an herb shop.

Despite his heavy work schedule, he always had time to call. Partly what I found so attractive was he didn't mind my brushing my teeth during a conversation. My spitting in the sink like a sailor hurrying for duty didn't disgust him because it was "just things people do" as Jim Casey, the wise preacher in the *Grapes of Wrath,* had said. We are all human, complete with flaws and foibles. We spit, we cough, and we fart, though I warned myself not to push that aspect too soon in the relationship—no pun to myself intended. For country people, the world is filled with excrement and vile things causing the average city person to wretch but which seem completely natural to us. As for Steve and me—the natural world and the things people did on a daily basis resonated with honesty and the phrase "It is what it is."

Each morning I grabbed my notebook and clicked on Steve's profile page. I was a cougar after a tasty rabbit. Never was I disappointed, for there awaited his email. My heart twitched. His wavy gray hair lay mussed and sexy, and I imagined riffling my fingers through it during an exotic kiss. Since he was six foot three, I also imagined myself being luxuriously engulfed and dwarfed by him during an intimate embrace. Goose bumps did the Macarena up my arms. To be sure, I preferred a strong, manly presence over one like Adam, the Heidi-guy I met months ago at The Cork and Corkscrew. I wanted a man I could sink my teeth into, not one I could blow over with a sneeze.

For weeks Steve and I talked twice a day, once before he set off in his dump truck of chemicals, and once before my earthy prince drifted into a dead, but fitful, sleep. Steve often confided his dread of nighttime and sleeping. He shared with me his nightly battle with insomnia ever since his wife died of leukemia a year ago. Despite exhaustion, sleep eluded him, so anxious he felt without a good woman. He hated being alone—despised it—and was in search of a lasting relationship with the right woman, someone he could easily fall asleep beside.

I smiled, believing he might be prepping me for

that position, confident I would pass the interview. Still, our relationship was relatively new, and I had a promise to keep—with Bill—and miles of men to go before I'd sleep—with that special one. We vowed to keep talking on the phone with the promise to meet after the busy spring ended.

****

The day for New Hampshire Bill's visit had arrived. I considered investing in some feminine fussing at the local spa but didn't have a non-leaky pot to piss in much less extra money for a Wal-Mart makeover event. So, I got out a ratty eyelash curler, an old toothbare hairbrush, makeup from the 70's, and went to town. After showering, I spread a concoction of emu oil and talc all over my body, then blew out my hair until my bob looked perfect without resembling a WWII flying helmet.

Then I decided on an outfit and shoes, all of which Lance had bought me years ago. Leaning into the mirror, I applied my make-up—simple eye-liner and mascara with a tad of lip balm. Being a farm girl, I wasn't "into" fancy and believed most men preferred the au naturel look: unburdened under several layers of pancake make-up and psychedelic eye shadow. Surely Bill would appreciate my looks in their natural state. If he didn't, I would bet my heart on Mr. Green Jeans.

Advice from online dating gurus suggested meeting one's date in a public place to avoid encounters with men having Ted Bundy-like tendencies.

Right, Ginnie. Your date should be put wise to your undying admiration for Lizzie Borden.

I ignored my old-maid conscience—she was just jealous. I slapped on more layers of mascara. I simply couldn't justify forcing a man, tired after a long drive, to meet me at the local International House of Pancakes. If he was taking that much trouble to see me, then I wanted my sexy Caesar to alight from his chariot and collapse on my royal futon while this concubine fanned him and fed him grapes. It was the least I could do.

Sitting in the over-sized stuffed chair and perusing Bill's profile, I dreamed of the Imperial One reining in his horses and skidding to a stop in my backyard. I checked my watch—only fifteen minutes until his arrival. My face felt flushed like Cleopatra's dreaming of Anthony. Would he look different than his photos, especially the ones glowing next to his cheeky little mother? My heart skipped a beat as I smacked my smothered-in-Vaseline lips together.

An hour and a half later I squirmed, alone, back stiff, in my chair. Where was he? Another hour later I felt numb, discarded. Only my cat, Selena, sat, my faithful companion, in my lap. For sure, I was no longer envisioning that first ravenous kiss imagined in the past three weeks. I sat, consumed with anxiety, and, yes— anger. Had he jilted me? He was supposed to arrive at noon. My watch read two-thirty p.m. An hour ago I had texted him as to his ETA and present location. Silence. Did he just decide I wasn't worth the trip? Did he decide to go to work instead of driving what would surely be an agonizing, gut-busting drive from upper New Hampshire to mid New York?

The longer I sat the more horrors I imagined— from a bloody car accident to, even worse, complete disinterest in meeting me. I called my eighty-two year-old mother for advice.

"Well, he is driving five hours, ya know," she said. I envied her nonchalance.

"True." I picked a cuticle.

"Cripes—give the guy a chance."

"He's dissing me. I can feel it."

"What's 'dissing'? Speak English, for Christ's sake."

I sighed. "I should have figured no man was going to drive five hours just to see *me*.

You said it. I didn't. Joke's on you, Cleo.

"Shut up," I yelled.

"Who are you telling to shut up?"

"Never mind—not you, Ma. What an asshole I am—believing a guy would be so enamored as to drive hours just for a date. I'm all dressed up with no place to *go*. And I could be working around here instead of just sitting here sucking my thumb like a child's doll-baby."

"Give him another fifteen minutes. If he doesn't come by then, just chalk it up and get on with your day. 'Tis what it is. Maybe he woke up this morning and couldn't face the drive. You don't know."

"Well, he's not calling me, nor is he answering my texts. He's dissing me for sure—I know it." My shoulders slumped—I was like a drunk with his booze cut off. "Okay, then. I'm going outside. Gonna ride a horse. At least I can get that done and not completely waste my day."

So, I trudged back upstairs, took off my good pants and shirt, clipped my bob into a messy knot atop my head, and headed out to the pasture. Cursing under my breath, I led my horse, Barry, into the barn, saddled him up, and grudgingly led him out to the riding ring. Minutes later Barry and I were both lathered in sweat.

As I urged the animal into his faster-paced show rack, I saw a black car creeping up the driveway.

I craned my neck. Bill? He didn't blow me off? Nah—can't be. Unlikely—being almost three hours late. It's probably some lost soul looking for directions.

Then a hand waved from the window. It *was* Bill. I stifled any ebullience, the likes of someone spared the electric chair, and nonchalantly motioned him to park at the house. He drove past as I rode Barry from the ring and unclipped my hair. With self-confidence flooding my veins like sea water flooding the Titanic, I put my steed into his fanciest gait and followed Bill's car up the driveway. Then I parked Barry parallel to Bill's car. When he opened the door and smiled up at me, my feet went weak in the stirrups. The man was excruciatingly handsome.

A firework erupted somewhere next to my bladder.

I dismounted, holding Barry at a rein's distance while Bill enveloped me in a friendly hug. I smiled like a horse eating a gooey molasses treat and hoped he couldn't detect the last hour's sweaty desperation. We exchanged a few witty greetings, and I invited him into the barn where I unsaddled Barry, who then decided to take a huge dump in the middle of the barn aisle.

"Silly horse," I chirped. I grabbed a shovel and hoisted the steaming load into a muck bucket.

"Wow—big pile ya got there," Bill said. He looked around. "You weren't kidding when you told me you worked a farm. Very cool."

Bill and I walked into the house where we sipped a couple of iced teas. He told me about the heavy traffic he battled on Route 87, and I commiserated about long drives. "You're probably hungry. Want anything to eat?"

"Maybe a piece of fruit or something. Do you have any grapes?"

I almost choked. "No, actually—only grapefruit. I *figured* you must've been held up in traffic." Selena, who was sitting on the kitchen counter, shot me a "stink eye." "At least your long drive is over. That 87 is *always* jammed up like a parking lot." I cleared my throat hoping he couldn't detect the quaking in my voice. Appearing too anxious or too interested was a woman's death knell.

"Wanna go for a hike?" I said. I stood, straightened my riding shirt, and immediately regretted the suggestion. It wasn't bad enough the poor guy drove a quarter of a day to see me—now I was going to drag his ass up the side of a mountain. Sometimes I could be such a stooge.

"Sure." He wrapped an arm around my waist. "I'd love to go for a walk with you. You are a beauty—you are. More beautiful than your pictures." His voice was deep, baritone—like Selena's when she purred.

I smiled confidently, all sweetness and molasses-lipped. "Thank you. You are so kind. And you're not too bad-looking yourself."

"Come on. Let's head out."

I offered him a six ounce bottle of Merlot to carry in his pants pocket. For sure the wine manufacturers had Bill and me in mind making those small, portable, plastic wine bottles for romantic hikes. So nice of them, and so convenient for us old-fart daters. He thanked me and stuffed it in his pocket while I put mine in my jacket pocket.

So, we walked hand-in-hand onto the north side of

my woods toward the state game lands a half mile away. If we were lucky, we might see turkey, pheasants, and, most certainly, deer while we confided our dreams and fears to each other. And perhaps, if I was lucky, he would kiss me.

My worries about his being a serial killer disappeared almost immediately, despite all the warnings from my well-meaning girlfriends. Charlotte said, "Okay, don't listen, my know-it-all friend, but if he puts a knife to your pussy out in those woods, don't call *me*."

During my venture into the world of online dating, anyone, even people I had just met, rained on my dating parade, and they didn't hesitate one bit to warn me about meeting strangler-strangers. When I splurged on a cute panty at Macy's and mentioned the panty's role in an online rendezvous, the Macy's store clerk "tsked" me a warning, her tongue sucking against her front teeth. As I started backing away with my purchase, she came in for the kill. "Watch out—that's all I can say. You can't be too careful with those kinds of men. All they want is sex. They're all weirdoes."

"Thanks. I appreciate your concern."

Yeah—since I have only met you for one frickin' second. You sound like Jack. Go find someone else to mother.

Everyone I met offered a history to relate—and not a good one—of women meeting men online and enduring as deadly a situation as a fly in a microwave. And men, even more than women, were the worst of the "black curtains." After all, other men regarded themselves as the sages of all sages, based on the fact they were privy to the motives of dangerous men simply because they *were* men. That seemed scarier than the advice.

The advice was on-going. "Be *careful*." "Always meet in a public place for at least the first forty times—until you get to know him." "Ask first what he does for a living and how much money he makes. If he's poor, just leave." "Do not have sex with the man—for at least two years." "If you do have sex, make him wear a rubber, and ask him for a health certificate verifying he has no STD's, no HIV, or chiggers."

What the hell is a chigger?

The advice seemed endless and so easily disseminated by folks—never trust anything a man says." And the final, most proffered advice from women and men alike remained, "All men are jerks. You're better off alone."

With words from the wise-guys and gals echoing in my brain, Bill and I held hands and scaled the first hill where I marveled at his endurance and lack of heavy breathing.

"Oh, I'm in great shape. Did you ever hear of the Tough Mudder competition?"

"Tough Mother?"

"No, Tough Mudder, as in mud. It's the civilian version of Navy seal training—trekking over an obstacle course loaded with mud and cold water. This is the first year I'm attempting it. It's not for the faint of heart—or body. I have been training for a year now—run ten miles a day and do exercises for upper body strength. Biking is good training, too."

"Oh. Then I guess this little hike is peanuts to you."

"Yeah, sort of. But it's nice." His smile threatened

to melt me into a puddle. "This woods is a very beautiful place, rugged and lush."

A barrage of imaginary sparks shot out my ears. I whispered, "Yes, very nice."

Then he turned to me, told me I was beautiful again, took me in his arms, and kissed me. When our lips met, I luxuriated in the warmth, the softness, the yearning between us. Then, without my knowing it, he slipped his tongue past the pearly gate, tickling my teeth. This was no frantic, mackerel-tasting serpent by the name of Groping Grover. Au contraire. He had put me in a French state of mind.

Oh, mon coeur.

Bill's kiss was gentle yet sexual. My lips parted to allow him deeper inside. I inhaled deeply, tasting him, exploring his mouth eagerly but softly. Our tongues slid together, touched a "Hello," and then parted.

His kiss was to die for, and I thought I might, indeed, faint dead away like a Jane Eyre character.

Ah, ma cherie amour.

Then, just as quickly and strongly as he had taken me, he let go, gazing into my eyes, smiling, and licking his lips as though savoring the last of filet mignon. He took my hand and led me, drunk with desire, down the woodsy path.

If this is what you're supposed to be so afraid of, then don't run, Ginnie. Those naysayers don't know what they're missing.

Dizzy with ecstasy—like Dorothy at her first glimpse of Oz—I felt goose bumps erupt from my scalp to my toes. Had I never been properly kissed before in all my forty-nine years of life? What else had I been missing? Obviously, decent sex, which I had given up in 2001 when Lance blew a brain fart that ricocheted through his body and out his penis. From stories in magazines to those told by girlfriends, I knew I had had one of the worst sex lives of anyone—probably even worse than Lady Bird Johnson's. If Bill's kiss was so extraordinary, then his love-making would rival Richard Burton's.

Suddenly my beaver twitched. I stumbled over a rock.

"Careful, gorgeous," Bill said.

But we hadn't gone too far before Bill stopped, turned, and again took me in his arms. He drew me tight against him, and I melted. Then I looked up and was overcome by a strange urge—almost instinctual—to nip his neck. I sucked a hill of skin with my teeth, and, to my surprise, his knees buckled. He let out a tiny shriek. Then he clasped me even tighter. And he gasp-whispered in my ear. "You are gorgeous, you know? And you are an excellent kisser."

Holy shit. Did you hear that, Ginnie? Proud of ya, girl. Still got it in ya after all these years.

Then I felt it—the hardness against my thigh. It was swollen and ready—all for me! My heart skipped ten beats. No penis had been ripe for me for over sixteen years. At that moment I realized Lance's lack of sexual prowess had made me feel unnecessarily inferior and fugly even though, when I looked in the mirror, I saw Wonder Womb-an. Lance's penile pigheadedness almost managed to sap the woman out of me, but I hadn't realized to what extent until this moment when the Siren in me began to yodel.

Bill's kiss made me feel alive, eager, robust and renewed again. For a moment he broke away, looked

146

hard at me—with an almost animalian look. Then, with a quick intake of breath, he took me again and kissed me. And I responded in kind, pressing his manhood with my thigh. The sexual Virginie Snow came to life again like some kind of surreal desert flower, blossoming, and overflowing her own foliage and tendrils with emotion and desire. I was the royal purple flower of the Atacama desert, persuaded into a rare bloom by a hint of rain or a sensual touch.

What I couldn't risk, as my renewed self, was to inadvertently expose my sexual naïveté, even though I had plenty of book education with *Any Woman Can.* Struggling to keep my cool, I let go his grasp. Then, I bit his neck lightly, playfully, and made a chicken trail of soft licks up to his left ear, tracing its outline with my tongue. He gasped. And then he held me close, so close I could appreciate the outline of the oak branch in his pants.

I stood back and noted his grandness. "*Very* impressive. He's quite the guy, I see." My curiosity bested me, and I lightly touched him.

"That's what every man wants to hear." He leaned into me.

"Well, it be not a lie," I said in my finest Shakespearean voice. Only a bit of comedy deftly used could dampen some of the fire between us, for I had long ago resolved not to allow sex on his first visit. And, like a prince, he had graciously agreed. Teasing him, getting him "up and running," and then abandoning him in favor of a platitude wasn't fair.

Sir Erectness—beneath Bill's khakis—shone in all his wonder and glory. More humor might ease his pain, though he was clearly enjoying the moment.

Like Lucille Ball, my finger against my lips, my eyes looking to the sky, I quipped, "Now what direction do you suppose he's pointing? North or north northwest?"

Bill laughed. He thought for a moment. "I think he's pointing toward you."

Tears of gratefulness welled, but I held them back as he kissed me again. I was incredulous at my own desire for this man—at this time, in this part of the world—consumed by me, a sexual has-been, a sensual cipher, a neophytic nympho, an aged granny who, for the greater part of her life, had suffered an emptiness unimaginable to most other women. When Lance decided to reward another woman with his pendulous penoid, no doubt having its first stiffie in twenty-some years thanks to a probable healthy dose of little blue pills, I felt even more undesirable than ever. But Bill viewed me not as some aberrant asexual being but as a full-bodied, full-blooded woman with all the sensualness of one. And with that realization, I felt so grateful for his offering me the "rope" to escape the suffocating rapids. He was anointing me with the affection I had grown accustomed to living without, almost as though that solitariness, that vacuity, was a deserved punishment. Bill had fashioned me into an object of affection, attraction, and desirability, the reality of which I found almost undeserving. I was as happy as an oyster plucked from the boiling pot.

Bill released me, and I stood back, almost dizzy with delight. He smiled and said, "Hey, there. Ya know, it's a bit hard for me to walk with this broomstick in my pants."

I giggled. "I imagine it would be. Remember—no

sex. We agreed."

"Yes, we did. I'm perfectly okay with that." I kissed him lightly on the cheek. You're a really sexy guy, ya know." Then I sang the chorus to Amy Winehouse's "Our Day Will Come."

Wow. A guy who didn't just want sex. Jack and the Macy's clerk were wrong.

After two hours in the woods, we climbed the hills toward home, stopping every hundred yards or so to kiss. We were like a couple of nineteen-year-olds, not a forty-nine-year-old woman with a fifty-three-year-old man. But I defied any young adults, no matter how experienced in the dating scene, to rival our kisses. What we had going was nothing short of *jalapeno* hot.

Suddenly Bill yelled. I followed his stare toward the ground. I was horror-stricken at the sight. His crotch had suddenly turned a dark bloody purple. I felt faint-kneed.

Oh, no. What did you do to him, Lizzie? I knew you'd do something to ruin it all. All that pressing and stroking. Now the poor man is hemorrhaging!

"Oh, no! The bottle's leaking," he yelled.

"What?" Surely I had maimed his schvonsticker.

"The wine leaked."

I gasped relief—I hadn't almost killed him. "We're almost home. We'll throw them in the washer."

We rushed back, and as soon as we stepped into the kitchen, Bill went into action. Before my eyes he unbuckled his belt, unzipped his stained pants, and whipped them off. My eyes grew as wide as a slow loris' as this hunk stood before me in his skivvies.

"Oh, Great Mother of God!" I gasped. Standing catatonic with my hands over my mouth, my eyes wide as frying pan lids, I watched him as he rushed his pants to the washing machine, stuffed them inside, poured detergent over them, and pressed the start.

When he emerged from the laundry room with his six-pack abs and slim waist so delectable, I doubted my ability to resist. While I stood in horrified ecstasy before such a honed, excruciatingly handsome male specimen, he took me in his arms and kissed me again, his tongue dancing softly against mine, his lips firm but moist and lingering. And then, predictably, his underwear began to billow like a sail caught by the wind.

But this time his penis was much closer—only a few fibers of cotton away. Curiosity finally got the better of me—if I couldn't have sex with it, I, at least, wanted to see it.

I rationalized any guilt away because Lance hadn't exactly been fair to me in the sex category, after all. I had been Lance's faithful girlfriend and wife from the age of seventeen to forty-nine. So, I was sorely indigent when it came to sexual experience and the number of penises in my life. Unfortunately I had only ever seen one set of male genitals. If that wasn't living life deprived—a sexual anorexic—then I didn't know what was. Perhaps I could add another set to my paltry stash if I made my desires known. For now, however, Bill was behaving himself as best he could—his monstrous penis still caged, like some ravenous wild thing, inside his underwear.

I giggled. If it let out a roar, I would just *have* to tame it.

Guilt and warnings from girlfriends flooded my brain. But common sense along with instinct argued more loudly. I *only* wanted to *see* it.

Mind yourself, Ginnie. He won't get it out if you don't. He's a gentleman.

My conscience could be such a drag. *"Fuck you, Conscience. I haven't seen one of these things for half a century. I feel like Columbus discovering the New World. What if I never get another chance?"*

How unreasonable could I be to just let him stand there with a happy hard-on and not at least acknowledge it with a stroke or two? It wouldn't be right—or nice. And what else could I have expected of myself, of him, a good, polite—obviously well-endowed guy—who had driven eighty-five hours to meet me? Denying him and myself any sexual contact at all was plainly cruel, inhumane, and stupid. We were adults, after all, and fairly old ones, at that—pawing at the grave. Time was of the essence.

Stand tall. Don't waiver, Ginnie. He won't respect you afterwards.

Bullshit. You're jealous!

The two angels sitting on opposite shoulders battled non-stop until Bill himself interrupted the argument.

He kissed me again, and, again, I felt him rising to the occasion. His erection was glorious. As if he could read my mind, Bill murmured, "Would you like to see him?"

My conscience caved. Maybe she really does have my best interests at heart, or else she was getting a twinge in her nether parts, too.

Go for it! You've only seen one penis in your lifetime. You're a female abomination! He's offering you a look—just a look. No harm in that.

151

"I would love to see him." I moved against him.

He smiled. With the washing machine sloshing in the background, and Selena sidling around his bare legs, he pinched open the waist of his jockeys. He reached inside as though plucking a prize from a bag and drew himself out.

I could hardly contain myself—my second *penis*!

I gasped, my knees weak. I cursed my light-headedness as he lowered his shorts with one hand and proffered his manhood in the other. Truly "he" was exquisite, with a very distinct head and a beguiling face—quirky—its length interminable.

"Oh, he's *so* handsome." I kissed him on the lips and moaned. And then all the rules I had set up dove completely into hell. I took *him* in my hand and stroked him back and forth. He liked it, rippling beneath my grip. And then, without thinking, I said, "I'm sorry. I shouldn't be doing this. I'm voiding my own rules, and it's not fair to you." Nevertheless, unwilling to let go, I stroked him again, watching, mentally measuring, admiring the appendage coming to life under my touch.

I was a voyeur of the worst, most pathetic sort.

"He's *huge*." My gaze was locked onto his cock.

"We can do other things besides have sex, ya know. How would you like to give him a hand job?" He looked in my eyes and drew me close. He knew how to work a woman who hadn't had a sniff at a dick since the signing of the Magna Carta.

I choked. "I would love to."

"Then I'll follow you to your bedroom."

And with that we climbed my staircase—to heaven. In the bedroom he threw himself, naked, onto the bed and smiled like Alice's Cheshire cat. A glimpse in the mirror showed my eyes wide and pupils dilated by the shock and awe occurring inside me. I needed this as much as an alcoholic needed a drink.

"Go ahead." His penis was as erect as a soldier.

I lay down, fully clothed, on the bed beside Bill. Though I hadn't seen one of these creatures since the Jurassic Era, I wasn't afraid or intimidated. This was all about living in the moment. I wanted him—wanted to take him on a cruise to a watery Shangri-La.

Ooh, la la.

He kissed me and murmured in my ear "Go ahead. Work him over."

I thought for a moment. "We got a problem, Houston."

He sat upright on his elbow. "What?"

"I don't really know how." I winced.

Oh, that's a real turn-on, Ginnie. Real good. Next you're going to tell him you haven't had sex in sixteen years. That'll seal the deal. No sex for you.

Bill looked up from the pillow, his mouth agape. I owed him a more thorough explanation. His cock listed, unsure, to the side.

"I know…I know. I'm forty-nine years old. I've gotta know *something*, right? Well, I've read a book about certain sexual activities, but giving a hand job was not one of them."

Clearly he was shocked silent. After several moments, he sighed. "I'll instruct you. And then he began giving directions. I followed like the good student I had always been, and in two minutes his penis burst into song, spraying its notes all over Bill's six-pack.

Oh, Glory Be to Thee, Oh, Christ. Not even two

153

minutes, and he came all over himself.

I had done it—all by myself! I was like a kid after riding her first two-wheeled bicycle.

Fucking amazing, Ginnie. You did it like an expert. Doesn't matter that Bill thinks you're a sexual dumbass. You did it, and you're back in business. No more celibacy for you. You are now officially out there. Forty-nine years old and back in the game. Yessiree. Lance hadn't really killed it. It's been in you all the time. Hoo-boy, baby. We're cookin' with gas!

That evening, after I made Bill a sirloin steak, green beans, and baked potato dinner, I kissed him good-night before he left for his friend Dave's. He promised to visit the next evening after spending time with his friend during the day. But the next day Bill called to say his friend had arranged the day off work and was looking forward to spending all day and evening with him. He was sorry but would definitely see me Sunday before leaving for New Hampshire.

I was disappointed but still riding my surfboard of happiness with my renewed sexual self. Sunday morning at eleven o'clock would be fine.

So, Sunday morning I prepped myself as usual in anticipation of Bill's arrival, but when eleven o'clock came, I found myself checking my watch, an ear alert for sounds coming from the driveway. Nothing.

Suddenly my text bell sounded. It was Bill. He had just left his friend's place, had to gas his car, and would be over in an hour. That would put his arrival time at noon. No big deal, I thought. Then another text came through: "Had a late night last night. Am hung over."

My conscience flipped out.

He's fucking hung over? You will have no more

than an hour to spend with this guy before he leaves, and he's hung over? Yeah, a real turn-on—having the guy hanging all over you smelling of stale beer. Oh, yeah!

As I typed robot-like on my phone, I read my response aloud as though I were somehow detached from it. "Don't bother coming. I am no longer interested." I hit "send," and sat, next to tears, immobile in my chair.

There I sat for over an hour, my ego deflated like a torn Macy's Day balloon. Hadn't he realized last night while he was partying with his long-time friend, he would need to be fresh for me and the drive back the next day? Hadn't he given that a thought at all? Had he no respect for me—thinking it perfectly fine to show up on my doorstep with a hangover? The last thing I wanted was to kiss a guy reeking of booze and having the judgment of a high schooler. What a turn off.

And then I had to face the hard possibility that, perhaps, because I had given him a hand job, he *didn't* really respect me. And that made me feel even worse. Thank goodness I had held out on the full-blown sex. At least that had been a good decision. At least I retained that smidgen of self-respect. Nevertheless, I smiled at the memory of Bill's penis in full bloom—he had liked me, very much.

Even if I had lost Bill's respect, I had released the tiger from its cage and stroked him 'til he roared.

Still, Bill would never visit me again, especially after getting that text. With a renewed sense of self, I thought awhile.

"Next!"

That afternoon as I swept out the barn, my phone

went off—Jack. He could help me fix horse fencing tomorrow for a few hours.

"Thanks, Jack," I said. "I'll see you tomorrow morning, then, around nine.

Chapter Eleven
It Is What It Is

The next day, as usual, I awoke at six in the morning to begin the morning feeding. I was Noah with many hungry mouths to feed, and the animals wouldn't accommodate my lingering in the sack for much longer. Once the animals' bellies were full, I sipped my coffee and ate peanut butter toast in peace—better than having cats meowing and goats and horses shrieking from the barn.

Uncommonly frigid for a March day, though my insulated underwear and high work boots were warm, the day shone brightly in anticipation of spring. Heaven had gifted the East coast an unseasonably warm winter with more forgiving lower-than-usual fuel oil bills. Since Lance had left, finances were tight, and I appreciated every break, including any offer to help on my farm.

Jack—Lois had often mentioned privately—was nothing if not an efficient, almost obsessive-compulsive type when it came to manly labor. His kind of Mr. Fix-It I desperately needed for an afternoon, and Lois had long ago suggested Jack would help me out if I ever got into a bind.

Before Jack arrived, I gathered all the fence-repair tools in a plastic bucket and loaded them, some wooden and metal fence rails and posts, and the heavy post "slammer" into the farm truck. Jack arrived on time and immediately began to strut around cawing orders, his machismo kicking in since fence-fixing signified serious man work. But because he was nice enough to help me, I didn't say much and let him crow and flex his wings. With a heavy sigh I climbed into the truck, Jack alongside, and we headed toward the horse pastures.

With a portable screwdriver, Jack drove a deck screw through a twelve-foot hemlock rail into a fence post. "You know…" His voice was deep, serious.

My back was already beginning to hurt. "What, Jack?"

Deafening silence.

Propping the rail on my knee, I waited for some proclamation. He was obviously prepping me for a major announcement. He sighed with heavy resolve. "Lois doesn't like this idea."

"What idea?"

"You and me working on the fence together. She doesn't like it at all."

"Why not?"

"Because she knows we'd be working together. She's jealous…."

"You're kidding me, right? Lois is not the jealous type. She's the one who suggested you help me if I ever needed it."

He shook his head and glanced sideways. "Oh, you can't believe how jealous she is of other women. You have *no* idea."

"I don't believe it. Surely she doesn't think we are involved with each other? We are just friends—*real* good friends—and she knows how much I could use a guy's help around here from time to time." I paused. "Why would you make up such a story?"

"Well, just so you know—she's insanely jealous of other women being around me." His eyebrows knitted into one slash across his forehead.

"Really? I don't think so. I *know* Lois."

"And I think she thinks I'm attracted to you. In fact…" He drove another screw into a rail. "She once told me that if you had sex with me, you'd know what good sex is all about."

"She said that?" My eyes bugged, disbelieving.

"Yes, she did." His lips were pursed. "I told you she wonders about me and other women. You know, she's a bit self-conscious of her being overweight and stuff. And I think she's jealous because you're thin."

"Yeah, well. I can't help I'm thin. I've lost a lot of weight through this damned divorce."

"Yes. You're really too thin. Not very appealing."

"*Thanks* a lot. Am I a turn-off because I'm too thin?" The deflated Macy's balloon syndrome hit me again. My shoulders slumped. "I'm a nice looking woman, and I'm slender. Isn't that what most guys want?"

"No, it isn't. You see, I really like Lois' body type—a bit overweight but not too heavy. I like women built like brick shithouses."

I shuddered. "Well, I think that might be a bit out of the norm, Jack. Besides, I feel better thinner than heavier, and my clothes feel better on me. I like myself this way."

"Nope. You're too thin." He sounded like a chastising mother.

"I can't *help* it." He screwed a screw into the post.

I let go of the rail and threw the next broken fence rail into the bed of the pick-up.

We finished repairing fence within two hours—a very awkward and silent two hours. I was pissed, frustrated, and morally deflated all at once—in a vulnerable enough state of mind without a dear friend telling me my body was distasteful. On top of that, I sure didn't need discovering his live-in partner and my best friend felt jealous of me. What I needed was a break from stress and emotional baggage because I had had enough in my life to fill a shipping container destined for the Czech Republic.

We finished, gathered up the fencing tools, slung everything into the bed of the truck, and drove back to the house. I thanked Jack for helping me, and he left. I stood in the driveway, like a chimp without a banana, feeling miserable about myself and my situation. I could not trust Lance, and I realized my best friend didn't trust me with her beau. Lance had set off a chain of events when he left me—every friend and acquaintance of ours was fearful that, similarly, such a horrific thing like Lance's going astray could happen to them, too.

That evening my farmer Steve called. For two hours we talked—about agriculture, how nice the weather was getting, my animals, his job. What each of us wanted was to hear the other's voice responding, quipping little flirtations, and just being there for the other. The presence of that person, his and my taking our precious time and devoting it to the other, became the crux of the conversation, not the actual conversation itself. Neither of us cared about each other's cats or what each of us had for dinner or how sweet the honeysuckle would smell in just a few more weeks. What we did care about was that the other was taking the time *and* the effort to be present—if only on the phone—with the other. After an evening of quiet talk, we said goodnight and hung up, the other's voice a final note of happiness.

****

The next afternoon Jack dropped by while I was mucking horse stalls. He strode from his truck, his voice nonchalant. "Lois is going out with girlfriends for dinner tonight. She suggested it would be nice if you and I went out for dinner together since she knew we would both be alone. Wanna go?"

Some jealous friend, huh, Ginnie? If she were that jealous, she sure wouldn't be sending you two out together for dinner. He's giving you a line of shit.

Jack could be such a drama king sometimes.

"Sure. I could use a night out." Sweat beaded my brow. Then I gave the wheelbarrow a huge push toward the barn door. Jack scooted quickly to the side, and as I blasted past him with my manure-filled wagon, he leaned nonchalantly against the doorway. I smelled the keen aroma of cologne as I passed. "Wow," I said. "That's some really good-smelling cologne you have on there. You smell like a musk-ox wearing a garland of lavender and patchouli."

"It's just bath soap. I don't wear cologne."

He was all dressed up, looking more spiffy than usual, his goatee shaved close, his hair coiffed.

I dumped the loaded wheelbarrow on the steaming manure pile, "You look like you're all ready to go. Is it okay if I just put on a clean pair of jeans and a nice shirt? You look pretty fancy. I don't have to get all dressed up, do I?"

He cast me a quick glance. "No, no. You're fine—just going to that biker bar, The Cork and Corkscrew. They have great wings, if you like wings. You've been there before?"

"Yeah." I pushed the wheelbarrow back to the barn. "All the time with my girlfriends. As a matter of fact, I went there with a couple of my online dates. One time they burned my buffalo burger, but I like the atmosphere—it's fun. They have decent drinks. I could sure use one after today. Hey, maybe you could help me out deciphering this letter I got from my attorney. I don't have a clue what she's talking about. She wants an assets and liabilities sheet, and I don't have the faintest idea how to prepare one. After all, Lance always took care of all the finances. I'm fairly ignorant about money stuff." I propped the wheelbarrow up against the barn wall and pulled my coat tighter against a chill. Jack stood in the doorway smirking at my winter overalls and old snorkel coat. The March air was unusually chilly as the season debated whether to go out like a lamb or a lion.

"Tell ya what. Why don't we meet in separate cars—it's easier. And why don't you—on your way to The Cork and Corkscrew—stop off at my mountain home before we have dinner? You've always wanted to see my cabin anyway. I'll fix us a few drinks and take a look at your attorney's letter. Maybe I can help." He smiled. "You look like you could use a refreshing drink, and I can make a pretty good Long Island iced tea."

"Okay. Sounds good. Then, when we're done, it's a shorter distance for each of us to drive home. It'll be fun to see your hunting cabin."

When Jack's wife died seven years ago, he stumbled into a huge inheritance that drowned him in money much like a fly in honey. His grief was bittersweet—he was painfully alone but unexpectedly rich. Always wanting a shack in the woods, he finally found his dream cabin and purchased it—much solace amid the forest and its creatures. He and Lois didn't frequent the place—she hated it, with its being so far removed from civilization and the shopping malls.

Four years ago after I introduced Jack and Lois, she promised if he moved into her apartment, she would spend every other weekend at his cabin in the woods. With familiarity discontent looms. After years of living with each other, her well-intentioned promises dropped to the wayside like so many lukewarm coals. Lois had confided to me each weekend they were to visit his cabin, she made excuses why she couldn't go. Though disappointed, Jack conceded most every time and stayed in town.

While he seldom stayed at his cabin, he loved it, nevertheless, and made frequent trips for cleaning and upkeep. During the winter when Lois visited friends during the day, he drove there and stoked the fires, cut wood, and set out corn for the deer. He even had named some of the deer coming to his feeders. He hoped one day Lois would share the same love of the outdoors and be willing to spend at least one weekend a month at the cabin. She didn't, and she wouldn't.

So, even though I was best friends with Lois, I had never seen Jack's cabin in the woods—only heard tidbits about it. I had only ever been invited to the little in-law apartment in town they shared together. And being a nature lover and woodland creature myself, I was excited to see it.

When I drove up Jack's driveway, I was stone-shocked silent. This was no cabin from which one hunted groundhogs and other varmints. Jack's house was a full-blown mountain home sitting in an elemental wild woods atop the Catskill Mountains.

I gasped. "Oh, my goodness. This place is gorgeous."

I shut off the car and marveled at the solitude of the woods, so isolated, so pertinently alone and without neighbors—it spoke to me as no other property, except my own, ever had. The trees, their vines and delicate branches, enveloped me like a bevy of kind grandmas.

Jack opened the door, and, once inside, I gasped at the loft whose entrance was gained from a lovely Art Deco staircase. The living room featured a royal blue sectional sofa resting grandly beneath a cathedral ceiling. Before the sofa a wood fire roared in the fireplace.

The place was astounding. "It's absolutely gorgeous, Jack. Lois doesn't like it here? She's *crazy.* Anyone would feel lucky to live in a place like this." I ran to the little kitchen—just big enough to prepare a meal—but cozy, undemanding, with a bay window looking out to the deer feeder beyond. "Oh, my goodness, Jack," I said in complete awe. "This is hardly a cabin. This is a castle in the woods—just beautiful."

He smiled proudly and pointed to the deer feeder.

"I know. I saw it." I looked to the woods beyond.

"Missy and her two fawns from last year feed from it," he said like a proud daddy.

"Lois doesn't like it here? Can't fathom anyone not

loving this place. I could live here in a heartbeat if I didn't have my farm."

He showed me the grill outside, and then we stepped off the porch and walked about forty feet into the woods. The air smelled crisp, moist, like piney mountain air—invigorating.

"I can't believe Lois doesn't love it here."

"Well, she doesn't. All she wants to do is sit around, drink, and buy junk on TV. Don't get me wrong—I like our apartment, but I love this place, too, and Lois and I had made a deal long ago to spend every other weekend here. Wanna know when the last time we stayed here was?"

I shook my head.

"Nine weeks ago. It's not fair to me. Lois says I can come here and stay overnight anytime, but I don't want to be here by myself. It's not fun when I can't share it with someone."

"I know what you mean. I know exactly what you mean." I shook my head. "Well, if I were Lois, I'd rather live here than where you guys do now—for sure."

I smiled, and he looked softly at me. His love for this place resembled my love for my farm. We both felt tied to the land, to nature, to the animals. Lois was denying him an essential part of himself, and that was inhumane.

In minutes Jack rustled up a few drinks. We took them into the living room and set them on a side table. The wood fire danced, spitting and sparking flames that calmed me, and suddenly I was filled with regret that Lance and I were not an item anymore. Such a romantic fire made me nostalgic for decades ago when my husband and I were young, in love.

Jack sat down beside me on the sofa and turned off the lamp. Immediately we were surrounded by the silence, the dark remoteness of the woods, the comforting arms of his woodland home, and the cozy fire. For one of the first times since Lance left, I felt as though I were in a right place, a safe place. But, then, I always felt at home in remote settings in the middle of a wild and natural environment.

I leaned back into the soft sofa and sighed. Then I remembered my lawyer's letter. "Oh—my attorney's letter. Help me out with it, Jack." I reached for my purse, drew out the paper, and began reading the list of all items qualifying as assets and liabilities. Just reading the letter aloud with all its legalese intimidated me—a wife who had never done any of the bill paying or banking. I was clueless and scared of this legal divorce stuff. Tears formed, and my voice quaked. "I have no clue what she's talking about or how to tally assets."

I turned toward Jack and apologized. "I've had it pretty tough these last few months." I wiped my eyes. "I try to be strong, forget about the betrayal and get on with my life, but at times like these, it all becomes too much. I'm on a frickin' rollercoaster to nowhere. In the meantime, while I'm trying to find some semblance of normalcy in the absurdity of this divorce, Lance goes on with his life, living with his whore. He is living the life *he* wants, and *I* am left, abandoned, picking up the shards of *my* life and trying to piece them together again."

"I know." He put a caring hand on my back.

"You and Lois are such good friends." I sniffed back tears. "I don't know what I'd do without you two."

I sipped more of my drink, smiled, and he cocked his head and smiled back. He looked so relaxed—oddly so—for Jack. He was usually so uptight. "Thank you for all you've done for me, and thanks for helping me yesterday with fencing."

"You're welcome." His voice was a whisper.

The heat of the fire warmed my face—so warm, so soothing, so safe. Then I placed my drink on the side table and leaned back into the sofa. So thoroughly relaxed, even though I held the attorney's nagging orders in my lap, I was oblivious to my surroundings, like a bird in a cave.

As I lay back, eyes half-closed, enjoying the sounds of the crackling wood fire and the fire dancing along the walls in the darkened living room, I sensed something. Jack had moved closer. Before I could object, he gathered me in his arms and kissed me, softly at first, and then ravenously.

And I kissed him back.

Oh, this isn't good. It's not good, and it's not funny. Ginnie, cool it! Are you crazy?

He held me, and I him. He nuzzled his face in my neck, and I sighed, relaxed beyond relaxation. Was I dreaming? If I were dreaming, why would Jack be the one? He kissed me lightly, tenderly, on the neck, and the scent of his bath soap made me smile. My lips parted as a hundred sparks, like fireworks, roared from my pussy, much as the embers from the fireplace leapt and danced in the wood fire before us.

Stop already! Before it's too late—not right!

We kissed, open-mouthed, for minutes that seemed like days, consuming each other, rubbing each other, feeling each other's skin and hair. The sexual energy in the room heated to an all-consuming conflagration before the fireplace. And the only sound in the silence of the woods was the crackling of the wood fire punctuated by our moans.

"I've been wanting you for years, Ginnie."

"Oh, Jack. Oh, Jack." I shuddered beneath his touch. "Do you think we really are attracted to each other as Lois said?"

And with the utterance of the word "Lois," we abruptly separated and stood up. I looked hard at him and shook my head as though clearing a fog. "What are we doing, for Christ's sake? What about Lois? She's my best friend. You're *her* man." The realization finally set in, and I was suddenly horrified. "What in the world are we doing?"

Jack held his head in his hands. "I don't know. All I know is I've been wanting you for years, and I want you now. I still love Lois, but she's been eating at me with all her drinking. When you fussed over my place here, I knew I was right about you. Ginnie, I want you. Have me—will you?—right here, right now—before the fireplace. Let's have each other." He took me again in his arms, and despite my horror, I melted into him.

No!

I felt his hands unhooking my bra, and then, as though disembodied, my hands went to his belt buckle. Any moral sense I had flew out the window to the woods beyond. I was dizzy with desire. Before either of us really knew it, we were standing before each other half naked. He looked at me, his face stern, serious. Then, he nuzzled my neck and slid my panties around my ankles. With that I dropped to my knees on the carpet. And Jack met me there, engulfed me with his body, now naked by his own doing.

No. No. No! What in the world are you doing, Ginnie? Have you, have I, no sense at all? Yes. Yes. Yes! The first parting of these tired old rusty gates since 2001. Bring it on, Baby. Open the floodgate—of hell!

As the wood fire gyrated and danced its magic, so did we—right before it. The sparks generated by our sexual passion could have set the entire mountain home, along with the whole mountain on which it sat, ablaze. We had each other—long, lustful, and luxurious. Finally, he and I cried out together as the fire roared like a menace.

When it was over, I sat up, my cheeks puffed. "I can't believe we did that. Now what?" Embarrassed by my nudity, I hooked my bra and slid on my blouse.

"Nothing. It is what it is." He pulled up his pants. "We have an attraction to each other, and we satisfied it. Neither of us wants to hurt Lois, and we have just promised each other we won't. We won't. Whenever you or I have the need, we can meet here or at your place. Lois never has to know."

My guts recoiled. "No, never again. Promise me. This was a once and done thing, Jack. I can't betray Lois like that again. I feel just awful." I was next to tears for the second time in one night. "What have I become? I have become, through this whole thing, a woman who has lost her moral compass. I'm no better than Lance's whore." I moaned with the self-realization. "I'm no better."

"Yes, you are. Don't forget you have been without sex for quite a while. What? Sixteen years? You deserve some affection, some attention. You need someone to satisfy you, hold you, appreciate you for the gentle beauty you are."

Gentle Beauty? That's a line of shit if I ever heard one.

"But you don't love me. You love Lois."

"Yes, I do love Lois. But I love you in a special way, Ginnie. I'm very attracted to you. If you insist, this will be the last time."

"I am going home." I gathered my purse and keys. "I'm not at all comfortable with what we've done, though it was exciting as hell. I can't go behind my best friend's back like this. I eat her fusilli, for Christ's sake! What kind of monster am I? I never expected anything like this to happen."

"Didn't you?" He smirked. "Really? Didn't you?"

I stammered "Well, well, I always considered you a catch—was always happy I introduced you to Lois years ago because you guys are so good for each other. Had I known Lance would be leaving me, perhaps I'd have been interested in you myself. But I gave you away to Lois, and that's how it should remain—you and Lois together—forever."

"Yes. We shouldn't let this one-time fling ruin Lois' and my relationship. I do love her, after all. Let's promise each other—here and now—this will be our only fling. We hereby make a pact to not do further damage to our relationship and your and our friendship."

We shook hands, and I climbed into my car, all thoughts of dinner turned sour.

Chapter Twelve
The Signal

I sped home that night as though fleeing the devil herself, but I couldn't escape her sitting in a red glow, grinning, in the passenger seat beside me. She was pleased. *"Way to go, Ginnie."*

Then my angelic conscience got in on it. *Really good, Ginnie. You fucked your best friend's boyfriend. Just wonderful. Now what are you going to do? You're no better than your husband's whore—no better. You walking vagina you. If you believed in a hell, you'd be serving time there. I'm really disappointed in you.*

Sleepy-Hollow-like shadows zoomed past the fir trees that so well covered upper state New York. I pressed the gas pedal harder. I became a modern-day Ichabod Crane tearing up the neighborhood in search of his head.

Where was my head?

What were you thinking?

Finally, I pulled into my garage, turned off the car, and locked myself in the house.

What *had* I been thinking? What would ever cause me to overstep my moral boundaries? I blamed the evil apparition riding shot-gun with me.

The devil made me do it.

Yeah, right! Blame the devil.

I stood in the kitchen, huffing and puffing, weak

with embarrassment and self-doubt.

Are you falling, too, Ginnie, into the ways of the modern world—devoid of ethics, sound sense, and self-discipline? Have you no scruples? You're no better than a soap-opera sex-fiend. How could you have betrayed your best friend?

That night I tossed between the sheets—nightmares of Jack looming over me with his massive hard-on, my surrendering to him, taking him inside me as though we'd been denied each other for centuries. Between feelings of complete disbelief at my deed and scoldings from my nagging conscience, I fell into moments of guilt and mental self-flagellation.

Go ahead and whip yourself until you're bloody. You deserve it, Lady Chatterley. Just because you haven't had sex for umpteen years doesn't mean you can bang your best friend's guy.

Sometime during my fitful rest I fell dead asleep and woke later than usual, the sun shining brilliantly through my bedroom windows. Barry and Red were neighing from the barn—reminding me their bellies needed filling.

I flung back the covers, dressed, and shuffled out to the barn. Then I stopped dead in my footsteps, and the previous evening washed over me like a mountain of wet rags. I shuddered, stepped into the barn, and took up the first scoopful of grain, plopping it into Barry's grain box. He tore into it like the animal he was. Then I gave the other horses their grain. Next stop—the goats.

Throughout the feeding, my conscience showed no mercy.

You're a no-good woman, reduced to a cipher like Hester Prynne. Guess you better go to the tool shed and get that can of red spray paint. Make a stencil and spray a big "A" on your T-shirt, Ginnie.

I let the horses out to pasture while a few sun rays peeked out from behind a cumulus cloud and warmed my cheek. I watched, smiling for just an instant, as my animals, both the goats and horses, grazed contentedly, nipping at the grass shoots. From somewhere a wave of self-forgiveness washed over me.

"Okay, sister." The teacher came out in me. "Last night I did the nasty with my best girlfriend's live-in boyfriend, Jack—a guy I'm really not in love with and who doesn't love me. It was just sex—that's all. No bigger a deal than eating a slice of pizza, right?"

You're rationalizing.

I scowled. "What's the big deal, anyway—I'm really no different from these animals here. I just did what came naturally—followed my instincts. Why should I hold myself to such a high level of morality? I'm a creature of nature, too, and have needs and wants. The rest of the world, most notably Lance and Yvonne, didn't give a hoot about having their affair. And Jack isn't married to Lois, after all."

Don't make excuses, Ginnie.

The sun came out strong and sharp from behind the clouds, and I began to imagine last night's experience in a new light—a once-and-done thing whose rumor will advance no further than Jack's and my worlds. And Jack and I made a pact to not "engage" again. The bottom line amounted to one fact—what Lois didn't know wouldn't hurt her. Jack and Lois would continue together as the more-or-less happy couple they were.

Chicken shit, Ginnie. You know damn well you won't refuse him again. You have become a sexual gourmand and, given the opportunity, you won't pass up another snack at the feast of fornication. I'm not talking to you anymore. I'm done—bad girl.

I hurried back into the house while the sun slid behind another cloud, its shadow following me inside.

Later that morning while I vacuumed the living room, Steve called. "Hey, hot stuff!" I smiled but quickly lost enthusiasm at the intruding reminder of last night's deed. Still, I was glad to hear his voice.

"This time of year is super hectic. This week the farmers are calling. They want lime spread on their fields. I'll need to deliver seed and other stuff—am looking at close to eighty-hour weeks, working Saturdays—my only day off being Sunday. But I'd love to see you this coming Sunday if you'd like."

Visions of my lavishly coiffed, gray-headed, gray-eyed suitor, brought a smile to my face. He was the perfect subject to take my mind off Lois and Jack. And next Sunday happened to be open.

"That would be perfect. I'll grill us something for dinner. What would you like?"

"Oh, I just love grilling. Let me make the stuff. I'll bring the meat; you get the rest, okay?"

"Sure thing. See you Sunday."

The week marched along as it usually does on a farm with many animals and acres of property to tend, and the errors of my pussy-fling fled into the sunset. I scheduled the pool opening, decided to make my first mowing stint around the property, and contacted a farmer to take away my brimming manure pile. Horse shit was the best fertilizer on earth, and the pile sat almost one-story high and twenty feet in diameter. Farm work, preparing the garden for the up-coming summer season, and writing snippets for my farm animal advocacy manuscript occupied my days. At night I curled up with my notebook to check out potential dates.

In the early evenings I visited with Jack and Lois. No one would have guessed Jack and I had had a fling just the week before, except for the overgrown loads of groceries I offered. One would have thought I were feeding an orphanage—bags of Coca-Cola and limes for Lois' favorite drink, bleu cheese, Italian-herb croutons, Vidalia onions for the salads, and fancy finger-desserts.

Lois gasped. "Jeez, Ginnie, why are you buying all this stuff? It's unnecessary. We can't possibly eat all this, and you're on a tight budget. We don't need all this food, for cryin' out loud."

Typically, Jack busied himself at the kitchen counter, cutting up shards of tomatoes and olives for the salads. I helped Lois set the table, all the while answering questions about my latest online dating experiences. "I'm finally going to meet Steve this coming Sunday. I've only ever seen three pictures of him—those on the dating site. But he looks pretty good, from what I can see."

"Where are you meeting him?" Lois asked.

"At my place—to grill dinner."

"I thought you were only going to meet guys at public places?"

I cut up a little hill of carrots for the salad. "Well, I have developed a policy. If my gut instinct tells me, after seeing nice pictures and talking with a man on the phone, that he's safe and decent, and, particularly, if he's driving a distance, then I'll have him come right to my place, like I did Bill from New Hampshire."

"Do you think that's a good idea, Ginnie?"

"Yeah, actually, I do. After a long drive, the guy can relax a bit. He can stay longer, not just go right back to rabbiting home after an hour's lunch or something. It's only fair. Besides, serial killers don't hang out on dating sites for older daters."

"Okay. Whatever you think. Just be careful. Oh, and maybe you and Jack would want to go out for dinner Wednesday night. I'm meeting some girlfriends. At least you two could keep each other company."

Jack had his back to us as he cut up pieces of broccoli to add to the fusilli. The knife scraped more furiously, harshly, against the cutting board.

"Yeah, that would be great, Lois—if Jack wants to go."

Jack threw the knife on the counter, and it flew to the floor. He picked it up and slammed it back on the cutting board. "Sure—I'll meet you at The Cork and Corkscrew at six." Then, he threw the last of the broccoli into the steam-pot.

I had already decided to redeem myself and my sin with Jack at this dinner meeting—no fucking around this time. I would not mention our extra-marital fling, not really extra-marital, however, because Jack and Lois weren't married. I promised myself to be nonchalant, detached. I would not meet him at his mountain home again—that would only be inviting that Cheshire cat-smiling devil back into the picture. We would simply meet at a restaurant, eat, and go home.

Dinner with Jack was about as awkward as a fart-cloud between lovers. We were like two gawking pre-teens at a church dance, the self-consciousness as thick as curdled cream. I entertained us—reading comment after comment on the dollar bills decorating the ceiling and walls. Jack played equally neutral, appearing rather disinterested in me and my comedic attempts. I, for my part, purposefully ordered French onion soup and a plate of messy hot wings so I couldn't possibly look tempting. In fact, my goal was to quell any possible attractiveness. Resembling a hippo would certainly put Jack off his game.

My strategy must have worked especially well, by the looks of the red-stained wet naps piled high at our table. I wiped off scads of hot sauce from around my mouth and under my nose, thus removing not only the sauce, but also any remains of makeup. No one, especially Jack, would find me an appealing sexual prospect.

After other superficial conversation about my attorney and the workings of divorce, we each split the bill and climbed into our cars—proof the monster was dead, finished—de-scaled and dried-up.

****

Thursday dawned a rather dreary April day as I sat, battling writer's block, at the computer. Moments like these were frustrating—sitting, waiting for a brain fart, fashioning the idea into the right turn of phrase, and then waiting stubbornly for the next idea to segue into my mind. A distraction was in order.

My brief prayer was answered with a telephone call.

"Hi, Ginnie. It's Steve. How are you?"

"I'm struggling with writer's block at the moment. So glad you called to break up the mental black hole."

He swallowed hard. "Uh, I think I might get out of

177

work early on Saturday afternoon. Would you like to get together one day earlier instead of on Sunday?"

My calendar was depressingly empty of other engagements.

"Sure, Steve. I can do that. What time?"

"Oh, good. I'll be out of work by twelve and can be at your house by two. Is that okay?"

"Yep. Sounds good, as long as you don't mind helping me feed the animals around four o'clock."

"Oh, no—that'll be fine. I love horses and goats. I'm bringing the steak for the grill—can't wait to meet you. All I've been doing is staring at your pictures on Facebook every night. You are quite an attractive woman."

"Thanks, Steve. You're not too shabby yourself. See you on Saturday, then."

Friday morning after farm chores, I sat down once again to write. The blank computer screen mocked me, defied me to put down a clever word. "Damn you, computer." I shut the lid. The eerie green glow oozed out from the sides of the machine. "Damn you." I stomped away.

Just then the phone rang—Steve again.

"Uh, uh, how's it going, Ginnie?" His voice was a tight as the A string on a cello.

"What's wrong, Steve?"

"Actually, nothing much. But I'm getting out of work here in a few minutes. Very odd that they're letting me go this early, but that's the way it is." His giggle sounded high-pitched. "Uh, I was wondering, uh, if you would like to meet this evening instead of tomorrow night."

I hesitated. "Jeez, you keep moving up our date,

Steve. What gives?"

"I just want to get it over with."

"What?"

He repeated words dripping with anxiety. "I can't take this anymore! I have got to meet you—to get it over with—finally."

"Well, that doesn't make me feel very good. What are you trying to get over?"

"The fact that, once you see me, you won't like what you see. You won't want me."

I didn't know what to say.

His voiced cracked. "That's right. I've seen all these pictures of you from your Facebook site—you're *so* gorgeous. And you've only seen three of me. When you see me in person, you might not like what you see. Then it'll be all over. So, I just want to get the rejection over."

Nothing like a good dose of no self-esteem to put the sexual fires out, huh, Ginnie? His three pics didn't look rhinocerian or anything. But he sure is working up an orgasmic rejection. Say something nice before he goes into a meltdown the likes of the Wicked Witch of the West.

"Sure, Steve. I'm sure I'll be attracted to you, but if you like, we can meet later this afternoon, okay?"

A blasting sigh sounded on the other end. "Oh, good—I'll be at your place by three, then. See you in a couple hours."

Steve's arrival was a good excuse to put the computer and my writer's block to sleep. After cleaning cat boxes, mopping the downstairs floors, and readying the animals' food for the evening feeding, I had to take a shower, do my hair, and plant some makeup on my

179

face.

And don't forget your skinny jeans, Ginnie.

My fat pants—pre-Lance's abandonment—lay on a pile. They were now three sizes too big. I laughed—farmer clothing wasn't exactly appealing.

I straightened up the house, called all the cats inside for supper, and was heading outside, newly showered, coiffed, and perfumed, when the phone rang in the barn. My watch read two forty-five.

It was Steve.

"Yeah, Steve. What's up?"

His voice was as strung tight as the female doctor's on the "dry-eye" TV commercial. He sounded two octaves higher than usual. "What's the signal going to be?"

Was this really Steve or was it Charlotte with laryngitis. "Steve, is that you? It doesn't sound like you. You haven't been sucking on a helium balloon, have you? What's wrong?"

"I need to know the signal." His voice was little more than a screech.

"What signal?"

"You know—in case you don't like what you see when I step out of my truck."

I frowned. "You can't be *that* bad-looking."

"See—I knew it. Oh, God—just give me a signal—if you like what you see, or if you don't like."

I didn't know what to say. He was so upset—frantic.

"Okay. Okay. Be there in ten. If you…don't like…what you see…give me a signal…after I get out of the truck…and I will just climb right back in and leave—no fuss, no muss."

You've got a live wire here, Ginnie. You know, with this level of psycho-sexual inferiority, he is, indeed, guaranteed to be fugly. Men know if they're handsome. No good-looking guy has issues like this. Your online sleuthing must've missed something with this one— must've over-looked a grisly scar across his nose or, worse yet, a non-existent bulge in his pants. Did you really analyze that full-body shot where he had his arms around his two daughters? Ah-ha, I knew it. All that screwing around with Jack has made you careless. Jack's dick sucked your brains out. Good luck with this one, Ginnie. And one last word—Karma.

How would I answer the piccolo-staccatoed man on the other end of the phone? Considering his own doubt, I began imagining the likes of Jimmy Carter showing up on my doorstep. And, despite how appealing Steve's personality had been during the previous weeks' phone calls, the right chemistry had to exist for me to even kiss him. The shallower part of me knew well enough that if he had teeth like a porcupine, eyes like a shrew, and ears like Obama, no way would I be able to get near him, much less kiss him.

I was starting to feel nauseous.

In answer to the frantic panting on the other end of the phone, I said, in as calm a voice as possible, "Okay, Steve. The second you get out of your truck I'll either give you a thumbs-up or a thumbs-down. How's that?"

The breathless huffing stopped. A moment of silence followed. "Okay. If I get a thumbs-down, I'll just get right back in my truck and head back home. I'll be there in five."

Nice job, Ginnie. You got yourself into a good one now. Wait'll this male abomination descends from his hell-coach. He'll be so friggin' repulsive—probably with festering face pustules, like the Cook in the Canterbury Tales—that you'll be running into the middle of next week to escape the pestilence. Karma, baby. Pay-dirt for doin' Jack.

In five minutes a small pickup truck pulled to a screeching halt before the barn. I didn't know whether to approach or keep my hand on the doorknob for a quick escape.

Very slowly the driver's door opened, and then Steve stepped out and stood, still as a taxidermied sheep, facing me. He didn't smile; he didn't say anything. He just put himself out there—right in plain view for me to size up and decide for myself—like a proverbial female bower bird—if he was, indeed, good enough for me.

And as he stood stiff as the statue of David, a cringe gripped my knee-caps. I struggled to stand straight, to keep from sliding in a heap to the macadam driveway. When I caught myself on the edge of a nearby wheelbarrow, he had no reaction. He was watching for the inevitable "thumbs-down" signal that would send him packing to the nearest Wawa for a half gallon of psyche-soothing ice cream.

When I regained my balance, I smiled at the six-foot, gray-haired, statuesque handsome creature before me and then shot him a resounding "thumbs-up" signal."

At sight of the skyward thumb, his whole body relaxed, his shoulders dropping, a light smile stretching across his face. He walked toward me and I toward him—shades of the TV commercial of a man and woman galloping toward each other on an isolated beach.

"All your worries were in vain." He took me in his arms and lifted me off the ground in an excruciatingly delightful bear hug. "You are one of the handsomest men I have ever met, Steve."

Then he set me back on the ground and pulled me close for our first kiss.

****

At Lois and Jack's two days later, Lois gave me the third degree on my first date with Steve. "Is he good-looking? Did he grill dinner for you? Is he hot? Did you have sex with him? When are you going out with him again?"

With Jack frantically dicing up cheese cubes—*tck, tck, tck, tck*—to accompany the night's salad, I explained in breathless excitement my attraction to Steve. "Not only is he tall and excruciatingly handsome, but he's very nice, too. He loves my farm. He actually likes cats, unlike most men, right, Jack?" Jack ignored me. "He's handy with machinery and loves farm work. I hope nothing goes wrong with this picture, but if he is all I think he is, I won't be needing the dating site any longer."

"Oh, I'm so glad for you." She beamed.

"How old is he?" Jack said. He had his back to us.

"He's forty-one."

"That won't last. You're almost *fifty*. He's too young for you. What would he want with an older woman, especially if he's that good-looking? He could probably get some young beauty. Nope—that won't last."

"Jack—don't say things like that to Ginnie. You don't know what's going to happen between the two of

183

them."

I said, "I did, as a matter of fact, tell Steve I was a complete package. It'll take him a bit of time to discover that for himself, too. Eventually, he'll come to put together all I am and have—I am attractive, slender, intelligent, creative, and I have a lovely place for him to live and enjoy the rest of his life. Let me tell ya—I'm willing to share it with this guy.

"Now, the only trouble is that he's going to be very busy spreading lime and fertilizer in farmers' fields this spring. I won't see much of him until sometime in July when his work starts slowing down. But that's only a few months, though almost half the summer."

"Well, if he's a good man, you can wait," Lois advised.

"Won't last. He's too young for you." Jack hacked up a bag of cheese cubes.

I could've stuffed those cheese cubes, single-file, up his ass.

"I happen to think that I look forty years old, maybe even younger, Jack. And I have lots to offer."

"Did you have sex with him on the first date?" Lois giggled.

"No, I'm proud to say I didn't. But it was close. He was ready—if you know what I mean. We were really into each other—kissing and cuddling—over the grill, cleaning up the dishes afterward, and watching the news on TV. I'm sure he would have embraced the nasty had I encouraged him, but we both were good. However, the next time we meet I'm not guaranteeing anything. I want a piece of this guy, and, from what I can tell, his piece is pretty large." I giggled.

"Well, it's just a matter of time," Lois said.

Jack was obviously silent, his back to us.

I was giddy with enthusiasm. "See, Jack—I *can* meet decent people on these dating sites. He's not only handsome, but he's a nice, kind, hard-working guy, too."

"It won't last. He's too young for you," Jack replied. His brow had wrinkled into too many furrows.

"Unfortunately, I won't be seeing a whole lot of him now, but we intend to stay connected—until we can meet again—through phone calls. In the mean time I intend to date others. After all, I don't want to do divorce again—want to be certain of any man, now more than ever, since the debacle with Lance. I don't want to make another mistake."

Lois, Jack, and I finally ate dinner. My excitement was particularly annoying to Jack though I hadn't intended it to be, but my interest in Steve was making me giddy with hope—he could be my final suitor. My roller coaster chugged happily toward its apex.

When I drove home later that night to Lady Gaga's album turned up to the max, a fleeting thought occurred—I hadn't heard from Richard Downing for a while. I would have to email My Colonel to see how he was doing.

Chapter Thirteen
No Bed of Lilacs

The next day I woke up determined to contact Richard for the latest military news. All this—the attraction to Steve and wanting to contact Richard, along with my manuscript and farm work—worked wonders as distractions to the abominable deed with Jack. By noon my guilt over Jack had all but disappeared, so I jotted off a jaunty email to my colonel. "Hey, Handsome. What're ya doing these days? Haven't heard from ya lately. Hope all is well with you and yours."

Really original, Ginnie. Yeah. You're some creative writer. So cliché.

I frowned in response to my conscience-with-an-attitude. She was becoming a real drag lately.

I continued, "Ya know—I'd really like to meet you sometime—actually meet the guy whose paper I helped write. What do you say I take that scenic drive down toward your academy for a visit sometime? Just as close friends, for now—no pressure—maybe more later. Or maybe we could talk on the phone if you're too busy to meet. I'd love to hear your voice."

Just as good friends, Ginnie? Who are you kidding? The handsome Colonel Downing is not just friend material, and you know it. Bet the colonel is packing a dick the size of a hand grenade in his camouflage pants. Sex with him could be energetic, quite explosive. He-he. Meet as friends—you've got to be kidding.

"Shut up, bitch." I said aloud. Then I hit "send," shut off the computer, and went to muck out the horse stalls.

Days later I lay in bed early one morning with my notebook on my chest, the green glow from the machine mirroring back my face in an eerie ghoulish cast. I turned away from the mirror-screen—*not a flattering look.* I looked like The Incredible Bulk. My inbox showed no messages from Richard—nothing.

My heart sank.

Then I turned to Safari and typed in the URL for the dating site.

Great Moby's Dick, Ginnie. You have three guys on your hook. Start reeling!

One was from Grover, a.k.a. "Wormtongue." He wanted to see me again. I remembered his kiss, the frenetic vermiform tongue that nearly made me retch my buffalo burger. A chill went up my spine, and I swallowed hard.

You really want to go out with Grover again? What if the worm has since grown into a full-blown python? Bet you wouldn't like that slithering past your lips.

I thought hard and considered I may have over-reacted to that first kiss. Wasn't it fair to give Grover a second chance? After all, he seemed nice, was good-looking, had hair and straight teeth, and said I was beautiful. And he drove a cute, maroon Mazda Miata.

Okay. Give the guy a break, then. Have at it.

I emailed him and told him we could meet again next week and to give me a call. I signed it with a resounding "Smooch."

Then I emailed the other two—Dan and Riley. I sent my phone number to both and remarked if they were interested to give me a call. Both their profiles portrayed them as gentlemen. Dan had posted two selfies wearing dark sunglasses. His physical profile looked nice—no saggy chin, aquiline nose, strong, no Cro-Magnon-like forehead. He also showed two shots of himself from a distance—without sunglasses—walking ankle-deep in the waves at a beach. He had a normal-looking body and appeared as calm as TV's Mr. Rogers.

Riley, on the other hand, posted pictures of himself kneeling with his two black labs in front of a fireplace. His labs were laughing, as only labs do, and Riley's face managed a huge grin—his lips stretched, much like his dogs'—from ear lobe to ear lobe.

So, now you've lowered yourself to dating clowns—just no end to your desperation, Ginnie.

"I'm not desperate!" I bit my lip, worried about my increasing habit of scolding aloud my smart-ass conscience—my Mini Me—perched on my shoulder. Then I emailed Riley to call me for a date. And, against my better judgment, I rattled off another "Come hither" email to Colonel Richard Downing. "I'm not *desperate,*" I yelled again. The email flashed off into cyberspace.

The next afternoon Dan and Riley had both called, anxious to hit the restaurant scene. Dan, Mr. Cool sunglass man, was scheduled Friday at the Boarhead Restaurant and Smiley Riley at a café outside of Coxsackie on Saturday.

Until I was able to meet Steve again, we kept in

touch via phone calls. He was often too tired to talk as his job was becoming even more time-consuming, keeping farmers in rural Connecticut and New York equipped with supplies, chemicals, and seeds. Still, we spoke nearly every day while he stopped for his lunch break.

Friday afternoon after I had finished my barn chores, I headed upstairs to take a shower, fix my hair and makeup, and dress to meet Ray Charles. I arrived at the Boarhead fifteen minutes early and sat down at an outside table, my back to the sun. He wouldn't mind looking into the sun since he seems so well-equipped to handle glare. A server set down my unsweetened iced tea, and just as I reached for the sweetener, the shadow of a tall, slim guy wearing sunglasses fell across my table. I looked up and smiled. It was Dan.

"Hello, Dan." I stuck out my hand.

"Hello." Then he pulled out the wicker chair.

Not bad. Full set of hair—not even gray. Tall, athletic type. Very nice. This one just might give Steve some competition, Ginnie.

He sat down and pulled his chair tight against the table. His smile was easy, inviting, the lips finely, lusciously drawn—a Da Vinci creation. *Ummm.* My pussy twitched, and I leaned forward. In that moment I broke my age-old vow to keep my instinctive tendency to lean forward under wraps—to not appear overly anxious. Long ago I had made a promise to myself to be the one woman men long for, dream about, chase, and fight for. I didn't *play* hard to get, but I *was* hard to get—something men find intensely appealing. But, in Dan's case, perhaps because his smile was so sexy and inviting, I wanted to prove I was distinctly interested.

In fact, in the span of a nanosecond I decided that, contrary to my previous dating behavior, I would compliment this man on his finely etched mouth. I leaned forward, and as I leaned forward, so did he. I smiled, looked into his sunglasses, and as he took them off and placed them deliberately on the table, I said, like little Red Riding Hood to the voracious wolf, "My goodness, what beautifully-framed lips you…"

Suddenly my words stuck in my throat like a bloated tampon wedged in a toilet. "You…" I tried to utter the compliment but was struck as silent as moss.

What I saw shocked me to catatonia.

As though I had just met Vlad the Impaler, I shuddered, my belly stiffening, my guts coiling into a pile of twenty snakes ready to strike. Yet I was determined the abomination before me wouldn't disrupt my cool. Somehow, despite the shock, I managed to plaster a noncommittal, though probably excruciatingly forced, grin on my face. I was nothing if not the master of nonchalance. Defiant of the most extreme shock-masters, this vision before me would not take me down—I *would* triumph over the hideousness sitting before me.

Eeeew! Nasty. Your conscience feels nauseous. You messed up, big-time, this time, Ginnie. Didn't screen this one well enough did you? Those close-ups of his face with sunglasses should've given you a coupla clues. You're getting careless, honey.

Dan stared at me deliberately, challengingly, his mouth set—he was testing my stamina and my stomach. Like a fortune-teller, he knew exactly what I was thinking and feeling, and he seemed not to give a damn, wearing a smirk. I struggled with my face to keep everything aligned against a pending earthquake-grimace.

Before me sat a man, the likes and lines of which bespoke all that is princely and handsome, except for the horror hidden beneath the glasses. Indeed, I struggled to catch my breath and regroup, but I couldn't take my eyes off the aberration before me. How cruel was I to stare at this unfortunate soul before me? Had I no mercy, no common decency for a man thus created? The person sitting before me was as hideous as Shelly's Frankenstein.

Suddenly Dan cleared his throat, and I startled. I mumbled a few incomprehensible words. I simply couldn't stop staring at the apparition before me.

Both Dan's eyelids hung at half-mast, burdened under *warts* the size of frisbees. A slit of a watery anemic iris peeked from under the heaviest eyelid—his left one dwarfed by a growth the size of a nickel. It trembled in an effort to stay open. The right eyelid, on the other hand, buoyed two similar, smaller dime-size warts, and it struggled just as admirably under their heft.

Dan sat, scowling and defiant, as I fought my own dis-ease of the moment. In a few more minutes a server coming for our orders saved me

Throughout the meal I kept my portions small and dainty as a favor to my upset bowels. Clearly I was not good in the company of a leper—I avoided Dan's glance, quipping aimlessly about the popularity of the restaurant and what other items I had ever ordered there. But every time he blinked, the bloated-liberal wart disappeared for a second only to reappear larger, nastier, and ever more wrinkly and tenacious. The two smaller, conservative moles, like two young fraternal twins, sat together on their bench-seat eyelid, merely along for the ride. They were just beginning to grow into beaming adulthood. At maturity they would likely grow hairs, too.

If I appear unsympathetic toward a man with such obvious facial warts, I make no apologies. Would one have me compliment him on their grandiosity, their character? I would reason that in his dating profile he had cleverly—dishonestly—hidden those warts under sunglasses, saving them as a nasty surprise for his date. His was a clear case of dating site misrepresentation. Moreover, if Dan wanted to attract a mate, why didn't he have a doctor remove those horny growths? Just as Dan chose to mask his warts, my choice was to reject him.

Better women than I exist in this world, ones who can appreciate Dan for the probably decent, though shrewd, human he is—ones who can altruistically look beyond a potential lover's physical abomination to the underlying goodness and kindness within. They should pursue him with vigor. Alas, I cannot, for his attempt to hide his true self on his profile defines the highest form of deceit and dishonesty. No matter how I convinced myself otherwise, I simply couldn't muster one iota of "sparkage' in the face of those blistery polyp lids.

At the end of the date, I insisted on paying my half of the bill. I could not accept charity from someone so stealthy. At least, if I paid for myself, I could walk away from the date feeling no obligation. The solitary drive home that evening was riddled with remorse coupled with resentment. Dan's was a clear case of deliberate guise—dark sunglasses on his close-up pictures, no glasses on photos too far away to detect the warts. He had done everything he could to disguise them from a prospective partner. But what he surely hadn't figured was that sometime he would have to meet a woman and put those eyelids on full display.

I remembered a conversation I had with another date, one in which we decided to be just friends. Our discussion revolved around online dating, its trials and tribulations, its positive aspects, as well. He had remarked about mature daters who misrepresent themselves. The fifty-five-year-old guy recounted the night he had been sitting at a restaurant waiting for a pretty blonde to meet him when an older, dark-haired woman tapped him on the shoulder and asked if he were John. He said, indeed, his name was John, but how did she know him? She said, "I'm from the dating site. My name is Sandy. Nice to meet you."

He couldn't believe his eyes. "But you're not blonde, and you don't look *anything* like your pictures. Who is the blonde you posted?"

She was embarrassed. "That's my daughter."

"Your daughter? You said you were fifty-eight!"

"My daughter *is* fifty-eight."

"Well, then, how old are *you?*"

"Uh, I'm seventy-four."

When I pulled into the garage that evening and went out to the barn to check the horses, I shouted at the starlit sky what had now become my mantra.

"Next!"

****

The following evening I was meeting Labrador Riley at a restaurant off Route 23 outside of Grand Gorge. The photo of him and his smiling dogs won me over, and he wasn't wearing sunglasses or featuring pictures of his standing behind bushes or anything, so I was semi-hopeful. Even so, I felt my first bad vibe after I suggested we eat outside at one of the lovely umbrellaed tables.

"Absolutely *not*. My allergies are bad. We are sitting inside." He sniffed loudly to prove his point.

"Oh, please," I begged. "It's so pretty out here on the porch."

"No!"

He's giving you orders already? Not a good sign, Ginnie. Careful.

Sometimes my conscience *really* could be my best friend. Like a cat, I was on guard.

So, on such a beautifully mild late spring evening I found myself sitting across from Smiley Riley at a teensy table for two inside a restaurant as dark and foreboding as a fruit-bat cave—no windows, no ventilation. Heavy blackness enveloped us. Feeling much like a dog on a tight leash, I tugged on my turtleneck to relieve the strangulation. As always, however, I could make the best of any situation. I had survived the suppurating eyelids—I could survive a date with a man who assumed women should subordinate themselves to men.

He pulled out my chair, which was a plus, and advised me on the menu's most popular items. But when I asked what he intended to order, he barked a decree. "I'm not telling you!"

"You're not telling me?" I frowned. "Why not?"

"'Cause I don't want to," he growled.

Yeah, you can really pick 'em, Ginnie. I'm losing faith in you now.

194

"Oka-a-ay," I said. "I'll have a Cobb salad, then."

We ordered, and I had already decided to play my libations conservatively by ordering nothing alcoholic, just a glass of iced tea. The vibes I was getting from Wiley Riley were a bit quaky, and I wanted no obligations for affection or commitments for any other dates.

The conversation began with a discussion about what he surely considered his impressive position within the surrounding local school districts. His job combined that of a high school administrator/disciplinarian, one who "floated" from school district to school district acting as a self-ascribed chief paddle-wielder and intimidator of recalcitrant teenage boys. He described in depth his infamous wooden paddle, handed down to him from his grandpa, which he lovingly called The Whopper. The board was honed shiny from consistent use on the most disruptive students, particularly members of the football team who thought they were studs.

What he didn't know was I had been a high school English teacher for many years and knew a thing or three about public school administrators, oftentimes promoted when they became failures as classroom teachers. The teachers' union made sure any teacher half his worth would not be fired but, instead, given an administrative position—a dangerous policy, in my opinion—in which he could do the least harm.

Yawning, I checked my watch for the fifth time. By seven o'clock the big, burly man with the thick skin-skull was still yammering on about the irresponsibility of teenagers and how they could benefit from water boarding. The braggadocio had an annoying

195

habit of snickering, his head cocked, as if to say, "So, what do you think of that?"

He laughed loudly at his cleverness, teetering proudly on the back two legs of his chair. How I wished those legs would collapse under him and send his ass crashing to the floor. In the one-sided conversation he had not asked me one question about myself; I felt as unwelcome and invisible as a germ. But I let him talk because it was apparent his talking about himself was a self-orgasmic experience. Had I peeked under the table cloth, I probably would've noticed his ego-induced hard-on.

Finally, the server put down our food. I dug around my Cobb salad, separating out the bacon because I don't eat pig. Then, stuffing a steamed clam into his mouth, Riley ran on to the next topic of conversation— his eighteen-year-old son. Like all the other high school students he saw on a daily basis, his son was just as clueless, undriven, and unambitious as all the rest— according to him. That morning Riley had ordered him to spread mulch on all the flowerbeds and around all the trees in the yard. "He doesn't have a clue," Riley spat. Then he threw another butter-dripping clam into his mouth. "Like you."

I looked up from the quartered hard-boiled egg on my fork. "Excuse me?"

Then Riley did something very strange. He stuck out his tongue.

I blinked, squinting in the darkroom.

Did he just stick his tongue out at you, Ginnie?

"You think I'm clueless?" I said. My eyes closed to slits.

"Yep." Obviously he was one of Christ's wise

men.

"Tell me something." My soft voice took over. "Were you a teacher before going into administration?"

"Yeah—taught health and phys-ed." He thrust out his chest and slammed another clam into his mouth.

I tossed an egg slice into mine, swallowed it, and laughed. "Well then—that explains it."

"Explains what?"

"You don't know I taught high school as well as college. One thing I understand is the path to promotion in a public school district."

"Yeah? So…"

I interrupted him. "It's this, Sorry Ass—if you *can't* teach, you get promoted to principal, disciplinarian, or super."

His face turned blue as a Jersey crab. Was the clam thankfully blocking his trachea, or was it my observation that had left him breathless? I decided to simply watch, unemotional, while he struggled in his chair in a paroxysm of coughing.

I continued. "Clueless, huh?" I said. I chewed a pickle. I looked up and cocked an eyebrow. "I don't think so."

Just then Riley cocked his head and out darted his tongue like the slidey part out of a party favor.

What gives with that fuckin' tongue?

I continued to eat, again—the master of nonchalance. If I could do Blister Lids, I could do Cobra Tongue. He was pulling nothing over me—I knew too well the workings of high schools and the promoting of the inept. As I munched another lettuce leaf, Riley changed the subject back to his son, a kid who had no idea or desire to discover the art of gardening. Ironically, Riley himself had mastered cluelessness because the only seeds his high school-aged son wanted to plant were his own—in the school's head cheerleader. Then, Riley enlightened me with the *correct* method of mulching—graduating the pile from the piled-high center to just perfectly even with the grass.

I looked up from my plate. "You're an obsessive-compulsive, aren't you?"

Shock drained the last of the blue color from his face, and his temples took on the greenish hue of cyan. "I suppose you could say that," he said in a smart-assed tone. Again he cocked his head to the side, looked at me, and stuck out his tongue.

Rip that fuckin' tongue right out of his mouth, Ginnie!

The conversation devolved from there. He had already sensed I was no more interested in him than in a heap of sanitary pads. So, he had nothing to lose—he could be even more obnoxious. He was, after all, a high school disciplinarian. He bossed people around as a career, especially ones he assumed were weaklings. He then began bad-mouthing his former wife, and I immediately understood her plight. I could hardly take this arrogant bastard for one meal let alone years in marriage.

Next he harangued football players way too cocky for their own good. When I commented his resentment was understandable considering in his school years he must've played the clarinet in his high school band, his tongue lashed out at me, whipping back and forth like a deranged dragon's. I had had enough of that tongue.

Abruptly I sat up straight, leaned forward, put

down my fork, and pointed at Riley's head with an index finger. "Ya know what? You need to keep that frickin' tongue of yours in your mouth where it belongs."

The tongue slithered back inside, and then Riley broke into a mischievous grin. He looked as though he was going to stick it out again, but he didn't.

Ugh. Can't wait for this torture to end. Must get through the obligatory adieu yet.

Finally, the dinner ended. I thanked him for the Cobb salad, offered to pay the tip, and we headed to the parking lot. The bright outdoors, in contrast to our bat cave setting inside, blinded me, so that when he walked me to my car, and I turned for the obligatory "Thank-you-for-my-dinner-handshake," I didn't really see what was coming.

As I readied my off-to-the side, noncommittal but friendly, "sayonara" squeeze, he moved in for the kill, obviously premeditated. He grabbed me, full throttle, by my shoulders, pulled me toward him, and injected that awful tongue right into my mouth.

A piece of cucumber lurched up my gullet—I swallowed frantically. My reaction came in an instant. I shoved the massive disciplinarian with all the strength I could muster, which nearly set him on his ass in the parking lot.

I took a deep breath. "That's it—I've had *enough*." Then, I leaped into my car, started the engine, and tore out of the lot toward home.

That, however, wouldn't be the end of Riley, the old lizard-lapping brute. I would hear from him via text message the next two days. He texted me that if I didn't acquiesce to his designs, I'd be forever regretful and promised to "*complete* me as no other man would or *ever* could."

I hit the keys with a smirk. "Thanks, but no, thanks. I am as complete as I have ever dreamed of being. I don't need *you* to complete me. By the way—don't contact me again."

I hit the send button and glared at the ceiling.

"Next!"

****

I met Grover again three days later at The Cork and Corkscrew where he professed my beauty to the dollar bills lining the ceiling and walls. His admiration made even the likes of me a bit embarrassed.

Luckily, a framed photo of Elizabeth Taylor sat on the wall. "There." I pointed to her. "Now *that* is what I call 'beautiful.' "

"Well, I think you're beautiful, too."

"Thank you, but, truly, I'm not. Good-looking, maybe—beautiful—no. But thanks for the compliment anyway."

Being in Grover's presence was like being in the presence of Oz's Good Witch of the North, who sees only the good in people. An attractive man with a deep voice, he gazed with dark brown eyes admiring me from the tips of my booties to the ends of my hair. Clearly, he was as nuts about me as Riley was about himself.

And I? Except for that fishy, over-enthused kiss of death on our first date—surely a fluke, no fish pun intended—I found him equally magnetic—kind, attentive, and unselfish. At least he didn't seem self-possessed or obsessed with mulch and such. I could possibly muster a few more pussy sparks.

After dinner we climbed into his Miata and headed for my house. In the kitchen, the two of us alone, this charming gentleman was overcome with sexual tension, and, admittedly, I enjoyed the compliment of his subtle erection growing in his pants. In fact, we ended up, somehow, in a maelstrom of affection that ended in a sensual tsunami on the sofa.

Wrestling with Grover on the couch, I was curious about his appendage that appeared bursting from its denimed seams. He had already removed my blouse and had expertly lifted away my bra. He was sucking on a ta-ta, his eyes closed to slits, when I heard the metallic *zing!* of his pant's zipper. And in seconds I had it in my hand. As we grappled each other, I noted the Seinfeldism: "I *took* it *out.*" He gasped, pressing down against me, my hand filled with him—caught between my thigh and his abdomen.

Then he began to move against me. That's when I became aware of something amiss. I frowned as he kissed me hard, his tongue behaving itself this time— soft, courteous, probing, questioning, but respectful— not reptilian. Our focus, now, was on our nether body parts. And something was definitely going on with his.

When it comes to sex, most women prefer being blind. While they may want to make love to their partners, they don't want to *see* themselves or their men doing the nasty, which necessitates their twisting themselves into compromising positions less than athletically desirable. Women prefer sexual acts done in a tent, at pitch-midnight, or inside a sleeping bag. Men, on the other hand, love to watch their body parts moving and reacting during sexual intercourse. Upon first kiss, men morph into creatures with the visual acuity of birds of prey. They watch, stare, analyze the sexual scene—the thrusting, the facial tension in their partners, the gyrating breasts, the jostling thighs. Women, though, being the more self-conscious, more modest, of the sexes, become creatures of the night wherein they are not continually reminded of their cellulite.

Unfortunately, instead of the "blind" signals evoking a pleasant, giddy feeling within my mind, I suddenly became possessed by something severely amiss in my fist. While Grover worked his magic on my mouth, I began taking mind measurements of his penis, which measured vastly shorter than my left hand. But that wasn't the alarming fact. What really wigged me out was the angle in the appendage. His erect penis came out straight from his body and took an abrupt right angle toward the ceiling.

"It's *broke!*" my blind mind's eye yelled. "His penis is *broke*."

Karma, baby.

Shut up.

The small broken dick begged for acceptance. Then, carefully, I tucked it back into Grover's jeans. "Not yet, Grover." I whispered in his ear. "It's too soon for me."

"Okay," he said. "I won't push you, though you know I'd love to make love to you."

"Not tonight, dear."

I admit I felt awful about refusing Grover. His broken cock was not his fault, perhaps, and I should have had the decency, the humanity, to overlook the handicap. But much as I wished with all my soul to be generous and magnanimous and urge Grover's broken arrow toward its target, my sour stomach overruled any sense of compassion. I had already endured a twenty-eight-year-long horrific sex life. If I was going to get seriously involved with someone, he had to have a decent dick, not one that resembled a T-square.

So, Grover and I held hands and watched the ten o'clock news that night, and as I watched his Miata drive down the driveway and out of sight, I ran back into the house, fired up my notebook and googled "broke penis." After lying in bed for an hour reading about penile fractures and Peyronie's disease, I made my final decision and muttered, sadly, to myself, "Next!"

Then, I checked my email—a note from My Colonel. I clicked on it and read the following:

"Dear Ginnie, You are one of the most beautiful and alluring women I have ever met, but I have been negligent and less than up-front with you on won issue. I can never realize you anywhere—ever—for I am married. The woman on my Facebook page is not my sister but my wife."

Gasping, I shuddered in my sheets and read painfully on.

"I truly love my wife but am hopelessly attracted to you. I must warn you that the Army would fire me on the spot if they herd of any affair. Extra-marital affairs are strictly verboten in the military, especially among hi-ranking officers. Though you are the most amazing woman I have ever not met, I must decline any kind of reel meating. Likewise, wheel never be able to talk on the phone because my wife pays the sell phone bills and would see you're strange number. Unfortunately, I guess this will be hour last conversation—in the interest of us all. Love, Richard."

Huge tears welled in my eyes, and I buried my face in my pillow. My world was as broken as Grover's penis. A blanket of depression rolled over me like a suffocating wet rag. What had Lance done to me? What had *I* done to me? My life had been forever changed—an emotional roller coaster struggling to provide for the animals and farm abandoned to me and trying to find love and self-respect again. I sobbed at the unfairness of it all—dating, flirting, and teetering on the edge of a new-found sexuality. Life certainly was no bed of lilacs for a forty-nine-year-old woman adrift in a sea of uncertainty. As I shivered into sleep, I nurtured one fleeting, hopeful thought.

"Next!"

Chapter Fourteen
The Void

I awoke to a splitting headache birthed from too many cocktails of warted eyelids, serpent tongues, broken penises, and untrustworthy male "friends without benefits." Ashamed of my behavior with Jack and what amounted to "life as usual mixed with moments of sobbing, not quiet, desperation," I soaked up the blame, too. I felt as weak and useless as a limp dick.

Thank goodness for Steve.

"Hey, good-looking." Steve's voice sounded eager on the other end of the phone. "How're ya doin'?"

"Okay, Steve. Sure wish we could get together."

"We will, hon. I'm so busy flying around delivering fertilizer and seeds to the farmers, I even forget to eat lunch. I'd love to see you but don't think this'll let up for another couple of weeks. Sundays are my only days for grocery shopping and straightening up my apartment. If only you didn't live an hour away, I could squeeze you in. But I promise I'm not dating anyone else. I just have to get the time to start going out again."

He sounded sincere, but after Richard's stunt, could I trust anyone? I wished him an easy Saturday afternoon at work and told him I anticipated our next conversation. I offered to marinate a London broil the next time he visited the farm.

"That's a done deal."

****

That Sunday evening Lois called. Would I like to come over for dinner? "And don't bring your whole pantry this time." She was making baked ziti with eggplant. Earlier in the week I had counted up the last of the week's allowance from Lance—a whopping twenty dollars left to splurge on something. So I bought Lois her favorite vanilla-flavored vodka.

When Jack heard about my Colonel's married state, he laughed so hard he almost split his ribcage wide open. "Told you that wouldn't work out!" he roared. He seemed inordinately happy with my disappointment. He laughed like a gleeful child at my tales of Mr. Wart-Eyes, Tongue-Thruster, and the broken penis guy. Lois, too, was laughing so hard at my latest dating abortions she almost peed herself. Jack shook his head and smirked through his moustache, "What are we going to do with you, Ginnie?"

"So glad my dating trials provide such swell entertainment," I said with a grunt. "Yeah, ol' broke dick scared the living shit out of me. No way is a cock with an abrupt *angulus rectus*—otherwise known as a right angle—getting into my kitty-cave. I felt sorry for him, but I was like Miss Muffet with her spider—the thought of that inside me made me physically sick. I couldn't go there." Lois roared with laughter, and Jack snorted, thoroughly amused. Surely he felt superior with his stick-straight dick.

Then Lois suddenly turned from the kitchen counter. "Ginnie! You *really* should write this all down in a book. I'm tellin' ya, it'd be a bestseller—good, racy stuff—stuff other women would flock to. Ya know, plenty of women are going through or have gone through divorce. And this dating stuff? Talk about a story that would speak to women all over the world?"

"Do you think so?" I raised an eyebrow. "I'm living some pretty heavy shit these days. Feels like I'm at an amusement park sometimes. One day I'm teetering at the apex of the roller coaster; the next I'm plunging down the other side, not knowing if my car will jump the tracks."

What I loved most about Jack and Lois was I could always be honest with them, especially Lois, when I battled rough seas. Lois was always the last to pass judgment on me—Jack wasn't always sympathetic but usually listened politely unless he had a "broom handle" up his ass. Both were my dearest friends and best supporters. And the one-night fling with Jack had passed like an owl in the night, never to take flight again.

"I just might turn these incidents into a book." I kissed Lois good-bye and headed toward home.

That night I crawled into bed early and drifted off to the latest episode of "Family Dad" when the phone jangled.

It was Jack.

"Lois is drinking her head off, and I can't take it anymore. Can I come over?"

My own head wasn't on straight, blanketed in sleep. Without much thought or vision I said, "Uh, all right. Come on over."

Soon headlights from a Dodge pick-up truck sped up the driveway. A few minutes later he was peering through my bedroom's French doors like an intruder from Investigation Discovery. I groped for the door, and he stumbled into my bedroom gripping a tall glass containing what had to be an alcoholic drink. The overwhelming aroma of stale booze hit me in the face.

"Phew—you *stink*. You better not be drunk, Jack." I fanned the air. "God, you smell awful. I'm throwing out the rest of this drink right now." I escorted it down the hall toward the bathroom where the last of it gurgled down the sink. "You don't need any more to drink. So, what's going on with Lois? Jeez, had I known you were drinking and driving, I'd have told you to stay put."

"I'm really not drunk." The blue glow of the TV outlined his clothed silhouette. "Lois is the *drunk* one. I can't take her anymore. The moment you left tonight she started in on me—said something about catching me staring at you tonight—looking at your ass or boobs or something. I didn't *do* anything. She's imagining it all. She's so insanely jealous of you, I can't believe it. She said you were giving me the eye, too."

"Me? I didn't do anything," I moaned. "You know I didn't do anything. We've both been pious since our little thing a couple of weeks ago." I concentrated, my senses slowly drifting back from a dead sleep. "Jack, I know the solution to this. Why don't you insist Lois marry you? That would end her jealousy."

"Hell no!" he roared. "I don't want to marry her. She drinks too much. She gets so plastered she can hardly walk. It's disgusting. I've tried to talk to her, have even pleaded with her to limit herself to one drink a night, but she says the more I nag her, the more she feels compelled to drink. She even admitted she drinks to spite me. Oh! And get a load of this—she says she also drinks a lot because I make her have sex too often."

"Jeez." I yawned. "That doesn't sound good."

"I want to sleep with you tonight, Ginnie."

"What?" I blurted. "*No.*" I pulled my nightshirt tighter around my neck.

"Yes. You've been sleeping alone too long now—here in this big bedroom in this huge king-sized bed without a good man beside you. Wouldn't you like me to sleep with you tonight? I don't mean have sex—I mean just sleep beside you, next to you. Wouldn't you like that, Ginnie?"

The last years of my invisible marriage amounted to two agonizing years of sleeping right alongside Lance without so much as a good-night kiss, certainly without any sex, with not even a word of comfort or kindness between us before drifting off to sleep. I hadn't realized how empty those years had been until he'd left me for his whore. The separation still shook me up. I always thought Lance and I would be an item, albeit a platonic one.

I looked at Jack, and he took my hand and looked hard into my eyes. "You're a beautiful, kind, wonderful woman, Ginnie. You shouldn't have to sleep alone—ever." I closed my hand around his and wondered if we didn't have sex, did it really matter that he slept in my bed?

"Okay, Jack. You can sleep with me. Then in the morning when you're sober, you make up with Lois."

He smiled and warmed my hands between his. His breath was thick with alcohol, but his eyes were soft, understanding. "Come on." He slipped from his clothes and pulled my nightie over my head. He tossed it in a corner where he stood naked before me. But he wasn't hard. "Let's get under the covers together." He turned off the TV, and the room went black.

We lay naked in the dark together, like two spoons, his torso and face against my back and neck, his arms around my breasts, his leg draped over my legs. I felt his hot breath on my nape. He squeezed me, his sign that everything was right with the world—two people together in friendship. I sighed deeply, feeling his body's warmth. Then I enclosed his left hand in mine and drew it under my chin. It *did* feel good to have a caring man in my bed. Naked, unabashed closeness without sex was good, soul-lifting, and the Goddess of Love, Aphrodite herself, assured me his being inebriated would stifle any erection. While he drifted off to sleep, I lay awake for close to an hour reveling in the peace of another human's closeness and warmth.

Around three in the morning, I woke up to Jack's stirring beside me. He had gotten out of bed to pee and slipped back under the covers. But he was restless. "Something wrong, Jack?" I whispered.

'I'm a little cold. Must be from the booze I had last night. I've got the chills." He snickered. His breath smelled of toothpaste. "Hey, can you turn on the fireplace, just to take the chill off?"

"Sure. Just need to flip a switch." I slid out of bed, took three steps, and turned on the propane stove where lovely embers began to glow. I crawled back into bed, stroked Jack's hair, and smiled as the flames lit up his face. "Go to sleep, Jack. It's only three in the morning." The light danced across his face. He looked strangely calm.

"I can't sleep with this hard-on, Ginnie."

I reached under the covers. His penis was in full bloom. I giggled and flung back the sheets exposing his manhood to the sparkling firelight in the room. "Ta-taaaa!" I sang. "Our latest wonder is Jack's cock, everyone!" I announced it like a night-show host introducing a newly discovered species of mammal to a live audience. "He's feeling big and strong this morning. And a bit frisky. Now cut it out, Jack. Go back to sleep. We aren't doing this again. We made a pact, remember?"

Jack wrestled me close, and my resolve began to drain away. I melted against him. He kissed me hard, gasping, and his tongue tasted my mouth in soft, whispery licks.

Before I could think, I responded, sliding my own tongue alongside his, tasting the mint, inhaling his fresh breath. I was helpless, and he knew it. Then he rolled into me and over top me, pressing his mouth hard against mine, driving his manhood into my thigh.

"I want you, Ginnie."

His hand groped me, and I slinked against him. He parted the gates, and a liquid surge erupted as I strained against him. I felt full—ripe for the picking. Round and round he stroked me while my body unconsciously moved in sync with his. His other hand clasped my back tightly. He had me wound tighter than the "E" string on a violin. Suddenly he grabbed a shock of my hair and pulled my face to his.

He stared, his eyes intense, his profile illuminated by the dancing fire, and I recognized the want, the yearning. He pushed his manhood hard against my thigh, thrust his tongue deeper into my mouth, and I took it all in, tasting it, relishing the moment.

Trying not to, I spread myself. And then like the male animal he was, he mounted me.

Very slowly, deliberately, he directed himself inside with his own hand. I gasped, feeling myself relax to accommodate him.

"Oh, Jack," I moaned. "This shouldn't be happening."

"Baby, you are so tight—so tight. Relax, and enjoy."

His breath came in fits, in rhythm to his sex moving inside me. Then, he repositioned himself deeper, and I watched, enthralled, as the flames crackled and bathed us in a sensual light.

I gasped as he began to move. Deeper. Faster. Harder. In that position made famous by missionaries, I angled myself toward him. The floor of my pussy rose like an elevator—Level One, Level Two, Level Three...

Last stop—everybody out!

Just as I was ready to jump out onto the rooftop, Jack yelled, his head back. In an instant he drove himself home and pumped himself empty inside me. I gasped, abandoned in mid-flight. The next second he fell out and, then, dismounted. He stroked my hair, smiled, and asked if I had come. It was all right I hadn't, that I had been awfully close and enjoyed every bit of it, nevertheless. He exhaled, wiped his brow, and curled alongside me where he fell immediately to sleep.

We lay in each other's arms, our faces caressed by the warmth of the fireplace's flames. Then a horrible dread washed over me—I had eaten Lois' food that very night, and hours later I was fucking the love of her life. And here he lay—fast asleep next to me. What kind of a monster had I become? A hidden one—hidden from all but myself. Hours later I fell fitfully into sleep.

At seven a.m. Jack's cell phone woke us with a text. He flung back the covers and leaped to the floor. It was Lois—apologizing for being drunk last night. She admitted she had a serious drinking problem she needed to fix. Could he forgive her? He texted back he would be there for her but that she must promise to get help.

We looked at each other. "Thank you for last night," I said. "It felt so good to have you sleeping beside me. It's the first time anyone has actually slept with me since Lance left. You made me feel safe."

"You don't deserve to sleep alone, Ginnie. You deserve better. I should be going back to Lois. Maybe she finally realizes last night she pushed me to my limit. Still, I loved sleeping with you. You helped me out at a time when I needed it, too."

We got up and dressed. Jack put his phone in his back pants pocket, and we went downstairs to watch the news while I fixed some toast and coffee. Cupping the warm coffee mug with both hands, I leaned against him on the couch. I took a sip—all felt right—cozy.

"Thank you for this morning. It really was something, wasn't it?" he began.

"Sure was. Very exciting. But we broke our promise, Jack. I feel awful—haunted—about Lois. We promised each other never to do it again—for her sake. You shouldn't have called me last night. It only stirred things up between us."

"Well, her heavy drinking got to me. And her jealousy thing has been eating at me, too. Where's that coming from?"

"She can smell it like a dog on a scent. But let's be

truthful—I know you love Lois, not me. You know you love Lois, and I would never come between you two. You belong together."

He thought hard. "She brought last night on herself. What she doesn't know about us won't hurt her. From now on, let's not expect the impossible from each other. As long as you and I don't try to break up Lois' and my relationship, it's okay to meet occasionally for sex, don't you think?"

Don't you know a line when you hear it, Ginnie. I'm so disappointed in you.

Two for the price of one.

I wasn't too sure about that. Karma could be a huge detractor. And, as naïve as I tended to be, I knew rationalization when I heard it. Jack wanted his cake and me, too. "I have to think on that one. By the way, I loved the fireplace accompanying our lovemaking. Didn't you?" I said.

"It really did heighten things for me." You looked especially beautiful in the firelight."

For the next fifteen minutes we talked about the spontaneity and excitement of the evening. And then nature called, and Jack excused himself for the downstairs bathroom. I watched the news with another cup of coffee, and suddenly Jack appeared, trembling, in the archway of the living room.

I sat up. He looked ashen.

"What's wrong?" I leaped to my feet.

"Lois just phoned me. Somehow, minutes ago while we were talking about last night, my phone dialed her number. She overheard us discussing it all—all the details, Ginnie. She heard our conversation about last night!" he blurted. "She told me, 'I hope you and

Ginnie had a wonderful evening together.' " He was nearly hysterical, his moustache twitching as he repeated the conversation.

My stomach dropped into a heap at my feet. The dread-wash had me reeling with dizziness.

"Oh, my God!" I said. My hands flew to my mouth. Visions of a friendship vacuumed right down the tubes of distrust and unfaithfulness flooded over me. I felt faint. My betrayal lay bare on Lois, my best friend of over twenty years. My brain imagined the eventual outcome, but I didn't have to think it through very long. We were done—this was the final straw. Lois would never forgive me for this.

I could never blame her.

Jack stood limp in the doorway. "What am I gonna do? What should I do? She told me never to come back. But I love her. I know she loves me—I told her I didn't love you!"

I winced. Though I knew that, it still didn't feel good to have it said.

"Yes, Jack. I know. We don't love each other. We were just temporary fuck buddies." The language sounded very high-schoolish.

"What the hell am I going to do?"

In the kitchen we stood together but apart, helpless and self-conscious in our fear and self-loathing. "You must go to her right now, Jack. You must tell her it was just a one-time fling and convince her you don't love me, that you love her more than anything. You've got to do it to save your relationship."

"Yes, yes, to save us. Ginnie, I love her so much. I don't want to lose her."

"I know, Jack. I love her, too. She is a very good

friend, and I did a horrible thing. I'm awful. This is it, Jack. We are totally exposed now. You and I are done—completely done. Lois will likely forgive you after a while, but she will be finished with me. I'm history as far as she is concerned—will probably never see her again. No more fun evenings with you two at your place. No more shopping trips or lunches out with you guys. No more talks. It's all gone now, and that's not being dramatic. No one could forgive a friend of such an abomination.

"I am totally alone now, except for my parents and two other friends. And ya know what? I deserve it. I *so* deserve it. I am so ashamed of myself I could crawl into a hole and never come out."

Jack stood in the kitchen, his right foot tapping nervously. "What am I going to do?" He could not have cared any less about my misery.

I had to forget about myself and help Jack and Lois, whose problems were more immediate. Perhaps their relationship could be saved. "You're going to go to Lois and explain yourself and the shallowness of our fling. And you're going to tell her you love her. And you're going to ask her for forgiveness. Get going, Jack."

And then he left.

Once Jack was gone, I dialed Lois' number. I almost expected her not to answer, but she did.

"Oh, Lois!" I cried. Tears poured down my cheeks. "I'm so sorry—so sorry. I have no excuses, only that it was just sex—like eating pizza. My behavior is inexcusable. I'm not even going to ask you to forgive me. What I've done is unforgiveable."

Her voice was almost matter-of-fact, dead-pan.

"Why do men always think with their dicks? I'm so sick of it."

"Please listen to me, Lois. Jack called me last night, upset, but I am as much to blame. He and I had made a pact to never hurt you, to never jeopardize your relationship. Try to believe me, Lois. I'd give anything to take back the last few hours. The sex was so not worth losing your friendship."

But my pleadings fell on deaf ears and rightly so. It was useless—my speech seemed cliché, even to me, though I was sincere. Canned sincerity. I sniffed back tears. "You can never forgive me—I understand that. But please give Jack another chance. He doesn't love me, and I don't love him. He only loves you. He's very upset right now, and he's on his way over. Please forgive him. I know I've lost both your friendships through this. You have no idea how sorry I am. I don't know what else to say. I wish to hell I had never done what I did. You were such a wonderful friend. And I am such a lousy one."

I was rambling in my hysteria.

She hung up on me.

I put the dead receiver back in its cradle. Then I bent over the kitchen counter, my forehead in my hands, and howled in absolute physical and mental pain. I cried and cried, remembering the sexual encounter, which now felt so wrong, so horrible— certainly not worth the loss of such a good friendship. I called myself every name imaginable, including the one I exclusively used for Lance's woman—whore. I was no better.

I didn't allow myself excuses other than the obvious—Jack gave me the opportunity to share a closeness I hadn't experienced for the past sixteen years. I took a gift not meant for me and ran with it— without thinking—without understanding the exact cost.

Sick with grief and embarrassment, I was bereft of any morality. I was like so many of the Western population who lack self-discipline and control, who throw themselves into love affairs, destroying marriages and families, entire personal worlds left, spent, in the wake of their destruction.

I didn't know what else to do with my broken heart except run, like a child, to my parents where I'd receive and soak up more verbal punishment, so entirely deserved.

My father couldn't believe it. "Oh, Ginnie." He was clearly shocked and, worse, disappointed. "You've lost a really good friendship. For what? She's gone now." He shook his head.

When I told my mother, she frowned, said much the same thing as my father, but offered me some consolation.

"Jack's the one who called you last night, but you'll get most of the blame because you're the woman. Men are better understood as randy creatures. She'll forgive him in the end, even though he's the one who initiated things. You are the one, though, who's left out in the cold. What a shame to have lost such a good, dear friend." She held me on the couch as I cried another river of tears.

This time no amount of time, promises, or excuses could fix my predicament. The only thing left was to buck up and take any punishment as bravely as possible—like a criminal in solitary confinement—

nothing to do except make the best of my situation. No self-castigation, apologies, or attempts to right the wrong would affect the outcome. I was alone.

I was staring at the void.

Chapter Fifteen
The Queen of Impotence

The imaginary maelstrom formed from my own wicked machinations had pulled me hopelessly into its vortex, the bottom of which reeked of whale shit. I lay in bed gulping like a dying fish—suffocating on my own malevolence. My betrayal of my best friend had been the ultimate act of selfishness and self-absorption—so contrary to my former self, so unrecognizable.

Had I, too, become a walking vagina—like Lance's whore? The destruction of self caused by Lance's rejection had been misery enough, but he was only partially responsible for so much of my descent into delirium. This misdeed rested solely on my head. Like one of Dante's characters clinging to the edge of hell's pit, I was racked with fear and self-loathing. Would I ever be able to forgive myself?

Days of moral wretchedness pursued me without dissipation. As punishment I worked myself to a lather on the farm—mucking stalls until not a horse turd was visible anywhere. For hours I mowed grass with the push mower, dropped hay bales from the loft and stacked them, weeded and edged gardens from sleepless morning until sleepless night. Exhaustion tinged with self-loathing followed me everywhere, even the pig sanctuary where I dove into mucking pig shit to cleanse my guilt. Farm work, formerly my solace, I converted into acts of self-flagellation.

Work, bitch! Work until you drop. This is your torture for being such an abhorrence. Dirty, nasty girl.

My only supporters were my parents and two girlfriends, but even in them I sensed distrust. Would I eventually betray them as I had Lois? Would I destroy their lives as I had Lois' and Jack's? No one, however, was more disgusted by my betrayal than me. Had I been living in early America I would've cheered from the stocks as villagers threw tomatoes and eggs at me—"Have at me, all! I *deserve* it."

Just when I was at my lowest, a trip to the mailbox put the final nail in my box—a letter from Lois. I gaped at the envelope, afraid to open it, knowing it would be scathing. On the other hand, perhaps the letter would reveal miraculously she and Jack were back together again and she had forgiven me.

The first sentences sent chills up my spine— "You are the most disgusting piece of shit on the face of the earth. You're nothing but a slut! Poor Lance—imagine what he put up with all these years. You're scum! You had your sights set on Jack from the very beginning and went after him—because you're a desperate woman!"

I folded the letter and tucked it into its envelope, unable to read anymore without throwing up. I struggled to support myself, my legs hollow, muscleless. Tears poured down my cheeks. Yes. A slut I was—like Lance's Yvonne. No better, for sure. Deserving of every hateful word, I filed the letter under the "Me" file in my desk, mopped my face with a towel, and trudged outside. At least my cats would tolerate me, no matter how many friends and relatives I betrayed. I could depend on their unconditional love, however undeserving.

Rankling depression followed me everywhere—to the grocery store, throughout my chores, at the pig rescue center, even while I tried to write another chapter for my farm animal advocacy manuscript. Normalcy was anathema, and sadness, self-hate, bottomless demoralization weighed on my shoulders, thick as slabs of bacon. Sunny summer days looked gray, overcast through my hollow eyes. The normally verdant greenery of mid-state New York had been sucked yellow-brown. I functioned poorly in a world colored umber.

I was drowning in the void of my unrecognizable self.

Not even occasional phone calls from Steve could cheer me up. He asked what was wrong, but I was too embarrassed to tell him. I lied that the summer chores were tiring me out, and I needed a vacation. What I really needed, however, was a vacation from myself. My living with me was exhausting—daily punishment of my psyche and physical body wore me skeletal. Still, I deserved it. My weight plunged twenty pounds. No chastisement short of death was too harsh—not for the crime I committed.

The unnerving isolation had me strung so tight that, at times, a rupture was imminent. My skin-seams were near to bursting, and my blood pressure measured higher than the electrical tower in the field behind my woods. My heart pounded fast, incessantly, and I waited, hoped, for the organ to rip wide open, thus ending my misery in one blood-bursting moment.

Finally, after the seventh consecutive day of mind-numbing farm work, I crawled into bed. With the pounding of my heart destroying any attempts at sleep, I picked up my notebook and turned to the dating site for company. In seconds I was chatting with a man from Iowa.

"Hey, handsome," I said. Enthusiasm for this game had left. "What are you doing all the way over there in flatland?"

"Good evening, gorgeous," he replied. I half expected him to say, "Good evening, whoremonger."

Bob and I traded emails for an hour. He was intelligent, nice-looking, and educated. And then I did what any seductress of my stature would do—I invited him for a conjugal visit.

"You actually want me to visit you?" His words sounded unfathomable.

"Yep." I felt no excitement. "I really need a change of pace, and it sounds like you do, too. We can chill out here at my place first and then go to the beach two hours away." The swells of the surf and the crashing of the waves pounded in my brain. I really *did* have to escape the farm and myself, or I would eventually self-destruct.

"What are the sleeping arrangements going to be?" he snorted.

I didn't hesitate. "Well, I don't suppose you want to come all this way to have a virginal good time, right? So, first things first—let's both get tested for sexually-transmitted diseases. I'll pick you up at the airport, bring you back here, and we can trade papers. No HIV or hepatitis, and we're good to go. What do you say?"

He paused. "Uh, okay, I guess. Sure, why not? You sound like a fun date. Let's have a ball. I'll make my flight arrangements. When do you want to do this?"

"How about next weekend?" I said. And then the lyrics to "Desperado" floated through my mind once again. That song had me pegged: I wasn't getting younger, smarter, and I walked through this world all alone.

Sleep came fitfully again that night. What had I done inviting a total stranger to my place and my bed? Another form of self-punishment? If I were, indeed, a slut, then I might as well reinforce the idea and live the part, right?—a weekend sex fest with a complete stranger.

Ginnie, have you completely lost it? What are you doing to yourself? Come back to me.

Was I crazy now along with being a complete wretch?

Crazy, lonely slut. Pretty soon you'll be banging down the gates to the Funny Farm. And even they won't want you.

Run fast, run far—get away from myself. The loneliness was taking a physical toll on me, along with a psychological one. I couldn't sleep, courted rapid heartbeats, was losing a pound of body-weight every day because I only allowed myself enough food to stay alive. I didn't care. Bob could be a good distraction—at least for a brief weekend. I had nothing to lose, really.

****

For the next few days I set aside my manuscript and went into high gear straightening up the house and landscaping in anticipation of my eager house guest. I stocked the refrigerator with goodies, bought beach food on my meager budget, purchased a set of cheap lingerie, and splurged on a revealing nightie. I raided a stash of bills in my bedroom for a couple bottles of wine and a block of parmesan cheese and bruschetta crisps. Then I washed windows, inside walls, and floors. *I* might not be clean, but my house would be.

Friday morning as I drove to the airport, a text from Bob rang through—his plane had arrived. I texted back I'd meet him in the airport lobby in ten minutes.

My heart fluttered.

The Virginie Snow of the past had been as morally untarnished and white as the downside of a deer's tail. Even in her barren years she had remained faithful in her platonic relationship with Lance, never considering infidelity. Ginnie had never been this forward, this outrageous, with a man before—until her recent transgression with Jack. The Jack thing had broken the dry spell. He had poked the first hole in the dam, and it was leaking profusely. Virginie Snow was some wild thing now—on the loose, on the prowl—a creature of the night preying on the male species. She was not simply a *walking* vagina—she had become a rabid, galloping vagina. In her frenzy, she could devour both men and herself at the same time.

****

Bob walked into the airport lobby carrying his overnight satchel. I immediately recognized him from his pictures—gleeful, sexy eyes, nice, classical lips smiling like an imp. His cheeks rivaled those of the mother of my suitor from New Hampshire. He walked over, cased me up and down, and set down his case. Perhaps he detected the past weeks' bruising beneath my skin. I shrank, self-conscious. Then he took me in his arms and planted a huge kiss on my mouth.

"My goodness!" You are *strong*, and you are

225

handsome. I think we're going to have a very nice, relaxing weekend."

"Oh, from the looks of you, we are *definitely* going to have some fun times." He picked up his bag, and we walked, his arm around my waist, to the car.

Bob and I stopped at a nearby café for lunch. I got my usual—Cobb salad. He ordered a hamburger. From the moment we sat down I liked him. He was witty, charming, and flirty. He was interested. If he could find something about me to like, perhaps I could like me, again—some year down the road.

At home he put his stuff in the spare bedroom. Of course, I assured him with a wink he would sleep in *my* bed, unless he didn't feel comfortable. He grinned, took me in his arms, kissed me hard and deep. I could feel his eagerness against me and the strength of his well-developed chest, his chiseled arms.

Then he reached into a side pocket of his satchel and produced a paper—his blood work for the sex testing. "See. Clean as a whistle." I breezed down the list of tested diseases, set the paper on the cedar chest, and offered to run for mine.

"Never mind. I believe you're all right. Kiss me."

I melted in his arms, his kisses of the European bent, his tongue delicately flossing my teeth, squiggling alongside my own. I inhaled him, devoured him. We were ready.

"I want you, Ginnie. Right now. I want all of you."

Red-faced, he looked stern in his sexual energy. I became soft, yielding, his for the taking. I stood back, smiled, and drifted into him while he scooped me into his arms. And then, as I buried my face in his neck, he carried me down the hallway and into my bedroom.

There he gently lay me on the bed and regarded me intently.

"Take me, Bob." I uncrossed my legs as he leaned over me, his shadow falling across the sheets.

"I want you so bad, baby. I want to fuck you so bad." The profanity escaped me. His face was serious, lips tight but parted, too.

He undressed my upper body, one item at a time. After he unfastened one article of clothing, he threw it to the floor. Then the next flew to the carpet as well.

I lay exposed, vulnerable, half-naked. He sucked in air at sight of my breasts. "Oh, God. They truly are exquisite, woman. Quite inviting." As with most of the men I had dated, this one, too, was very visual. For men, it's all about the visual. They could be deaf or have no feeling in their fingers, but the bottom line was that sex and making love to a partner was all about vision—seeing the breasts rolling like the tides during the act, seeing the woman's lips part and exhale at the moment of orgasm, seeing her eyes roll back in her head. Sex was a picture to be experienced physically, yes, but, more importantly, in the mind borne through the eyes.

Next he tore off his shirt and threw it into the corner. And then, all the while staring at me prostrate on the bed, he unzipped himself, tore off his jeans and tossed them aside. And, then, in only his jockeys he straddled me, supporting himself on his hands. He kissed me again, leaning into me, desiring me.

I felt at once like an innocent fawn, not only being entertained as wolf's quarry but also protected by a parent. The experience felt extraordinary, at once predatory but paternal, too. And, then, suddenly, and all

227

the while staring intensely into my eyes, he tore off my jeans and then my panties, flinging them to the floor.

At sight of my bare thighs, he moaned like some desert beast of Ethiopia. Then he ripped off his underwear from which his solid, stolid manhood jumped. I felt scared. He was huge, lovely, inviting, and, truly, his swollen cock was his invitation for me to join him in a sexual dance. I reached toward it, feeling, at once, innocent, protected, and, yes, hungry.

He groaned again, his teeth set, animal-like—his eyes slits. He roared aloud as I stroked the massive length of him. It grew more, straining against its own skin, and then, suddenly, Bob opened his eyes and glanced hurriedly around the room. He spied the tube of K-Y gel on my side table, grabbed it, sat back on his haunches, and quickly squirted the liquid on his huge erection. I positioned myself for entry, taking him in my left hand and supporting myself in an upright position on my right elbow.

"Oh, God, I need you." He stared, slavering, at my spread legs. I eased my pelvis toward him—his invitation.

"Come, take me, Bob. I want you inside me, all of you, inside me."

I lay back—his second invitation. Then came the most enjoyable moment of the sexual experience—the mounting—that feeling of being taken, of vulnerability, of feminine knowledge of male desire for me alone—when the excited male can no longer put off penetration. I cherished that moment when the male has reached such a heightened sense of desire, attraction, and unrelenting need to consume his female in a sexual way he simply cannot delay the taking any longer. Then

I am everything to him—when he can no longer romance me—because his need is too overwhelming, too strong to resist. This is a powerful, very sensual, sensuous moment for a woman. At this time I belonged to him exclusively. I became his rare, delectable possession—one he won't fathom losing.

He groaned again. Then his back arched, and I winced as the dragon broke through the castle walls. The pain was fiery, momentarily excruciating until I adjusted to him. Then I floated with him as he moved, strongly and swiftly, inside me.

Bob's mouth hung slack, his eyes slits, though he watched me, almost vacuously. His arm muscles bulged under the strain of supporting himself, and his torso muscles rippled under the thrusting. With every movement, I tightened myself around him.

"Ah, God," he moaned to his deity. "Oh…oh…I'm already ready to come.

"Yes." I moved against him.

Suddenly, his eyes opened wide, and then he slammed himself against me and held himself there. I pressed into him, waiting. I could feel the slight pumping of the sperm into my tank. I lifted myself higher to meet him, to join him in his ecstasy.

"Oh… Oh… Oh…" He grabbed my hair, my boobs, and anything else he could. "Oh— Great God in Heaven!" The last of him drained into me.

Then he withdrew himself, stared at the ceiling, and we lay side by side in the aftermath.

I turned to the wall, and tears poured down my face.

That evening we enjoyed dinner at a local club where the company was fun, the conversation stimulating, the food and wine unusually good. There was no better partner to erase momentarily my betrayal of Lois. He insisted on paying the bill. Later we curled in bed together, fell asleep, and didn't awaken until the next morning.

After a hasty breakfast, we packed day bags and headed to Pleasure Beach near Bridgeport, Connecticut. One could hardly deny the chemistry between us. He couldn't take his eyes off me and held my hand as we drove the three hour ride. He smiled through the entire ride, as if he had just won the lottery. He regarded me as lovingly as Jesus himself. We two strangers both realized our rendezvous could have ended in a complete flop. Instead, our time together grew more sensual and intense with every moment.

We walked along the beach, holding hands and snapping pictures of each other in the surf. Then we ate a picnic lunch. I fed him spicy olives and offered him a glass of wine. On the drive home we held hands over the gear shift and smiled at each other at every stoplight. In general, we were giggling and behaving like a couple of randy teenagers. For the moment my inexcusable deed had been forgotten.

That evening we ran down the hallway and leaped into the sack. Beneath the sheets he enveloped me in his arms. "I think I'm falling for you, hon. We had such a good time today. I feel so connected to you. This is not turning out as I imagined. I expected to just come here for a good fuck. I never dreamed I'd be so attracted to you and you would feel so good in my arms."

I blushed.

He continued, "It's remarkable, really, how in the space of less than two days you've become, not only my lover, but my best friend, too. I just feel so close to you."

We spooned together before the blue light of the TV, and before I knew it, Bob was snoring in my ear. I smiled, enfolded his hand to my chest, and, as tears welled in my eyes, I fell asleep.

****

On Sunday we hiked the property behind my farm. We walked hand in hand, stopping to kiss every hundred yards or so. Then we went for a golf cart ride, fed the horses treats, and fixed some fence. He proved himself not only an expert lover but a fairly good handyman as well. Maybe it was a sign. Perhaps this long-distance meeting was meant to save me rather than punish me, as I first intended.

That evening we had dinner at the club again. On the veranda we gazed at each other as though no one else were around, for, indeed, the world was ours alone. I asked him if he was enjoying himself on his mini-vacation from Iowa. He smiled, "Most definitely, sweetheart."

"I love having you at my farm."

We didn't linger beneath the umbrella very long. After all, my bedroom awaited. And in another hour we were dancing happily toward the bed.

Another round of love-making began with Bob's remarkably soft, lizard-quick tongue kisses. I savored his breath, took his tongue into my mouth, and sucked him inside.

"I think I may be falling in love with you," he whispered.

I smiled and patted his head. Then he glanced at his penis, his signal for oral sex. So, I went to work stroking, sucking, and nibbling. Then he turned me over, stroked my pussy, and bent toward her.

He was hard as a rock.

Only Lance had ever attempted—one time—to give me oral sex—when we dated in college. He emerged from my pussy spitting and hacking in disgust. "I don't like that—it smells."

I said, "It does? Okay, Lance—you don't have to do that." So, I sucked his dick, and, then, we had two-minute sex. I should've taken his inconsiderate comment and run like hell in the opposite direction. Instead, I married the ass.

During Lance's and my early marriage, he expected me to relish sucking him on a regular basis. Of course, *his* dick had no objectionable odor. Oh, no—not Lance's dick. Anyone could ask him—his cock was fucking *pristine*. I should've been so grateful to stick his peeing device in my mouth. Neither was Lance considerate of my gag reflex. During an outdoor movie, in a moment of oral ecstasy, he became over-zealous and jammed his cock into the back of my throat. I retched and damned near lost my popcorn right in his lap. I should have hit the road then, too.

Remembering sex with Lance, I had been particularly deprived. My sex life, all sixteen years of it in my twenty-eight year marriage, really sucked—one of the worst of all tales.

Foreplay? *One token kiss should do it.*

Finger my pussy? *How? A coupla pokes should be good enough.*

Lick my pussy? *"Nevermore," quoth the raven.*

Female orgasm? *There is no such thing.* So, when Bob went to give me oral sex, I almost laid an egg.

"What are you doing?" I yelped.

"Pleasuring you, sweetheart. Just relax and enjoy it." And he swirled his tongue and did other stuff to my clueless, but sensitive, clit. Somehow, however, I just couldn't adjust to the surreal picture of a human head wedged between my thighs. Perhaps it was all the years of sexual barrenness, which had me thinking like a Puritan, but I had to admit seeing a head down there was a bit disconcerting.

I tapped on his scalp. "Love me now. I want you *inside* me."

He looked up, his lips shiny wet, and he smiled. "Yeah, baby." Then he mounted me.

I directed Sir Hardness inside, and then, as he moved within, I lightly called his name. "*Bob. Bob.*" I gasped. "I *want* you." The thrusts kept getting stronger, deeper, and then I wrapped both legs around his waist and squeezed. But that same move that drove Jack wild weeks ago sparked absolutely no reaction from Bob. Then, just like that, his cock fell out.

What the hell? Where did it go?

I looked up at Bob—he wore a look of horror. I reached around and felt for his member, which was hanging limp as a bean sprout. I began to pump it with long, tight encouraging strokes.

"No, no—that won't do it!" His brow was knit. He glanced down at himself. Then he grabbed the recalcitrant thing and began pulling furiously on it while I watched and waited.

"Oh, Bob—I want you so bad. Make love to me, will you?"

"I'm tryin'! I'm tryin'!" He spit into his hand and rubbed it all over his flaccid penis, and then he began to

233

jerk it around again. I watched with some amusement as the head flew from side to side. I stifled a giggle—when dicks are small, they are so incorrigible and, so, well…teensy. Seeing it being man-handled like a stubborn child, while Bob's face remained so stern and intent, made it all the more amusing.

I stifled a laugh.

"Here, come on!" he roared at me. He grabbed my waist and turned me over. "Let's do it doggy style. He likes it better that way."

If there was any sexual position in which I felt as though I were just being fucked, it was doggy style. With no touching or ability to kiss my partner or be kissed, I felt like one of those blow-up dolls men buy at Condoms Carry-Out. Doing it in the doggy position is not love-making—it merely uses the woman as a vessel in which to ejaculate. It sucks.

Still, knowing he was having a bit of a problem with his erection, I conceded. So, much as I didn't want to, I grabbed the bed posts like a sailor aboard a tossing ship and hung on for dear life. Behind me I could hear the workings of his juicy hand job—*flick, flick, flick, flick, flick, flick*—like a woodpecker against a beech tree. Fast and furious he worked himself over, and then he directed the hard tip into me.

"Get it in the right hole," I warned. All my desire had evaporated.

"Don't worry!" His voice was as high-pitched as a cat's.

He stuffed it inside and then went to work, banging me as though he was pounding a fence post into the ground. My guts shook with the force.

Geronimo! Yee-haw—ride 'er, Cowgirl!

I gripped the bed, buried my face in the pillows like an ostrich, and pointed my ass in the air. What an embarrassing position. Hated the doggy thing. Hurry up and get it over with. Then, suddenly, it dropped out.

What the hell?

I turned over. Bob had sat back on his haunches and was frantically working his penis again. He was sweating profusely trying to get it to cooperate. He couldn't maintain an erection for the love of me or God.

"It's okay, Bob. Let's stop already. I don't mind at all. Maybe we can try tomorrow." His face was red, his hand foamy from the scads of lubricant. His dick hung, mopey—a wrinkly worm. With a set jaw he muttered, "Why does it always *do* this to me? Seems every time I begin to develop feelings for a woman, my dick does a number on me."

In a way, I felt flattered. "I think I may feel love for you, too, Bob. Let's forget about it for now—give the poor thing a rest. Soon you're going to rip it in half. Let's wait until tomorrow, but I have to get you to the airport by eight a.m. for your nine o'clock flight. Come on—put your head on my shoulder, and let's watch TV."

He kissed me lightly, and that's exactly what we did.

Early Monday morning I slipped away to feed the animals before climbing back into bed for our final love-making session. I curled up against Bob and wrapped my arms around him.

He stirred, rolled over, and kissed me, smiling.

"Make love to me," I whispered.

I reached down. He was hard. With a confident smile he raised up on his hands and mounted me, directing himself inside.

I moaned. "Oh, Bob. You make me so horny. I want you."

He began to move, slowly at first, his eyes slits, his lips tight, a look of concentration on his face. I moved with him, toward him, and moaned.

And then it fell out.

Suddenly Bob sat up and then threw himself back onto the bed. "*Damn*."

"What?"

He was gripping his head in total frustration—a painful grimace beneath his hands.

He said, "I can't take it when you *talk*."

"*What?* You don't like when I whisper your name?"

"No. It disrupts my mental state."

"*Oh*." My eyes were wide. "I thought men *liked* to hear their names uttered during sex." I paused. "Sorry."

"And the angle's not right!" He was clearly irritated.

"*What angle?*"

"Where my dick enters you. Last night during the doggy position, the angle wasn't right either, and it's not right now. That's why I lost my erection. Your legs are too long."

"*My legs are too long?*" I was puzzled.

"Yes. That's right. It puts the angle off. That's why I fell out. And that's not all either."

"*What else is there?*"

"You try to take over the sex act!" He was massaging his brow as though easing a migraine.

"*Huh?*"

"When you wrap your legs around my waist,

you're trying to take over, control everything. I don't like it."

"I wasn't trying to *take over*, Bob." I was matter-of-fact. "But I won't do it again. You want to try again before we need to leave?"

"*No. I can't.* Ya know, I'm an older man, and I *can't* be expected to be rock hard anymore. Your pussy is so frickin' tight I have a tough time getting my dick into you. You can't expect me to be so *hard*."

I can't help my pussy's tight, either.

He jumped out of bed and sauntered down the passageway. He was done.

I shouted after him, "Well, what do you wanna do—drive a *bus* into it? *You* need a frickin' *cave* to fuck. Then, once you get it in there, you're not going to *feel* anything!"

I was done, too.

While he dressed and performed his morning constitutional, I lay in bed shell-shocked. I felt overwhelmingly undesirable and inept, like some kind of sexual neophyte, which I guess, technically, I was after all these years of inaction. But I thought men liked a woman uttering their names and wrapping their legs around them. I thought they liked tight pussies, which, by any analysis, would give them more friction and sensation down there.

Tears welled as he went downstairs to gather his things. What was wrong with me? First Lance and now Bob.

You are the Queen of Impotence, Ginnie. The frickin' Queen of Impotence. Karma, baby. Inviting a complete stranger for a weekend rendezvous? What woman with any sense or decency would do that?

Then all the ugly memories of Jack and Lois came flooding back. I felt sick, sick at what I had done to them, and, then, looking around me, I felt sick at sight of my disheveled bed—sick at what I had become.

I finally got up and dressed. Downstairs I grabbed my keys as Bob stood, his overnight bag in hand, stolid and serious in the doorway. He thanked me for a nice weekend, and I motioned to the car. Then I drove him to the airport, stopped the car, and without so much as a good-bye kiss, said, "Here ya go, hot stuff. Have a good flight back. And don't let the door hit you in the ass."

As I drove toward home, I put my head out the car window and shouted.

"Next!"

Chapter Sixteen
A Mountain High

Back home from the airport, I took stock of myself—my needs, my motivations, my past behavior.

Let's have a review today, class. Now, just what is it you want out of life? Do you just want men to fuck, or do you want love?

As I sat on the swing with Selena, I answered aloud. "I want to fall in love with a kind, attractive man, one who really loves me for the special woman I used to be. I want him to put me above everything else in his life, love animals, and country living. And it would help if he had a job."

Where was I going to find someone like that at the age of damned-near fifty? Though I did look between thirty-five and forty-five, the real number followed me like a haunt—a member of the Medieval team. Maybe Jack was right—no man in his early to mid-forties would want me. Did I really deserve love? Seems I had fairly many faults, the chief one—betraying my best friend. She had loved me once—no doubt she hated me now.

I had made a fistful of mistakes in my online dating experiences, one of them being too sexually enthusiastic, too available, offering myself as more of a door-prize rather than making them earn my love and sex. *Bingo.* Even though I knew better, I was a sexual

239

push-over. Deep down I knew men didn't fall in love through sex. They fell in love because they felt emotionally connected to a woman.

Course: Intimacy 101. Grade: F minus. Summer school, Ginnie.

My morale floundered in the pits—lower than whale shit. I tapped out Charlotte's number on my cell phone.

"I am a colossal failure," I wailed. "My friends can't trust me, and I *truly am* The Queen of Impotence. I'm destined to be...ah...ah...a piece of unpopped popcorn."

"What?"

"You know—an old maid."

Charlotte scolded me in a stern voice. "I'm coming over there. We need to talk."

****

My self-described epithet, "The Queen of Impotence," had been a standing joke between my friends and me after Lance had left. The separation had so demoralized me I decided to reveal the dark secret plaguing our marriage for twenty-eight years—I had been a sacrificial heifer to an impotent husband.

The announcement couldn't have left them more stunned. "Lance and you didn't have sex for the past sixteen years? That's so abnormal it's bizarre." But my friends were even more astounded I had never had an affair or sought a divorce myself.

"Yep, that's right," I said feeling like an ass the size of Kentucky. "He is a very *im*-po-*tant* man. Not that he didn't *want* to do it with me, mind you. Oh, he *wanted* to make love to me, all right. But Lance can be a pretty obsessed, anal guy. When his dick decided—

one time—to pitch a fit, it refused to cooperate thereafter. His cock fucked him over every time—as contrary as a miserable teenager."

"Well, how does he do it, then, with Yvonne?" they had said, incredulous.

"Back in 2001 when he had problems, they had few sex pills. I have no doubt he's using ED drugs now. But I know better. The Pillsbury Dough Boy has nothing on Lance 'cause Lance is the biggest softie going. You could've twisted his dick into a pretzel."

When Charlotte pulled into the driveway, I had barely given her enough time to exit her car before I burst into tears. "What am I going to do?" I moaned. "My legs are too long for sex. I take control during the act. I can't keep my big mouth shut while a guy is trying to come. And worst of all—my frickin' pussy is *too tight*. What am I supposed to do about that? Use my boot stretcher?"

"You're not using a boot stretcher, for Christ's sake."

"I'm doomed.*"*

"Hold on there—too long legs?"

"Yes. They threw the angle off, he said."

"The angle? What angle? Who said?" Her brow furrowed. "Too tight a pussy? You take control during sex?"

"Yes, evidently. 'Cause I wrapped my legs around him. I guess kinda like a baby possum clinging to the bottom of its mother."

"I thought men liked that?" Her mouth hung open.

"Yeah. I thought so, too."

"Boy, you can't do anything right, can you? Who's telling you this shit? The Bob character, the one from

Iowa?"

I looked down at my feet. "Yeah, Bob. He couldn't keep a stiffie. It's all my fault, I guess. Just like everything else probably is—the end of my marriage, the destruction of Jack and Lois. Everything. I'm like the community terrorist. Mayhem follows wherever I go.

"I'm more depressed now than since Lance left— lower than a hole within a hole. This Bob thing sealed the deal. I feel so undesirable, like a pox. I'm so stressed out I feel about to blow an aneurysm. I'm about to detonate, Charlotte. Talk to me, girlfriend, before I tear open a cuticle." More tears welled as we walked to the swing.

Charlotte sat beside me. "Listen, sweetie. Not a man alive takes responsibility for his own sexual problems and other inadequacies. They grow and function in a cocoon of sorts—all charged up with themselves and their transformation into what they think will be the handsomest, most macho butterfly of all time. The trouble is most of them remain in the pupa stage, and we know that's not nice. Then, when a woman, like a giant bird, comes along, they blame her for pecking at them. They can't admit they are nasty, wormy things anyway and deserve to be eaten.

"Just look at Lance, for Christ's sake. Said he couldn't stand your personality. He had you so blind-sighted you went to a shrink to see if you had a personality disorder, for Christ's sake." Her tone became sarcastic. "He had only been married to you and living with you—not even with one evening apart—for twenty-eight years! All of a sudden he couldn't stand your personality? Big red flag there, honey.

"And what was the real reason he left you? He was having a *stinking* affair with his office housekeeper. *You* are the one who should've had the affair after all those years of putting up with his gumby dick! Now it sounds like this Bob guy has a pissed-off penis, too, he can't control. What is it with men and their dicks?"

She thought for a while, and I shook my head.

The answer to that question would make the entire world a different place, Ginnie.

Suddenly Charlotte lit up. "I'll tell you what. Men's cocks are like animals. Alligators, rhinos, monkeys, horses, even cats and pigs react according to instinct and momentary need. They're rebellious, all existential creatures. And penises are *no different,* all with *minds* of their own. Did you notice how *little* those heads are in comparison to a real human head? Some are as small as soda caps. That's the first clue as to why men react the way they do. It's because their cocks have no brains, have no connection to their skull brains. And they have a limited vocabulary. They only know one word—pussy. And one other word—get."

I laughed. Already Charlotte was easing my pain.

"Yep. Not a whole lot going on in those tiny heads," I said.

We laughed.

Charlotte continued, "So, Ginnie, don't blame yourself. Sure, perhaps you shouldn't have had this Bob come for a weekend visit, especially so soon on the heels of the Jack and Lois fiasco. You were lonely and feeling lousy about Lois. You were looking for comfort and attention from someone you didn't really know. And maybe a shrink would suggest you dove into this guy to punish yourself, too, because a weekend rendezvous with a total stranger can't possibly work for the long-term. You can only get hurt doing that. You can also contract a disease. At least you asked for health papers—good move. You're smart, Ginnie. Deep down you had to know it would be a disaster. Still, *his* problem is not *your* problem. Don't ever forget something. *Men are jerks*."

I sighed and nodded appreciatively.

"And just for the record about your not being a friend to be trusted. You've always been there for me. You helped me bury my dear dog when I couldn't even think straight—you came with a pick and shovel and dug that hole like a man while I could only watch and sob.

"Give yourself a break and stop beating yourself up over what happened with Lois and Jack. You've apologized to her incessantly, only to receive a hate letter in return, which she probably wrote in a drunken rage. You tried to get the two of them back together again, but she refused to forgive him and take him back. And you haven't seen or been with Jack since the incident. You tortured the shit out of yourself afterward, working yourself to exhaustion. I was so worried about your having a stroke or something the way you were beating yourself up. So, you've paid your dues. Get over it."

I wiped tears on my sleeve.

She continued. "You've been on the biggest roller coaster of your life since Lance the Lacking left you. So what if you had sex with Jack? They weren't married, and Jack confided to you he wasn't going to marry her because of her drinking. That night *he* called you three sheets to the wind. *You* didn't call him. You need to forgive yourself, once and for all. You've spent far more time punishing yourself over that mistake than any court of law would have. I think you need to learn to get over it and like yourself again."

I looked up, put my arms out, and gave her a big hug. "Thank goodness for you, Charlotte. I'll try to work on giving myself a break."

****

The following evening I was back in bed with my notebook. I sent out emails to five men. In seconds my phone was ringing. "Hello," I said in a chipper voice.

"Hello," said a male voice on the other end. "This is Bruce from, uh, what's it called? I can't remember. You know, the elderly dating site."

"Elderly dating site?" I farted a tight laugh into the phone. "Uh, I may be going on fifty, but I don't consider myself elderly." I thought about Charlotte's proclamation about men being jerks. "I'm training for a triathlon and really can't see any old men right now. Toodle-doo." I hung up. "Next!"

Earlier I had emailed one interesting male specimen who was forty-eight and had never been married. Asking him why he had never been married before was a legitimate question. He wrote, "So, why are you separated? Bitch."

Not to be out-done, I wrote back, "You're right. I am a bitch." And then I blocked the bastard. "Next!"

The following morning as I was mucking horse stalls, my cell phone went off.

It was Steve.

His voice sounded particularly sexy. "I've got tomorrow off. Can I come over? I haven't seen you in

245

so long, and I can't take it anymore. You're all I think about."

This guy is dreaming about The Queen of Impotence? Grab him and hang on like Grim Death.

"I'd love to see you again, Steve. It's been so long I was afraid you'd been run over by your fertilizer truck or something." I laughed. I was nothing if not witty. "No? That's good. I'll see you tomorrow around one."

"Sounds good. I can't wait to kiss you again."

Sunday morning I rushed around straightening up the house, cleaning the litter boxes, mucking stalls, and mopping the floors. Then I ran upstairs and began plucking a few stray hairs from my chinny-chin-chin. I removed any trace of moustache with depilatory cream, jumped in the shower and exfoliated my body with a mixture of olive oil, half a cup of sugar, and half a cup of salt. I exited the shower with red-raw skin and coated myself in a layer of horse-hoof dressing. Then I stood like a mannequin, arms akimbo, while the cream sank into my skin. Finally, I pulled on some clothes, did my hair and face, and walked outside.

I sat on the swing drinking an iced tea when Steve's little red pick-up came up the driveway. We hadn't met for so long I almost forgot what he looked like. Again, my knees felt weak when he climbed from his car—a six foot three handsome man with blue eyes and wavy salt and pepper hair. He had broad shoulders and a male-slim waist.

He strode toward me, took me in his arms, and lifted me off the ground, something Sir Lance-a-Little had never done.

He kissed me so passionately I melted into him, my body molding like candle wax against his chest. His skin radiated warmth, and though it was summertime, his intense masculinity and heat drove me delirious. We kissed for several minutes.

This time I vowed not to open myself up for sexual contact too soon. Steve and I would have to become good friends first before I'd surrender and take him inside me. The passion and sparkage occurring between the two of us, however, would make that promise extremely difficult to keep. I felt as if Fourth of July sparklers were firing from my scalp.

As we sat down on the swing with iced teas, I asked him about his summer.

"Hectic as hell." Selena jumped into his lap, and he smiled, petting her on the head. "I am at the shop at six thirty every morning, including Saturday, and I don't usually get home until eight or nine o'clock. That's why I haven't been able to call much. All I want to do when I get home is grab something to eat and crash. But now the workload is finally starting to let up."

"I'm glad. I've missed being with you. And I've missed kissing you."

He put his iced tea glass on the ground. "Come 'ere, sweetie. We've been waiting too long for this moment." And then he drew me close, staring into my eyes and then back to my lips. "Kiss me, beautiful."

Steve's mouth resembled Da Vinci's David's mouth—classical lips, so well-defined, so perfectly shaped. The teeth behind the lips were no less stellar, naturally brilliant, white as cream. Everything about him was striking. How lucky was I to have attracted this forty-one-year-old man? After all, I was eight years older than he, even if I did look like other women his age. Do men really enjoy the company of older women?

247

I couldn't exactly qualify as a cougar since he was already in his forties. On our first date I had asked him if my being that much older bothered him. "Not at all." He smiled. "I'm in search of true love. Age doesn't matter. I want the right woman—sure don't want to do it all over again."

Then he kissed me again, his lips soft but firm, pressing against mine, orchestrating the kiss so that my lips opened in sync with his. Then the maestro slipped his soft tongue inside my mouth, and I relaxed, taking him in, inhaling deeply to taste his breath, his moistness, his excitement, his good, warm male smell. Intoxicated, he wrapped his arms entirely around my back and drew me closer than ever. He lifted and turned me toward him so that I was nearly sitting in his lap like a small child in his arms.

For at least an hour we kissed and held each other, making up for lost weeks, lost passion, lost companionship. He clasped my face in his hands, stared into my eyes, and drew an imaginary line down my nose. He traced my jaw line, all the while staring intently. He reached across and kissed my neck, sucking, and licking until goose bumps paraded up and down my arms. When he paused, again to look, to analyze my reaction, my desire, I returned the favor, licking an ear, nibbling on its lobe. I whispered his name. "*Steve.*"

Unlike Bob, Steve appreciated my murmuring his name. He was erect, and from a few glances, I could see we would fit like a plug and socket, his plug having both exquisite length and breadth and my socket being tight and well-adjusted. But this time I vowed to take my time. If I wanted this to last, I had to make that emotional connection before the act. I was like Jerry's friend George, who decided one day, to do everything contrary to past actions. Yes, this time Ginnie was going to wait—she didn't know how long yet—to make love to this remarkable man. Steve would have to tame his hard-on—keep the lion in his cage—until he loved Ginnie the woman. Later he could take her to bed as Ginnie the lover.

Yet, as our kisses became more and more voracious, I had some doubts I could last. This very conundrum surely plagues older daters, especially men whose sex drives had matured at age seventeen and whose best erections typically resembled day-old Jell-O. For men a sexual encounter amounted to a dash to the finish line before their cocks lost enthusiasm and went mopey, heads hanging.

At what point do mature daters have sex? Most agree that no specific number of dates or passage of time should determine when two people "get it on." A better gauge would be the level of connection and attraction. And most would say each partner should be within the same comfort zone of approachability, each according to his or her own needs.

Accordingly, age usually affords people certain qualities young people tend to lack, i.e., wisdom and self-understanding. Young people are neither wise, nor are they aware of their true needs and natures, though they may certainly think so. Most mature daters have already tired of playing games. Paved over by mates of the past like pitch over cracked macadam, they seek honesty and authenticity from a partner. Most know what they want from a relationship. Along with age usually births wisdom and the ability to allow a relationship to develop naturally without rushing things and without evidence of desperation. They are more able to go with the flow and do what feels right, considering the other person's relationship history and that elusive sense of connection.

After what I'd been through so far, I could open my own therapy school—Intimacy Instruction for the Sexually Inept and Insane. I would be my first patient, and everyone could call me Zelda.

Above all, older daters tend to search for themselves in a potential mate. For instance, if they value their own independence and ambition, they seek those qualities in the opposite sex. If they have thick eyelashes, they may value fluttery eyelids over straight teeth. The older, more self-confident, financially-established person will value those same qualities in a mate. We seek our twin in the opposite sex.

"Let's go inside," Steve whispered. He stood up. His erection in his pants had become insistent.

I stayed put. "I can't make love to you yet, Steve, as much as I really want to. When we have sex, I want you to want Ginnie, only Ginnie. I don't want to lose us to passion. I want to express my love for you, too, in the same way, to appreciate the man, Steve, before I make love to him. Let's go, instead, for a hike behind my farm, can we? It's beautiful back there, and we can talk."

He smiled. "I thoroughly respect your decision. In fact, I was hoping you'd say that."

"Good. I really like you. I don't want things to get screwed up between us."

We drove the golf cart out through the recently-cut alfalfa fields until we came to the edge of the woods where the bridle path started. Once on foot, the path would take us up and down wooded trails where deer and turkey gathered. The woods grew verdant this time of year, the wild honeysuckle scenting the air—the perfect place to build a romance.

We climbed the first hill, hand in hand. He told me about his first marriage of seventeen years and the reason he had left his wife—diagnosed with schizophrenia. His second wife died a year ago from leukemia. In the lousy economy and while his second wife lay dying in his arms, he lost his plumbing business. For a while, he told me, all he had had to eat was buttered noodles. He struggled with poverty and starvation but had recently begun to claw his way back out of the hell hole. Things were finally starting to look brighter.

"It must be hard for you to begin dating again since your wife died," I said. "I'm so sorry about that. This dating at an older age is a little baffling for me, too. After what you've been through, you might worry about losing another woman to disease or divorce again. Your life hasn't been easy."

"No, it hasn't been. I've had a rough time of things lately. My solace is my two grown daughters. Mandy just got married, and until she and her husband get on their feet, they're living at my house. They keep the loneliness away. Of course, I love my job. Can't get any better than being outside in this beautiful weather, helping out the farmers and stuff. I have a few friends, too. As a matter of fact, a very good family friend and I are going out to dinner this week. I'm excited about that."

"When you're going through a divorce or getting

over the death of a spouse, family and friends are key to keeping your sanity," I admitted. Then I told him all about Lance—*all about him*—Sir Lance-the-Least.

For two hours we hiked the woods behind my farm. We talked, we stopped to kiss, and then we headed for home. At home he helped feed the animals, and then we cooked up a light dinner.

By the time he left, I already knew Steve was quite different from all the others, particularly Lance, Jack, and Bob. He knew how to behave with a woman. It came naturally to him. When we were eating dinner, he held my hand in his, stroking it while looking into my eyes. He had me mesmerized, his light, blue-gray eyes piercing, intent. For those moments he was the Earth, and I was his Moon. He inhaled my beauty, my femininity. I felt his attraction to me right down to my toes.

Steve was an easy date, too. No stewing about what he thought of me, if he thought my chin hung a bit slack or if he had noticed the dark spot newly erupted on my cheek. His glance, his words, spoke volumes. He cherished me; I knew it. I needn't worry or doubt him. I needn't ask. An intensity emanated from him as he stroked my hand, my back, as he leaned toward me, the only woman for him.

Not only was his undivided attention very flattering, his complete admiration allowed me to see myself in a different light. Perhaps I really was the beautiful woman he was so mesmerized with, not only on the outside but on the inside as well. Our conversations that afternoon and evening spanned religion, education, relationships, needs, and desires. Our discussions had been both accepting and revealing—deep, thoughtful. He liked the person whose name was Ginnie. And, for sure, I liked the man whose name was Steve.

Before he left, we hugged and kissed in the kitchen. Again he drew me closer, tighter. No one had ever held me so tight. With my head leaning against him, his soft heart became my cushion, his strong chest my steady anchor.

You're falling for this guy, like a sinker into a quarry. Be careful. Ginnie's falling in love.

****

My girlfriends approved of my taking Steve slowly, "one step at a time."

"Don't hurry the sex," Sharon warned. "It'll happen when you're both ready. And don't forget to use protection. You don't know how many women he's been with—really."

"I don't think that many. His wife died last year of leukemia, and he's been too busy with work to have dated much."

"Well, mind-reader, you don't know for sure. Buy a stash of rubbers at the drugstore, just in case."

"I think he might be an Extra-large. Do rubbers come in different sizes?"

"Ya know. You're showing your age when you call them 'rubbers.' The proper term is *condoms*."

Before Steve came to visit the following Sunday, I drove to Walgreens. I had never had to purchase what seemed to me a rain slicker for a penis before, and I wasn't looking forward to it. But my eighty-two-year-old mother flatly refused to do it, so I had no other choice. Perhaps I could just slip in, grab a box, run it up to the register—hopefully with a female clerk—and have her quickly take my money before anyone noticed.

Of course, buying a box of rubbers would never be that easy for *me*.

When I sidled up next to the condom display, a myriad of choices vied for attention—ultra-thin, encased in its own lubricating fluid, extra-sensitive. Having the condom station so close to the prescription desk wasn't very comforting either. There I stood, Ginnie Snow, an almost fifty-year-old woman of the Cro-Magnon era—perusing the condom section instead of the incontinence aisle where she belonged.

I looked around. No one. I squinted, leaning closer to the display to check each box for sizes. One box had "Magnum" written across the front. How apt to name a rubber after gun ammunition. I discovered much later that "magnum" referred to the larger size and really meant "bigger" which, necessarily, in the world of sex, always means "better." "The Missile" or "The Torpedo" or "The Washington Monument" would've been better descriptive names.

One thing shocked me—the prices were outrageous, especially for someone like me who, in order to save money, made her own ketchup and poked the dirt out of vacuum cleaner bags to reuse them. I looked around again. Still, no one watching. Good. Perhaps Dollar General would have cheaper ones.

You get what you pay for, Ginnie. Just get *a box, for cryin' out loud.*

I picked up the ultra-thin condoms and searched both ends of the store for a female cashier. One stood, register ready, up front. As casually as I could, I tossed the box of condoms on the counter, along with a pack of gum. Yeah, gum and fresh breath came first, and if I was lucky, the box of rubbers would be next.

You're dreamin', girl.

I handed her the twenty dollar bill, and the young woman returned four dollars. She stuffed the box in a paper bag, tore off the receipt, and stuffed it inside the bag. With a quick "Thank you" she turned to the photo machine and began to extract pictures from it.

"That's it? That wasn't so bad." I walked proudly to my car. Too bad they didn't have my favorite nasal spray. The pharmacy at the other end of town would have it.

Empowered, I drove to Rite-Aid. I walked inside, and right there, inside the doorway, sat the condom display. I stopped to check the prices.

"Eight bucks!" I yelled. I gripped the box of rubbers in horror. The twenty-something male clerk looked up, startled, and I shrank toward the Gatorade display, the box hidden at my side. When I got to the laxatives, I felt more in control. I examined the box. I was right. This box had the same number of rubbers and was *half* the price as the one I had just bought across town. I couldn't afford to just throw away eight dollars on marked-up condoms. Returning the first box, however, would be excruciatingly embarrassing.

I faced a conundrum—take the money hit on the more expensive rubbers and be out eight bucks, but keep my dignity intact, or demand my money back on the first box and reveal myself as an old woman with the sex drive of a hamster.

I took a deep breath, grabbed the cheap box of condoms and bought it, forgetting all about the nasal spray. The very situation I had initially dreaded was about to happen. In a small town pharmacy where everyone knew your name, I had to return the first shittin' box of rubbers for a full cash refund. I already felt like a scuzzball for having purchased them in the first place. What turned out, initially, as an easy deal morphed into an excruciatingly miserable one.

I walked into the first drugstore again where eight people stood in line at the only active cash register. I got in line with my package and waited…and waited. In the long minutes I waited to return my frickin' box of rubbers, five other people queued up behind me, which meant they would be privy to my return.

I contemplated walking out. Instead, when it came to my turn, I took a deep breath and made my annoyance clear to the same young girl who had checked out the same box a half hour ago. "I want my money back for these rubbers. The very same ones—ultra thin—are at Rite-Aid for half the price. I'm not paying double."

I had no idea what the people in line behind me were thinking. I heard a snicker. Then, all became as quiet as moss.

The cashier replied in a nonchalant voice, "Oh, I know these are very expensive here. You might want to try the Christmas tree place in the mall by the airport. Their condoms are really reasonable."

Did she have to say "condoms" so loudly?

She gave me my money, took the box, and shoved it to the side. I muttered a quiet "Thank you" and bolted out the door.

****

Steve phoned every evening. He remarked how much fun we had on Sunday and how much he enjoyed the walk in the woods. He mentioned he loved kissing me, too. He had gotten a particularly big thrill riding on the golf cart and next time wanted to ride the horses.

The following Sunday we drove to the Catskills to hike a trail. This would be a good test. If he had any doubts about being with an older woman, I could allay them by proving I had the stamina and aerobic capacity to climb a steep mountain in record time. If I had any luck, I'd beat him to the top where he'd be so impressed with my fitness level, he'd ask me to marry him on the spot.

So, dressed in hiking clothes, we drove toward Cairo. On the way to the mountain, he agreed to stop at a bar for a quick drink and an appetizer.

We split a chicken quesadilla, and I ordered an iced tea. Steve, however, sucked down two pints of beer in a half hour. Though I could have warned him loading his stomach with that much booze probably wouldn't be conducive to climbing a mountain easily, I didn't want to nag. All I said is, "Remember—we will be hiking up the side of a mountain in twenty minutes." And to that he smiled and ordered another pint.

"I'm in excellent condition," Steve bragged. We began the first ascent up the mountain. "I love hiking, don't you?"

"Oh, yes. I really do. You can get such a good workout and do it among nature—can't beat the combination." Lance and I had been to Kaaterskill Falls many times before. I knew the unmarked paths in much of the Catskills as well as I did those in my own woods. I also knew the climb up the mountain was quite steep and physically taxing, especially for the unfit or unaccustomed. Still, Steve was used to physical labor— he would do fine.

Not even a quarter of a mile up the boulder-strewn path, Steve began to lag. Ever vigilant of companion hikers, I asked if he was all right.

"Just fine, sweetie. Just fine." His cheeks puffed out. He was struggling. "You go ahead. I'll be right behind you."

So, I kept the lead, mindful of the load of beer and quesadilla that had settled in his guts like a load of concrete. This hike was no walk in the park. His body would be taxed inordinately, both with trying to digest the booze and supplying a good amount of oxygen to his heart. Luckily for me, the hike proved me his physical equal.

Several times he had to stop. While he struggled to catch his breath, I contemplated a rock or a pile of moss. Hauling himself up another path of boulders, Steve was visibly taxed. He couldn't understand it. "I *really am* in decent shape." His cheeks were blown out with exertion. He was huffing and puffing. "I'm so embarrassed." I told him it was the beer making him sluggish, and I absolutely believed he was in far better shape than what he was demonstrating at the moment.

Finally, we reached the lookout from which hikers enjoy a stunning view of the length of Kaaterskill Falls and the surrounding mountains. Once Steve had caught his breath, he climbed onto a huge boulder and marveled at the panoramic view. "Oh, God—it's absolutely beautiful." He pointed out a hawk flying well below us, probably hunting fish over the river. "This is just awesome and well worth the torture getting here."

"It's one of my favorite spots on earth. Would you like to take a short walk to a rocky out-cropping? Not many people know about it, but the view from there is even more striking. We can have our picnic lunch there."

We hiked toward Kaaterskill High Peak and Round Top Mountain until we found Hurricane Ledge. "Here it is." I ran to the massive rock, which had been carried and stranded atop the mountain by a glacier eons ago. Hanging three thousand feet over the forest floor, this was the perfect place for a romantic picnic.

I invited Steve to sit beside me while several large birds, though mere specks below us, glided, intent on hunting. Steve gaped, awestricken. "It's absolutely beautiful here. Thank you for this." He looked at me. "Thank you—for you."

"You're very welcome, Steve. This was worth the climb, wasn't it? No other person around. Like we have the entire mountain to ourselves. It's as if this boulder was made for us to enjoy together."

"I can't get over how awesome this is. Look, do you think that could be a bald eagle?"

"I don't know. It's too far below us to tell."

He turned, took my face in his hands, and kissed me. "You are so beautiful, Ginnie. I really, really like us together."

Chills rippled along my arms. He liked us together. Wonderful.

Don't spoil things, Ginnie. He's falling in love. All you have to do is be yourself.

We sat together on that boulder for two hours. We kissed, held each other, and watched for birds of prey coursing the drafts along the mountainside. Steve leaned against me, and I wrapped my arms around his chest while he put his face in the crook of my neck. The trust, the vulnerability emanating from him was as natural, as sure, as the natural scene surrounding us. For the moment we sat, entwined, enjoying the fresh air of the mountains and the scent of each other.

Chapter Seventeen
Gone

Steve and I soon became an item. On Sundays we were like a couple of characters from *The Real McCoys.* We weeded chickweed from the garden, chain-sawed brush from the woods, and mucked horse stalls. In the evening we rode in his little truck through the countryside, finally ending with a drink around the fire pits at The Cork and Corkscrew. He loved taking scenic country drives in his pickup, and I enjoyed his *drivin' Miss Ginnie.* I was proud of my catch and rapidly falling in love.

As for Steve, he was equally smitten—obvious as we went about our chores. His love burned in his eyes moments before he threw down his shovel and caught me up, laughing, in his arms. Then he kissed me, his lips firm, his tongue soft, loving.

"You are a master kisser," I told him.

"And you. You amaze me. You are a fabulous kisser. I never knew kissing could be so erotic."

My decision not to have sex too soon was paying off with big benefits. One of those was developing a true appreciation for the kiss. Had we jumped right into the sack, the kiss would've probably taken a back seat to our pulsing sex organs. With that knowledge stirring my imagination, I envisioned a cartoon fit for a porno mag in which the two most revered and superior sexual organs—the penis and vagina—are caricaturized. In the cartoon a penis wearing a white fedora is driving a van. Its skinny little arms have a firm grip on the steering wheel, and its crack of a mouth is turned down on one side into a scowl. Beside him in the passenger's seat sits a huge, fleshy vagina wearing a pill box hat with black veil. And strapped into the back seat like two little kids, ride a set of lips and a tongue, both wearing sneakers and brandishing lollipops. And the bubble above the penis says, "I want *quiet* back there—no backseat drivers! Your mother and I are driving the bus, kids."

So, in delaying the co-joining of pussy and cock, Steve and I allowed our mouths the fullest expression of love. Really, when it came right down to it, French kissing—really good, intense French kissing—was tantamount to sex. Not inferior to regular intercourse, kissing was all about moisture, penetration and intense touching with one's tongue and lips. With it came no less moaning, no less desire, no less satisfaction. The added benefit for Steve was not only could he enter me with his tongue, but I could penetrate him in return. Kissing became our extreme sport in which the ability to realize love actually was much better served by mouths rather than by standard sexual organs.

Kissing, somehow, perhaps because our lips were located closer to our brains, made us more aware of our feelings for each other. Each could breathe the other in, inhale the essence of the other. I tasted the farmer in Steve, the earthy soul who preferred walking through an alfalfa field to watching a football game. When he kissed me, he smelled the good, distinct scent of horse on my shirt. He stared into my eyes and recognized the creativity brimming. The kiss, the grand maestro of sexuality, conjured closeness and connection as no other sex act.

Still, no matter the luxury in the kiss, instinct drove the inevitable. Even though our kisses were intense, highly erotic and sexual in themselves, we were fast guided by the larger organs driving the passion bus. And one Sunday evening as we stared into each other's eyes, we knew it was time.

The afternoon before that inevitable evening, we had taken a ride into the Catskills, finally ending up at Upper Ulster Lake where we walked hand in hand along the water's edge. We laughed so hard as the wind pushed us along, as though to hurry us toward something more spectacular and far more urgent. As usual, we talked and giggled, flirted, and told each other private stories to which no other was privy. Then, at the lake's edge, we jumped to a large boulder, and, surrounded like a tiny island, sat down and opened up our picnic basket. We fed each other garlic-stuffed olives and drank wine from plastic bottles as the waves lapped along the edge of our rock.

I felt Mother Nature most certainly approved our relationship which seemed as authentic and real as she. Together, Steve and I were a reflection of all things earthy and grounded, as Nature herself. When we played outdoors together, not unlike wild creatures under her watchful presence, she deliberately encouraged us with her own natural beauties—a waterfall, a secluded wooded area, a mountaintop with a view—all with the idea of leading us toward a larger sensual experience. Together Steve and I had become a microcosm of the natural world—our playing in the woods and along the lake stimulated us, subliminally, into believing we were as natural together as two deer in a woods.

That evening after we fed the animals and walked back into the house, we stood in the kitchen and smiled. As I looked into his burning blue-grey eyes, I knew he loved me. While I put away the picnic leftovers, Steve came behind me and wrapped his arms in a solid hug. His hands skirted my breasts, and his arms locked across them. We stood "spooning" in an upright position. I leaned back to lay my head against him, but before I could, he kissed me voraciously on the side of the neck. Goose bumps sprung wickedly across my shoulders and down my arms. I yelped.

Eyes closed, I turned, and he took the cue, sucking up a small triangle of skin. I shrieked again, and my knees collapsed, nearly sending me to the floor. With a laugh he caught me. Then he turned me toward him and kissed my neck like a man possessed.

"I want you." My voice was weak, gasping. "I love you, Steve."

He looked hard into my eyes. "Make love with me, Ginnie. I need you." He slowly slid a hand down the front of my pants but paused before my doors, awaiting the invitation. "I want you more than you'll ever know."

"Take me—all of me." I squirmed under his touch. For a moment I recognized the cliché, yet it wasn't cliché, for I did want him more than I had ever wanted any man.

We didn't even have time to make it upstairs, so fast, so furious our minds and bodies were colluding toward the consummation. The clothes flew, littering a trail into the living room. Then, breathless, we stood, holding each other, naked, in the dark.

"You're so incredibly soft." He stroked the skin along my arms. His eyes were slits as he consumed me visually. "You're so hot, Ginnie. Oh, God, I want you so much!" He moaned.

"Oh, *yes*," I panted, kissing his mouth. "I need you, want all of you—inside me."

I gasped at sight of him naked. His body was exquisite, like Michelangelo's *David*, his erection huge, eager, crimson. Then I took him in my hand, looked down at his glorified attention, and then the oddest sensation overcame me. I needed to taste him there, to take into my mouth the length and breadth of him. So, I led him by the hand to the couch. He leaned over to kiss me, but I stopped him. He looked quizzical, but I merely smiled.

"Sit down, sweetheart," I said. "I want to pleasure you."

Then I slipped to the floor and softly spread his legs where I knelt as though praying to a god.

Steve's cock stood at attention—swollen-wild. I looked up at him, his eyes wide and sparkling, his lips drawn into a flattened "O" as he stared at my up-turned breasts, my slim waist and flat belly, my angular hips. Before him, at the altar of exquisitely sculpted maleness, I said a silent prayer and fisted his penis.

With one hand on the shaft, I began to lap my ice cream cone, slowly first, then, luxuriously. Head back, Steve groaned, his breath hissing through his teeth. The performance of oral sex, done under the right motivation and direction, is no less than an art form that, ideally, builds toward a symphonic climax. It must be executed perfectly. Remembering back to the book Sharon had given me, *Any Woman Can*, I traveled to the most sensitive side of his organ—the underside. There, right beneath the head, I flicked my lover lightly, as a banjo player strumming his instrument.

With that Steve yelled. "Good God, girl, you're killing me! You're driving me *wild*." His eyes shone wide, disbelieving the myriad sensations coursing through his member. "Ah, God. It feels *so* good. Dammit, Ginnie. I love you."

As thanks for his declaration of love, I lapped him with brush strokes of the most sensitive, careful artist, stroking and sucking in one rhythmical motion, my mouth and hand working together in a symphony of movement. Then, with my left hand I lightly cupped his balls and began massaging them.

"Oh, jeez. I'm close to coming, hon. He gasped, his breath shallow. And I want to come inside you, in your pussy. I want to save it for you, baby."

With a few more flicks to the underside of the penis and a few nibbles to the head, I sat back on my haunches. "I'm ready, Steve. Take me, baby. I've wanted you for so long."

He leaned forward, his eyes flames now, enfolded me in his arms and stretched me out on the floor before him. His ice-blue eyes were burning so brightly, watching my naked body writhing toward him under the dim light of dusk, I thought he might self-combust.

In another second Steve mounted me, his erection raw, insistent. Then he took a deep breath, leaned toward me, and guided himself with his own hand, into me. I winced as he entered my ring of fire, strung tight as a tambourine. I concentrated on relaxing that part of myself to allow him in, but he was so large even my releasing the tension did little to ease the delightful pain. I felt like a virgin.

"Easy," I whispered. "You're an awfully big guy. Let me adjust to him."

"Whatever you need, baby. I don't want to hurt you."

He eased into me and then pulled back a little. We needed no lube, the two of us as wet as oceans for the other. Finally, I was able to relax enough to accommodate his girth. With knees bent, I began to slowly move against him.

"To the very tip," I gasped. "I want to feel all of you, Steve, driving inside me, slowly. Let's watch our bodies moving, enjoying each other—watch you move in and out of me. I want to see him disappear and then reappear."

"Yes, Ma'am." He groaned and smiled. "Aa-a-a-ah, you feel so good around me. Such a tight, wonderful pussy you have."

The rhythm was slow, the thrusting deliberate and deep. Then he moved more shallowly within me in order to nuzzle my breasts. He scooped one breast into his mouth and sucked hard against it as he drove deep back into me. I arched against him, deeper, and he cried out. I wiped away a drop of saliva at the corner of his mouth and licked it from my finger.

For perhaps two minutes we moved in sync, like musicians in a symphony orchestra, and I watched his slim waist and his groin area moving, rolling with me, watched as his muscles rippled with the force, as he drove forward then back, forward then back in a most natural rhythm. I watched, awe-stricken, as he withdrew his penis to the head and watched as he drove it inside again. I could hardly breathe so exciting was the panorama of our sex, and with each stroke I tightened my pussy harder around him

For several minutes I watched him, consumed, his eyes aflame with the sensation of me, and then, suddenly, I noticed an abrupt change in his demeanor. The flame in his eyes turned to embers and, then, suddenly, snuffed altogether. Like a black hole—a bright star collapsing into itself—the fire in Steve's eyes had moved inside himself and lay burning somewhere in his mind. In his ecstasy his eyes looked vacant, like that of a blind man who "sees" within, staring more within himself than at the outside world. For all purposes, Steve had left me. He was momentarily *gone*. His sexual fire raged in another world, in another dimension.

At the exact moment when I detected the vacuous look in the eye, our rhythm increased. His mind, his urgency, had, indeed, taken him to an otherworldly place, a place where no one, no outside sound or stimulation, could disrupt the sexual sensations consuming him like a conflagration. He was for the moment, *gone*, absent from the room and totally within the vestibule of himself and overwhelming sexual passion.

Though his energy, his force, had left, his body remained with me, moving, thrusting, urgent, driving toward climax. Knowing he was close to release sent me toward the edge of my own ecstasy.

I resisted the urge to cry out as something in me was drawn tauter than an archer's bow. Steve's delirium was titillating, his absence a measure of his having turned inside himself to enjoy with purity and without distraction, the imaginary sea of female pleasure and ecstasy. I delighted in his vacant moment, loved that I had caused him to disappear inside himself. He needed me, needed to escape the real world and fly on sexual wings, on the wings of love, to another place and time.

At the same time my own climax was building. I was still with it, not as gone as was Steve but felt myself rising higher, lighter, like riding a gondola from a hot air balloon. Orgasm was unfamiliar to me, thanks to Lance, but I had the feeling I was being stretched toward something rather spectacular.

Oh, Goddess on Olympus. Don't tell me we're about to come! Hang onto your shirt, Ginnie!

Suddenly a tsunami shook my insides. I shrieked, and, with that, Steve's eyes fluttered. He witnessed my moment, and that was all it took. Back arched, he drove himself hard into me, a singular pressing into me, propelling his sperm as deep inside my body as his ancient male ancestors had fashioned him.

I felt his surge, the pumping inside me lasting for probably a full minute. Then, with a great outward rush of breath, he collapsed in my arms and buried his face in my neck. I kissed his moist forehead, his eyelids, his nose and ran my fingers through his hair—my precious gift.

But his orgasm hadn't ended. The second coming was almost as earth-shattering as the first. As he lay, spent, in my arms, his whole body began to shudder. I had never experienced such a thing with any man. What must have resembled bolts of electricity coursing through his body lasted for two or three seconds followed by stillness of about seven seconds. Then another round of trembling occurred, followed by quiet. The quaking happened about five times, and then, with a flutter of eyelids, Steve was back.

He had arrived home.

He looked at me, kissed me tenderly. "Oh, my God. That was *so* fabulous. I love you, girl. Don't you ever leave me."

Still entwined on the living room rug, we held each other as he shuddered one last time. Then he pulled out and lay on his back. He kissed my forehead and drifted off to sleep in my arms. I whispered, "I love you."

Chapter Eighteen
Whatever Comes of the Broken-Hearted?

We made love again early the next morning, and then Steve left for work. I felt thrilled, ecstatic as I waved goodbye while my lover's little red truck roared down the driveway. The following weekend's visit seemed so far away I didn't think I'd be able to survive.

Back in the house I fired up the computer. While it booted, I sat at my desk, chin in hand, thinking about Steve's and my relationship. Our connection, developed and strengthened over time, sealed us together emotionally, emphatically. Conversation between us was easy, honest, playful. Together we laughed, pleasured each other with our minds, our hands, our lips, but, mostly, our hearts. Sex between us was exquisite—at times both slow and intense, sensual and playful, tender and rough. Love became the driver of our sexual energy. For sure, I was done looking for a mate, and I was pretty sure he had found his one-and-only, too.

Each day during the work week we texted each other—snippets of caring and protectiveness. We flirted with each other, had true oral sex—texting sexual innuendos to each other—verbally professed affection for each other in as many different ways as was possible. We were in love.

While he worked in Connecticut spreading

271

fertilizers on farmers' fields, I sat at the computer in Climax, New York, a nearby hamlet of Coxsackie, putting the finishing touches on my farm animal advocacy manuscript. Creativity burst easily from within when my heart was calm, loved, self-assured. Steve's admiration for my writing gave me the ambition to produce more on behalf of the animals who sacrificed their lives for human dinner plates.

Love and anticipation for the weekend became the catalyst for ambition, not only in my writing, but also in every other aspect of my life, too. Like a person on steroids, I not only cranked out poignant pages describing the farm animal's plight but also ramped up my farm work—gardening, riding the horses, tending the landscaping, and fixing fence. Love had energized me in all respects. In turn, I loved not only Steve, but everything in my life, even the reckless drivers I met on the road. Being in love had a way of mellowing me out, perceiving life through rose-colored glasses. Similarly, in other ways it slowed me down, allowed me to appreciate a tender moment with one of my animals. It allowed me to smile at annoying people and their habits. Love had transformed me into a teddy bear.

By the sixth month, the two of us were true partners, as close as a couple of rectal polyps. We couldn't keep our hands off each other. The energy between us smarted, it was so keen, so over-powering. We even had to laugh at ourselves, at the quickness in our steps, our enthusiasm for the world around us, our need to be within forty feet of each other at all times.

Then, one Thursday before our up-coming weekend together, Steve hadn't called, as usual, to firm up our plans. I brushed it off—he was probably busy at work. Besides, our relationship had become so solid, so habitual at this point, he probably considered his visit a "given." I'd just wait for him to show up, as usual, Friday evening.

Before he arrived that Friday, I busied myself dusting, washing the bed sheets, sweeping the barn, and cleaning the house. Then, I ran upstairs, showered, did my hair and makeup, and put on a pair of black jeans with a pretty turquoise top. Blue was Steve's favorite color.

Later that afternoon when I heard his truck's familiar purr up the driveway, I smiled, sipped the last of my whipped-cream-flavored vodka, and uncrossed my legs. My prince had arrived. The engine shut off, and I could already feel the goose bumps erupting on my arms and down my legs.

As he strode down the stone-path leading to the front porch, I stood up to greet him. He took me in his arms and kissed me. I kissed him back. "Yum. I love you, Steve. You're home, baby." We had always kidded he was home—no matter where he was—as long as he was with me.

He turned away and sat down on a wooden step.

I looked at him, still smiling, unaware.

"We need to talk, Ginnie." His eyes avoided me.

I stared and bit my upper lip.

He wiped his brow.

I stepped up to him, touched his cheek. "Okay, sweetheart. Is something wrong?"

"A little bit."

"Talk to me, honey." I held his hands.

"Could I make myself an orange vodka first?" He got up and nearly ran into the house. Moments later he appeared, glass in hand.

"What's going on, Steve? Is something wrong at work?"

"No." He took a large gulp of his orange vodka and tonic water. "I feel really bad about this, Ginnie, but I swore I'd always be honest with you." His face looked gray, his eyes empty.

No. I don't want honesty. I just want us—forever.

My guts twisted inside me.

"Remember a few weeks ago when I told you I was meeting a family friend for dinner?" He was still looking down at the porch.

I took his chin in my hand and made him look at me. I looked into his eyes, searching for my Steve, the one who loved me more than he did himself. "Yes," I remember," I said. I heard my own lifelessness echoing back. I felt sick, wanted to flee.

Oh, Ginnie, my love, I'm so sorry!

"Well, that family friend is a woman. Her name is Jill. I've known her for thirty-three years. And, well, I've always had a crush on her. I've been wanting her since I was eighteen-years old."

"Oka-a-ay." I gulped. Somehow I knew this was not going to turn out in my favor. "What about her?"

"That night when we met for dinner, I told her I was in love—with you. Then she told me her husband had been cheating on her. She is getting a divorce. At that time I hadn't thought too much about it because, for all these years, she has never encouraged me in any other way other than just as friends."

"Yeah. So, now she wants you, right?" I was nothing if not perceptive, a master of human motivation.

"Yeah. She called me this week and said she wants to be more than just friends." My heart quaked, and I put my hand over it.

Dirty bitch. Kept him hanging for all these years until Ginnie appears. Rotten cunt.

My innards were wound as tight as violin strings, my teeth and jaws set, my mind reeling. My hands curled up into fetal fists. I felt instantly nauseous awaiting his answer, which I already knew.

"I hate doing this to you," he said, looking down and petting Selena.

My heart split open. I was bleeding inside.

I wiped away a tear. "Go ahead, Steve. Spit it out already. I already know what you're going to say."

He couldn't even look me in the eye, this man who, only weeks ago, had professed his undying love for me. He stood, now, disconnected from all we had shared for the last six months. Had this woman the power to snuff all that out during one dinner meeting and one phone call? Could our love have been so superficial, so tenuous as to be destroyed so easily?

"I've *got* to go for it, Ginnie," he pleaded. "I'm so *sorry*. I never wanted to hurt you like this. *Never* wanted to. But I've been chasing this woman for thirty-three years. She's finally giving me a chance now."

My heart lay in pieces somewhere alongside my bladder. I felt faint, sick inside. My eyes were welling with tears, but I blinked them back. Then, in another moment I found my former self, my pre-Steve self. The hurt morphed into anger. How could he *do* this? He's jeopardizing our love because of a fantasy he's been chasing for thirty-three years? Totally bizarre.

I couldn't contain myself. Despite the knot in my

stomach, I laughed—the laughter of mockery. The guy I had fallen hopelessly in love with had finally shown his true colors—as stupid, as clueless, as a stone.

"*Wonderful*! Just *wonderful*," I shouted. I blinked furiously. He looked at me, shocked. He had never heard me speak in a sarcastic tone. "For thirty-three years—*thirty-three fucking* years—you've been bearing a torch for a woman who has kept you at arm's length, a woman who refused *you* in order to marry *someone else*. Are you *fucking* nuts? Have you no self-respect?"

Fuck, too, the renowned internet relationship counselor whose tips I had been following for months. Her advice—speak to your man according to how you honestly "feel," but never be accusatory. Use "feeling" terminology and resist blaming your lover. Instead of saying, "You make me so angry because all you do is think with your *little* head instead of your *big* head," say something like, "I'm feeling anxious today. I feel as though we aren't communicating well. What should we do about that?" She warned men don't take well to criticism, so avoid using the word "you" in any conversation in which you are unhappy with your man's behavior.

Fuck her and the ship she rode in on!!

"*You* are a total *ass*," I said. I lurched toward him. He backed away. "Can't you see what happened here? Have I meant nothing to you? You are a complete, unadulterated *jerk.*"

Go for it, Ginnie!

His shoulders sank. Then he chugged the rest of his drink.

I sucked in one long breath and filled myself up like a blow fish. My hair stood up on my head, and I stepped forward, took his face in my hand and squeezed until he looked me in the eye. "Have you no self-respect, pursuing a woman for thirty-three years? One who married, not you, but *someone else*? Now that she's being dumped, you're finally good enough for her?"

He disgusted me. Truly.

Then I acted the part of Jill talking to herself in a moment of self-reflection. I mimicked her in a high desperate voice. "Oh, poor me. My husband is cheating on me, and I feel lower than a turd from a titmouse. I feel fat and homely as a halibut now. Woe is me. How could I possibly feel better about myself? I know. I'll go yank Steve from under that rock where he's been lurking for the last thirty-three years. Steve'll make me feel like the Queen of Fucking Sheba again!"

Steam was pouring from my ears.

"And that's exactly what happened, didn't it, Steve?"

He looked at me with a pained expression.

"During that bogus friendly dinner date, you told her you had moved on and had fallen in love with someone else. Then, after being dumped by her husband, she found herself about to lose the only other guy who ever wanted her. Don't you get it? She reeled you in, not because she loves you, but because she couldn't bear the sight of herself without a man."

He looked down again, his shoulders slumped.

Any love I had had for him ran right out of me like imaginary diarrhea. I felt hurt, angry, and betrayed, all over again.

"Don't look *down. Look* at me!" He reminded me of a bad child and I his scolding mother.

On the outside I was as angry as a wild boar with hunted babies. Deep inside, however, I was broken-hearted, hurt beyond words. My knees struggled to hold me upright. I wanted to collapse into a sea of tears. I also recognized my wrath would not dissuade him from that woman. Likewise, I knew no amount of my understanding his situation, no amount of reasoning, cajoling, pleading, or crying was going to change his mind, make him see things rationally or in a clearer light.

In fact, nothing would persuade him in my favor because Steve, though he stood with slumped shoulders, was, literally, on top of the world. The woman of his dreams had finally given him the go-ahead. Finally, his fantasy could be realized. He was like a prisoner sprung from jail, a young man who finally got his muscle car after being disappointed for the previous twenty Christmases. As I stood cawing at him like an angry crow, I had, even before he arrived that day, become negligible to him. Though he had been brave enough to tell me this in person, he was not sorry, at all. Inside he was ecstatic.

"I'm so sorry. I didn't want to hurt you. I never wanted to hurt you," he said, shaking his head.

"Well, it's too late!" I hissed, my wings flapping. "I *am* hurt. *Excruciatingly* hurt. I'm confused. And *disappointed in you*. I can't believe you can write us off so easily. Ya know what? You don't really care we're done because you're so full of yourself right now—deep down—so ebullient over this Jill dame because she has finally seen the light that is Steve, right?

"You are a fool, Steve, for letting yourself get sucked in by this woman. For heaven's sake, she *didn't* marry *you*—she *married* someone else."

I looked at the sky, shaking my head. I wasn't finished, feeling driven to clue him in on some facts. "Do you know anything about the way many women think, Steve? Do you really know?"

He looked at me and shrugged his shoulders.

"Well, I'll tell you. Women want what they think they *cannot* have. Yvonne did it, too. Yes, that's *right*. Throw yourself in front of a woman, and she won't give you the time of the day. Be hard-to-get, and suddenly she can't live without you. They know how to manipulate men, and the men are too stupid to see it. Women are masters at burning their cupcakes and eating them all, too."

He looked at me, his eyes set. The spark that had been there for me was gone, sapped dry. Any ounce of love he had for me was gone. My fury had destroyed the last drop

But I didn't care.

Against the advice of that internet relationship counselor and with the knowledge that no amount of understanding or forgiveness would ever bring him back to me, I let him have it. Why? Because it made me *feel* good. That's why! In his heart he belonged to Jill now. I was a cast-off.

I couldn't contain myself. I would have my day in court. I made a proclamation, eyes blazing. "For thirty-three years you *wanted* her. You allowed her to reject you every single, solitary day you were pining away. You were right there, curled under your rock, hoping she'd look under it and take you out to play. But she didn't until a few days ago, when, feeling rejected herself, she peeked under that rock and discovered you were gone. Like a starved thing, she called you back, and you came bounding back, tongue lolling like a beaten cur."

I sighed, spent from anger, trying to control the urge to cry. "And now I'm an even bigger fool for thinking you actually loved me, as you told me. The sight of you sickens me now."

"I really, really *like* you," he said. His was a school boy's voice.

I cringed. Then I pointed to the door and said quietly, "You need to leave."

His shoulders slumped. "But I don't want to leave. I'll stay the night and help you with chores tomorrow."

I snorted. "Are you crazy? That's *not* going to happen. I can't stand the sight of you, looking as though you're so damned sorry you've hurt me when I know full well you are so frickin' happy—giddy, really—because this Jill has *finally* given you the green light. You've been wanting this woman for thirty-three fucking years? You aren't sorry at all. You're fucking *ecstatic*. You need to leave, Steve."

"Can I get a few of my things from upstairs?"

"Yeah, take it all. I don't want any reminders."

"I'm really sorry. I really am…"

"Just get out. Take your sorry ass and get out."

He went inside, gathered his toothbrush, high blood pressure meds, and the pin-striped black shirt I bought him for his birthday. I stood, my teeth and jaw set, my arms folded across my chest. With his paper bag of stuff under an arm, he opened the door to the outside.

Please don't go. Please don't leave! I loved you. I so loved you.

"Good-bye, Steve," I said.

"I didn't want it to end this way."

"Don't let the door hit you in the ass."

He left.

I walked, numb from my head to my feet, to the large chair in the living room. Then I burst into tears.

An hour later I went to the bathroom mirror. My undereye circles shown a keen purplish-red, my hair disheveled. I looked as though I'd been in a car accident. I washed my face, put on some make-up, styled my hair, and put on a different set of clothes, ones that were body-skimming and sexy.

I looked in the mirror, sniffed back tears, and quietly said, "next."

****

On the elderly dating site once again, I posted another gaggle of pics—my puckering up an imaginary kiss to an admirer, my sitting, smiling, on the grass surrounded by a slew of cats, my posing, model-like, before my front door—all very flattering pictures of myself. In a few hours my inbox lit up with an entirely new group of men. The gallery pages of older gentlemen from the dating site smiled at me like jolly suspects in a line-up. One guy whose face was turned down, eyes closed, looked as though he was in a deep sleep or a coma. Three others wearing tight head scarves and black leather jackets sat proudly astride their "chrome turds." Another held a huge, probably smelly, fish at chest height. Those I deleted with no sense of compunction, as well as the guy singing at a karaoke bar. A guy playing a piano I saved as a "favorite," and I "favorited" another one holding his cat in front of a Christmas tree.

I was becoming a bit gun shy after Lance's

unfaithfulness and that unexpected rejection by Steve. In fact, both had demonstrated how easily a man could throw away a woman he claimed to love, like a used oil rag. In the beginning, I wasn't carrying any broad-based bitterness toward men in general. When Lance had walked away from me, I attributed our problem to his and Yvonne's selfishness. Compared to the amount of baggage other divorcées were dragging around, I lugged little more than a change purse.

However, with the Jack fiasco the change purse morphed into a handbag. With the Bob weekend, the handbag transformed into a suitcase. With the Steve thing, I felt as though I were dragging around a steamer trunk the likes of those sunk with the Andrea Doria. I had more baggage than Beyoncé prepares for a month-long trip to Bali.

With some trepidation I sent off an email to the self-described cat man.

Chapter Nineteen
Next!

Cat man and I met at the Bonefish Restaurant in Coxsackie the next Saturday night. The good, clean smell of the Hudson River enveloped me as I drove into town. He had a table reserved when I arrived. A nice-looking man with a respectable job as director of information technology for a small business, he was a chatterbox when it came to his four cats—how mischievous they were, how Toughy awakened him each morning with a bite to his ear, how Waxy begged for treats, and how he managed the litter box cleaning schedule. I imagined him naked and holding a pooper-scooper. My interest perked.

You thought other women were threats? Wait'll you meet his cats. They'll scratch your eyes out.

After the third public date with Evan, I suggested he make the hour trip from Dalton, a suburb of Pittsfield, Massachusetts, to see my farm. As he stepped from his car, my own curious cats, like a gaggle of Wal-Mart greeters, trotted over to him and sidled against his legs. I fought my way through the pride of felines and offered him a hug. But instead of taking me in his arms, he skirted past me and launched himself into the bevy of mewling beasts.

My cats are expert at detecting a cat fancier, and they had immediately sniffed Evan out as bait. In minutes cats swarmed all over him like maggots on a carcass. As he sat on the grass among them, twenty-some cats slinked and sidled against him, along his back, against his arms and legs, some crawling into his lap and kneading on his stomach, others creeping up his arms and meowing into his face. Evan was in heaven, but I found it all as entertaining as *The Autobiography of Benjamin Franklin.*

That evening Evan and I grilled a couple of steaks in the outdoor kitchen. Afterward we went inside to watch a movie, and Selena immediately planted herself in his lap, thus making any romantic involvement next to impossible. While he cooed and stroked her, I clasped a pillow and focused on the TV. After the movie, he yawned and said he'd better be going, and, then, without a good-bye kiss, he got into his car, reached down to pat Kramer the cat good-bye, closed the car door, and drove away.

The next time Evan came to visit, I had forged a plan for myself. If he spent more time talking to my cats than me, I'd put my paw down. I was not about to take a back cushion to the Boots Brothers. Who needed a purr-fect lover anyway? All I wanted was one that noticed me.

As usual, after dinner we retired to the living room where I'd hoped he'd kiss and cuddle with me enough to provoke a hard-on. After all, nothing is more flattering to a woman embraced by a man than feeling him swell his pants. Fuck any comments from a man about my beautiful eyes or hairstyle. When it comes to dating, talk is cheap. A growing erection is the ultimate compliment.

Wishful thinking, however, was just that—a

fantasy. Instead of taking me in his arms and holding me tight against Sir Surly, Evan ignored me, instead baby-talking to my silver-tabby, Lillikins, and scratching her luxuriously under the chin.

Hey, Idiot. You've got another pussy dying to be scratched here. And that one can offer you something in return.

Instead, Evan chattered on about his own cats and stroked Lilli into feline ecstasy. The drone of his voice made me almost cat-atonic. By evening's end I had had about enough. Would he pay attention to me if I coughed up a hairball? With late evening approaching and the "I really should be going" comment imminent, I put my plan of attack to the test. With one swipe I elbow-blasted Lillikins out of his lap and onto the carpet where she landed with a thud. Then, with a heated, sultry look, I leaned toward him and proffered my lips.

Instead of melting toward the human temptress by his side, he was shocked. With a frown he began to scold me. "Hey, don't be *mean*. Lilli just wants lovin.'" He retrieved the cat, put her back in his lap, and apologized by way of giving her a full, fifteen-minute feline body massage. Then he uttered the inevitable "I should be leaving." As usual, I walked him to his car where he climbed inside and started the engine. I stared, transfixed like a haunt, as he smiled from his car window.

Five dates, and he's afraid to kiss you, Ginnie. This guy's got to go.

Evan put the car in reverse, but before he could go two feet, I wailed. "Do I have bad breath or something?"

As though I had hit him with a cattle prod, he threw the car into park, leaped from the vehicle, grabbed my shoulders with both hands, and planted a hard, quick kiss on me. Then, he jumped back into his car. It hitched backward, and he sped down the driveway.

I stood as dumbfounded as a cantaloupe.

The next weekend he came bearing gifts—for the cats. With delight he fed treats to the cat swarm meowing at his knees. Obviously this date was going nowhere—again—so I went into the house and stuffed myself with Doritos. Other weekends passed similarly, and I soon began to believe he was visiting me only to see my cats.

Each date passed similarly—no more than dinner and a few pecks on the lips for me while my cats lay like so many demanding Cleopatras in his lap. The cat immersion seemed almost like a religious experience to him, the transfiguration of the tabby trinity. When he and they had their fill of each other, he excused himself and headed for home.

Finally, I had had enough nonsense. After dinner the following Friday night, I sat next to him and again knocked Lillikins out of his lap with a well-aimed elbow-swipe.

"*Hey*, what'd you do that for?" he yelled.

"Damn it, Evan. I can't take this anymore. You can't make love to a cat, so wake up. You're in the presence of a beautiful, entertaining woman. Pay attention to *me* for a change." Then, I sidled, cat-like, next to him and began opening the buttons on my blouse.

He stared at my looming breasts, and then he

brought me to him and began to kiss me with an open mouth. I took him in, coaxed his tongue through my lips, and then he took in a hard breath and held me close. *Finally.* He was a tiger, his kiss ravenous, devouring. Surely this was not the same Evan, the hard-mouthed, virginal, harried kisser of prior dates. This one was eager for me.

I reached down, and he was hard as a baseball bat. Then I slipped my blouse off and watched his reaction. He glanced down, saw my breasts cupped in a sexy white-lace bra, and suddenly his eyes grew wider than Lilli's. He slid his hand slowly around my waist and then moved it toward my chest where, once there, he moved the bra away and sucked a nipple into his mouth.

I squeaked like a mouse, and he pounced again, playing with the elusive breast, swatting it back and forth with his face and biting it, pinning down the elusive creature. And I squeaked again and writhed from under him.

"Wanna go upstairs?"

Evan, not much for words except while conversing with one of my cats, growled. "I want you."

We slinked to the bedroom, and I first undressed him and, then, myself. I handed him a rubber, which he dutifully put on his erection, and then lay on the bed with a come-hither look "Come get me, King of the Jungle."

With that he leapt like a tomcat on a female in heat. He was wild for me. Biting my neck, he hung on so hard I'd swear a bloody mark would mark the spot the next day. I lubed his member, and he mounted me with a curdling howl. His ferocity made me hiss with delight

287

as he entered, his back arched, his teeth bared. I clawed his rump like a wild thing as he drove hard into me, back and forth, rhythmical, deliberate. Then I drew my legs around him and snarled as he came inside me, pumping his all inside my precious pussy.

In that moment he roared. "Oh, God. You are beautiful, Ginnie. That was *terrific*."

"You're not so bad yourself, Tiger," I said with a smile. And in the spooning position we fell asleep until the next morning.

Evan stayed the weekend. The sex was pretty rabid, and he was likeable enough. What it did for me, more than anything, was affirm I was still desirable. The Queen of Impotence melted away like Oz's wicked witch of the west. Evan's manhood stayed interested and attentive toward me and my pussy for the entire weekend.

Ding dong. The Queen is dead.

Through the next month and more, Evan and I were fast becoming best friends as well as lovers. After a while his love for my cats impressed me as a positive thing, along with his sexual stamina. Unlike Lance and Bob, Evan got it up at the mere sight of me a hundred yards away. I walked around very sure of myself and my ability to cause swelling. Evan had spit at the Queen of Impotence, and she had slinked, beaten, away. In her place erupted the Vixen of Virility.

Still, we didn't just stay in bed like a couple of lazy cats. We took a day and drove to the beach, hiked a mountain, chain-sawed a bunch of broken branches on the farm, and attended summer festivals hand in hand. Love between us was growing much like one of the seedlings in my garden, every day growing even more.

Unlike the love-at-first-sight thing between Steve and me, Evan's and mine was developing slowly, steadily, more assuredly with every meeting.

One day we decided to make a bucket list. Since we were older daters, we had a number of things we both wanted to do before the Grim Reaper came calling. Evan wanted to go on a tropical vacation, and I wanted to go to the local water and amusement park. I booked the flight to St. Lucia, and he paid for the house on the ocean. We were giddy at the thought of snorkeling and drinking piña coladas and getting caught in the rain.

Evan bought tickets for the water park, and though he couldn't go on any circular rides forcing a stomach roll, he loved the roller coasters and all the water rides. That day we both felt like kids again. In particular, we loved the Lazy River. We floated down the lolling stream of water in a double-holed inner tube, holding hands, and avoiding the overhead waterfalls and other watery obstacles. We came home that afternoon exhausted but happy and hopeful for a long-term relationship.

The next evening, sitting alone in the living room, I opened my computer. An email from Evan. I glanced at its length before reading. What could he possibly have to say he couldn't have said yesterday at the amusement park? As I read, my guts began to twist. Though he had begun on a positive note, referring to our fun day at the water park, the tone of the message shifted quickly to a somber one. He commented on the growing seriousness of our relationship, the excitement he felt, and where he saw it leading him. Because he felt himself being pulled so strongly toward me, possibly even falling in love with me, he had to think rationally about the situation.

He continued, saying though he loved my farm, agricultural living was not his lifestyle. He definitely loved the cats, especially Lillikins, even though she was a bully to the others. The real issue that plagued him, however, was the distance between my home and his work. He could not envision himself driving an hour to and from work every day. Knowing I loved my farm and couldn't live in a suburban development like his, he saw no way around the circumstances. He thought it better we separate before becoming even more emotionally involved with each other. As was Evan's style, he was very rational and collected about his assessment of things.

And as was my style, I was not.

"Fuck you, Evan!" I shouted to the ceiling. "You could have at least *called* me to discuss this, not done it through email."

I beat out a response on the keyboard. "You sent me a Dear Jane email? *Coward.* We spent the whole wonderful day together yesterday, and you couldn't so much as phone me to talk about this?"

I waited fifteen long minutes but got no response.

I phoned him. I would not let him get away with dissing me in an email. He would have to face me.

No answer. When the tone sounded for me to leave my message, I didn't stifle myself. "You dump me in a frickin' email? How could you? Selena and Lillikins hate you now. I paused then hit him with the worst news. "And so does Kramer!" Then I hung up.

I sat, tears near to erupting but sniffed them back, set my teeth, and deleted his email.

"Next!"

****

One would have thought my online dating was proving a disaster and I should have taken Lois' advice months ago to set up a tent at Wegmans in order to meet single men on the prowl. "But they're at the grocery store to buy fucking *eggplant*, not pick up a *woman*, for Christ's sake," I had said. Maybe she was right.

Back to the computer I went. After all, I had met and dated around ten men so far, all found on the internet dating site for people forty years and older. For the most part, I had picked nice, friendly guys. None had been really nasty, except maybe for that high school disciplinarian with the cobra tongue. No serial killer had snuffed me out. No one had even closely resembled Ted Bundy in appearance or emotional instability. They were all normal guys looking for a decent woman, so long as she was a knock-out and sported big tits. Other than that, they all wanted to develop a serious relationship with a really nice lady.

I did meet the occasional man sent my way by well-intentioned friends. One of those was Raoul. I met Raoul at Riverside Park in Climax where we fed the ducks and sat on a park bench and talked. He told me I was beautiful. I politely disagreed. He said all the right stuff and delivered one hell of a French kiss.

My friend would tell me later he was smitten after just the first date. Thereafter, every day Raoul texted and phoned me. He was like a druggie needing a fix.

When we met a second time at an Italian restaurant, I asked him how old he was. He said he was thirty-three.

"*Holy shit*. You're just a baby!" I was horrified.

"Oh, no, I'm not. I'm very mature for my age. Age

has no relevance as far as I'm concerned."

"I'm fucking *fifty*," I said. "You're way too young for me. Why don't you find yourself a nice, young, tight-assed chick?"

"I've always been attracted to older women." He smiled.

We walked to the parking lot, and he opened his car door for me. Then he suggested we just sit a while and listen to some Latin love songs, chill out.

My friend said he was always a gentleman and not a serial killer. "Well, I really think I'm too old for you." I climbed into his SUV anyway, and he closed the door.

"Stop saying that. You're beautiful. You look thirty-five at most."

"Well, that's very nice of you, but the fact is I am seventeen years older than you. Do you even know who the Beatles are? We wouldn't have anything in common to talk about. You're from a different generation."

"Cut that out. Age makes no difference to me. I'm attracted to strong, independent women, and I find you fascinating. You've been through so much, yet you've survived admirably. For instance, you've conquered that ass-hole husband of yours."

"I appreciate that."

"And I can compete with any of those geezers you may be attracted to. Look at my package." He pointed to his crotch. "It's pretty amazing, don't you think? Can beat any of your fifty-year-olds." He was smiling like a proud father.

A package, huh? I looked down and smiled dutifully at his crotch. It looked as if he had a large bag of plums stored there.

"Very appealing," I agreed without embarrassment.

"Nice, indeedy. I see he prefers hanging to the left. Must be a liberal."

"Yes, he sure must be."

We laughed. There was a long pause.

Lance's abandonment had left me bereft of carnal knowledge. I totally believed I had probably re-grown my hymen much like an unused ear-piercing closed shut. Virginal once again in mind and body, I felt as though I wore a dunce cap shaped like a penis head. But my recent dating experiences had graduated me to the top of all genital graduates. I was fast becoming an authority on anything penile.

Raoul continued to persuade me over to his youthful, virile side. "Would you like to see him?"

I choked, and my breath mint landed in my lap. "I'm sorry, Raoul. I can't do this. You're a great guy, and you do have a very nice..." I paused, searching for the word, "*bag,* but I'm just not interested."

"*Package,*" he corrected. He looked annoyed.

"Sorry about that. Your *bundle* is really big. Anyone would love it. I'm *sure* even I would. But you need someone younger."

"*Package,*" he roared, scowling. He got out and came around to my side of the car where he opened my door like a true gentleman. I slid out, walked to my car, and got into the driver's seat.

When I pulled away and drove onto the road, I opened the windows and sang, louder than any bagpipes.

"Ne-e-e-ext!"

****

My mother and I had become like sisters after Lance left me. She was as devastated as I had been by his betrayal. When I told her I had sacrificed my sex life for him and that he had not had sex with me for sixteen years, she was astounded, almost speechless. "That was no marriage, you poor thing." She vowed to make my transition to independence as easy as possible and help me find a suitable male companion. That included accompanying me to the local country club to check out the action.

So, my mother and I sat at the bar one evening sipping wine when I spied a rather decent-looking specimen talking golf at the other end of the bar. I smiled, and he smiled back. Aaron, the bartender with whom I was good friends, asked me how my day had been.

"Terrific." I ignored the hoard of men talking loudly about their huge clubs, their scores, and the sixty-ninth hole or something like that. "This afternoon my girlfriend and I went out for a ride on my horses."

"Oh, great day for that," Aaron said. "This is gorgeous riding weather."

The men were listening now, eavesdropping, all talk of golf at a standstill.

"Yep," I said in a calm but strong voice. "My horse is a stallion. Today I had a *real* man between my legs."

With that the room got coldly, suddenly, still. Then, as the remark sank in, the men erupted in laughter. I laughed, too. I'd like to see any of those sissy club-swinging men ride and survive a ride on a goofy horse like Barry. My mother snickered. And suddenly, the good-looking gent motioned for the bartender to buy the two of us drinks. In another minute he had planted himself on a barstool next to me.

I thanked him for our drinks, and for several

minutes we traded barbs, some with sexual connotations, others double entendres and gentle sarcasm. He cocked his head, looked at me as though I were a complete wonder, and then took a sip of his own drink. I sat back and enjoyed the vibes of attraction oozing from him. I let him do all the work, asking me all about my horses, my farm, the usual small talk.

He said, "Do you play golf?"

"Oh, horrors, *no*. I hate games involving a ball. Are you married?" I was nothing if not direct.

He managed not to choke on his drink. Then, he cocked his head, looked into my eyes, and with a look of confidence set his jaws. "No. Indeed, I am not."

"Interesting." My mother was stirring her wine with a cocktail straw, trying to act nonchalant, but she was bursting inside at her daughter's shamelessness.

He was smitten. "Perhaps we should trade phone numbers. I'll give you a call, and we'll go out."

"I would like that." I handed him my number on a cocktail napkin.

My mother and I ordered a light dinner of hamburgers, flatbread barbecue pizza and eggplant fries. My admirer ordered chicken fingers. Throughout the repast we talked as though we had known each other for years. He offered to buy me another drink, but I thanked him and said one was my limit. I told him I liked his personal style and found him physically attractive. He told me I was a good-looker, and I didn't argue, for a change.

Then, his face lowered. He leaned toward me with a serious expression. "I have to tell you something."

Once again an empty feeling grabbed my guts, even though they were digesting dough and fries.

He said, "You're such an honest, open woman, and I must tell you that, though I'm not married, I *am* living with someone."

The hamburger flipped inside me. I raised an eyebrow.

"Well, you asked me if I was married, and I'm not, technically. I'm really not happy with the woman I'm with. We fight all the time, and I'm looking to get out of the relationship.

I stared.

He whispered, "You and I could meet, see if we get along, and then I can leave her as I've been contemplating for months now. She's a real bitch, and we really don't get along."

"Thank you for the drinks, but my mother and I really must be going now."

He looked devastated. "Give me a call sometime, really. I like you."

My mother and I stood up from our barstools and gathered our purses. She looked expectant and finally whispered, "Well, what are you going to do?"

Then, as we walked to the door, I said, loud enough for the entire bar to hear.

"Next!"

Chapter Twenty
And the Beat Goes On

Fall was quickly approaching. A year and a half had passed since Lance had left me. I had heard, via the grapevine, that he and his housekeeper whore were growing fat and unhappy together.

Karma, baby.

Our divorce was at a standstill. I refused to accept the peanuts in support he was throwing my way, and he refused to pay me anymore. Each day I struggled to feed my animals and myself and keep the landscaping as sculptured as when Lance had been around to help. He would not best me. Neither would his relatives, as they drove past my farm, be able to gossip how I was letting the place grow up in weeds. No, sirree. I was determined to survive by myself on the farm and do it admirably. He had made me the loser in the beginning. I would not be the loser in the end.

As far as the dating scene was concerned, I felt like a teen again, but this time around was different. My teenage life years ago had been as boring as chewing cardboard—I had met Lance at the age of seventeen and never had another date. Thinking back on it, I had really missed out on dating other guys, experiencing their kisses—as different as dawn and dusk—their hugs, their different personalities, going to parties, holding hands, and having fun. I watched my girlfriends in college march off to the fraternity parties while I sat at night, ever faithful to Lance, in my dorm room. What a waste of my best years.

But that was then, and this was now.

Luckily I had maintained my shape and overall appearance through the years well enough to spark interest from the opposite sex. Every morning I had several emails from eager suitors in my dating site inbox. I perused them at my own convenience, between stall muckings, mowing the grass, and writing another chapter on my farm animal book. The world of men—at least those on the ol' farts' dating site, which is how I jokingly referred to it—seemed at my fingertips. I could pick and choose my dates according to my specifications and time schedule.

One afternoon after I had finished all my barn chores, I came inside to the computer and began documenting all the dates I had had so far. Behind each name—if I couldn't remember his name, usually I could remember what state he was from—I jotted down a few notes about the guy—if he was polite, if he had bought my dinner, if there were sparks, etc., if he had potential for a long-term relationship.

A few men hadn't liked my refusal to date them exclusively. They didn't like my seeing others while going out with them—possessive bastards. That attitude puzzled me. After all, I had joined a *dating* site, and that's what I intended to do until I had found someone who floated my boat. Those guys who took umbrage to my dating others usually said something sarcastic and alluded to my being a "game player" and not looking for a serious relationship. They could not have been more wrong.

What I wanted more than anything in the world was to discover the love of my life. I thought I had found him long ago in the seemingly devoted and adoring Lance. Who would have ever thought we'd be divorcing after almost twenty-eight years of marriage? Certainly not I. If I had been wrong about Lance—and I obviously was—then I needed to be even more careful, more analytical, more vigilant, and more discriminating in my search for another mate. I was determined not to make the same mistake twice and have that fail, too. Yes, I longed for love from a man, but it had to be the right man.

Steve had fit the love-bill in all ways—my soul mate, my partner on the farm, my lover. But, as it was with older daters, little had I known he came calling with his own baggage—a fanny pack stuffed with thirty-three years of a woman named Jill. A year later I still remembered him with fondness—how large his hands were compared to mine, how he stared deeply into my eyes, his own eyes sparkling, admiring the beauty that was his. In just a few months he had become the love of my life, but, in one ego-deflating afternoon he was gone. Gone. I had lost my second love.

So, this time around I vowed to taste-test all interested men as one would fine *vinos.* One thing was for sure. All my dates would be vintage. I just had to separate the robust, mellow, well-aged ones from those turned to vinegar.

I stared at the list of men I created. I guesstimated my total would come to around twenty or so. Beside each one I jotted a few comments, whether I had sex with them, the quality of the sex, how it ended, whether they were salvageable, whether they measured up as long-term material.

After I wrote down the obvious ones, like the guy from Afghanistan with whom I had Skyped, My Colonel, Steve, and Evan the Cat Man, I scribbled down all the other, more fleeting ones, in between. I had completely forgotten about Brian from Cherry Hill, NJ, a guy who bought grungy, worn-out homes in Philadelphia and flipped them, selling them for a handsome profit. How could I have forgotten him, an excruciatingly handsome specimen with a perfect set of teeth—always a sexy trait for me. Good lips and bright, straight teeth were a turn-on. I must have developed that fetish later in life because Lance's teeth were an orthodontist's dream—as crooked as the up-rooted fence in *The Wizard of Oz*.

Despite his beautiful choppers, however, Cherry Hill Brian wasn't really interested in me. He, much like Steve, carried within him a heart that was broken, bashed in by a ravishing, independent Asian woman. He confided she took her massage business back to China and left him behind with no more than an afterthought. He admitted, too, he had a penchant for Oriental women. He loved their looks and something else. In contrast to American women who, he felt, were too boisterous and bossy, Asian women tended to be more passive, more agreeable with their men.

It didn't take me long to figure out that Cherry Hill Brian, who got a hard-on for a subservient woman, definitely was not my type.

"Next!"

Next on the list was Roy, a recent widower, who admittedly needed to regroup and get on with his life.

His profile pictures were enticing—wavy gray hair and blue eyes. When I met him at the restaurant, he was all decked out in golfing attire. He admitted he found a woman who enjoyed golf and tennis enticing. I told him I hated any game that involved a ball. For the next ten minutes we stared at each other, not knowing quite what to say or do.

But during lunch, after I remarked I had rescued twenty-something cats from the New York City kill shelters last spring, I had my answer.

"I *hate* cats." He gagged on his salad. That confession, along with his obsession with the two most boring sports in the world, as well as his nauseatingly thick calves protruding from his golf shorts, sealed the deal.

"Next!"

Another Stephen from upstate New York had the most gorgeous blue eyes. When I complimented him on them, I expected, as a matter of course, a compliment in return. Most anything would do. "Oh, the arthritis in your pinky isn't too disfiguring." "Your nail polish matches your outfit so well." *Something*. Most anything would've been satisfactory. Instead, he remarked his blue eyes were nothing compared to his daughter's. Thereafter, the course of our conversation revolved around his daughter, Chrissy. And, just like Evan and a few others, this Stephen also hadn't the slightest clue how to talk to a woman. He rattled on and on about vacations he and Chrissy took year after year and how that had become a tradition between the two of them. They were so close I found it a teeny bit bizarre. I wondered just where I would fit in, as a budding girlfriend, in that cozy tradition between him and his love-child.

That wasn't Stephen's only disturbing trait. Quite by accident he began to recount a story of his last love. In short, he had broken off a relationship a few months ago with a woman he said he was "totally into," totally committed to but who was not "into" him. He had been living with her for four and a half years and had wanted to get married, but she turned him down—shades of Steve and Jill. As he told his story, I began to detect a slight odor of rotten eggs in the air. I asked him if his old girlfriend was dating another man now or had married someone else, and he replied she had not and was currently living alone. I asked him if he ever talked with her. They talked about once a month. They were still friends.

Right then and there, I smiled and said, "I made a promise to myself I vowed to keep." He looked long and hard as I paused, trying to come up with just the right words and phraseology. Then, leaning toward him, I said, my eyes hard, "I will not, under any circumstances, become involved with any man carrying a torch for another woman."

He blubbered over his sandwich something to the effect he really was over her. He had really moved on. But it was too late. His words fell on deaf ears.

I purchased my own sandwich that evening and ended the date.

"Next!"

I wasn't too sure about going out with Don, a football coach at a local college, simply because he was four years older than I, but he had a full head of nice gray hair and straight teeth. I could forgive his age if he were healthy, fit, and kind. Our date out to dinner at the country club went nicely except for the conversation which centered around football boot camp, an event soon approaching. During that time he would not be able to go out with anyone because he'd be too focused on the training camp and his duties as a coach.

I asked him about how his previous wife liked his football coaching. "She couldn't tolerate my love for football." He broke into a grin. "Hey, it's what I do. I love coaching football."

"Was your wife a football widow?" I casually munched a fry.

"Yeah. Can you imagine? Said I never spent enough time with her. Said I was obsessed with football. Imagine, she was jealous of a *game*."

"You *do* know I can't tolerate any sport involving a ball. That's stated in my dating profile."

He choked on his beer and looked at me. "You're very beautiful." He looked into my eyes and took my hand.

I slid the plate of fries to the side. "Thank you, I'm not, but I can't stand golf or tennis, and I absolutely *detest* football."

His shoulders slumped, and he looked out over the golf course. "I guess we probably won't work, then, either."

"No. We probably wouldn't. Let's just enjoy the rest of the night as friends and then call it quits."

"Too bad."

"Yeah, really."

"Next!"

"I *hate* games with balls!" Isaac shouted gleefully during our phone conversation late one evening. "I *never* watch Monday night football."

"That's a good start. What do you do most days?"

"I'm a volunteer fire-fighter, and I'm studying for my EMT degree. I graduate next March. Once I have that, I can get a paying job. The other thing I do is cook. I just *love* to cook. You say you have an outdoor kitchen? How about if I bring you an entire meal, from soup to nuts, and make it on the grill for you? My specialty is grilling. I'll make us a flank steak marinated in my special lime-garlic sauce. The rest will be a surprise."

"Oh, yeah, spoil me rotten, please. You will find me an appreciative gourmand."

"Huh?"

"I love to eat."

The following Saturday afternoon Isaac arrived in his Mini-Cooper. The oak trees languored under the heat in which the pines stood more resilient, but we decided to cook and eat outside anyway. I helped him cart a wheel barrel full of vegetables and the steak marinating in a plastic bag out to the outdoor kitchen. I kissed him, handed him a requested non-alcoholic beer, and told him he was just too kind for going to all this trouble. I confessed I hated cooking as much as I hated sports involving a ball. We both laughed.

"And wait'll you see what's for dessert." He turned over a piece of broccoli on the grill. He didn't wait for me to guess. "Grilled pineapple with a black pepper and pomegranate sauce. It's spectacular."

Never a slouch at any meal, I sat down at the picnic table as the birds began their evening roost flitting into the bushes and undergrowth in the woods around us. I slobbered like a wolf at Isaac's scrumptious repast and dove right in. Looking less like a "beautiful lady"—as he called me, I probably more resembled a starving Amazonian. Always pressed for time, even when I truly wasn't, I gulped my food, had ever since I was a kid. I swallowed, almost whole, big chunks of scrumptious juicy steak. Nothing tasted quite so delicious in a while. In my shark-like feeding frenzy, I forgot all about being petite and lady-like. I laughed, mouth wide-open, complimenting him on his expert culinary skills. Though I wasn't aware of any cringing on Isaac's part, I later wondered what he must have thought. I must've looked like Gulliver at a Brobdingnagian wedding celebration.

I believe, however, Isaac felt complimented by my robust eating display. He smiled as I mounded forkful after forkful of broccoli, potato, and garlic-rubbed steak into my mouth. As we ate, he and I laughed and talked, and as I went back for my third helping of steak, my appetite came to a screeching halt.

"Oh, my *goodness*." I sat back in my chair. "That was all so scrumptious, Isaac, I didn't even realize how much I was eating. I better stop before I end up with a bellyache."

"Yeah, me, too. I'll start cleaning up. You go relax inside in front of the TV."

"You're just too kind." I held my guts and hoisted myself out of the chair. I walked into the house and wedged myself into an over-stuffed chair and increased the volume on the TV.

Shortly Isaac walked into the living room. "Everything's cleaned up."

"Come sit here with me, handsome."

He climbed beside me into the one-and-a-half chair and kissed me. I kissed him back, turning my body toward him in the chair.

And then it started.

"Oh, excuse me," I said. A burp erupted from my innards.

"Really enjoyed your meal, I see."

"Sure did. It was the best. But I think I ate too much."

"We both did."

But he wasn't burping. I felt another pint of gas building inside my stomach, and then another burp—just a slight "pop" from my mouth—flew out. I caught it in my hand.

Remind you of anything, Ginnie?

When I had first started dating Lance, his mother invited me to Sunday dinners consisting mostly of pot-roasts or roasted turkeys. No one had warned me Lance's family had made belching a veritable art form. I could still remember the scene as though it were yesterday. As I sat at the dinner table forking a sliver of turkey into my mouth, a vomiting sound suddenly rocked the dining room. Horrified, I kept my gaze glued to my plate. A wave of nausea overcame me as I imagined a huge mound of vomit splashed across the dinner table. At the sight of something like that, I'd be sure to lose it, too.

So, I did the only thing I could do. I lay down my fork, allowed a few seconds to pass, and then slowly peeped to either side. No puke anywhere. I couldn't believe my eyes! Surely someone had become sick at the dinner table. I had heard it. But as I glanced around I was relieved. Forks scraped against plates as Lance's family calmly chewed, intent on their meals. I shook my head in quiet disbelief, shrugged my shoulders, and picked up another forkful of food.

And then, in another instant, the same noise ricocheted off the walls. I looked up. Again, nothing. And none of his sisters or parents or brothers seemed to notice. Had no one else heard the awful retching? Someone among us surely was sick. Yet nonchalance dominated the table.

It wasn't until later in the meal, as I was talking across the table to Lance, that I heard the vomit noise again. My head spun around like an exorcism's victim. It was Lance's brother, Jerry. "Excuse me for interrupting," he said. Then he snickered.

My burps after Isaac's dinner hadn't reached anywhere near the decibel level of Lance's brothers' and sisters'. To be sure, each one of them had perfected the art of air-barfing. I soon discovered dinnertime had become a competition as to who could muster the loudest, most vile-sounding belch. In fact, Lance's brother could even burp *without* eating. Jerry was happy to demonstrate how he could gulp air and then force himself to eructate like a cow. I found it absolutely gross, but Lance's family prided themselves on their competitive spirit when it came to oral gas emissions.

In comparison, my burps were rather silent, sounding a petite "urp" behind the back of my hand. "Excuse me, Isaac. Must be all the olive oil you were using."

"That's quite all right. You really ate quite a lot. No wonder you're gassy."

"Yes, really too much, I've come to realize."

I really did try to respond to Isaac's kisses as we sat smashed up against each other in the one-and-a-half

307

chair, but the longer we kissed, the burpier I became. I didn't want to burp in his face, so each time I blasted it toward the fireplace.

"Jeez, I'm so sorry. I feel so bloated." I was starting to feel somewhat queasy, but I couldn't let him know. Puking on one's date could possibly kill a romantic encounter. Furthermore, blowing my dinner all over the room wouldn't be very complimentary to Isaac's cooking.

Suddenly my lower belly cramped. Oh, for *Christ's* sake. Not now, not diarrhea, not while we're making out. My body rarely had mercy on me, especially when I needed it most. It'd break with the shits in the stupidest of places, at the worst possible moments, like during a hike one time at the Grand Canyon.

Another belly cramp hit. "Uh, Isaac. I must go to the bathroom. I guess your cooking doesn't quite agree with me." And then I raced for the steps and bolted upstairs.

In minutes I squeezed back into the chair beside him. I felt limp.

"You okay?" His lips came toward me for a comforting kiss, but I turned away. The last thing I felt like doing was putting something else into my mouth. For sure I'd hack my whole dinner right into his lap.

I felt another cramp rock my guts. "Oh, you dirtball body. You really have no mercy on me, do you?" I thought.

"I must run again." I raced for the upstairs.

Back downstairs, I stood in the hallway and called weakly to Isaac. "Isaac, you need to go. I don't feel very good."

He stood up and was looking strangely at me. He

looked terribly disappointed. "Guess my cooking didn't agree with you, did it? I do cook pretty rich, lots of olive oil and garlic." He reached for his bags of leftover vegetables, his wok, and cooking oil and, with them in tow, walked dejectedly to the door. "Next time I'll make something more bland. I promise."

He gave me a peck on the lips, and as he went out the door, I muttered, "I'm so sorry. I certainly didn't think this would happen. Call me again."

As it happened, he never did.

"Next!"

Chapter Twenty-One
The Penis Chart

My next prospect, Robert, was a good-looking man in his mid-fifties who stood at six foot two. He, too, sported a full head of short gray hair, and his eyes were as green as a leprechaun's. He did woodworking, a self-described wood artisan. I sent him a flirt, and he replied he enjoyed my profile and pictures. Would I want to go out?

Since we were two hours from each other, we decided to meet halfway, close to the 4-Mile Point Preserve outside Coxsackie on Route 385 overlooking the Hudson River. The next Saturday afternoon, wildlife experts at the preserve were featuring a bald eagle demonstration.

"Oh, I'd love to see that," I said.

We decided to meet, see the eagles, hike, and have a picnic lunch. I would design a couple of gourmet subs, and he would bring my favorite, a jar of garlic-stuffed olives.

The day shone brightly, and I arrived at 4-Mile Point Preserve only five minutes late. At the entrance to the information center, Robert stood, slightly bow-legged, in a blue polo shirt and a pair of cream-colored shorts. I walked up to him, smiled, and then leaned in for the welcome hug.

In my years of online dating experience, I learned a

few things when meeting a potential mate. Typically, the two parties have never seen each other, except for online photos. They are acquainted only through email or phone conversations. Some have rarely even talked before racing into the meet-and-greet. So, the problem of intimacy as well as the correctness of the greeting, including one's exit strategy, particularly dependent on the amount of "sparkage" between the two people, remains a conundrum. Whether one kisses, hugs, or shakes hands during the first few moments is entirely up to each individual. In short, any kind of touching— no matter how much or how little and for how many minutes or seconds during an online date—is a crap shoot.

Robert seemed fine with my quick, noncommittal welcome hug, and then we searched the area for the eagle demonstration. Together we sat in the crowd of bird aficionados, and he held my hand as the experts talked about the majestic creatures perched on their forearms.

"They are amazing birds," I whispered into Robert's ear. He smiled and nodded and squeezed my hand.

After the eagle demonstration, everyone dispersed, some to hike the short trail to the look-out point where everyone was encouraged to count the different kinds of hawks. Robert took out the map of hiking trails and recommended a path less traveled. "Let's hike this one. The elevation is fairly steady. We won't kill ourselves climbing boulders, and we can get into the heart of the woods and away from the crowds and kids. What do you say?"

"Sure. Don't want to hear screaming kids in such a

beautiful setting as this."

And so we headed out onto the path, one taking us out to a boulder field. We sat side-by-side on a large rock and marveled about the ferocity of glaciers and how unbelievable that frozen water could move such huge rocks. Then, he leaned over, took my shoulders, gazed into my eyes, and kissed me. I melted into his arms, the natural setting around us and the sunny day encouraging romance and playfulness. Our lips parted. "I feel something."

"You do?" I giggled.

"Yep. I think it moved."

I glanced at his crotch. "Oh, my. I think he wants attention."

"You just may be the one to give him some, someday. How do you feel? Are you interested in me? Got any sparks going?"

"Yes, actually, I do." In order to assure him, I put my hand along the back of his neck and drew him close for another kiss. We sat and kissed, our world silent except for our sighs. He rubbed my back, caressing me, and stared into my eyes as though in search of something. Whatever it was, I believe he had found it.

In an hour we were back on the trail heading back. I over-tread my ankle at one point, and when I sat down to rest, he rubbed it and expressed concern as Lance once had whenever I was hurt. Robert was kind, romantic, level-headed, and a bit shy. Happily, he was not gabby, which I found off-putting in one of the male sex. I liked my men strong, confident, and reticent, except during a romantic encounter. Then I preferred the language to reflect their attraction to me. Selfish bitch I could be.

Back at the parking area, I retrieved the cooler from my car while he found a cozy picnic table. We set the table with plastic ware and dined on hoagies, cheese nips, and garlic-stuffed olives. This time I guarded my appetite. Didn't want to ruin another date by galloping to the portable toilets.

During lunch we talked about our exes, as is the topic of conversation during many online dates. After all, almost all of us had lived through the circus and horror called divorce. What I found common to all the stories from the men was their spouses were always to blame for the break-up of the marriage. Never did any admit their fault. I couldn't fathom all the women who had affairs on their husbands, when, from what I always gathered, lotharios are mostly male.

Robert, however, didn't reveal much negative stuff about his ex-wife. They simply hadn't gotten along and had stayed together—as is the case with so many couples—for the sake of their three boys. When the youngest one began college, he felt it was all right to divorce. Robert was nothing if not kind and rational.

In a half hour we had finished lunch. We sat at the picnic table for a while, and then he suggested we go for another hike. "I really enjoyed your kisses. You're a great kisser. Would you like to go farther back into the woods to get to know each other better?" He smiled, and his voice was as soft as his light green eyes. I couldn't resist.

"I'd love that." I tossed the empty cooler into the back of my car, and we headed out beyond the parking lot and into the woods, far beyond the hiking paths, and far beyond any solitary hiker.

Finally, we stopped, and he took me in his arms,

his back against a broad tree. I reached up and kissed him, and softly he inserted his tongue in my mouth. He tasted me, inhaling hard through his nose as he drew me closer. He made me feel so desired, so protected, so sexy. And, then, like clockwork, the stronger grew his kiss, the more breathless I became. In an instant his erection grew hard and insistent against my thigh.

I drew away from his kiss and looked down. Then I looked up at him and smiled. "Thank you for your interest, Sir." He snickered. I stared down again, marveling, at the length and breadth of the erection in his shorts, "My goodness but you must be a big guy."

"Would you like to see him?"

"Here?" I paused. "Right here in the woods?"

"Why not?"

More than anything I wanted to see his manhood, feel it, see it move and squirm under my touch. But to take it out here in the woods? A hiker off the beaten path certainly would have a rude awakening stumbling upon two old gropers.

I didn't have to think long.

"Yes. I would love to see him." While he enveloped me in his arms, I kissed him and slid my hand down his pants. His swollen penis was pointing toward the West Indies, and I took the full breadth of him in my hand, mentally taking measurements, as I had with all my willing dates.

Let there be no misunderstanding—I wasn't always an easy lay. I had my standards. However, I had come from very poor, very meager sexual beginnings, as the impotent Lance's wife. Having always been faithful to my husband, from a teenager to an adult of forty-nine years, I had had a rather elementary, rather stunted development in the area of sexual experience. My lack of sexual contact, however, hadn't made me ravenous for sex. I had not turned to the promiscuous, dark side of humanity. I was no nympho. But my distinct backwardness concerning anything sexual had left me a curious woman.

Up until a year and a half ago, I had only seen two penises—my high school sweetheart's and Lance's. From what my girlfriends had said, I gathered Lance's wasn't exactly the meatiest of the meaty. From lack of exposure as a young woman, I developed a fascination about all things penile. So, when Robert had asked me if I wanted a viewing, I could hardly keep my enthusiasm in check.

With his hardness pulsing against my hand, Robert unzipped himself, lowered his shorts enough so that it popped out into the piney fresh air of the forest. The logistics of the scene struck me as totally surreal, and I snuffed a snicker. He would not appreciate my laughing at his erection, and truly, his member was truly inviting, hardly laughable. What was funny, however, was seeing an unclothed, raw penis exposed in the middle of the greenery of nature. Though it shouldn't have been an anomaly because one's sexual organ is a creature of nature herself, it was. Rabbits, deer, turkeys, insects, spider webs, and the flora accompanying the fauna are expected as part of the scenery. A raging naked cock was not.

Once I overcame the initial shock of what we were doing, I looked down and grasped the enormity of the thing as well as the enormity of this experience, so lacking in my previous life as Lance's girlfriend and wife. Before me stood the king of all cocks—a gorgeous specimen by any female's account. His length rivaled a shoe box, his width an energy-drink can. His enormous size was just the tip of the ice cream cone. The head was excruciatingly large, smooth, almost youthful, and inviting, the little slitty mouth already slobbering with excitement.

I had no other choice, could not help myself. A fleeting thought of "No, you can't. *Not here.*" shook me, but, just like that, the guilt disappeared. Literally melting into my knees, I looked up at Robert, and he saw the admiration in my eyes. He went to kiss me. Instead, I squeezed his manhood, stepped back, looked him in the eye, and licked my lips. Right then and there, in the middle of the woods with not a soul in sight, I kneeled before the Master of Men, the King of all Cocks, took the Prince in my fist and encircled that lovely head with my lips.

Robert could have rejected my advances, but I pushed on, confident I had read his signals correctly. I had. Robert placed both hands on the back of my head and drew me closer. He groaned softly as I worked him.

Oh, Heaven and Earth. Praise be to the most luscious of all manhood ever to be in my presence.

Then, as I strummed his "banjo," a pang of guilt gripped me. "What could he be thinking of me?" He groaned softly. Giving him oral sex on a first date?

Ginnie, you'll be lucky if you ever see him again. He won't have any respect for you now."

My conscience made me stop. I stood up, and his eyes fluttered. "You are one beautiful man," I said. "But I have over-stepped my bounds. He was just too luscious for me to resist." Then, I put his raging penis back into his shorts. I zipped him up and kissed him.

"I'm sorry. Please excuse me, and don't think poorly of me." Just maybe I could salvage a shred of dignity.

"I don't think badly of you at all."

"He was just so gorgeous, so over-the-top, that I felt drawn toward him in that way."

"Thank you. I take that as a compliment. I think we better go back to the parking lot before I jump you right here and now."

"Yeah, probably a good idea." And we walked hand-in-hand back to our cars where we kissed and said good-bye.

That evening I shot off an email to Robert apologizing profusely about the blow job in the woods. "I should have never done that. That's not like me at all. I'm really not a slut."

"No, I never thought you were. But, woman, you have been seriously deprived over the years. It's no wonder your curiosity got the better of you. And make no mistake—I truly enjoyed it."

With that response, I felt a bit better. He didn't think I was whorey. Good. I would be more careful next time. Another man might not be that understanding. Robert and I decided to meet at my place the following week.

****

I was in the barn feeding the horses when Robert pulled to a stop in my driveway. Striding over to him, I reached toward him, and he pulled me tight. We kissed and headed out behind the property to the woods. An hour and a half later we were back home. I offered to show him my place, and when we got to the bedroom, he sat down on the bed and patted the cover next to him.

He pulled me onto my back and all six foot two of him straddled me in a position intimating sexual desire. "I want you, Ginnie," he whispered in my ear. He began to undress me.

His Eager Eminence blossomed into the most spectacular sex spear of all. Forget Lance's self-conscious dick, this Romeo had no lack of self-esteem. He knew he was King of the Tallywhackers. And the King desired a ceremonial copulating with his Queen of Hearts.

Our lovemaking was furious, wicked. The massiveness of Sir Sirloin filled me up, and the friction was intense, all-encompassing. We raged on for several minutes, and just as I had stepped onto the edge of nowhere, Robert yelled, setting himself as hard and firmly into me as he could. He clung to me, and I squealed with delight but stepped back from the edge, totally caught up in his orgasm.

Admittedly, orgasms came hard for me, if they did at all. I was a typical woman in that I could only orgasm with someone who loved me. Without that, I could become excited enough to hover on the brink, but I could never fall into the lovely abyss. I just couldn't, not without love. Still, I enjoyed the experience immensely, more for what I did for my mate than for what he could do for me.

My greatest pleasure was watching the excitement build in the male, seeing his need for me driving him onward, faster, faster until he was about to climax. What a sight to behold. With the release he drove hard into me and held himself there, tight against me, spewing his love juices. And, though not all men shuddered immediately after an orgasm, I welcomed that vulnerability, held him while he lay spent, useless, on my ribcage. I loved his weight on me as much as a heavy blanket on a cold winter night. The male climax was so dramatic, so intense, so otherworldly, and I felt flattered by the attention and the fact I had caused it. My comeliness, my personality, my intelligence, my sense of adventure and my humor and earthiness—the combo of all of it—could take them to another place in time and space. The result was emboldening.

Afterward, Robert groaned in my ear, rolled over, and fell asleep. I smiled, dressed, and went out to feed my animals. Hours later, after we had dinner and sat around talking, he got in his car and drove home.

****

Days later I was out running on the path around my woods when overhead a *"whomp, whomp, whomp"* sounded. I had startled a bald eagle. I was so excited I had to tell Robert, so I reached into my pocket and dialed his cell phone.

With much excitement I told him I was going back to the woods to find a possible nest. I was, after all, somewhat of an expert after hearing the eagle demonstration at 4-Mile Point Preserve. Then, he asked me to wait. He needed to talk.

"Sure, what's wrong?" I was still happy as shit a bald eagle had flown overhead.

"I wanted to be right up-front about us." I detected a somber note in his voice. "I just don't feel any sparks for you."

"*Oh*?" A chill paraded up my arms. "That's odd. That wasn't the impression I got from you from our two dates. I thought you really liked me."

"I do like you—can be good friends with you. But I

just don't feel it. You're beautiful and fun and nice. It's just that there's no sparks going on for me."

I thought of his lovely dick I would never see again and wanted to say, "Did you inform your one-eyed pocket lizard that you felt no chemistry because I think he'd disagree." But I didn't. "Okay, Robert. You know how you feel. I do wish you well and hope you find a woman who gives you goose bumps. Thanks for everything. We had a couple of good times together."

And then I hung up.

"Next!"

Robert's rejection hadn't upset me in the least. I wasn't in love with him, and, though he was a sexual catch, I knew deep down we weren't compatible. Though I had felt sparks with him, my gregarious nature and ebullience overshadowed his shyness. I was loud; he was quiet. I was quick-witted; he was pondering, deliberate—a bit slow. We weren't a long-term match. Still, I felt happy I had seen his proud prick, for it was, indeed, the loveliest of them all.

Concluding I had developed a penis fetish through all my years of sexual deprivation and its resulting self-doubt, I ran to my desk that afternoon and wrote down all the names of the men whose penises I had been privileged to imagine, see and/or manipulate. I scribbled down Lance's name first, along with some negative comments. And, then, one by one, I mapped out my conquests. Any penis I had had described to me, glimpsed, given a hand job, a blow job, or full-blown sex, I categorized on an Excel spread sheet—complete with comments. Finally, I rated each one a "skill set" number from one to ten, ten being the most skilled of all. And for a woman, whose pussy, for most of its life, had been ignored, un-used, and, virtually, invisible for most of its life, a life resulting in a lack of personal and sexual self-confidence, I realized I hadn't done too badly for myself.

"*Nine penises!*" I shouted to the ceiling. "In the last eighteen months, I've experienced nine of them. I'm a *cock* professor."

And, then, like a train arriving at the station without brakes, it hit me.

"*I'm free,*" I yelled to the ceiling.

Goose bumps rose on my neck. I sat taller and squinted with a smirk at the paper. The penis chart not only validated my own desirability, my sexuality and femininity, but it had set me free. I was no longer a victim of sexual slight and inexperience. Not at all. The penis chart, with all nine cocks analyzed and mapped in an organized row, allowed me total objectivity with men. The chart equalized the playing field in this dating game. From now on I wouldn't feel indebted to a guy or worry if one might not be attracted to me, if I was forced to flatter him, watch his favorite TV shows with him, or cook up his favorite meals in order for him to want me. The penis chart validated my worthiness, my desirability. Furthermore, it revealed I was any man's equal, possibly his superior, even though I didn't have a cock of my own, because all those penises had become my subjects, my vassals, if only for a few minutes of a day or week or month. I had the ability physically, mentally, and emotionally to captivate men's most valuable, most vulnerable part of themselves—their dicks. In my hands, their cocks were helpless, putty turned to concrete. With the playing field leveled, all things being equal, I could evaluate each guy for his rightness for *me* instead of how I could be more accommodating and better for *him*.

"Thank you, Lance, you old bastard, for giving me life again." I grinned like a giraffe eating stickers. "Alongside Sir Impotence I would've faded slowly away into the vapid void of selflessness."

For an hour I sat, amused, at my desk. I finished the chart of my penile conquests, like some Columbus discovering a third world, and I was proud as hell. I looked over my diary of dicks and giggled. The memories of each one came flooding back. Which girlfriend mistakenly told me, in an authoritative voice, that all penises looked alike? Like hell they did! Penises looked as different as pumpkins in a patch. That much I knew without ever meeting any of a race different than mine. Imagine those lucky women who had *that* experience. In comparison, my nine-count cocks made me seem rather virginal. Still, I was proud—look where I had come from? Many fifty-year-old women had no interest in their husband's dicks or anyone else's dicks, for that matter. Women my age gag at the sight of an erect penis. I, however, found myself blossoming into sexuality at the ripe age of fifty fucking years old. How lucky could I be?

I sat, my chin set, my eyes merry, my penis chart in my lap. I perused the descriptions, the secret nicknames, each one's ambition or erectile ability, and the ratings and comments on their skill sets. And, yes, the nine penises I had met all had different personalities, from the most self-conscious, as was Lance's, to the most proud. Some were ravenous, as was Jack's; others were polite, as was Evan's. But they *all* had different personalities.

With my penis chart in hand, I poured a celebratory whipped-cream flavored vodka. With nine on the chart, I had finally arrived at the harbor of my own destination, not a destination someone else had arbitrarily set. This chart, this experience was mine. I owned it. At the age of fifty, I had finally realized, through the penis diagram, my sexual side and my acceptance of myself. During my marriage in which I had labored to be faithful to my husband and his disability, I had completely wiped out my own needs—the wants and desires of the sensual realm. Now this penis chart had become my sheepskin, my diploma.

Ginnie, you made it. You have graduated magna CUM laude!

And I read the names of the men whose penises decorated my chart under the following headings: Penis Owner; Nickname; Description; Personality; Ambition; Skill Set (1-10)

Owner: Lance

Nickname: Johnny Come Never

Description: can't remember, "average" comes to mind

Personality: dull, stubborn, recalcitrant, mind of its own

Ambition: N/A

Skill Set: minus 5. Recommendation—studies in Kama Sutra.

———

Owner: Richard

Nickname: The Chief of Staff

Description: unknown

Personality: eager, creative, stealthy, undercover

Ambition: projected to be "excellent"

Skill set: "X" (incomplete)

———

Owner: Grover
Nickname: Twisted Sister
Description: truncated, last two inches perpendicular to ceiling
Personality: shy & introverted, self-conscious, good sport, courageous
Ambition: dysfunctional, performs to ability
Skill set: 5—exerts good effort; should apply for disability.

———

Owner: NH Bill
Nickname: Handy Andy
Description: six inches, stocky, well-defined corona
Personality: entertaining, enthusiastic, agreeable, courteous, user-friendly
Ambition: patient, projected to be excellent
Skill set: 8 for hand job; 10 for testicle juggling

———

Owner: Jack
Nickname: Polyphemus
Description: average in length & width; poorly defined corona
Personality: selfish, arrogant, unfaithful, ravenous & insatiable, entitled
Ambition: bordering on priapism
Skill set: 8—master of every sexual position.

———

Owner: Bob
Nickname: Have Dick Will Travel
Description: long and wide in girth; appealing

glans

Personality: psychotic—manic-depressive; self-defeating, blaming

Ambition: traitorous, unreliable; undependable, squirrely

Skill set: 2—psychological adjustment needed along with blue pills

———

Owner: Steve

Nickname: Moby's Dick

Description: 7" long, 2" thick, superior specimen

Personality: loving, vigorous, appreciative, eager, enthusiastic, experimental

Ambition: vigorous, turnaround time less than an hour

Skill set: 8—champion

———

Owner: Evan

Nickname: The Cat's Meow

Description: 5" long, skinny

Personality: non-committal, careful, obedient

Ambition: steady as he goes, hopeful

Skill set: 4—mastered basic skills; needs advanced work.

———

Owner: Robert

Nickname: Hawk Eye

Description: King of Cocks: long, thick, magnificent; finest specimen

Personality: proud, unafraid, flattering, theatrical

Ambition: spectacular performance, confident, unselfish

Skill set: 10 for oral sex; 9 for intercourse.

Standing ovation.

Next, I went to the computer, typed out the list, and taped it to the wall behind my desk—the evidence of my arrival as a free, independent, complete woman: The Penis Chart. I was *ecstatic*.

****

Though I was proud of my Dick Diploma, I didn't take it to bed with me. Instead, that night I fired up my notebook. I did a search for single, widowed, and divorced men in New York, and a most handsome man popped up. Only two pictures displayed, which was good enough for me. I had to check out if he was a smoker. If he wasn't, I'd rattle off a come-hither email.

His profile said he was a retired officer in the military and dabbled as an entrepreneur. He played classical piano and could cut a mean *pasa doble*. *Holy cow, he does ballroom dancing.* When I saw he also could scuba dive, I hit "Send message" and began to compose a letter.

"Hey, soldier!" filled my subject line. "You must be an extraordinary specimen, one I would love to meet. I, too, can scuba dive and dance, all at the same time. :) I am looking for someone just like me, a guy who likes to cha-cha, hike, ride horses under the fall leaves, and dive in tropical climes. I hate any sports with balls, except for sex. Straight white teeth are important for me as well as intelligence and wit. I'd love to talk. You fascinate me. I advised him to google "Virginie Snow" and jotted down my phone number. Then I hit the "Send" button.

That evening while I sat at the kitchen table with my parents, my cell phone rang. It was Richie, the dancing scuba diver. "How are you, sweetheart?" were his first words.

"I'm just fine, Handsome," I laughed.

"Baby, you are gorgeous."

"Yeah, and you aren't half bad yourself."

He laughed hard, a lean, raspy laugh. "I googled you, and I'm very impressed. You're one bright, intelligent woman."

"I am aware. I *am* aware. But thank you."

Mutual admiration at first conversation.

For two months we talked at least once a day, and we texted each other every few hours. Something always seemed to prevent our meeting, but I was content getting to know this particular man at a snail's pace because something about him was extra special, enticing, and I wanted this one to last.

Although we haven't had time to meet, we think we may be in love. We have even "mock-married" each other over the phone. Others scoff, but stranger things in this world have happened, like not having sex for a third—the good third—of one's lifetime and then racking up nine penises in eighteen months.

In two weeks Richie and I will meet for the first time. I imagine the two of us like the two in the TV commercial, running toward each other on the beach and into each other's arms. If I'd be a lighter weight, I'd jump into his arms in a giant hug, and we'd fall to the sand and kiss like long-lost-and-found lovers.

How do I think our first meeting will really act out?

When he gets out of his car, I will be shocked catatonic at sight of the man I *may* love—the man who *thinks* he loves me—stricken still in his presence, blinded by the brilliance of his prophetic love. Likely

327

he, too, will gape in awe at sight of me, for now I wear a halo of self-confidence not easily dismissed. We will stare, smiling, each at the other, at the intelligent, witty, kind being across the way. Eager to kiss, we will be fearful too, afraid the feelings might not last, that something in the future, might ruin it all—the fantasy that could morph into lasting love.

And if, when we meet, our meeting should fall flat, I can rest confident in myself, for, through it all and with the help of all my gentleman callers, I have finally arrived—strong and reinvigorated, sexually and personally complete—assured. With penis chart in hand and with stamina and freedom, I will find my other half.

Epilogue
Spring Solstice

A year and a half later and knee-deep in cardboard boxes during a session of spring cleaning, I stare down at my penis chart. I smile and finger its smooth face. Honed with the utmost care, a product of experience, lust, and love, its edges are frayed, the page coffee-stained. I handle it lightly, passing it beneath my nose for any scent reminiscent of sperm. Some entries forged in pencil are barely legible, as though a butterfly, its wings dipped in fairy water, had fluttered over the words and smudged them. I hesitate to over-trace the entries with a pen, for that would disrespect the past and taint the moment as I had recorded it that day. Doing so would somehow deflate the immediacy surrounding that particular penis and my relationship with its owner.

Now, so much later, I smile fondly at my dick diagram, the summary of a two-year sprint of dating-while-divorcing. For me it represents a very abbreviated bible of sorts, a report card, a coming-of-age at a mature age masterpiece, a reflection of my rebirth into late-sprung womanhood and wisdom. My penis profile, even now, allows me to look back on tough times overcome with grace, astuteness, and humor. This piece of paper reminds me I have survived, conquered, and learned much about myself, friendship and betrayal, the world, men and women, social justice, and how it all operates and interacts.

My penis chart has become the vehicle of my journey. Some of my "on the road" penile encounters, back then, touched my heart—a masquerade of tenderness—even love. Not all the sojourn was loving nor uplifting, however, and it needn't have been. Now, evaluating the entries with an objective eye, much more of them I could dismiss with a scoff and a punctuated laugh. They were mere day trips on the road map of life.

But that's okay. If I didn't approach the bummers as just a few cat turds in the shitpile of life, I would drive myself crazy questioning it all. Yet through it all I had triumphed, grown—blossomed like a happy, hooligan dandelion growing solitary, defiant.

Thanks to my penis chart, the memories encapsulated there and all it reflects, my new object of love, as I have come to discover, is no longer *any* of the men featured therein, recent ones, or those of the future. In fact, though this new love of my life has been birthed from the flaccid blueprint in my lap, this person has not become an entry on the map itself. That is because my new love is female, and since a female has no outside genitalia, she does not qualify for inclusion in the chart. Yet she exists and thrives *because* of the chart.

In fact, my new lover, lustful of life and living, has few characteristics of the male species at all. My new lover is *myself*. I stifle a giggle at the thought. I can hardly have sex with myself, nor is it in my character to use a tool with which to masturbate my parts. Yet because I am in love with myself, I am more complete. With this realization, like a groom with his new bride, I am committed to defending her, taking care of her, satisfying her most primal, sometimes immoral, needs and desires, guaranteeing she survives the holocausts of life in the best, most humorous, and least trusting of ways. As a direct result of these penile conquests, I love myself more—my body, my energy, my intellect, my instinct to survive, and my sense of humor, which I embrace as the most liberating force of all.

In fact, thanks to the experiences embedded in Ginnie Snow's penis chart, I am well on my way to becoming *more* than myself. The new me may not be as traditional, as pure, as bound by morality and responsibility, as submissive, as trusting, nor as serious as the old married one, but she is by far stronger, more independent, funnier, sexier, self-confident, and more, unapologetically, honest. Thanks to my experiences with penises and the men who own them, I have become one of the world's wisest, most learned, most existential iconoclast.

I am the love of *my* life.

About the Author

Virginie Snow graduated college with degrees in English before moving to Climax, New York, where she has been hunkered down writing articles advocating for the well-being of farm and factory animals as well as writing women's fiction. She works at a local pet pig rescue for fun and to help the animals.

Her advice for readers: "Live life with humor; love yourself, and everything else will fall into place."

~*~

Visit Virginie at
www.nextonlinedatingadvice.wordpress.com

~*~

To chat with Virginie Snow and other Wild Rose Press authors of erotic romance, join us at
www.groups.yahoo.com/group/thewilderroses.

Also Available from
The Wild Rose Press, Inc.

A War Like Ours
By Saffron A. Kent

A liar...

Three weeks ago, James Maxwell's wife died in a car accident, but he hasn't been able to tell his five-year-old daughter the heartbreaking truth behind her mother's death. Instead, he packs them up and leaves for a summer resort in upstate New York to spend a few peaceful weeks and to gradually break the news. But a spirited and outspoken maid at the resort has figured out his secret.

A hater...

After witnessing her mother's violent death at the hands of her stepfather, Madison Smith has turned aimless and bitter toward the world—men, in particular. Her dead-end job at the local resort and her convenient girlfriend are barely keep Madison from falling apart. When she meets James, however, she's driven to protect his child from the darkness she sees inside him.

A forbidden kiss...

But Madison doesn't expect to find that very darkness irresistible. Drowning in guilt and memories, James doesn't expect to be drawn to the sharp-witted woman who has made his life miserable. When their tempers flare, a brutal kiss triggers a need that blurs the lines of hate and desire. As their lust spins out of control, they must decide if their attraction is worth fighting for or if love is the real enemy.

Also Available from
The Wild Rose Press, Inc.

Screwed
By Mike Owens

Somehow, it's always about the money. Sharon Saluda, in her junior year at Pisgah College, doesn't have nearly enough of it, and a diploma is her ticket out of the narrow confines of small town life in Jacob's Bluff, NC. A career as a stripper seems a promising solution, but when that ends badly, a desperate Sharon capitalizes on that most basic of needs—sex—by matching up college coeds with faculty clientele.

Her job description takes a dramatic uptick when Connor Shaw arrives and wants her as his own—for a very good price, of course. She takes the plunge, body and soul, because this man is gorgeous, ridiculously wealthy, and the sex is out of this world. But there's always a catch...right?